CHRISTINA BARTOLOMEO

The Side of the Angels

~ A NOVEL ~

 ST. MARTIN'S GRIFFIN ✺ NEW YORK

www.stmartins.com

Designed by Kyoko Watanabe

Library of Congress Cataloging-in-Publication Data

Bartolomeo, Christina.
      The side of the angels / Christina Bartolomeo.
          p. cm.
      ISBN 0-312-32366-2
      EAN 978-0312-32366-0
      1. Women public relations personnel—Fiction. 2. Washington (D.C.)—
Fiction. 3. Catholic women—Fiction. 4. Single women—Fiction. I. Title.

PS3552.A7677 S53 2002
813'.54—dc21   2001057709

First published in the United States by Scribner, a trademark of Macmillan
Library Reference USA, Inc., under license of Simon & Schuster

First St. Martin's Griffin Edition: September 2004

10 9 8 7 6 5 4 3 2 1

The Side of the Angels

To my darling buddy Dan,
who gives me laughter, courage, and love

Acknowledgments

This book was fortunate to have two wonderful editors. Jane Rosenman vastly improved the first versions with characteristic kindness and wisdom, and an unerring eye for where it needed to go next. Jake Morrissey shepherded it through successive drafts and publication, giving generously of his time and expertise to a manuscript that he "met" midway through development. Thank you both, more than I can say. Warm thanks also to Rachel Sussman of Scribner, for guiding this book through final production and giving her time and talent generously to its promotion.

Thanks always to my agent, Henry Dunow, for his encouragement, support, and friendship. As agent and fellow author, he truly understands the highs and lows of the business of writing and has seen me through all of them. Much gratitude to Lucy Stille of Paradigm, for past miracles and for her enthusiasm for this book, and to Ethan Friedman of Scribner, who gave me a crucial character, and was always there to reassure. For another gorgeous jacket, many thanks to designer and illustrator Honi Werner, as well as Kyoko Watanabe for a lovely text design. And, for stepping in to get this book through its finishing touches, many thanks to Brant Rumble.

For their camaraderie and advice, my thanks to writers Karl Ackerman, Angela Nicholas, Leigh Bailey, Larry Doyle, Timothy Murphy,

Elinor Lipman, and Mary Quattlebaum. Special thanks for the stellar teaching of Richard Bausch. For getting me through this book and so much else, love and thanks to Susan Lieberman, Sarah Bulley, Roy Raymond, and my D.C. Tuesday night and Maine Wednesday night therapy groups.

Thanks and affection forever to my former colleagues at the American Federation of Teachers. For teaching me all I know about union organizing, special thanks to: Tom Flood, Jerry Richardson, Norm Holsinger, Rick Kuplinski, Juanita Dunlap-Smith, Don Kuehn, Pat Jones, Tom Moran, Ann Twomey, Candice Owley, Ray Mackey, Marty Keegan, Rich Klimmer, Bob Jensen, and Chuck Iannello.

For their great goodness to me during my time in New England and after, my heartfelt thanks and love to Denis and Noreen Murphy; warm thanks also to Jean Foley and Bonnie Spiegel.

I am blessed to count among my friends: Laura Baker, Jason Juffras, Christopher and Christy David, Kate Bannan, Mike Long, Vandana Reddy, Jared Schwartz, Kate Innes, Danielle Oddo, Kate Callison, Andrew Young, Sam Wang, Peter Darling, Jon Givner, Shannon and Michael Spaeder, Mary Jones, Sylvia Mapes, Carol Goodman, Kathy Dillon, and Peter Leopold. Marybeth Kelly Evans and Ivan Klein have died since this book was begun but I will never forget them or their belief in me. Matt Jacob and Jeff Campbell have been there for every joy and sorrow, the truest friends in the world.

Deepest love and gratitude to my family: my mother and father, John and Dorothy Bartolomeo, my loyal and loving sisters and brothers (Mary, Anna, Angela, Nick, and John) my terrific sister-, brothers-, and niece-in-law (Phil, Eddie, Annie, and Kate), and my darling nephews John, Brendan, Cristian, and Samuel. Love and thanks to our extended family, especially Mary and John Heneghan, Gary Lattimore, John Schlecty, Kim Christiansen, Andy Lee, and Leta Davis. Special thanks to my nephew Devin, no mean writer himself, who read this book in manuscript and rooted for it all along the way. I love you all so much.

The Side
of the Angels

· 1 ·

MY COUSIN LOUISE and I ate lunch together twice a month at her office, no fail. That's what we were doing the first Wednesday in November when my boss's call came, the one that threw Tony and me, if not back into each other's arms, into each other's orbit. Don't you love it when life suddenly behaves like a movie? There we were, Louise and I, speaking of a man I'd just left—not Tony, another man—and I was on the verge of remarking to Louise, "At least I'm not the mess I was after Tony," when the phone rang.

Tony was my old flame, the man who got away. The man whose getting away had so thrown me off my game that I'd fallen into a series of stupid romances, the most recent of which was a three-year-long involvement with Jeremy, a self-enamored British expatriate who'd been cheating on me for six months before I discovered it and kicked him out on his tweedy, two-timing ass.

"The thing about Jeremy," Louise had commented a little earlier as she laid out some pink linen napkins and secondhand china (Louise likes to beautify even a weekday lunch), "is that he's the kind of man who's never happy unless he's exercising his talent for persuasion. Which makes a day-to-day relationship difficult, unless you have some strange arrangement where you pretend you're dumping him every other week, or you wear different wigs to bed, or costumes."

"I would say I was playful in bed," I said defensively. "I read articles and stuff. Once in a while."

"I'm not faulting *you*, Nicky. You could dress up in a lion tamer's outfit one night and a French maid's the next and it wouldn't be enough for Jeremy."

Louise had never liked Jeremy. Suave, educated, well-spoken types held no charm for her. She preferred her men artistic, tortured, and generally unbathed. Though perhaps she discouraged Jeremy's potential reemergence because she wanted to try her hand at digging up prospects for me. Louise is a professional matchmaker, a harebrained occupation at which she's surprisingly successful. She'd always wanted a shot at seeing what she could do for me. Like a temperance worker with a tippler in the family, she was frustrated that her dedication and devotion to the cause were of no use to her own kin.

"My trouble is, Louise, I can never spot Jeremy's kind until he's stomped on my feelings so badly I don't want him anymore."

"Which, of course, makes him come after you with renewed interest. Look at how he's acting now, like you're the Holy Grail. Where was all that appreciation these past three years?"

Jeremy had been doing his best—his persuasive, most grandly romantic best—to get me to give him a second chance. I'd dumped him in July. Needless to say, time had not yet dulled the wound.

Louise's phone rang. We let the machine pick it up—she still has one of those old-fashioned manual answering machines, now considered as primitive as long-playing records.

"Nicky," came Ron's voice through the static, "I know you said not to bother you, but this is important. Call me."

It was always important. Ron liked to pretend he lived in an atmosphere of crisis. He was an ardent fan of those medical dramas where the doctor races through the hospital corridor shouting angrily, "Get me a CBC on that kid, stat." Ron wished with all his meager, little heart that he could someday say "Stat." Unfortunately, there wasn't much call for that sort of thing when you headed a second-rate PR firm that specialized in hopeless causes. Not only was Ron's firm second-rate, so was his taste in names. He had christened his business "Advocacy, Inc." despite all my persuasions. I cringed whenever I glanced at our letterhead.

Ron clicked off. Then the phone rang again. If Ron applied only half the single-minded devotion to his clueless, charity-bent clients that he did to getting his own way, how much better off the widow, orphan, and unspayed house pet would be.

"Just ignore it," I said to Louise.

"Nicky, if you're there having lunch with Louise, and I know you are because you told Myrlene that was where you were going, please pick up. It really is important. I mean it. I'm sincere. Please pick up."

This was a man whose last honest emotion was when he cried at the baptismal font.

"Shouldn't you call him?" said Louise. "Maybe it's some sort of personal problem."

Louise is good in ways I'll never be. Serene and unflustered, Louise manages to be lovable despite the fact that she floats down the river of life as if on a golden barge.

Nine months younger than I am, my cousin Louise has been at hand for nearly every major event of my life, from my first Communion to my first pregnancy scare. She is my sounding board, my reference point, my unshakable ally. When we were teenagers and nearly every other girl I knew was cruel or unapproachable, Louise was my friend. Because of her, I had survived four years in one of the meanest, snootiest convent schools on the East Coast, the St. Madeleine Sophie Academy for Young Women. Our parents had scraped and saved to send us there; the parents of the other girls considered themselves deprived if they didn't fit in a second trip to Europe every year. We were made to feel this difference. But, because of Louise, the petty hurts inflicted year after year, the sly daily nastiness that adolescent girls are such experts at, hadn't done lasting harm.

Louise got there a year after me, being younger, and a month into her first semester my cousin's uncrushably lighthearted presence transformed the place, for me, from a daily incarceration stretching endlessly before me into a temporary stint, a launching pad, a joke. I'd not only survived high school, I'd largely forgotten it—because Louise was there too, looking out for me in her unobtrusive way.

Lest she sound too good to be true, Louise is also impractical, maddeningly slow to put any plan of her own into action (though she's usually sure of what I should do), and chronically, outrageously late, to the extent that I always bring a book when I go to meet her in a restaurant. Most annoyingly, Louise spends much of her time in a bright mist of hazy, optimistic pseudo-spiritualism. There are few side roads on the journey to enlightenment that she hasn't explored—group therapy, tai chi, vegan purification diets, past-life regression—and it gets on my nerves sometimes. It's one thing to keep an open mind. It's another to seriously consider joining your local witches' coven.

The phone rang again. I threw down my forkful of chicken in tarragon mayonnaise (there is an excellent gourmet shop around the corner from Louise's business) and snatched up the receiver.

"Ron, I specifically told Myrlene to tell you not to bother me. For one hour. One lousy hour."

"I know, but we've got a problem," said Ron's mellifluous voice. In his college days, Ron earned extra money as a radio announcer.

"What problem?" I injected some controlled fury into my voice. Ron is like a dog—he responds to tones more than actual words. "This better not be that Mallard Pond thing again. That's your baby."

Three years ago I would never have used a phrase like "that's your baby," but you can't touch pitch and not be defiled, I guess. I only hoped that Ron's effect on my moral fiber was less insidious than his effect on my vocabulary. It wasn't as if I'd been overburdened with moral fiber to start with.

The Mallard Pond account was more trouble than it was worth. Mallard Pond was a tiny, algae-filmed lake near a planned community in northern Virginia, a spot that had been farmland when I was growing up. The Mallard Gardens Homeowners Association had hired Advocacy to get some press attention for their fight to save this pristine if not particularly scenic body of water from rapacious developers. The homeowners, I suspected, were more concerned that the arrival of video rental emporiums and movie cineplexes would lower property values than they were about preserving nature's beauties. Their aim was noble enough for *our* standards, though. Our standards were not high.

I'd warned Ron that this account would require a level of client coddling out of all proportion to the money we'd see from it. Did he listen? Of course not. I can count on one hand the number of times my opinion has influenced Ron's behavior.

"Not to worry, Mallard's under control," said Ron. "The *Loudon County Observer* just came out on our side. 'Save Our Southern Walden.' That was the title of the editorial. My idea."

The Side of the Angels ~ 15

"Great, Ron. Now go visit a library and see if you can find out whether General Lee ever recorded in a letter home that he let his horse, Traveler, bend and drink from Mallard's cooling waters. Then we'd be home free."

"What?"

It was possible that Ron had never heard of General Lee. He was from Minnesota, where history seemed to be measured in droughts and blizzards. He probably thought Pickett's Charge was a new kind of credit card.

"If it's not Mallard, then what is so damn important?"

"This is for the Toilers Union," Ron said. "A nurses' strike in some blue-collar town in Rhode Island called Winsack. It's about twenty miles northeast of Providence. The nurses there have been in contract negotiations for twenty-one months and the hospital's not budging, so they're close to walking. I told Weingould we'd be over at two o'clock. Myrlene can clear your calendar."

A strike. There went all my free time until Thanksgiving, perhaps until Christmas. The only bright spot was that taking this assignment would give me an unimpeachable excuse to refuse Louise the request she'd been leading up to when Ron interrupted.

"Ron, what am I supposed to tell Janet Stratton-Smith about the planning meeting for the Campsters Christmas gala?"

"Wendy can meet with her."

Wendy was my assistant, an exhaustingly perky twenty-five-year-old whom Ron had hired as a favor to his tax accountant, whose niece she was. Ron owed his firstborn child to his tax accountant, for reasons I preferred not to think about.

"Janet won't like that."

"Wendy can smooth her down. She's good at that. Tactful. Sweet. Unlike some people."

"Fine. I'll see you in Weingould's office at two. Who's he got on the ground there?"

"A guy named Tony Boltanski. You know him?"

For a moment I couldn't speak. No one I knew, except Louise and my mother, had mentioned Tony's name to me for five years. Most of my friends knew that I liked to pretend that Tony had been lost at sea in a tragic marine archaeology expedition, or been blown up in a fool-hardy but courageous attempt to crack a Columbian drug ring. Any-thing rather than the knowledge that he'd gotten over me, that he was out there doing the job he'd always done, the job he'd preferred to me by such a large margin. I was not the sort of generous soul who bids her lovers good-bye with earnest wishes for a happy life, a wistful, philo-sophic smile, and "What I Did for Love" playing softly in the back-ground. I wanted them all to suffer.

"Tony Boltanski? I knew him a long time ago. A campaign in New York. He's capable."

"Better than capable, according to Weingould."

Tony and I had lived together for a year and a half. I'd thought I was going to marry him. With Tony, for the first time in my life I'd felt I was home safe. More fool me.

"Could you meet me in the lobby at a quarter of to discuss strat-egy?"

"Don't push it, Ron."

He clicked off. He knows that note of finality in my voice.

"I have twenty minutes," I said to Louise.

"You're going on assignment?"

"Yeah. Rhode Island. I hear it's lovely there this time of year."

"And Tony's involved?"

"I'll tell you about it later."

She pushed a plate of warm pecan brownies to my side of the table. My favorite. I began to gobble, though I knew Louise had provided this delicacy specifically to soften me up for the pitch she was about to make: namely, that it was time I availed myself of her services, as it seemed that every other desperate single person in the Washington metropolitan area was doing. Her company, Custom Hitches, sole pro-prietor Louise Geary, stood ready to cure my solitary state. This pitch, which had never had much of a chance, was doomed to failure the moment I heard Tony Boltanski's name for the first time in five years.

Damn Ron. Leave it to him to put together the perfect combina-tion: working with an old lover from whom I'd parted bitterly, for Weingould, the compulsive looker-over-the-shoulder, on a strike that already sounded more like a siege than a winnable campaign, up north, as winter started. Faced with this cheerful prospect, I was in no mood for Louise's canned lecture about how the Universe held a mate for each of us if we would just make room for love in our lives.

My name is Nicky Malone. Nicky is short for Dominica, the middle name of my mother's Neapolitan mother, but no one ever called me that except my mother in her more dire moods. My full name is Dominica Magdalen Regina (confirmation name) Malone. I like the short version. It sounds like the name of the hero in one of those forties detective stories. "Nicky Malone here," I could see myself barking into the phone, my hand caressing the fifth of scotch in my drawer, my eyes lingering on a hunk in a fedora and a pinstriped suit who, at any minute, would attempt to seduce me to throw me off the trail.

I have two brothers, and would have had more if something hadn't gone wrong with my mother's insides during her last labor and deprived her and my father of the six kids they'd have liked to bring into the world. My older brother, Michael, is gay, to the eternal lamenting of my mother, who refers to Michael's gayness as if it were a disease ("I should have *seen* it coming on. If only I'd made him stay in Little League").

Michael is dark and slim with coal-black hair. With his heavy-lidded black eyes and long straight nose, he resembles one of those beautiful, melancholy youths in Etruscan portraits. No trace of Irish blood in him. If it wasn't for our eyes, you would not know we were brother and sister, to look at us. He's an investments counselor—he shows people who have a certain amount of money how to make even more money by carefully, carefully playing the stock and other markets (or, as Michael would say, "developing a well-balanced portfolio that will yield sustained and steady long-term growth").

My younger brother, Joey, whose snub nose and mischievous grin mark him as a mick from twenty paces away, is married and has a new baby, a baby new enough that it still scares me to hold him. Since my father's death from a heart attack four years ago, Joey has managed River Road Auto, the car repair shop that was the reason my dad brought us all down from Boston when I was five. The shop is a fancy place now: foreign cars, computer diagnostics, twelve bays with hoists, ten employees where there used to be four.

Our cousin Johnny Campbell, who came to live with us when he was thirteen, is Joey's head mechanic. The best mechanic I've ever known, and my father was pretty damn good at his job. My dad had talent and an attention to detail, but Johnny has intuition and at times pure genius. There is nothing on wheels that Johnny can't fix. When he flexes his long fingers over the hood of a fractious automobile, it quiets itself like a horse being gentled

Johnny is loping and kind, with long, deep-set blue eyes. His Irish half is tempered by his father's blood, a mix of Lowland Scots and French Canadian. He's steadier, more equable than Joey—but of the two, you'd rather cross Joey, because Johnny never forgets a betrayal.

Johnny was in love with Louise, who is no blood relative of his. Johnny's mother is our father's sister, and Louise's father is our mother's brother. Louise was unaware of Johnny's feelings, probably because Johnny had accidentally gone and gotten engaged to someone else and was due to marry her next June in a tasteful ceremony in some Connecticut suburb.

That's all of this generation that live here, although we have numerous cousins up in Boston and on Cape Cod whom we rarely see. And so, as I've said, Louise is the closest I'll ever have to a sister. She knows what that means to me, and sometimes she trades on it—as she was about to do now.

She refilled my coffee cup and gave me a second brownie.

"Have you ever thought it might be time to do something about freeing a path for a man in your life, Nicky?" Louise said, as casually as she might have said, "Don't bother to clear up, I'll do the dishes later."

When Louise wants something from you, she always approaches the subject with a throwaway air and a deceptively mild directness. I took a wolfish bite out of my brownie and glared at her. She clasped her hands in her lap and gazed at a point just over my head, as if to encourage me to join her for a moment in reflecting on my priorities.

"I don't need a man in my life, Louise. I just got *rid* of a man in my life, remember? Having men in my life is what got me in the mess I'm in today."

Louise dropped the Buddha act.

"What mess? You're gorgeous, you've got a great career, a great apartment, great friends."

"If my life is so great, then why are you so hell-bent on seeing me paired up?"

"I don't mean that you need a man in some *groveling* sense, like it's a terrible tragedy to be thirty-two and single. All I mean is that it's time to try."

"You're going to break into the chorus from *Georgy Girl* next."

"I just think you've felt bad about Jeremy long enough."

"Felt bad? That's for when you miss a lunch appointment or tap someone's bumper, Louise."

"You know what I mean. He's still looming way too large."

"Ma put you up to this, didn't she, Louise?"

To my mother, my being unattached at this advanced age was a dire circumstance, as if I had leukemia. In fact, a life-threatening illness would have been preferable. In that case, she would be "poor Mrs. Malone, bearing up so bravely" and not the failed mother of a daughter who might now never get married. Sad, sad, sad.

For years my mother had been trying to get me to young-adult dances at her parish, St. Ignatius, and when I got too old for those, to Catholic professional singles groups where I might meet some nice Timothy or Patrick who'd soon convince me that birth control was an invention of the devil. Now she was resorting to Louise and her half-baked clearinghouse for lonely hearts. She must be really desperate.

I wasn't ready yet to consign my romantic future to the tender but muddleheaded mercies of my cousin. I'm not gorgeous by any means, despite Louise's encouraging words, but I get my share of Saturday night dates and sidewalk glances. What's most noticeable about me is my hair. It's auburn with gold strands twining through it, and it's thick and long and wavy. Providence must have given me good hair to make up for my cup size, a B on a good day.

My eyes, a legacy from my Italian grandmother Antonella, are so dark a brown they look black. My skin is creamy and pale and without a freckle, though on the debit side it's a paleness with olive undertones that can look sallow if I wear the wrong color (Grandma Nella again). My legs are long and I'm five foot seven. I'm not every guy's type—not like Louise, who has the classic appeal that comes with being blond, petite, and reasonably stacked—but those whose type I am, I am *indeed*, if you know what I mean. Surely fate had something better in store than Louise's wifty maneuverings.

"You promised me that you would think about dating in the fall," said Louise.

"Isn't it against your yenta code of ethics to rush me?"

"Sometimes we all need a little karmic shove."

"Spare me, Louise."

Louise knew that I didn't fall for her pose of New Age nanny to the lovelorn. Having survived the brainwashing of the Catholic Church, I wasn't about to succumb to the mush of self-help lingo, Horatio Alger pep talks, and warmed-over Transcendentalism she served up to the despondent and discouraged who sought out her advice. What's more, Louise and I had had the same English teachers. So I could spot every borrowed line in the superficially profound patter that worked with her clients. With me, she couldn't get away with cribbing from Matthew Arnold or Edna St. Vincent Millay, or, God help us, Christina Rossetti. I knew all her sources.

"This karmic shove is coming from my mother, isn't it, Louise?"

Louise does not like to lie, so her avoidance of this question was all the corroboration I needed.

"What if I at least prepared a roster of possibles for you? I've had some great men sign up recently. Good, solid men. Men you could count on."

"I'm still convalescing, okay?"

Louise assumed the expression of the sympathetic Mother Superior counseling Julie Andrews in *The Sound of Music*, and said, " 'Let us grieve not, but rather find strength in what remains behind.' "

"Louise, that's from Wordsworth, whom you know I can't stand, and it's 'we will grieve not,' and that poem is not about breaking up with someone who screwed around on you, it's about Wordsworth's stupid childhood."

"It still applies," said Louise.

"You know, your clients may think you're so wise, but really you're just exceptionally well read."

Louise looked hurt, but shelved her feelings for the moment.

"You don't have to go through the preliminaries," she said.

"Boy, my mother must really be in a hurry to get me on the market."

This ready-set-go approach was a departure from Louise's usual playbook. Louise normally put her clients through an intense "pre-dating" course of preparation. I wondered why her customers put up with it, but I guess they figured that Louise was like a personal trainer: anyone who made you work *that* hard *must* be good.

Louise's methods had proven so successful that, had she wanted to, she could have bought a nice Edwardian condo in Kalorama, rather than the seedy apartment she rented on Capitol Hill. She could have afforded a reliable car instead of the old Chevy Cavalier that broke down six times a winter. But Louise was uncomfortable with her comparatively recent security. She still feared that Custom Hitches would collapse, or that the IRS would find fault with her scrupulously honest tax returns.

Louise had nothing to worry about. She had found her vocation and would continue to thrive on her uncanny intuition for what made one poor slob right for another poor slob. You had only to look around her office to know that she was a natural for her job. The rooms (the third floor of an old storefront in Woodley Park, above a yoga center and a florist's shop) were painted a dusty, womblike pink. Wedding invitations and engagement announcements lined the windowsill. See, they mutely testified, this could be *you*. Dim lighting, bowls of potpourri, and faded rose brocade curtains turned the office into a scented, firelit cave, a refuge where you could confide the ridiculous dream of finding someone to love you who'd actually love you back.

I had no interest in Louise's offer, though. I was still bewildered, still wondering how I'd been so unsuspicious. Jeremy had cheated on me with Virginia Sprague, the head of admissions at Laurel Hill, the girls' college on Boxwood Road where he taught modern world history and was far too spoiled with attention and admiration. Laurel Hill was a glorified finishing school for not-too-intellectual young women of good family, and Jeremy was a star on its underachieving faculty. It's not good for a man like Jeremy to be too long in a place where he's top dog. He starts thinking he can get away with anything.

I'd met his honey once at a department dinner party. Virginia was cool and poised, gracious but not friendly, a forty-year-old divorcée from Charleston with a lilting Carolina accent that recalled Civil War love letters. It was funny, how she'd never lost that accent after ten years in D.C.

"Virginia is nice, but she's not very warm, is she?" I remembered saying to Jeremy after that dinner party. Virginia had wafted in during the second round of cocktails, wearing a lilac organza blouse so fragile and expensive that only a woman who never, ever spilled or tripped would be confident enough to purchase it.

"She's very closed off, isn't she?" he'd agreed. "It's quite unattractive." By which I should have known he found her very appealing. Men make those immediate denials of interest solely about women who do, in fact, interest them intensely.

Maybe it was that voice, sweet and cool as the wisteria-shaded corner of a veranda on a hot summer afternoon. Or her often-silent self-containment, so challenging to a man like Jeremy, to whom women presented confidences and confessions like bouquets. Or maybe she'd simply wandered into his enclosure just as he started to feel restless.

Now, listening to Louise extol the virtues of a fresh start, I wondered at her faith in happy endings. I'd thought Jeremy was trustworthy. I'd thought we had something good going on, something that merited his keeping his pants zipped up at the office. What accounted for Jeremy's straying? And what was so great about Virginia, with her outdated Grace Kelly pageboy and her cultured pearls?

"What about the process?" I asked Louise.

"You don't have to go through the process. I know you well enough, don't I?"

She poured me more coffee, her own special almond-hazelnut blend (she uses hazelnut coffee and pours a tablespoon of almond extract on top before brewing).

Before she sent you out on your first date, Louise cataloged your romantic history, asked you to write down your dreams for a week, and made a genogram of your extended family to pinpoint any possible "intimacy roadblocks." If something in your past or present was getting in the way of your finding a lifetime partner, Louise would discover it faster than a drug-sniffing canine at the Miami airport sussing out a cocaine stash in a duffel bag.

Not to worry—if you *were* a subconsciously reluctant lover, Louise guided you through a free monthlong "unblocking" course, with personalized prescriptions for opening yourself up to love. These ranged from juice fasting to singing lessons to spending a weekend alone in a mountain cabin "to fall in love with yourself first." Louise even led rituals for saying farewell to past loves, in which souvenirs of the unfaithful departed were burned, buried, or, in one case she told me about, spat upon. "Nothing else really seemed to express how she felt," Louise said. "It was incredibly cathartic."

On the rare occasions when a client left in dissatisfaction or gave up after encountering disappointment, Louise mourned for weeks. Once in a while she'd confide in me about a particularly difficult problem. I felt honored and pleased when she did that. It meant that Louise knew that underneath my pessimistic surface I rooted for love just as fervently as she did, though with less faith. It was like being a Red Sox fan. You prayed the Sox might make the play-offs, you cheered them through every victory of the season, but history told you that they'd never win the Series. Somehow it always ended with a heartbreaker in the bottom of the ninth.

But it was one thing to cheer for the home team, and another to be shoved out onto the field after a disastrous spring training.

"You have nothing to lose, Nicky. There are three great guys I can think of offhand that I know you'd have a terrific evening with, and that alone would be a boost for your confidence."

"I don't know, Louise. I somehow don't have the courage for meeting a lot of new men right now."

"I'd hold your hand every step of the way."

"You can't come on a date with me. You can't feed me the right lines while I make chitchat over dim sum. I promise, Louise, when I'm feeling up to it I'll give it the old college try, I really will."

"Then I won't push you."

"I'll tell my mom you did your best."

Louise smiled.

"I can handle Aunt Maureen," she said.

They understand each other, Louise and my mother. In fact, if my mother could have chosen a daughter, she'd have chosen someone like Louise, someone who, like my mother, was as delicate-looking as a calla lily and as tenacious as bindweed.

"Thank you," I said. "I know you mean well. Unlike my mother, who's just bossy."

"Go to your meeting."

As I was dusting bits of brownie off my skirt, there was a perfunctory knock, and our cousin Johnny ambled in. I noted Louise's expression: initial joy, followed by an immediate reining-in of the thousand-watt smile. On Johnny's face, I could discern no emotion other than easygoing affection, but that was Johnny. He played his cards close to his chest.

"Cousinettes," he said, his nickname for us together.

"What brings you here in the middle of the day?" I asked.

"The same thing that brings you here. I wanted a decent lunch."

He scooped some chicken salad into a folded-up piece of wheat bread and began eating, hanging over the table so as not to mess up his clothes. Today he was unusually dressy for Johnny: spotless jeans, his only good blazer with a black T-shirt underneath, and clean sneakers. Over his arm was the classic and becoming charcoal-gray tweed coat that Louise had persuaded him to buy at a flea market in Salisbury, Maryland. Before Betsey came along, Louise picked out most of Johnny's clothes. Now he would occasionally appear in something suburban and cutesy, like a pine-green cable-knit sweater with snowflakes dancing across the chest, and we would see Betsey's hand.

His light brown hair, as usual, was flopping into his eyes. At the shop he had to tie a twisted bandanna around his head to keep it back.

"I came to ask Louise if she'd go shopping with me," he said. "Betsey's parents are coming to town this weekend and I need to look nice."

"What's wrong with what you've got on?" I said.

"They want to take us out to dinner. Betsey said no sneakers. I thought Louise might want to advise me on some nice dress shoes."

It was always Louise, and still Louise, whom Johnny turned to for advice on how to get on in the real world. At the garage, Johnny knew exactly what to do. But outside the shop, he constantly struggled with a void of information about how regular life should be led.

Johnny came to live with us a week before his fourteenth birthday because his mother drank. She was also, even more scandalously, divorced. In the months before he came to us, the nuns at Johnny's school in Gloucester, Massachusetts, noticed that he was arriving at school every day without a lunch, his uniform unpressed, his hair growing longer and longer. The parish priest investigated, a family conference was held, and Johnny was taken in by my mom and dad.

If my parents had suspected the situation earlier, he'd have been rescued from neglect years before, but Johnny's mother was a charmer, Dad's adorable, flighty little sister, Peggy, who knew how to keep up appearances—until one day she couldn't anymore. Johnny's dad was notable only for his spotless record of absence and his reluctance to contribute to his son's financial support. The result of this haphazard upbringing was that Johnny, although he put up a good front, still guessed a little at what regular people did about things like buying dress shoes. And Louise was the only one he allowed to assist him with the things he didn't know. It had always been that way. It was Louise who'd told him what flowers to get for his high school girlfriends on Valentine's Day and how much to spend on them, Louise who drilled him for tests and proofread his papers when he was getting his BA in business administration at Towson State, Louise who ordered him his first business cards when he became co-manager at the shop, Louise who encouraged him in the aw-shucks politeness that was such an asset with his customers and his lady friends.

For her part, when Louise broke up with someone and I was on the road, it was Johnny she called to come hold her hand. Johnny made sure she had her snow tires each winter and that her crummy apartment was equipped with enough locks and window bars to discourage an entire chain gang of escaped Lorton inmates. Johnny did the books for Custom Hitches. He even changed her lightbulbs.

But lately Louise had seemed impatient and distracted in Johnny's presence. I knew that she'd seen him a little less than usual this fall, and this change was not due to Betsey, a diligent and industrious type who had so many evening classes, book discussion groups, bridal workshops, and knitting festivals on her schedule that she often left Johnny at loose ends these days.

Louise said, "I can't go, Johnny. I'm booked for the rest of the afternoon."

"Maybe tonight?"

"Shouldn't Betsey help you with this? She'll know what sort of place her parents would take you."

The old Louise would rather have gone out to buy vacuum cleaner bags with Johnny than be taken to a four-star restaurant by anyone else.

"Betsey has her class Halloween party tomorrow. It was delayed by the flu. All the kids got it."

Betsey was a second-grade teacher, and she was always busy with tasks that struck me as overwhelmingly boring, like putting up bulletin boards in celebration of Arbor Day or visiting the arts and crafts store for origami paper. Betsey was . . . well, the only word for her was *damp*. There's something about teaching grade school that does it.

What did Johnny see in her? Maybe the shakiness of life with his mother rendered cautious, reliable girls like Betsey attractive to him; they'd always been his type. Betsey would remonstrate with Johnny when he got a little wild. He would shock her by driving a hundred miles an hour down Dalecarlia Parkway or going "cliffjumping" up the river with the guys from the shop. He'd take a road trip to Atlantic City for a weekend and lose every cent he brought with him, just for the hell of it. Betsey would reproach him for these excesses and suggest some safe outlet for his energy, such as learning golf or coaching Little League.

Betsey, as the pop psychology crowd would say, "grounded" Johnny. I didn't think this sounded like a good thing.

"I can't go shoe shopping this afternoon, Johnny," Louise said, sounding more fractious than I'd ever heard her.

"How about tonight?" He began beating a tattoo on the back of one of Louise's overstuffed rose-velvet client chairs, a sure sign that he was anxious. Johnny isn't normally fidgety.

"I do have a life," Louise said.

"Sure, but you told me yesterday that Hub is on the road. You know how I feel about shoe stores. I hate those guys with the foot measurers."

"You're thirty-one years old," said Louise.

"No guy should have to go shopping alone," said Johnny. "We get panicky. I'll buy the first pair that fits and they'll be all wrong."

"Fine," said Louise. "But I'm not making dinner afterward."

She would, though. She'd end up broiling a steak and frying potatoes while Johnny hung around the kitchen imitating every salesman and customer they'd encountered that night to make her laugh. Did anyone but me think it was odd that the woman Johnny turned to for companionship, reassurance, and truly excellent fried potatoes was an entirely different woman from the one he was marrying?

It irked me, Johnny's unspoken assumption that Louise was at his disposal. Louise was just as good-looking for a woman as Johnny was for a man. Male clients fell for her in droves, though she would never have dated one of them. In her eyes, that would have constituted malpractice. There's something soft and endearing about Louise: her profusion of baby-fine, dark-golden curls, her round chin and cheeks and elbows, her very slight plumpness. Louise has the pretty pastel tints, mild blue eyes, and long spidery lashes of an eighteenth-century miniature. Her upper lip curves upward ever so slightly in the middle, giving her an impressionable air that endears her to men.

And Johnny saw none of it. Johnny's image of Louise was fifteen years out of date. As a teenager, Louise had been overweight by twenty pounds, which made all the difference on her small frame. Used to his plump cousin with her acne-ridden, squeaky-voiced suitors, Johnny hadn't seemed to notice when, a little later than her contemporaries, Louise came into her own. Her metabolism stabilized, her fashion sense crystallized, and she let her hair grow out from the butch layered cuts that hairdressers inflict on chubby women with the excuse that short lengths "draw attention to the face."

Louise's metamorphosis only slightly improved her taste in men, unfortunately. She was currently dating a guy named Hubbard Wentworth Gruber III, otherwise known as Hub, a trust fund brat of thirty or so who sang in a semi-successful folk group that would never make it to the big time because no one in it was hungry enough, but had enough of a groupie following to keep going. Distasteful as Hub was to me, with his ostentatious vegetarianism and false artistic suffering, I was happy that Louise no longer put up with the dismissive, critical types who had been the abiding theme of her love life until she "grew into her looks," as my mother liked to say.

Johnny ridiculed Hub with a fierceness that should have told him something about himself. There he and Louise were, perfectly right for each other, right in *front* of each other, and still apart. It was like watching a yellow jacket trying to get out an open window, bumbling all over the windowpane, knocking into every corner of the sill, always just missing the route to the open air.

Johnny was still hanging around when I left, going through Louise's desk drawers for a postage stamp, singing "Don't Cry for Me, Argentina" in a smarmy falsetto to make Louise laugh. As she walked me to the door, Louise tucked the last two brownies, carefully wrapped in green cellophane, into my briefcase. That was what you had to love about Louise. In the midst of proffering spiritual consolation, she still remembered to send you off with baked goods.

"Make Johnny take you out to dinner," I said to her as I hugged her good-bye.

"He's playing pickup basketball at nine."

"No, he isn't. Not now. Get him to cancel. It's the least he can do for dragging you out shopping."

Louise hated shopping of any traditional sort. Noise and crowds and stacks of bright shiny merchandise overwhelmed her. Her favorite stores had names like "East of the Sun, West of the Moon," and featured soothing mandolin tapes playing in the background, a smell of patchouli in the air, and odd ethnic apparel hand-loomed by gallant peasant artisans from Tibet, Peru, or Nepal.

"Johnny," I called back to him, "you *are* buying Louise a meal after this shoe expedition."

"Glad to," said Johnny, and grinned at Louise. "There's a new rooftop bar in Adams-Morgan where they have free tango lessons and half-price tapas after ten P.M. Want to tango, Louise?"

"No."

"Fox-trot at the Chantilly Ballroom?"

"No, thanks."

"Go waltzing at the senior center?"

He grabbed her by the waist and began twirling her around the room. Louise had taught Johnny how to waltz for some debutante cotillion he'd been invited to, the spring of his freshman year in college. I watched them circling together, laughing and treading on each other's feet, and remembered Louise at nineteen, patiently counting out the box step with Johnny in my parents' living room five nights in a row so that he wouldn't embarrass himself at the dance with another girl, the girl who counted that particular week or month. The girl whose name he probably couldn't even remember now, though I was sure Louise would.

Sometimes it seems to me that, for every happy couple fate brings together just in the nick of time, there are five other pairs who miss each other by inches or miles. Do human beings just not want to be happy, deep down, or is it that we snatch at the easiest, most comfortable happiness, not the hard-won kind? And who was I, I thought as I ran down Louise's stairs, to aim that question at anyone but my sorry self?

· 2 ·

BY SHEER LUCK I found a cabby who drove with furious energy, cutting in and out of the narrow inbound lanes on Rock Creek Parkway, then hurling us across to Independence Avenue and through the clogged side streets. I was early, and of course there was no sign of Ron, who, after hurrying me through my lunch, would arrive at the stroke of two.

Entering the headquarters of the International Union of Toilers and Wage Laborers always plunged me into depression. If the Toilers' coffers were as fat as the right wing portrayed them to be, it certainly didn't show in their national offices. Erected in the 1970s—that Dark Age of architecture—the building was a brick-and-glass pentagon tinted the brown of watery coffee. Its twelve floors overlooked a desolate inner courtyard in which no one ever lingered. A few years ago, due to shoddy construction, stray bricks had begun to fall off the outside walls of the building, narrowly missing students from Georgetown Law who were trudging down F Street. A wire mesh cage had been set up to catch any falling masonry until the problem could be permanently fixed. Structural repairs, of course, would have cost almost as much as it had taken to build the place originally, and the mesh was still there, giving the whole building the look of some odd artistic "happening," as when that guy out West wrapped an entire island in white sheets.

These infrastructure difficulties had put a crimp in the Toilers' budget that was apparent in the office decor, which hadn't been spruced up with so much as a philodendron in the three years that Ron and I had had the account. The walls were hung with Eastern European paintings picked up by the Toilers' recently deceased president, Frank De Rosa, during his years of undercover missions to dissident unions in former Soviet bloc countries. These depressing works depicted sad-looking Yugoslavs playing cards in smoky bars, and Ukrainian villages under a bruised-looking sky. There were a few abstracts too: a gouache of angry eggplant-colored triangles whirling and snarling, and a black-and-white etching of what seemed to be either a spiderweb or a net.

In an attempt to cheer things up, a cut-rate decorator had at one time installed purple and orange rugs on all the floors open to public view. The rugs had acquired rips and tears that tripped the unwary, and were now halfheartedly patched with silver duct tape that was grubby and peeling at the edges.

I asked Phyllis, the receptionist, if I could use the small phone perched on a spindly fiberglass table in the lobby. Although the phone is meant for guests' convenience, Phyllis delights in telling people it's off-limits.

"Is Ronnie boy coming by, too?" she asked me.

"He's late already."

Phyllis snorted. She expected no man to be dependable. At fifty-one she had buried three husbands, and thus had a dark view of life. Oddly enough, this robust pessimism didn't repulse potential suitors. Phyllis might have been full of negative energy, but at least it was energy. She enthusiastically attended art openings, charity walks, community theater, and family weddings no matter how distant. She'd been on an inland-passage cruise in Alaska, an archaeological dig in Egypt, and a kayaking expedition down the Columbia River.

Phyllis dressed with the refined good taste she deemed suitable for a receptionist at a classy, mob-free union like the Toilers, but her vitality couldn't be confined in the conservative career separates she bought at the mall. Her henna-red curls stood up exuberantly from her forehead, her cloisonné earrings from her weekend in San Francisco swung wildly, her silver fake-Navajo bracelets purchased on her trip to the Grand Canyon jangled, and the bright pink nails, which she got done once a week at Darla's House of Manicures, drummed impatiently when she was still for even a minute.

Uncharitable coworkers claimed that Phyllis wore her three hapless spouses to death, but I thought the explanation was simpler. Opposites attract, and Phyllis drew quiet, spiritless men who could be dragged along, men who'd been divorced by first wives who found them hopelessly boring, or who'd been left at loose ends by the death of a saintly mother. Such men, by their very nature, are probably doomed to a fairly early demise. At least with Phyllis, they got to live life to its vicarious fullest before retiring exhausted to their heavenly reward.

Phyllis liked me for some reason, perhaps because she had little use for Ron and enjoyed watching me push him around. She'd once said to me, "We redheads have to stick together, even if I bought my color and you were born with yours."

"He's in one of his moods today," Phyllis said.

"He" was Weingould, the Toilers' director of organizing, a man so constitutionally nervous he should have worked in a library, not as chief of a bunch of unruly union agitators, as Weingould's organizing reps liked to be called.

If Weingould was jumpy it would not be an easy meeting. I sighed, and dialed my mother's number. I had a few things to say to her.

"Hello," came the faint, wispy voice my mother thinks is ladylike on the phone.

"Mother" (she thought "Mother" was more upper-class than the Bostonian "Ma," though none of us could stick to it), "Mother, why did you pressure Louise into trying to sign me up? You ruined the only free hour I have today."

"Hold on a minute, let me turn down my story."

I could feel my mother gathering her forces at the other end of the line. She would be folding laundry, wearing the sensible black gabardine stretch pants, long thick sweater, and black Keds she considered suitable home attire, and watching *All My Children* (her "story") with a childlike intensity. My mother would never be seen in trousers in public, with the exception of the grocery store, but they were practical for the thousand tasks she found to do in a three-bedroom house in which only one person lived. The bulky sweater was for two reasons. She didn't think women over fifty-five should "show off" their figures (although my mother still had the tiny waist and lovely legs of her youth) and she kept the heat down to sixty-three degrees until January.

My father had been able to leave my mother comfortably off, thanks to the success of the business she had bullied him into starting. But she acted as though she still had to watch every penny, another trait she had in common with Louise. When I urged her to relax her stringency a little, she'd sigh and say, "I would, but I worry about you kids. You're not married yet, and Michael isn't going to marry, I suppose."

"You suppose? Ma, Michael is gay. He may marry, but it won't be a woman. And I'm not suffering for cash."

My mother would go on as if I hadn't spoken. "And who knows how many Joey's going to have before Maggie Ann is finished? I'll save my money."

Maggie's easy pregnancy and short labor with her first child had been a great disappointment to my mother, who would have liked a fresh obstetrical trauma to swap with her friends in the Ladies Sodality at St. Ignatius parish. The tale of her thirty hours in labor with me was a little stale, after all, even the part where the priest gave her extreme unction and she said to him, "Father, I don't care about myself. Just ask God to save this baby!"

Now my mother said, with wounded innocence, "I didn't pressure your cousin into anything. We were talking about you, very casually, and the subject just happened to come up."

In other words, she had summoned her niece to the house for tea and some of her awful soda bread and had blackmailed Louise into doing the will of a poor, frail widow who only wanted to see her daughter well settled before she died.

"Ma, you know I'm not in the market for a husband right now."

Phyllis was openly eavesdropping. When not answering the phone, she was supposed to type or file, but she ignored the office manager's attempts to turn her into anything but a receptionist. "If I wanted to be a secretary, I'd be a secretary," she would say. "I like working with people, even if most of them are jerks."

The office manager didn't press the issue. With the tight labor market, finding receptionists who spoke clear English and would actually take messages was a daunting task. Better to keep Phyllis, who was so zealous that if you were out of the office and your optometrist called to say your new eyeglasses were ready, she'd track you down at a rest stop on the New Jersey turnpike.

"Retiring from social life to nurse a broken heart is fine for a twenty-five-year-old," said my mother. "But at thirty-two, every month counts. You have children after forty, they'll all turn out retarded or worse."

"People don't say 'retarded' anymore, Ma. And lots of women have perfectly beautiful children after forty. Besides, I don't even know if I *want* children."

Phyllis nodded emphatically. Her twin girls, Patrice and Lettice, caused her nothing but heartache with their credit card bills, their no-account boyfriends, and Lettice's recent fling with lesbianism, which Phyllis felt was calculated specifically to annoy her.

"You say that, but every woman wants children. It's unnatural not to want children."

"My ovaries have at least eight more good years."

"Fine," said my mother. "But you'll be going to college graduations when you're sixty, and how will you feel then?"

"I'm not worried about that. You'll probably have hounded me into an early grave long before my children finish high school."

My mother sniffed plaintively. She is a redoubtable warrior, but take the hostilities into her territory and she acts more helpless than Ingrid Bergman in *Gaslight*.

"I'm glad you called," she said after a pause long enough for me to have fully realized my unkindness. "I need you and Louise to help me plan the engagement shower for Betsey."

"Doesn't Betsey have any close friends to do that sort of thing?"

"Most of her family is in Connecticut, and her college crowd is scattered all over. I think she said her best friend from school lives in Dubrovnik or some terrible place like that."

I didn't understand the compulsion demonstrated by many of Betsey's friends to join the Peace Corps or spread the gospel of liberty to nasty places in the Balkans. Was America suddenly short on poor people? And was our own democracy so perfected that we had nothing left to do but export it?

"You'll have to plan the shower without me, Ma. I'm going out of town, probably right away. For a nurses' strike."

That would shut my mother up. We had not traveled so far from Boston that Ma could forget she was a good Democrat, an old-fashioned Democrat. My mother had never crossed a picket line in her life, and she still shopped with a keen eye out for the union label, though finding it was a lot harder than it used to be. While other children were sung to sleep with "Froggy Went A-Courting" and "Oh, Susannah," my mother's lullabies to us had been "Bread and Roses," "Joe Hill," and "The Mill Was Made of Marble." She'd alternate these with Irish ballads of loss, such as "Freemantle Bay," or "Grace, Please Hold Me in Your Arms," this last being the farewell of a man to his new bride hours before being hanged for the Easter Rebellion. It was a wonder we weren't all in therapy.

But I still get tears in my eyes when my mother sings "Joe Hill" while she's doing the dishes. Joe Hill, as Ma had explained to me years ago, was an organizer in the Utah copper mines who was framed for murder by the copper bosses and executed in 1915. By the time she gets to the part where Joe says, "What they forgot to kill went on to organize," I'm reaching for one of her dish towel calenders to sniffle into. I have a whole drawerful to choose from; my mother's collected them since somewhere around the time of the Cuban Missile Crisis.

To such a mother, a loyal union gal, you'd think a strike would be a valid excuse for failing in my girlish duties to Betsey. But no.

"You can at least design the shower invitations," she said.

My degree in studio art and the layout skills I'd learned on the job meant that I was obliged to help with flyers for the parish carnival, funeral programs for distant relatives, song sheets for neighborhood caroling, and every other circular or notice my mother thought would look better "done up nice."

"I'm going to be busy, Ma. A strike is no picnic. This one will probably be messy."

My mother was proud that I earned in a year more than my father had earned in two when he was my age, but she didn't want to hear about my job. She wanted to hear what color eye shadow I'd worn on my last date.

"You'll have a spare half hour here or there. Look, Betsey may not have been our first choice, but we should still welcome her to the family."

"What if I don't feel like welcoming her yet?"

It had been a dark day for all of us when Betsey brought her cranky Toyota into River Road Auto, smiled trustingly up at Johnny and asked for rush service. For all her flowered, drop-waisted dresses and unpowdered nose, Betsey was no slouch in the man-catching department. She had reeled Johnny in with patience and skill, not letting up until he was, so to speak, flopping on the floor of her boat.

Ten months after they met, Betsey was playfully dragging Johnny into Tiffany's to show him just what sort of engagement ring she'd prefer—platinum, with a pear-cut diamond. (Of course, my mother had sent Johnny straight to an old customer of my father's who had a connection on Amsterdam Avenue. She wasn't about to let Johnny go into hock so that Betsey could have a glittering trophy to show off to her friends. Johnny himself was enough of a glittering trophy, in my mother's eyes.)

"We owe this to Johnny," said Ma, with the false firmness that meant she agreed with me completely but was trying to set a good example.

"Hey, it's a long way to a June wedding. You know as well as I do that if ever a couple illustrated the phrase 'meant for each other,' it's Louise and Johnny."

"And what do you suggest, Nicky?"

"You're his aunt. Talk to him."

"You're my daughter, and talking to you does no good."

I sidestepped that one.

"At the very least, you don't have to take this shower on, Ma, do you? We'll all be standing around, gritting our teeth, and Betsey and her little kindergarten-teacher friends will be cooing over cat stuff."

Not only did Betsey have a cat, but she was one of those people who collect whimsical cat-related objects. That seemed to me grounds for being jilted by any man worthy of his salt.

"I wasn't going to get involved, but Johnny asked me to," said my mother. "And he asked me to ask you to do something pretty for the invitations, with your artistic talent."

"Ma, you know Johnny never said any such thing. We could do the invitations on construction paper for all he cares."

"Nicky, have you thought that maybe Johnny loves Louise like a sister?"

"No, Ma, and neither have you. He loves *me* like a sister. His attitude to Louise is very, very different."

"Okay, Dr. Joyce Brothers. You may be right, but that doesn't mean we can treat this girl like dirt. If Louise had wanted Johnny she'd have done something about it by now."

"Ma, Louise can barely manage to get her car inspection renewed every two years. We're not talking about someone with a life plan here. She'll float along until the week before the wedding and then it'll hit her and it'll be too late. Besides, she was definitely prickly with him this afternoon. I think that's a good sign, don't you?"

"Has she dumped that long-haired boyfriend of hers?"

"It's only a matter of time, Ma, you know that."

Joey had said once, when asked if he liked one of Louise's beaux, "I've learned not to get too attached to them." None of Louise's boyfriend oddities lasted long with her, which is what you'd expect from a woman who convinces herself she's fallen in love every nine months just to distract her heart from the subconscious pain of wanting what it can't have. In her own eyes, Louise was still the fat cousin who listened to Johnny talk about his evening when he came home from a date. A noncontender.

My mother would have agreed readily with this analysis. It was amazing how many things we could agree on and still fight constantly. The quality I share with my mother, and which keeps me reluctantly convinced that I am her blood child, is an insatiable nosiness about the true facts of other people's lives and an overpowering desire to see to it that the lives of those we love turn out the way we think they should. It always surprises both of us that the rest of the world is so willing to deal on the surface, when we feel it's a waste of living not to know what's *really* going on, not to address the real and interesting problems.

Ma said, "Enough about Louise's love life. What did you two agree on at lunch today?"

"If you're talking about matchmaking, we agreed on nothing. If you're talking about the new knee-length skirts, we both think they're hideously unflattering."

"Everything's a joke to you, Nicky. Do you want to be alone when you're forty?"

"I thought I was going to be a gray-haired mother at forty, isn't that what you said? Make up your mind. I have to go now, Ma. Ron will be here any minute."

"Fine," said my mother, in a voice that meant, "If your slick, glamorous career means more to you than your own mother, so be it."

"I'll call you before I leave town."

"I put something in the mail for you," my mother said. "Maybe you'll get it before you leave."

As I hung up the phone under Phyllis's interested gaze, I wondered what my mother had sent me this time. Probably another pamphlet in what Joey called the "Catholic, Come Home" series. They had titles such as "It's Okay to be Angry at the Church," "Are You a Lost Sheep?" and "Our Lady's Tears: How the Blessed Mother Leads Catholics Back to God."

My father had not said a word when I ceased going to church, one month to the day that I left to live at college. I hadn't gone far, just to College Park and a soulless dorm room at the University of Maryland, but it was far enough to pull loose the never-very-strong roots of my faith. Ma, of course, had said plenty. But Dad had always subtly encouraged the rebellious streak that ran through all his children. It was my father who'd bought me my first set of oil paints when I was only eight, bought them despite the fact that my mother didn't understand why I couldn't be satisfied with temperas in plastic jars and drugstore watercolors.

It was one of the few times I ever witnessed my father disagreeing with her. He said, "If she wants better paints, she should have better paints. We can call it an early birthday present." That was my father. He never seemed to notice anything—he was certainly not like the prying, vigilant, cheerful fathers so common on television in those years. He worked hard, and he was silent with exhaustion most nights when he came home. Then, out of nowhere, he'd do something just perfect, something that required an intuition for children and how passionately children want what they want.

Oddly, Ma never lectured Louise about being lapsed, perhaps because Louise was afflicted with an originally Protestant mother, my Aunt Pamela, who'd grown up a Methodist in Chambersburg, Pennsylvania. Ma once commented to my aunt that Methodists "seemed to do nothing in church but sing." All that singing was clearly too enjoyable to have anything to do with religion. No wonder Louise had imbibed the idea that faith was supposed to make you feel good. The poor girl never had a chance.

In books and movies, the grown child learns to appreciate the aging, difficult parent who has never been properly understood. It turns out that behind all the crotchetiness, there always beat a vulnerable, sensitive heart that hungered for filial affection. I waited for any sign from my remaining parent that this was the case, but clearly my mother was going by a different script, one that included the lines, "You weren't a pretty child, but people always noticed your hair," or, "If you ever put me in a home, don't even bother coming to visit. I won't want to see you."

My kind and silent father was gone. My grandmother was a memory, a woman with eyes like mine and a will so fierce that it had dragged an entire family onto the boat to America when no one but her really wanted to go. A will so fierce that she had been the hands-down victor in every fight that she and my mother had ever had. I missed seeing that. And I missed my father's interested approval, an approval I'd never had to win.

I still had my mother, though, and the beautiful relationship we might develop in her golden years. Somehow, that wasn't much comfort.

"YOU'RE LATE," I said to Ron.

"Last-minute crisis at the office," he replied.

In other words, he'd had to floss his teeth and admire his profile in the luxurious privacy of his executive washroom. Ron took an innocent delight in his own beauty. He had windswept hair—dark with a gleam of silver here and there—that fell in Regency locks on his forehead, a square chin with the proverbially dangerous cleft, and broad shoulders shown off by the war correspondent trench coats and black turtlenecks he affected. Another woman might have been weakened by constant exposure to his melting good looks, but there was something slightly wrong about Ron's mouth that put me off; it wasn't quite resolute enough, and the general outline of his lips wasn't defined enough for my taste. Besides, I knew better than to fall for a man who appeared in black turtlenecks anyplace but on a ski slope or during a burglary. Somewhere along the way a man like that has looked in the mirror once too often.

Ron wound up in public relations because communism collapsed, leaving him high and dry, James Bond looking for a day job. In the golden last days of the Cold War he'd been a hired hand for the American Foundation for Freedom, a quasi-governmental organization that funneled a lot of money to Poland and Cuba and worked closely (many said too closely) with the most staunchly anti-communist AFL unions—and with other more sinister organizations, perhaps. Maybe it wasn't for nothing that it was sometimes joked about as the "AFL-CIA" back then.

In his single days, Ron liked to hang out with the World Bank cocktail-hour crowd and tell stories about sneaking into Havana or taking secret video footage of Mexican factories violating NAFTA by dumping toxic waste. (The truth, I suspect, is that Ron was just a glorified delivery boy, getting cash into the right hands but not clued in on anything else.) Among D.C.'s plentiful Euro-snobs and embassy hangers-on, he became a ubiquitous lounge lizard. Women in those circles would smile dismissively when his name came up: "Oh, yes, I know Ron. *Everybody* knows Ron."

Then he met Dana in line at the Department of Motor Vehicles. Dana was a stunningly attractive child psychiatrist with a firm yet sympathetic air ideal for managing Ron and, I assumed, her small clients. Dana knew malleable raw material when she met it. Three months after their first dinner together, Ron was married to Dana and living in a split-level in Bethesda. Six months after that, he was promoted to account exec at the prestigious PR megafirm Swinton McClaine. And four years later, he went out on his own.

Ron's character was flavored through and through with a conniving sleaziness, but his wife, who had few illusions about him, kept his worst excesses in check. If it weren't for Dana's restraining influence, I wouldn't have gone to work for Ron. Even so, there had been plenty of times when I regretted my decision. For example, the week I first came on board with him as "creative vice president," renouncing my secure berth as a copywriter at Swinton, Ron shook my never-very-robust faith in him by entertaining the possibility of the Mothers in Motion account.

Mothers in Motion was a group of right-wing female fundamentalists leading a thousand-woman journey from California to Capitol Hill to lobby for private school vouchers, an end to sex education, and a return to the values that made this country great. Unfortunately, on the third day of the walk, a few of the more overzealous Mothers had the inspiration of throwing smoke bombs and firecrackers into a Planned Parenthood clinic in Nevada, leaving MiM in need of some speedy damage control. Ron received a hysterical early morning phone call from a Florida senator with uncomfortably close ties to this posse of Mrs. Cleavers.

"You can't be serious," I said, when he broached the idea of pulling MiM's irons out of the fire.

"What do you have against motherhood?" said Ron.

"Nothing. I just have a problem with felons in flowered aprons."

"Those were just a handful of fringe members."

"Save it for the press statement."

"Shouldn't feminism mean that all points of view are embraced?" said Ron, quoting perhaps from some Heritage Foundation radio program he'd turned on by accident once in the car. Like all good PR men, Ron was a magpie. Without being especially thoughtful or perceptive, he could pick up snappy phrases like this and retrieve them when the occasion called for it.

It was only by pointing out to Ron that our left-leaning clients were likely to blacklist us if we started shilling for MiM that I persuaded him to pass on the project. In the past few years, I'd slowly managed to convince him that since we couldn't compete for the kind of big-dollar accounts the major players went after, we should carve a niche as the plucky little firm that gave its offbeat, affordable best to every noble but underfunded cause from carpal tunnel syndrome to the rights of circus elephants.

In our first year together, we won a few big victories that put us on the map. We got a pro-gun-control state senator elected in Montana. We kick-started the fund-raising efforts of a well-meaning but naive women's health services collective, raising enough money to open a shelter for victims of domestic abuse in downtown Memphis. Ron enraged me by calling it "Tempura Home for Lightly Battered Women" in private, but he drummed up a million to open its doors.

"I told you, you wouldn't regret it," Ron said when he took me out for sushi on the anniversary of my first year with him and handed me a bonus check that brought my Advocacy, Inc. salary up to nearly two-thirds of the one I'd left behind at Swinton McClaine. It was typical of Ron that on this occasion he chose a sushi bar, never inquiring if I had any taste for raw fish (I don't) or saki (I do). I ordered shrimp teriyaki and let myself bask in the five-minute glow of Ron's gratitude.

"When did I say I didn't regret it, Ron?"

"Nicky, Nicky. Working with you has been an adventure. We're like Lewis and Clark."

"I'll be Clark. I think Lewis had syphilis."

"You know, if I weren't married, Nicky, I could really go for you."

"There's a thought to keep me awake at nights," I said. Ron took this as a compliment. He liked to flirt with me in the hammy way that reformed rakes adopt, but I never felt threatened for a minute by his smarmy glances and regretful allusions to his lost single state. If Ron were to be, say, run over by a bus, Dana would grieve but she would go on, personally and professionally. Ron might stray occasionally—though I had no firsthand knowledge that he did—but, if the reverse happened, Ron would wind up a wreck of a man, living with his married sister in Wisconsin, selling used cars or model homes.

Why did I work with Ron, whose morals were flexible on a good day and priced for quick sale on a bad day? Probably because he didn't care that I wasn't a real public relations professional. He knew that I'd gotten my start at Swinton when, after I'd temped there for six months, they decided to keep me around rather than go to the trouble of training a new junior copywriter. Ron knew I had no ad agency experience, no communications degree. He didn't care, because as a business team we were perfectly complementary. Ron could put together long-range media plans as beautiful and inventive as da Vinci's blueprints for a flying machine. He was a fountain of what that brilliant adman David Ogilvie called "big ideas," the overarching concepts without which no campaign is truly a campaign. For my part, I turned out snappy copy that combined sincere emotion with low-key credibility. I laid out ads and brochures for clients who couldn't afford a real graphic designer. I even pinch-hit as an events planner when I absolutely couldn't get out of it.

While I would never have Ron's flashy way of pitching a story, I grew to know a reliable handful of reporters at key dailies and magazines who'd return my calls because I tried not to waste their time, and who could be counted on to give our side a fair shake in their coverage. Once in a while I hit lucky with TV coverage. Ron was our star media relations guy, but he'd taught me enough that I could back him up when his plate got too full. The whole setup worked far better than I'd hoped.

"Because we're small, we do it all" was the motto Ron wanted to put on our stationery, until I convinced him it made us sound like a rental car company.

Trade union clients like the Toilers were a fairly recent development for Advocacy, Inc. Back when big labor really *was* big labor, the unions didn't need much help from spin doctors. Now, with union membership down to 18 percent of the workforce and with some politicians putting unions on their hit list right up there with single mothers and evolutionists, a few of the more forward-thinking honchos in the AFL had begun to realize that something was needed.

We'd come to Weingould's attention a few years ago when we helped win a first contract for the janitors and maintenance workers union at Windsor Real Estate, the owner of luxury high-rises across Pittsburgh. Ron came up with a "Custodians with a Conscience" campaign, in which lovable members of Local 802, dressed in caps and denim overalls, picked up litter in city parks. This feel-good gag so won the public's sympathy and the media's praise ("Big Labor Cleans Up Its Act," ran the approving editorial in the *Steel City Clarion*) that the janitors wound up with a 6 percent raise and family health insurance benefits. Weingould was impressed with our performance, and one meeting with Ron convinced him that together they could turn the Toilers into the little union that could.

"Can Wendy handle your other assignments for the next two weeks or more?" Ron asked, as Phyllis phoned up to the Big Guy to announce our arrival.

"I guess so. She'd work twenty hours a day if we let her."

"Pack heavy. It's cold and it's damp," Ron said.

"I'll charge my new longjohns to the office account."

"You seem less than enthusiastic, Nicky. It's not like you."

"It's just that this strike couldn't have come at a worse time," I said. "We've got the Campsters thing, and the Joseph's Kitchen canned food drive, and the Reading Ready adult literacy fund-raiser. I don't know *what* we're going to do for that."

"Wendy suggested a book-themed house tour. Get six or seven of the board of directors who have fancy homes in Georgetown or Dupont to lend them out and deck each mansion out in a theme from some famous book, like netting and harpoons for *Moby-Dick* or fake Spanish moss for *Gone With the Wind*."

"I don't think that Tara had Spanish moss, Ron. And I have trouble believing Wendy's ever read *Moby-Dick*. Or *Gone With the Wind*, for that matter. I'm not sure she has the mental staying power even to sit through the movie."

"Give the kid a break," said Ron.

"You give her a break. It's your ass her uncle is saving from being dragged through an audit."

"What do you think of her idea, though?"

"They'll like it. Who doesn't get a kick out of looking at rich people's homes? No facility rental costs, either. Our Wendy comes through in the clutch again."

"I realize that she gets on your nerves, but you know you're lousy at the adorable stuff, Nicky, and she always nails it."

"You're right. Wendy's great. She's great. She really is."

There, I had done my good deed for the day. So what if Wendy would just as soon throw herself into planning a book-*burning* bash, if that had been what the client wanted? So what if her enthusiasm was undiscriminating and her mind a shallow turquoise pool with goldfish darting and pennies winking? She gave her all, and she was, in her own way, irreplaceable.

"Ron," I said, "I've worked three strikes with you, but I've never worked a strike on my own before. I'd say I have the potential to really screw up."

"You can do it. It's your sort of thing. Storming the barricades. Fighting the good fight."

"Going down with the ship."

"They can't be much worse off than they are already, so nothing you do can hurt them any," said Ron.

"Gee, thanks. I feel better now."

The elevator, bouncing on its frayed cables, carried us up to Weingould's office. Its inspection notice was three years out of date. Wasn't there someone in the city government in charge of these things? Who was I kidding? In this city, it had been cause for prolonged celebration when the murder rate finally dropped below New York's.

As Ron adjusted his pocket square and assumed the entirely misleading air of competence and alertness with which he greeted clients, I had a feeling of impending doom that, as it turned out, was entirely accurate.

· 4 ·

WEINGOULD WAS ON the phone when we walked in, but he motioned us to the couch and waved an ink-stained hand to indicate that he'd be with us in a minute. Unlike many of our clients, Weingould tried to keep his appointments on schedule. Unfortunately, he agonized over the simplest decision, and it slowed him down. Like a doctor, he was always lagging behind by midafternoon.

The couch, as usual, was stacked with folders, contracts, and the yellow legal pads he scrawled ideas on and then forgot about. We cleared space enough to sit, Ron barely refraining from dusting the crumbly leather before it made contact with the seat of his pants.

Weingould's long-suffering secretary, Mary Bridget, handed us "Proud to Be Union" mugs of acrid coffee and a paper cup full of packets of lightener mixed in with a few venerable sugar cubes. What seemed from its aroma to be soy sauce stained the bottom of this cup, which was clearly the receptacle for condiments of all kinds. I decided to take my coffee black for a change.

Weingould was wrapping things up.

"Okay, Bill, let me make sure I've got this. You're saying they can't get the phone list ready until the twentieth. We're paying them twenty goddamn thousand dollars for a quickie poll and they can't do better than that? They can't make it the eighteenth? We wait much longer, the Teamsters'll be in there handing out free windbreakers and then we're really screwed. . . . Okay, okay. Tell them if they can manage the eighteenth, we'd appreciate it. . . . Okay, just do your best. I've got a meeting now, but you tell them from me the eighteenth would make all the difference. God Almighty, I'm sending this guy's kids to college with what I pay him, he could move his butt for a change. . . .

Okay. Okay. . . . Yeah, I know it's a long shot. . . . Okay, I'll speak to you when I speak to you."

This was a typical scene. Weingould, a victim of the age of office technology, lacked focus, and I had never entered his office for an appointment without sitting through the tail end of his frantic, pacing phone calls. He loved to shout into his speakerphone while scrolling down the ninety-two e-mails he got every hour, ripping open overnight-mail packages, and dictating memos to one of the three secretaries who indulged him and ran his life. Rumor had it that Weingould had remained on the telephone throughout his brief honeymoon, consummating his marriage only with the help of one of those headband receivers long-distance operators wear.

Weingould was heavily built but not overweight like so many of his cohorts—the reason being that he could not eat and talk at the same time. His ties were always crooked and his shirttail was always out, but his clothes were beautiful, tailored to a perfection Ron only aspired to. His wife picked them out, for Weingould never left the office until after all the stores closed.

Alan Weingould had grown up in the labor movement. His father, Jacob, had been an early leader of the garment workers, a man remembered both for his courage in facing down the sweatshop bosses and his early and generous assistance to Jews fleeing Hitler. Jacob Weingould had the heart of a lion. His son had the heart of a St. Bernard on acid, always bounding forward into snowdrifts too high for him. Thanks to his chaotic and devoted efforts, the Toilers had become one of the fastest-growing unions in the AFL-CIO. Driven and demanding he certainly could be, but in a town full of shills and operators, he was a refreshingly true believer.

"Now, what are you here for?" he asked Ron, shifting some of the piles on his desk and putting on his reading glasses.

"The St. Francis strike," Ron said.

"St. Francis," said Weingould blankly, as if conjuring up visions of Assisi's lover of wolves and sparrows and wondering what it had to do with us.

"In Winsack," Ron said. He was accustomed to these preliminaries. "Rhode Island."

"Yeah. Yeah. That's right. The nurses."

The Toilers had only recently started organizing nurses in a big way. Most of their members worked in some form of civil or public service, from garbage collectors in Trenton to professors at city colleges in Philly and Queens. Jerry Goreman, the bureaucratic little man who'd succeeded the legendary Frank De Rosa as the Toilers' president, had no fire in his belly for winning new members. Goreman's goals were simple: he wanted to spend his years as president watching the current membership dues pile up in the Toilers' treasury, thus funding his junkets to international labor conferences in Madrid and Tokyo.

But Goreman had made a lot of enemies during the three years he'd played a watchful Stalin to De Rosa's Lenin, and his political base was far from strong. Weingould wrested money from the union's executive board by assuring them that health care was the new gold rush territory. Under the HMOs, even the American Medical Association was talking about getting doctors organized. If M.D.s were that desperate, Weingould reasoned, the time was ripe to prospect for nurses.

And he was right. The Toilers' nurse membership, which had once consisted of a few straggling locals in state mental hospitals, had grown to twenty thousand in the last three years. Nowhere near the size of the heavyweights, but still very respectable. Weingould had been vindicated, but he was unprepared for how tough these organizing drives were. In the public sector, workers' rights were protected by better laws and long precedent. But in the largely unpoliced Wild West of the private sector, the hospitals had proven themselves nasty adversaries—dragging out contract negotiations for years, hiring union-busting lawyers to come up with perfectly legal schemes for intimidating employees, and delaying elections until ordered to hold them by the courts, by which time all the union's original supporters had been fired or pressured out of their jobs.

What Weingould really needed were seasoned experts with a track record in private-sector organizing. What he could afford, thanks to Goreman's budget pinching, was Ron and me, flying by the seat of our pants.

*   *   *

Without even looking, Weingould put his hand on the one manila folder he needed in the stack of thirty on his desk. As he did so, pink message slips and penciled reminders from his secretary fluttered to the floor and were rolled to shreds under the wheels of his desk chair.

Ron pulled out his engraved Mont Blanc pen and the leather-bound notebook with his initials stamped on the cover. He brought them to every client meeting. Ron loved obvious executive accessories. Like any actor, he needed a few props. I dug out a steno pad and a Bic.

"We have a situation here," said Weingould in his verbal shorthand. "Our local at St. Francis is a fair-size local, maybe one hundred, one-fifty nurses. Catholic hospital in a small blue-collar mill town. *Used* to be a mill town, anyway, like all those towns up there, depressing as hell. Hospital's been operating since 1910, was run at one time by the Little Sisters of St. Francis with lay nurses added over the years. We won our first election in 1979, actually bargained pretty decent contracts since then. Clare Murray is the local president there. Done well for the past eight years. Well respected, not just at the hospital but at the state level."

Ron inscribed, "Murray—well respected" in his notebook. His handwriting is large and sprawling. You can tell he never went to parochial school.

"Murray grew up right there in Winsack. Always had a good, productive relationship with the administration. Two years ago the hospital was acquired by a big for-profit chain, Coventry Inc., and things are going to hell in a handbasket. Take a look at this."

"This" was a petition from the St. Francis nurses on the medical-surgical floor. A med-surg floor, I could gather from the wording, was a regular hospital floor, rather than an intensive care or cardiac unit. The nurses were asking the hospital to remedy certain dangerous conditions in their unit. The problems listed made me hope I never needed my tonsils out.

I read the petition text over Ron's shoulder.

"*We are alarmed by a nurse-patient ratio that has gone from one to three, to one to eight in the past year,*" the nurses had written.

"One nurse to eight patients?" I asked Weingould.

"That's the first step these for-profits take. Cutting labor costs, and nurses are expensive labor."

We read on. "*Incident reports include: a sixty-year-old male who waited more than an hour for a herapin drip due to equipment shortages . . . some patients going ten hours without vital signs taken because the two night nurses were occupied with higher acuity cases . . . inadequate nurse training on infusion pumps which could result in fatal dosage errors, including one incident in which an exhausted nurse in the fourteenth hour of her shift keyed in 82 milligrams of morphine instead of 8.2 milligrams before realizing her mistake . . . a patient assigned a bed in the supply room because all other rooms were overcrowded already.*"

What surprised me most was that the petition, according to Weingould, had been signed by every single nurse in the med-surg unit. You almost never saw that. Hospitals did not look kindly on nurses who were "troublemakers." Conditions must be really lousy at St. Francis.

"Negotiations were a disaster from day one," Weingould said, loosening his tie. Ron loosened his too. I had nothing to loosen, so I crossed my legs.

"The nurses were focusing on staffing and safety issues," Weingould went on. "No big-money demands. We knew we were in trouble when the hospital waited two months past the official start of bargaining to submit its bargaining proposals. When they did, we weren't even close. Management offered no staffing relief, no patient-safety concessions. Nothing on forced overtime or floating. Needless to say, no raise. The hospital's crying poverty, which is a load of crap."

"Financial statements?" Ron asked, leaning forward. He loved money talk.

"I'm getting a specialist to take a look. At a glance it seems like the hospital had a stellar past five years, which is probably one reason Coventry snapped it up in the first place. But there's a few weird things going on with wholly-owned subsidiaries that I'm curious about."

"Excuse me," I said, breaking up their little tête-à-tête. "But how come these nurses are so ready to walk out? They're looking at a strike that could go into Christmas."

"The hospital's sent every signal that they're not going to budge, and the nurses know it. They're practically being locked out as it is."

"Any allies on the board of directors?"

"One or two. We have a source on the board who should come through for us in a day or two on that."

You had to hand it to Weingould, he never threw you into a situation without thoroughly prepping you. Mary Bridget might have to program reminders of his wife's birthday into his computer for him, but he knew the details of what was happening in every single one of the forty campaigns he had going nationwide.

"What's our time line?" said Ron.

"The local took a strike vote that goes into effect at the will of the bargaining team, which could be soon if there continues to be no movement. The vote was at ninety-three percent. Can you have Nicky up there pronto?"

"By this weekend. Who's the MFWIC again?" Ron asked. (MFWIC, pronounced "miffwick," was an old campaign acronym which meant "mother-fucker-what's-in-charge.") "Tony something?"

"Tony Boltanski," said Weingould in clipped, flat tones, as if he were some sort of FBI agent filling another agent in on Tony's sordid past.

"What's his story?"

"We got him from SEIU. He ran that Connecticut election that won the whole Fairhaven system. A month into that campaign the hospital had him roughed up by some security guards. He told them he'd take it out of their sorry asses, and he stayed there, getting in their faces for two years, until they won that thing. He's a good guy."

Tony Boltanski was a good guy, all right. The best. The American worker had no better friend than Tony Boltanski, veteran of the Smithson Mine strike, the Superlink Telephone lockout, and the Hedgerow Farms blueberry pickers' famous 1989 boycott. The tougher a fight looked to be, the faster Tony was there.

Tony Boltanski was a real pro, and the Toilers had been smart to hire him. He was also a self-centered, pugnacious, uncompromising emotional deaf-mute whom I had no wish to see again, let alone be cooped up with for the duration of what promised to be a bitter and prolonged strike that the public would regard with little initial sympathy. Nurses leaving their patients was right up there with police officers or firefighters walking off the job.

"And Murray?" said Ron. "Anything to watch out for there?"

"Just take a look at her," Weingould said, grabbing a videocassette from a shoe box, which he then kicked under his desk. "This is from the Nurses' March on Washington last January," he said. "The ANA was there, SEIU, AFSCME, everyone who's into nurses. Murray was one of the leadoff speakers. You'll see she knows how to handle herself. Damn it, what happened to the volume? Wait."

He fiddled with a few push buttons, turning off the videocassette player by accident. Noisy static filled the screen.

"Mary Bridget!" Weingould bellowed. She was already at the door. They had a sixth sense, Weingould's secretaries, like that of a mother who can hear her baby stir in its sleep from three rooms away.

Properly started by Mary Bridget, the tape revealed nurses marching down New Jersey Avenue and East Capitol Street with signs that read, "Every patient deserves a nurse," and "Patient care first, profits last." It was a very cold day, you could tell that from the flat, bright blue sky and the wind that whipped at the signs and blew the banners. Most of them were wearing sensible coats or down jackets over their uniforms. Contrary to *Playboy* fantasies, nurses in general are far from glamorous.

"The rally was pushing for a whole series of measures on patients' rights, most of which never made it out of committee," Weingould said. "But a lot of politicians turned out, since health care is everyone's favorite issue these days. Okay, here she is."

The camera cut to a woman in a navy blue coat standing at a podium with the Capitol rising behind her. Her dark hair was confined in a low, ladylike ponytail. She wore a small union pin on her lapel, and her hands were gloveless and chapped-looking.

Not many people appear to advantage at a podium. They hang over it, or back gingerly away from the microphone, or mumble into their chests. Clare Murray didn't look half bad. She was tall and sturdy, with wide shoulders held straight back and a rather straight-up-and-down torso that would probably be prone to solid stoutness in later life. My brother Joey called a certain Celtic cast of feature "potato-faced Irish," and Clare was one of those, with her square forehead and chin and slightly fleshy cheeks. Her eyes were her greatest beauty, wide-set and straightforward.

Clare's speech was about the need for a national whistle-blower act to protect nurses who spoke out against hospital cost-cutting practices that endanger patients.

"It's not about our being heroes," she said. "It's not about us against management. It's about our patients. Nowadays, some hospitals are even calling patients 'care consumer units,' as if by taking the humanity of patients away, it will be easier to forget them, to forget that they're the reason hospitals are there, not the other way around. Well, we're here to say we won't let the patient be forgotten. Not by our hospitals, not by the insurance industry, and not by this Congress."

The crowd broke out in enthusiastic applause. Clare Murray nodded once and stepped away while the clapping and cheering were still going on.

"She's good, she's very good," said Ron absently. He was eyeing the next speaker on the tape, a popular blond actress justly respected for her devotion to liberal causes. He was probably picturing her naked. Sometimes I wondered if Ron was strictly faithful to Dana. Some men had a roving eye. Ron's entire persona roved, searching new worlds to charm and seduce. His romantic bravado in the days of his singleness had made Rudolf Valentino look self-effacing in comparison, and it was hard to believe that marriage, even a prospering marriage, had changed him entirely.

"Yeah, but Clare Murray may not be able to hold this thing together," said Weingould. "This thing's a war of attrition. Basically, can our nurses stay out on strike long enough and cause the hospital enough grief so that it's less trouble for them to deal with us than to fight us? That's the question."

Without glancing in my direction, he handed me the St. Francis file, then two five-pound binders of background material for light reading.

"How fast did you say you can get her up there again?" he asked Ron.

"I just have to tie up a few loose ends," I said. "You can address me directly, you know. I'm sitting right here."

"Sorry," Weingould mumbled. Ron glared at me.

"It's lucky you're good at what you do," he said in the elevator. "You'd never survive on tact and charm alone."

"That's what I have you for."

· 5 ·

THERE WERE MENNONITES in the dining car singing hymns. I scowled in their direction. Being forced to listen to other people's religious views is as bad as being forced to breathe secondhand smoke. Here I had temporarily escaped my mother's doom-laden reminders to repent, only to be lectured in song by people who had the path to unmechanized salvation all mapped out and were looking awfully smug about it.

I took a large sloppy bite out of my tuna sandwich and opened my copy of *Murder on the Orient Express*, which I was rereading for the third time. I glanced over at them. The women's faces were placid under their unbecoming caps. The men looked self-assured and jovial. For a moment it seemed so tempting: a healthy, hardworking life. The assurance that you were living the Lord's way. Perhaps a nice, strapping husband you had married at eighteen and a few plump, sweet-tempered children.

Then I thought of other sweetnesses, of a picnic with Jeremy at Carderock in the middle of March, when we necked on a blanket like teenagers and pulled the blanket around us when it started to rain. I thought of how in the beginning we'd slept so late and made love so long on Saturday mornings that we didn't leave the house until hunger forced us out for a three o'clock lunch. I thought of all the boys I'd dated in college, of one in particular who drew me valentines in red crayon and kissed like a very angel. Perhaps I would try to become good in extreme old age, when men didn't want me anymore and I needed to settle accounts with my Maker, just in case it turned out he had noticed what I was up to all those years.

I had a whole table to myself. Not many people on this 7 A.M. Friday train to Providence. Ron fussed about my taking trains because it removed me from his reach for hours, but like most people who have to fly frequently on business, I've grown to hate flying. Besides, I love trains. They're still somehow both cozy and adventurous. You can walk around. You can eat whenever you want to.

Best of all, even Ron couldn't expect me to phone him from a train, since there is usually only one phone booth at best, and it's always taken. I had refused to purchase a cell phone on the grounds that it would give me brain cancer, though the real reason was that I didn't want one more electronic shackle in my life. Ron had scoffed at me, but immediately went out and bought one of those gamma-ray-shielding earpieces, or some such device. Ron was wonderfully suggestible that way. He had an air purifier in his office, a radon detector at home, and a special alarm on his car that would alert the police departments of five counties to his location should he ever be carjacked.

Johnny had driven me to Union Station. I'd told him not to bother, but he'd insisted. We were barely a block from my apartment when he started talking about Louise.

"She was so damn fussy the other day," he said. "Not fussy about what shoes we bought, but fussy with me. She picked on every word I said."

"Now, Johnny," I said. "Think back. What word was it in particular that she picked on?"

"I don't know. How can I remember?"

"You're right. It was a whole two days ago."

He swerved expertly to avoid a jeep whose driver, yammering, of course, on a cell phone, seemed to think that the lane markings were just suggestions for him to take or leave and that red lights were for other, less fabulous people. I gave the guy the finger and a look of death.

"Nicky, I've told you not to do that," said Johnny. "Haven't you ever heard of road rage? You never know who has a gun these days."

"That little snot doesn't have a gun. He'd piss in his pants if he ever saw a gun. He just has a tiny member and a great, big SUV."

"Well, it's a bad habit. Every housewife is packing a pistol lately."

"Which is why you tailgated that guy who cut you off at the Georgia Ave. exit the other day and got out and yelled at him at the first traffic light until he cried."

Johnny has a wide, thin mouth and a long, easy grin that tilts up and sideways. When he smiled, I saw my father's smile again.

"Louise," I reminded him. "You were going to put your cute little mind to remembering what set her off."

"How should I know about Louise? I can't do anything right with her these days."

"The other night. Think back, Johnny. You can do it."

"We went out to White Flint and got the shoes and I thanked her, and I even took her to dinner in Georgetown at that place she likes, La Pommette, and then we walked along the canal down by the lock where the touring barge is tied up, you know where that is."

I knew. It was a beautiful spot where the path wound down among maple trees and old row houses. Very secluded.

"Then I asked her if she'd be a reader at the wedding and she said she hated getting up in front of people at these things. And I said, what about Cousin Andrea's wedding, where you got drunk and tried to do the Texas two-step during the bride's dance with her father? And she said, why didn't I ever remember the times when she acted charming? Why did I only remember the times she made a fool of herself? And I said I thought she *was* charming at Andrea's wedding, I even said adorable. Then she got really mad, said I was making fun of her and that she would prefer to be a guest at the wedding just like everyone else. And then she wanted to go home."

Poor Louise. Shopping for him as if she were his wife, eating dinner together in the gauzy light of La Pommette's back room, strolling along the most romantic stretch of the towpath. Then being asked by Johnny not if she'd ever thought of him as more than a cousin, but if she'd agree to read from Kahlil Gibran at his wedding to Betsey. If he hadn't been driving, I'd have slugged him.

"Johnny," I said, "did it ever occur to you that you could have, how can I put it, feelings for Louise?"

"Feelings?"

We were almost at the corner where Mass Ave. doglegs over to the station. There was no time to be tactful.

"Romantic feelings. It's not like you're actually related, you know. Not blood related."

"Are you crazy, Nicky?"

"Johnny, Louise is the only person you've ever really trusted one hundred percent. Even with me and Mike and Joey, you keep your guard up that one little tiny bit. I'm not blaming you. But Louise has always been the exception. So why are you planning to spend the rest of your life with someone else?"

I almost said, "with someone as boring and stupid as Betsey," but I didn't want to push it.

"Louise has always considered me like a brother," said Johnny. "She's never given me a second thought."

"A second thought? Louise would donate a kidney for you."

"A romantic second thought, I mean. Has Louise ever said anything to lead you to believe she cares about me in any romantic way?"

"No, but I know. I *know*, Johnny."

"Excuse me if I don't want to bet my future on your woman's intuition, Nicky. Besides, if I ever say anything to Louise and she looks at me like I'm certifiable, there goes our friendship. I could never hang out with her again."

"Johnny, you're not going to be able to hang out with her much once you're married to Betsey. You think Betsey's going to let you out of the house every Wednesday night to watch *Law and Order* with Louise? You think she's going to let Louise pick out your ties? You think she'll let you go racing over there when Louise calls crying at one in the morning over some loser?"

He was quiet, appearing to digest this. You never know with men. Sometimes they look as if they're cogitating, when all the time they're just playing the NBA theme song in their heads.

Finally he said, "I would be nuts to screw things up with Betsey. She's a wonderful girl. She has so many great qualities."

"Which of course is why you marry someone. Because they have great qualities."

"You want me to marry someone *without* great qualities?"

"I'm saying it's not quantifiable. There are only two reasons to marry someone, Johnny. One is that she's pregnant and her father is in the Mob. The other is that you want to, for reasons you could never list."

"I don't know, Nicky. Why'd you have to bring all this up right now?"

He was scowling and uncomfortable, but he was still managing to drive wonderfully, avoiding taxicabs, Metro buses that took up two-thirds of the road, and diplomats who, as we all know, can bump off a few people on their way in to work without fearing legal retribution. There's a reason the subway is so popular in this town.

"Because I thought that it might be rude to bring it up at the rehearsal dinner. Just turn it over in your head, Johnny. I won't bug you for another week or two."

"That long?"

The station loomed up before us. Whenever you were late for a train, traffic was awful. Be early, and in the middle of an engrossing conversation about affairs of the heart, and every light turned green for you. I leaned over and hugged my cousin, and told him not to come in with me. He knocked the side of his head lightly against the side of mine, his version of a cousinly embrace.

"Go get 'em up there, Nicky. And if I find myself needing advice for the lovelorn, I'll know who to call."

"Anyone but me."

"Right."

Watching the Mennonites unwrapping their homemade sandwiches, I wondered if I was even remotely qualified to boss Johnny about his romantic choices. After all, I was passing up Jeremy despite his sincere repentance, a move that spoke volumes about my unyieldingness, my stony heart. Was there something to be said for Christian forgiveness, a precept that had been drummed into me since I was five and beat up Jamie Raley next door for painting my bicycle black? Then again, what had always irked me about Christian forgiveness was that it was never presented to me as a choice. As soon as you can toddle, you're just ordered to turn the other cheek, even in situations that violate the keen sense of justice that every child possesses. This is hardly the way to raise mercy-minded adults. After all, the reason most people don't like lima beans is that no one ever asked them if they did or not.

The train rounded a curve and knocked coffee over the page where Hercule Poirot discovers the mysterious pipe cleaner left at the scene of the murder. Poirot, of course, would not be fooled by the intended implications of that pipe cleaner, or by the grease spot on the Countess's passport, or the strange complication of the doorknob and the sponge bag. He would never let a bunch of singing Mennonites, even if any had been permitted to board the Orient Express, distract him from the task at hand.

My own wits wandered more easily. Half my mind was on Johnny and Louise as I read.

During the Gulf War. That was the first time it came home to me that Johnny might love Louise, that Louise might love Johnny.

My little brother, Joey, who went through college on an ROTC scholarship, was in the air force reserves, and it looked for a while as if his unit would be called up. This was before he met Maggie, and he wanted to go. Joey's job in the reserves was repairing the exteriors of damaged aircraft, sort of like bodywork on a car. This duty wouldn't have put him directly on the front lines, but there was no predicting what could happen in a war, and Joey was not one to stay put just to be safe. He would just shout "Yahoo!" and charge on in. I'd have worried less about my brother Michael, who, although he is brave beyond doubt, does not get intoxicated by risk. In this way Michael is fundamentally different from Joey and Johnny.

It was Joey's birthday that January night I'm speaking of, and we were all there: Mike, Joey, Louise, Johnny, me. And some girl of Johnny's (there was always some girl of Johnny's) who had to meet other friends after dinner. Joey's unit had been put on alert two days before. We went to his favorite Mexican restaurant, Cactus Cantina, on Wisconsin Ave., and made our way through two pitchers of margaritas, all of us except Michael, who rarely drank. The only time I'd ever seen him plastered was at my father's wake.

After dinner, we piled in Joey's truck with Michael driving, minus Johnny's girl, and drove down to the Jefferson Memorial. It was bitingly cold for going outdoors, but the memorial at night was a favorite place of ours. In the night quiet there, you can hear the sound of the breezes in the pine trees all around and sit on the wall of the Tidal Basin and dangle your feet above the black, lapping water.

We'd stopped for coffee on the way down. Louise ordered hot chocolate, as always. Johnny teased her about being a baby who still needed her cocoa at night, then drank most of it. We sat on the steps overlooking the water. Louise asked for Johnny's sweater and he gave her his coat instead, leaning against her to keep warm. Joey started to horse around, singing a corny old song about a young man off to war, "Billy, Don't Be a Hero."

In the song Billy commits some fool act of bravery and all his fiancée gets, all that's left of him, is a letter from the army praising his courage. Joey sang high and squeaky for the fiancée parts, then he started singing, "Billy, don't be a queer-o," shoving Mike in the arm and laughing. I watched them clowning around. As different as they were in looks and character, a stranger would immediately know that they were brothers. You could see it in the quick turn of their heads when something took their interest, in the way they had of collapsing at the middle when they laughed.

Louise said to Johnny, very quietly, "It's a good thing we've never had a real war."

"Why?" he said. I could barely distinguish their words, but years of eavesdropping had sharpened my hearing.

"I would never have let you go."

"I'd want to go. Talk about an adventure."

"If you wanted to go I'd have to knock you in the head and put you in the trunk of my car and not stop until we got so far into the Canadian wilderness you'd never make it back."

"I'd be mad at you if you did that," he said, but he didn't look mad. Louise was staring out at the water. Below us on the plinth Joey was doing a little soft shoe to "If I Only Had a Brain." He was three sheets to the wind.

Louise didn't see the way Johnny looked at her then. Her lovely hair was blowing back from her face, and Johnny took a lock of it between his fingers. If I hadn't been drunk, this might not have struck me as anything but the usual cousinly affection. But I saw something

I hadn't seen before, and Mike saw it too. I remember Mike looking at me, to see if I noticed.

Joey did not go over to the war. It ended too quickly, to his deep disappointment. There's always been a kind of halo around that night for me, though. If not war, the shadow of war, and if not love, the beginnings of love.

The Mennonites left the dining car, and I read for a while in luxurious solitude. It was such a pleasure to read my old Agatha Christies, especially now that Jeremy was no longer looking over my shoulder, commenting on my frivolous taste in reading, and trying to interest me in some dreary, waterlogged modern novel set in the English Midlands or a depressing, newly released anthology of World War I poets.

That was Jeremy—he never stopped trying to broaden my insufficient horizons. He thought my musical education was lacking, so he would force me to listen to Bartók, or to the sort of aimless, circular jazz that makes you feel as if it's 2 A.M. on a stifling summer night and you've just become aware that life is meaningless. While I wanted to play Chopin, Eartha Kitt, and the Gin Blossoms over dinner, Jeremy wasn't happy unless he was inflicting upon me the latest album by one of those lamenting, undernourished females singing bitterly of inadequate men in eerie, angelic voices.

"You should challenge yourself more," Jeremy had objected when I refused to attend an exhibit by an acquaintance of his who worked exclusively in neon.

"I don't think something you have to plug in is art, that's all. Unless it's a Tiffany lamp."

"You're so hidebound, Nicky. You can't spend the rest of your life visiting the Turners in the National Gallery and reading *Middlemarch*."

To me it seemed there was no reason I shouldn't go on doing exactly this. But Jeremy, who was in truth a gifted teacher—I knew because I had visited his classes—was bothered to his core by ignorance. It truly upset Jeremy, for example, that I didn't know or care much about world affairs. I believed that the British should leave

Northern Ireland and that we should stop trading with the Chinese until they stopped selling sneakers made by preschoolers, but beyond that I got lazy. I am ashamed to admit, for example, that I never did figure out the difference between Croatian Serbs and Serbian Croats.

Only when Jeremy entered my life did I start taking the morning paper; I did the jumble while he read about who was slaughtering whom these days, sharing the more gruesome bits over bacon and eggs, an ungentlemanly habit, I told him.

When some man has done you wrong, it's wise to dwell on his faults. But Jeremy had a lot to recommend him otherwise. He was intriguing, sharp-witted, funny in a cynical, sophisticated way. And he was the first man since my breakup with Tony whom I could stand for any length of time.

Oh, and he was romantic, Heathcliff-romantic in a way you wouldn't have expected of a man whose scone-baking, weepy-letter-writing, America-hating mother still knitted all his sweaters. We had even met romantically.

It was at a crowded party one spring night, at a Dupont Circle penthouse without enough furniture (our host preferred to sink his money into rent and entertaining; he spent most of the time between festivities flat on his back on a mattress on his bedroom floor, with a cool washcloth over his eyes). Jeremy was pushed into me by a large, red-faced girl of very good pedigree and terrible manners, whose out-flung arm made him stumble and spill champagne down the front of my dress.

I teetered on my high-heeled evening shoes and turned an ankle. He grabbed my shoulders with both hands to steady me, and I looked into his eyes—intending to lambaste him, but stopped short. Those eyes. Jeremy's eyes are such a color, a gray-green in which the gray does not dim but somehow enhances the green. I've seen pictures of Ireland, though I've never been there, and his eyes reminded me of those green, green hills shrouded in mist. He claimed not to have any Celtic blood in him, but those eyes made me wonder about his mother's milkman. His hair was lovely, too: dark, heavy, lustrous curls clipped close and a beard that hid his only flaw, a slightly weak chin.

He helped me hobble to a corner couch, brought me strong liquor to ease the pain of my twisted ankle, and talked to me all night about . . . I can't remember. One of those everything-under-the-sun conversations. He took me home in a taxi and walked me to my door. Then he called for a week to see how my ankle was coming on, just like Willoughby did for Marianne in *Sense and Sensibility*. At the end of that week we went out for dinner. At the end of that month we went to bed.

We were wonderful in bed. Chemistry surrounded us in a golden cloud. After more than a year together, we still kissed on park benches. We still left dinner sitting on the table whenever passion distracted us, which was often. We were rowdy and hot-blooded, and when he swore he'd never known anything like our lovemaking, I was fool enough to believe him. I was fool enough to think that only with me did his face take on that expression of wonder and absorption, followed by anguished bliss, followed by sleep. Only with me, I thought.

We hadn't been a perfect couple, but we'd had so much that was good, and he'd treated it as casually as a chipped old coffee cup you use every morning but wouldn't miss if it broke.

I threw away the debris of my lunch and lurched back through the rocking train, on the way accidentally grabbing the shoulder of a woman in a lambskin coat who started up, probably fearing that I was some animal rights activist about to spatter red paint on her. Back in my seat, I read with a concentration that had served me well in the past months. With a stack of books by your bed, you can survive any heartbreak. In the watches of the night, reading soothed me as hot toddies or Valium never could have.

In an Agatha Christie mystery, Jeremy would be the slimy stepbrother or the not-too-grieved widow's opportunistic lover—some character too self-preserving to have done the murder, but handy for adding confusion to the plot. I could learn to dismiss him that way, if I practiced long enough. In the meantime, I was suddenly glad to be leaving town, glad of the comfort of having a job to do. It beat staying here in Washington, being bombarded by self-pitying love notes from Jeremy and reproachful telephone calls from Ma. If distance did not bring me perspective and healing, at least it would make it harder for them to find me. No small blessing.

As the train flew up the coast, I thought of all the times Jeremy had looked at me with laughter and desire, how his eyes at such times would do what men's eyes in my mother's romance books did: they would actually change color, the mist on the green hills coming down, veiling and intensifying their beauty. He would never look at me that way again—or if he did, how could I believe him?

I huddled in my seat and watched Wilmington and Philadelphia go by. In my mind's eye I was rocketing up the coast like an arrow, shooting straight up and away from all of it, all the mess and noise and exhaustion of my daily life. Even if all I traded it for was *another* brand of mess and noise and exhaustion, the trade alone would be a relief. If one could not always demand liberty, as Charlotte Brontë said, one could at least ask for a new servitude. I let my hair drop over my eyes to block the light, and fell asleep.

· 6 ·

"I SEE YOU'RE still doing that *Girl From Uncle* thing," said Tony when I walked into strike headquarters. "Or is it *The Avengers?*"

For the train trip, I'd chosen a black pinstriped pantsuit that zipped up the front, with a hip-length leather jacket I'd bought with my first bonus from Ron. I'd wanted to look professional in a stream-lined and sexy way. Tony made me feel merely stagey.

"And you look the way you always did," I said, trying to convey by the coldness of my tone that this was not necessarily a good thing.

He had not, to my regret, run to fat or lost his hair. He was much the same as I'd known him. Tony had always had the air of an attractive roughneck, and he still did. The appeal of his blunt features lay in their mobility and humor rather than their individual handsomeness. He was the sort of guy that people instinctively trusted to know what to do in an emergency, the kind of guy you see on the evening news who, after saving three people from a house fire, says awkwardly, "I was just doing what anyone would do." The maddening part about Tony was that being this guy was not all there was to him. Observant, skeptical, and occasionally generous to a fault, he despised anyone who fell for his pose of tough-talking man of action.

Tony's eyes were the light blue you see on four of five Polish-Americans in the part of eastern Pennsylvania where he'd grown up. You'd think that color would look wishy-washy. Tony's, however, were quick and keen, and when they regarded me for the first time in five years, they didn't soften a bit, neither in gratitude for my assistance in this crisis or in appreciation of my female charms.

"Weingould warned you I was coming up here? He told me he would."

"I got a whole two minutes with him. He's still hemming and hawing about giving me a budget on paper, but he said he'd definitely pay for you. I don't know how your friend Ron managed to get in so good with him. Usually Weingould's on the phone telling me to make sure and order the cheapest brand of toilet paper, in bulk, for the campaign office bathroom, and here he is hiring high-priced consultants."

I disliked being made to sound like a hooker being given as a bachelor party gift, but said only, "I've never seen Weingould put a budget in black and white for any campaign he's used us for, so I wouldn't hold your breath."

"Yeah," said Tony. "If he doesn't get his ass in gear I'll just do what I always do. Spend what I want and tell him afterward he approved it in advance. He never knows the difference."

His demeanor was calm, and his handshake had been dry and brief. Right down to the sarcasm about my outfit, he came off as one jaded old pro greeting another jaded old pro. Well, if he could play it that way, so could I. Only, he was on his own turf and I was the newcomer learning the ropes. It gave him the advantage.

My first impressions of Winsack had not been happy ones. Driving into town in the rental car (which had developed a weird throb as if the camshaft were about to go on me), I saw the mill clock first. It was visible miles out of town. The dark red tower with its gilded numbers looked quaint and old-fashioned, but the sheer hulking size of the crumbling textile mill reminded me that one of the worst factory systems in the country had originated in this state. I had read this information in a library book entitled *Touring Historic Southern New England*. I like to learn a little bit about the places I'm assigned to, so that no one accuses me of that ignorantly smug "I'm from Washington and I'm here to help you" attitude.

The rushing Blackstone River had supplied the power for the mills and factories all through this area, the book said. Today, in the aftermath of a rainstorm, you could see why. The river rushed turbulently between its brambly banks, a dirty brown-green flecked with yellowish-white foam. The town was no more cheerful or appealing than the river.

I'd grown accustomed to the broad, leafy avenues of my adopted city, its low open skyline, its pink and silver marble and wide green parks. The palette and scale were different here. Winsack huddled on three lumpen hills, a study in maroon brick, gray stone, dingy white clapboard, black shutters, and black iron gates. Only the white spires of the Quaker and Congregationalist churches and the golden twin domes of the Russian Orthodox church showed bright against the sodden sky. You couldn't imagine anyone turning this place into a cheery little object lesson on the Industrial Revolution as had been done in Lowell, Massachusetts, and other locations. Of course, the people in Salem have created quite a nice little theme park around the witch trials, so I guess anything is possible.

The strike office was on a side street off the main drag. It occupied the first floors of two adjoining buildings that, by the evidence of unlighted neon signs out front, once housed a doughnut shop and a drugstore at some time in Winsack's more prosperous past. On the doughnut shop side, the original doughnut counter was still there. So was the tin ceiling on the drugstore side, lovely in its tarnished intricacy. That side had creaky hardwood floors that reminded me of the Woolworth's in Bethesda, Maryland, near where I'd grown up, even down to the comforting smell of the old-fashioned floor varnish.

The doughnut shop counter was even more hideous by comparison with this faded elegance. It was a bright orange elongated U, and the windows on that side were thin plate glass, open to daytime glare and the harsh light of streetlamps. Clearly this had been a java spot right out of an Edward Hopper painting.

The counter was piled with food although the local wasn't even officially on strike yet. People bring more food by a strike office than they do to an after-funeral lunch. There was a lemon layer cake at one end of the counter, and a huge tray of stuffed grape leaves at the other end, with assorted casseroles, cold cuts, salads, and huge fresh loaves of Italian bread in between. My stomach curled with hunger. I was damned if I was going to look hungry in front of Tony, however. He would probably interpret it as yearning for his strong, masculine physique.

"I'll need an hour with you and Clare Murray," I said to him, "and a place to work, and a few other things like the name of a nearby union printer. You know the drill."

"Clare's at a CLC meeting," said Tony. "That means Central Labor Council, in case you don't remember. She's drumming up support from the other local unions. God knows we'll need it."

When I first met Tony, I didn't know what a CLC was, or a work slowdown, or a blue flu, or countless other labor lore and trivia he'd clued me in on, including the legend that George Meany was buried with one of his favorite cigars in his coffin and that his ghost haunted the AFL-CIO office in D.C., smoking and wandering. Walking down an empty hallway in that cavernous building still gave me the willies.

"So when can Clare see me?"

"It's too bad you didn't get here in time to go with her."

"Yes, it is, isn't it."

I didn't say, "I got up at the crack of dawn to make the train," or "Do you know how many other clients need me right now?" I had learned a long time ago that it never paid to defend yourself against implied accusations that you weren't a sufficient martyr to the cause.

"You're here now, anyway. How's everything going?"

He could not have spoken with a finer detachment.

"Great. Just great. And you?"

"I'm great. Going out to Snake River after this is over with. Whitewater rafting."

"Exciting."

To Tony, it wasn't a vacation if he didn't have a chance to get hurt. His idea of fun was flinging himself into raging rapids on a rubber boat, or throwing himself down a western peak on two planks of wood—and believe me, in Tony's case, skis remained just planks of wood, not graceful instruments of near flight. He wasn't supposed to ski because of the bum knee he'd gotten playing high school football, but he taped it up and skied anyway. He'd broken an arm twice and an ankle once, on slopes where he had no business being.

"Is Jimmy still in the same job?" I asked.

"He got promoted. He has the prime route now. All the big accounts."

Tony was wearing a black T-shirt with "Milwaukee Gold Malted" written across it in big yellow letters. This was a gift from his younger brother, Jimmy, a salesman for a liquor distributorship. Thanks to this brother, many of Tony's possessions were promotional items for beer, wine, and spirits. His travel alarm clock was in the shape of a green plastic martini olive. His winter hat was a knit cap with the words "Clive's Red Rum" running in a continuous horizontal stripe around his head. His key chain was in the shape of a beer keg, and the only two drinking glasses he owned were embossed with the fake royal arms of a bourbon company. A temperance worker would have wept at the sight of him.

"You have a place for me to set up?" I asked him.

"We're a little cramped, as you can see. The best I could do was to give you that spot in the back there, squeezed in next to my desk."

I peered at the shadowy far corner that he indicated. "Is that a copying machine I'm almost sitting on top of? And the coffeepot's right behind me? How am I supposed to work that way, Tony?"

"No one else even has a desk. The rest of them are making do with card tables and folding chairs."

"Aren't I lucky."

"You want to sit at the end of the conference table and type while they're stuffing envelopes? Because that's the only alternative seating in the house."

The desk Tony had chosen for me couldn't have looked more unwelcoming. It was constructed of thin, splintery plywood you could have put your fist through, and a childish hand had scrawled curses on it with an indelible marker.

"That was Eric," Tony said, as I examined the varied inscriptions that decorated even the sorry blotter. "You'll meet him. He's one of our member's kids."

"Must be a lovely child."

But I said it under my breath. Already our little altercation had drawn a few looks. If I kicked up much more of a fuss, the people here would think I was some jumped-up, inside-the-Beltway brat who'd be no use whatsoever.

The office was humming quietly, but I knew from experience that the instant a strike was declared, it would be pandemonium. The space was cluttered with derelict furniture obviously brought from members' basements: folding tables, rolling desk chairs with wobbly casters, tarnished steel standing lamps too unattractive to be labeled vintage, and a long saggy sectional sofa covered in royal-blue burlap with sinister dark stains here and there. Piles of poster board and two-by-fours for picket signs were stacked in every corner, including the corner directly behind my desk, where I would discover that they had a habit of crashing over during the middle of important press calls.

Some of the picket signs were already finished. As I watched, a brisk-looking woman began to ink in the same slogans on sign after sign: "Local 507 nurses speak out for patients!" and "Keep St. Francis safe. Support striking nurses." I had no problem with those, but other stacks, already completed, seemed to have been lettered by a Bolshevik with heartburn. They read "St. Francis: bad for nurses, deadly for patients," and "Stop killer overtime before people get killed."

"Tony," I said, pointing. "You can't use those."

"You're here five minutes and you're telling me what slogans we can use?"

"Tony, people like nurses. They trust nurses. But they don't want to see nurses with their fists in the air like some bad imitation of Che Guevara."

"What are they supposed to do, sit in a circle singing Peter, Paul and Mary songs? Lie down in front of the Coventry lawyers' limo to make the ride softer for the fat cats?" said Tony. "We need to show some righteous anger here."

"Anger is okay, but it has to be *grieved* anger, principled anger, like the image people have of Florence Nightingale fighting for medical supplies for wounded soldiers in the Crimea. Motherly. Steadfast, calm, and caring. That's the way to go, don't you think?"

Tony made a gagging motion with his finger.

"Cut it out. I told you I was right, Tony," said the woman who was inking in signs. She had a funny little face, a strangely archetypal face that seemed oddly familiar. When I thought about it later, I realized it was the sort of face you see in a Colonial portrait. It was oblong with clearly delineated but sized-down features, and the small constant hint of a smile, severely restrained. She had light brown hair cut in a straight bob, capable hands with short nails, and a firm jaw and chin. I guessed her age at thirty-eight or so.

"This is Kate Kenney," said Tony. "Kate, this is Nicky, our PR flack."

"Hello. Good call about the signs. We've been fighting about this. And don't get all prissy and displeased with me, Tony," said Kate, shaking my hand in a parenthetical way. "Those slogans are way too inflammatory. We should get rid of them. There's plenty of cardboard."

"I wrote them out myself," said Tony. "It took me two hours."

"You get an A-plus for printing well and staying in the lines," said Kate. "I'll bring you in a gold foil star tomorrow."

"Fine," said Tony. "Fine. We'll be up until two A.M. the next three nights making more, but fine."

"We'll be up until two anyway," she said, turning back to her work.

"This is my desk," said Tony. He gestured toward a beat-up oak battleship from the 1940s. It looked like a stage prop from *His Girl Friday*, and it was inches from mine. I wouldn't be able to cough or whisper without him hearing me.

Do not react, I said to myself. He's trying to spook you. He wants you to bolt for Providence and hop on the next train you can find with a name like The Carolina Mockingbird, and not get off until you're well over the Mason-Dixon line.

He made a show of moving a stack of *Inside Labor* magazines off the top of my desk so that I could set down my portable computer.

"I've been writing the strike newsletter myself," he said. "I'm sure you'll come up with some improvements."

"That's what you pay me for. But it doesn't look half bad."

Weingould had given me copies.

"Who's doing layout for you on the newsletter right now? Did you learn a desktop program?"

"Margaret. You'll meet her. She does a lot around here."

Oh God. I knew the type.

"And how's Ron?" said Tony. "Still profiting off the suffering of others?"

"Someone has to," I said. "This strike alone should buy him a new dining room set."

"I'm glad we could be of use to you two," Tony said in a flat, phony business voice. His voice—his real, relaxed voice—was one of the things I'd always found most attractive about him. There's no way to describe it except that it was a "light" voice. Not a tenor, because that conjures up images of musical comedy. Just a grainy, scratchy voice, a voice that lay lightly on the ears. It was infinitely persuasive and casual, with that odd Pennsylvania inflection at the ends of his sentences that made his questions sound like statements.

"Ron likes to say, 'Causes pay bills.' Who knows, he may find some time to come up here and help us out, how about that?"

"That'll be the day," said Tony. "Can he even travel without a special suitcase for his mousse and manicure kit and cosmetics?"

"Face lotion is not a cosmetic, Tony. His skin gets dry in the winter."

"How does his skin get dry? Washington is a frigging swamp."

The outside door opened. There was a string of bells attached to it, and when the door was pushed the bells jangled like beauty shop bells.

"Margaret put those up," said Tony.

"What for?"

"To make the place homey, she said. She does a lot of that."

Through the door stepped one of the last people I expected to see here, and he was sauntering toward us with an air of welcome that did not deceive me.

"You've got to be kidding," I said to Tony under my breath.

"Goreman sent him."

If Doug Hamner had stepped foot within a hundred miles of one of Tony's campaigns, it could only be in the empty title of second in command. Had Hamner been forced on Tony in any other capacity, Tony would have quit. The antagonism between them was long-standing. The antagonism between Doug and me was pretty venerable too.

I unwillingly shook Doug's offered hand, which was moist, no larger than mine, and far too soft. I noticed that he was wearing his fanny pack, a zippered pouch that hung from his belt and held God knew what. He always wore it in front—like a colostomy bag, Tony had once said. It went oddly with his suit and tie.

"Are you ready to be put to work?" said Hamner. "I have a lot for you to do."

"Oh? You're helping Tony out, then?" I knew that would irritate him.

Hamner was nicknamed "the Hamster" by his fellow organizers, due to his slight overbite and his small, quickly gesturing hands. He'd hurriedly been brought on board at the national by the Toilers' new president, Jerry Goreman, when that old warhorse Frank De Rosa died. Doug was only one of the many yes-men from Goreman's Chicago local who rushed off to buy standby seats from O'Hare to Dulles while the last strains of "Solidarity Forever" were still echoing down K Street from De Rosa's funeral extravaganza at St. Matthew's Cathedral.

Doug was shoehorned into the organizing department, not because he had the faintest idea of how to run an organizing campaign, but because Goreman needed a spy on the ground in Weingould's territory. Weingould tried to neutralize Doug by assigning him to small races that were already in the bag, where he couldn't do much damage. Doug got very puffed up at these illusory successes, speaking frequently of his "win record" at Toilers staff meetings. One of the more venerable reps had commented to Doug once, on extreme provocation, "You know, sonny, it's easy to hit a home run when the pitcher hangs one over the plate." But since the only sport Doug followed was bicycle racing, it was feared that he had missed the point.

He'd gotten puffed up in other ways, I saw now. He'd gained about twenty pounds since I'd last seen him, and it wasn't flattering to his Germanic countenance or his age, which must be close to forty-five now. You wouldn't call him heavy yet, but the extra weight transformed what had once been a pretty-boy handsomeness to a curdled attractiveness on the verge of running to fat. So rosy-cheeked was he, so yellow-brown of hair and droopy mustache, that if you'd put a beer stein in his hand and stuffed him into a pair of lederhosen, he could have walked into any Oktoberfest in Bavaria and been taken for a native.

"Now that you're here," said Doug, "there are a few meeting notices Margaret hasn't been able to get to, and some ad copy for the Knights of Columbus banquet program which is due tomorrow. I think you'd better do the meeting notices first; we can hit the night shift with those."

"Actually, Weingould's hired me for some pretty specific writing and PR assistance, Doug, so I'm afraid I'm going to have to limit ad hoc favors like that. But if you like, I can look over anything *you've* written and give you some ideas."

His florid complexion, so unbecoming in a man, grew a shade redder. You can't win with a guy like Doug. Assertive females threaten him, and docile women earn only contempt for their pains.

I gazed at him blandly. He looked from me to Tony, but Tony's face was wooden. Doug laughed. He gave Tony a playful punch on the arm.

"Tell her to give me a hand, since she says you're the boss."

"I'm my own boss," I said. "And I don't want to promise away my time on insignificant tasks until I get a sense of what's on the front burner. In fact, Tony, I need to be brought up to speed, which means I need to meet with Clare. Any idea when that can be arranged?"

"Clare's still at the CLC," Doug said. "She wanted me to tell you, Tony, that Peter Arseneault from Channel Eight is going to be interviewing Bennett Winslow in front of the hospital in twenty minutes, and you should be there to get our two cents in for the eleven o'clock news."

Winslow was the president of St. Francis Hospital and Coventry's mouthpiece in all this. He'd been doing an adroit job with the press so far. I was curious to see him.

"Damn," said Tony. "You could have told me sooner."

"I was overwhelmed with joy at seeing Nicky," Doug said nastily.

"Your reunion brought tears to my eyes," said Tony. "Now let's get the hell out of here."

"Want to tell me where the hospital is?" I said.

"Skip this," said Tony. "I can get back in an hour and fill you in."

"I'm coming."

"I said you don't have to, Nicky."

"And *I* said I'm coming. Where is it?"

I was furious at him. He hadn't said a word during the exchange with Doug, just stood by and let me duke it out for myself. Not that I needed any Sir Lancelot sticking up for me, but Tony and I both knew that if Tony was silent when Doug baited me, Doug would see it as a green light for his feeble attempts to throw his weight around.

"Kate can take you," Tony said. Kate had come over in the last minute and was contemplating Doug with frustrated revulsion, as if he were a giant palmetto bug who had crawled in through the hot water pipes yet again, even though the exterminator had been and gone.

"Yes, I'll take her, since you paragons of chivalry haven't offered," said Kate. "And then afterward we're going to get something to eat. She's been traveling all day and you guys didn't even fetch her a cup of coffee. Where were you raised, in a barn?"

She handed me a large chocolate chip cookie and a carton of milk, took my briefcase from me, and shoved an extremely unbecoming brown-and-blue-striped wool cap over my ears and forehead. It reminded me of the ones my aunt Deedee used to knit and inflict on us as Christmas gifts. The last thing I saw before the swing door closed behind us with another beauty-shop jangle were Doug's and Tony's faces still turned in our direction. Tony was scowling, his face scrunched up like a rebellious schoolboy's. Doug was frowning petulantly, a frown of balked entitlement, as if he'd just arrived at the theater and someone else was sitting in his seat.

Outside the wind was ten degrees colder than it had been when I arrived. When I took a chilled breath, I realized that early November meant true winter here, winter fully arrived and final. Back home, the scent of loam and falling leaves and damp earth was still in the air. Here the leaves were all off the trees and if the air smelled of anything at all, it was of wet stone and car exhaust.

Ahead of me lay weeks of this same cold. I was going to miss the last of Washington's southern autumn, with its gentle blues and muted golds. I wasn't going to be able to dawdle along Skyline Drive with Louise as we'd planned, getting our last sight of the Blue Ridge before snow closed the mountain passes. I wouldn't be there for those warm Indian summer days when I could walk by the river with only a sweater and throw sticks down the rapids to see how far and fast they floated.

When I miss a season because I'm traveling on business, some small, barely noticed part of me feels wrong and off-kilter until the year rolls round again to that same season and I recoup the lost time. Someday, I wanted to settle down someplace where I could sit on my own porch and drink lemonade or mulled cider, depending on the weather, and plant an amateur rose garden, and stay still enough to watch four seasons scroll by me in beautiful, detailed entirety. Where this porch and rose garden would be, and how I would live this life of soulful leisure while still earning enough to keep myself in lemonade and cider and the occasional glossy magazine, I didn't know.

"Eat," said Kate. "You're going to need better gloves."

Her kindly hectoring reminded me so forcibly of Louise that I felt doubly homesick. I would call Louise when I got to the bed-and-breakfast, I decided. Then I would take a hot bath and finish *Murder on the Orient Express,* which I had left off reading just at the point where Hercule Poirot is amused to find the mysterious scarlet kimono stashed in his own luggage. I would feel better in an hour or two, or a day or two, or a week or two.

"You're the first person I haven't pissed off today," I said as we waited for the windshield to defrost.

"Hey, when I saw how angry you made Doug, I knew I'd like you," she said. "Finish that cookie, will you? This could take a while, and I don't want you fainting on me. It would look lousy for the news crew."

I finished the cookie, guzzled some milk, buckled up, and off we went.

7

KATE WAS A GOOD driver, rather fast but careful. I hate driving with people who don't know how to handle a car and compensate by whipping around corners and changing lanes in a slapdash, bravura fashion.

"Hamner is clearly delighted you're on board," she said. "I haven't seen him looking that upset since his first day here, when Tony wouldn't let him sit in on negotiations."

"I go way back with Doug."

"And it's clearly been a wonderful association."

"He's a snake."

"Tell me how you really feel."

In my first months with Ron, I'd been assigned to work with Doug on a school board campaign in Minnesota, in a district where the Toilers were joining the teachers' association in backing a pro-union slate in hopes of a better contract for their cafeteria workers and school bus drivers. During the course of the campaign, Doug blamed me for a printing error, an expensive error. It was a headline in a four-color flyer that read, "John Knutsen supports the best for our pubic schools." *Pubic* schools. Luckily, we caught it before it went out the door to the voters. But not before we'd racked up a hefty print bill that someone had to be blamed for.

That headline was an easy enough mistake to make when you'd been working round the clock. My only fault had been that when I'd asked Doug if he'd had the blue-line proofed by two people besides me, I'd believed him when he said yes. We'd run twenty thousand copies. Fixing it was not cheap.

Doug had asserted, with an air of injured innocence, that I'd told him the piece was ready to go. Advocacy ate the cost of the reprint, because Ron wanted to keep the Toilers' business. I'd have forgiven Doug for letting me take the fall if that printing fiasco hadn't been merely one of the ways in which he showed his mean streak over the course of that campaign. He was the kind of person who bullies the hired help just to feel important.

"How's Doug going over, anyway?" I asked Kate.

"He hasn't endeared himself to most of us. He'll never sit and stuff envelopes even when everyone else is pitching in. He never makes a pot of coffee or refills the paper tray in the copying machine. He asks us to fax things for him. Well, he tried to. That didn't last long."

"How's he doing with Clare?"

"He's buttering Clare up for everything he's worth, and she's a little off her game right now, so she doesn't see through it."

I didn't like the sound of that. Doug's MO was notorious: he hid his incompetence by assiduously currying favor with local leadership, until he became a New Best Friend. Doug did not care for hammering in those home truths and unpleasant realities that local pols needed to be reminded of when the chips are down. "Don't worry," said Kate. "Tony and I are keeping an eye on him."

We parked in a staff lot and walked up the circular drive to the hospital's visitors entrance, where the nurses would picket if a strike occurred. Like the rest of Winsack, the hospital had clearly seen better days. Its small but hulking main building had been erected somewhere around the time President McKinley was shot, in purplish-red brick with white wooden trim. It boasted an oddly Moorish cupola surmounted by a brass weathervane in the shape of a tall-masted ship. In its day, this edifice was probably the last word in forward-thinking modern architecture, but now the place had an air of having been the scene of involuntary commitments, lobotomies, and deaths in childbirth. Clumsily attached to the main building were three or four wings from the fifties and sixties, executed in glass and steel interspersed with those hideous aqua panels that were in fashion then.

In a bare, floodlit courtyard between the old and newer buildings stood a solitary statue of Saint Francis preaching to the birds and squirrels, an elongated bronze figure with a countenance oddly gaunt and Scandinavian for an Italian saint. I walked closer and saw that the statue was labeled with a plaque on which ran the lines of the saint's famous prayer asking God to let him be a "channel of Thy peace." There wouldn't be too much peace around here for a while.

I said, "Where's Winslow? Isn't he supposed to be out here doing an interview? I want to get a look at this jerk."

The news crews were setting up with their usual efficiency, but I didn't see anyone who corresponded to the description I'd had of Winslow. The only person in a suit was obviously the Channel 8 reporter, Arseneault. I was truly back in the north, I realized when I heard that classic French-Canadian name. Irish, Italians, French-Canadians, Poles—all brought here by the mills, once upon a time. They gave these towns what life they had, and living beside them—above them—was that dying breed still separate and distinct: the flinty, frugal Yankees whose family fortunes had been built on shipping and the slave trade. Kate, I took a guess, came from such a family, despite that Irish-sounding married name.

"You won't believe me, but Winslow's actually not that bad a guy," said Kate. "He's just in over his head. They imported him from their smallest hospital in Massachusetts, where Coventry's already gobbled up four facilities. That hospital was tiny, and it wasn't unionized, and it served a well-off, suburban patient population. I think Winslow was probably fine there. All he had to do was act executive."

"Is that him now?"

"That's him."

Winslow had just walked out of the hospital, which was looking positively Gothic as wisps of fog rose from the sidewalk and drifted in the beating light of the TV cameras. He threw a small nod our way, and Kate gave him a cheery little wave.

It was a blow to see just how personable Bennett Winslow was. If you were casting a sympathetic, dignified hospital CEO in a medical drama, Winslow would have been on your short list. He was in his late fifties, with silver hair, a high forehead, and clean-cut, noble features that were only looking more noble as age drew a few lines that gave the appearance of wisdom earned. As he chatted with the Channel 8 reporter, I could hear that he had a voice like Ron's: deep, self-confident, professionally modulated.

"God," I said. "He's right out of central casting. I was hoping for someone fat and squinty."

"Give it a few minutes," said Kate. "He starts out strong, but then he always adds something that screws him up."

We drew a little closer to listen in on the interview. Winslow was clearly used to television. He gazed either at Arseneault or straight into the camera, relaxed but not too smooth, without that nervous blink that afflicts anyone who doesn't have long practice in front of the lights. The opening questions were softballs: What was the hospital's position on staffing, was there room for movement at the bargaining table, would there be a strike or could a solution still be reached?

Then the reporter, a likeable, handsome guy with black hair and speaking dark eyes and a trench coat obviously modeled on Peter Jennings's circa 1990, said, "Mr. Winslow, would you comment on the recent death at St. Bernadette's Hospital? Wasn't that a case of inadequate staffing, just like the nurses here are talking about?"

Winslow was clearly rattled. His expression moved from comfortable benevolence to peeved surprise, then became downright cross.

"St. Bernadette's has nothing to do with conditions at this hospital," said Winslow, his forehead furrowing in a way that his media trainer should have warned him about. "St. Francis is not St. Bernadette's, and it would not be appropriate for me to comment on that case. The staffing philosophy is certainly not the same."

St. Bernadette's, I knew from Weingould's folder, was the Coventry hospital in Lawrence, Massachusetts, where a patient had died two weeks earlier from being given an incompatible blood type. It was a nursing assistant's error. Coventry would give the poor things six weeks training and then shove them into critical-care units with very little supervision or help. Coventry was hoping that they could replace nurses with large numbers of these low-paid assistants, as if nursing skills were as easy to pick up as running a cash register or flipping burgers. Lots of the hospitals were doing it, and the resulting horror stories were beginning to hit the news.

The case had been getting a lot of play, especially since the victim was a fifteen-year-old girl. Coventry hadn't come off well in the latest

newshour segment, which included footage of the bereaved family laying flowers at Lisa's grave and inviting the reporter into their living
room to look at photos of the deceased teen in her marching band uniform.

"Actually, isn't the staffing philosophy exactly the same?" said
Arseneault. "Coventry is gearing up to replace nurses with unlicensed
assistants here at St. Francis, aren't they?"

"One-on-one patient care by a nurse at the bedside is overrated in
terms of medical outcomes," Winslow asserted, obviously not familiar
with recent studies that showed just the opposite. "Most patients don't
need their hands held every moment of the day."

Tsk, tsk. Guess which quote from this interview would make the
evening news?

Arseneault, knowing he'd gotten his sound bite, finished up with
a few harmless last questions. Winslow regained his poise, and his
hand stole to the lapel of his navy suit jacket in an unconscious preen-
ing gesture. A minute later, the reporter was thanking him and turning back to the crew.

"Not as smart as he thinks he is," I said to Kate. "Thank God."

"The secret to Winslow is that he's just a big kid. Do you see that
fountain in the lobby, that black marble fountain?"

"It would be hard to miss it. Whose idea was the green and blue
floodlighting?"

"Winslow had it put in. He had the whole fountain put in. You
wouldn't believe what it cost. He was *so* proud of it. The day it was
installed he was just beaming, walking around asking everyone if
they'd seen it yet."

"It's awful."

"It was a running joke right from the beginning. Our people call it
'the million-dollar bathtub.' Even the doctors make fun of it. But all
the ribbing really got to Winslow. He wrote an editorial defending
himself in the hospital newsletter. He sounded so hurt, it was pathetic.
He gets to you, somehow."

"That guy gets to you? How big a pushover are you?"

"You'll see. He's coming over."

Surprisingly, Winslow was approaching, with the measured, almost ceremonial walk of someone who expects a lot of fanfare to surround his appearance on the scene.

"How are you, Kate?" he said, extending his hand in the way I imagine the pope does when you kiss his ring.

"I'm just fine, Bennett. This is Nicky Malone, from Washington, D.C."

"Ah, Washington. I was there for a while after the war."

"Korea?"

"Vietnam." He frowned slightly. "Washington is a lovely city. My favorite place there is a courtyard behind the National Portrait Gallery. Those enormous elms."

It was one of my favorite places, too, which was disturbing.

"Do they still have that upstairs Civil War gallery?" asked Winslow. "With the engravings of the *Monitor* and the *Merrimac*?"

"They did last time I went. Though the whole place is being renovated, so Lord knows what it will turn out like."

"I hope they don't change a thing. That place has memories for me," he said, and smiled sadly. Perhaps there had been some girl with whom he strolled in that courtyard, a girl who had died young, a girl who had married another man to whom she was already promised, a girl who had broken his heart. Suddenly World War II songs were playing in my head and I saw Winslow in officer's khaki saying goodbye under the elms to a Merle Oberon type.

Kate gave me an amused "I told you, didn't I?" look. I shook myself mentally. Here I was weaving a sad romance around Bennett Winslow, who was probably the type of person who visited a place once and then claimed to know it well, the type of person who said he had "friends" in cities where he'd merely made acquaintances. I had to give it to the guy, he had charm to spare. In a moment he'd gone from being a pronouncing, pompous stuffed shirt to a wistful, attractive older man, remembering days of his youth with just the right appealing ruefulness. As he adjusted his tie I saw that he had very nicely shaped hands. Masculine, but beautifully modeled. If you were casting a bronze statue of George Washington, you'd want to borrow Bennett Winslow's hands.

Kate said, "Nicky's going to help us with some of our strike literature."

Immediately his expression became pained, as if Kate had committed a terrible breach of manners.

"I hope it won't come to that, Kate. I certainly do hope a solution can be found, even now."

"If not you can wave to us occasionally from your office window."

Instead of taking offense, Winslow gave her a sidelong smirk, as if she'd just said something flirtatious.

"And will you wave back?" he said.

"I might not have a free hand. Those picket signs are pretty heavy."

He laughed as a Shakespearean actor laughs, with the sort of fake ho-ho you might hear from a duke or minor prince in one of the comedies, over some obscure joke that the audience doesn't understand but presumably people in the sixteenth century thought was a hoot.

"You take care of yourself, Miss Kate," he said, and nodded to me.

When he'd gone back inside I exhaled.

"Oh, boy."

"It's amazing, isn't it? You can't help warming up to him. Happens every time."

"It's like some immobilizing ray gun in a cartoon."

"The worst part is, you know he's just being smarmy, but it works anyway. For some of us. He has no effect on Clare."

"But Doug does?"

"There's no accounting for taste. Besides, Doug is versatile. He plays to his audience. Winslow could never change his act."

A car screeched up the drive and out jumped Tony in a tearing hurry. Hamner alighted from the passenger's seat more slowly; he seemed to have gotten caught in the seat belt mechanism somehow. To my dismay, Tony was sporting a disreputable old brown windbreaker that I'd tried repeatedly to remove from his wardrobe in the past.

Kate said, "I can't believe he wore that. Wait a second, I'm going to go tell him to take that off before he's on camera."

There was a brief disagreement, then she came back holding the windbreaker.

"Men," she said. "You should see the shirts my husband tries to hold on to."

Tony began by wisecracking with the crew and exchanging manly pleasantries with Peter Arseneault. He was as relaxed and affable as Bennett Winslow had been, though in a more down-to-earth, off-the-cuff way. The Tony of my day wasn't comfortable even on the phone with a reporter. Now he was waltzing through an on-camera interview with the aplomb of an old pro.

Arseneault went easy on him to start, just as he had with Winslow. Tony got to make his points about patient safety, about the recent death at St. Bernadette's, about the need for better staffing. At the end, though, the reporter threw in a tough one.

"How do the union nurses justify walking out on their patients?" he said. "Isn't that the last thing a nurse is supposed to do? Firemen aren't supposed to strike, or policemen. Why should nurses?"

Tony paused, as if to get the camera glare out of his eyes for a minute. He'd learned the trick of taped interviews: since you're not live, you can play for time. They aren't going to show you on the news scratching your head and thinking for twenty straight seconds.

Then he turned to Arseneault.

"Sure, our nurses are going to worry about their patients if we go out. They're going to worry a lot. That's why they've waited this long. But think about it, would you want your mother in this hospital? With what's going on here? Good nurses can't work in unsafe conditions without speaking up. There's still time to avoid a strike, if the hospital will take our safety concerns seriously."

The sound bite for Tony would be, "Would you want your mother in this hospital?" and it would make a nice counterpoint to Winslow's "Patients don't need their hands held."

The reporter said, "I think that wraps it up," and very quickly he and his crew were gone. Tony took his windbreaker back from Kate, who said, "Not bad, Boltanski."

"It would have been better if Clare could be here."

"Don't be modest."

He ignored me, so I didn't offer him any compliments. Was he going to pretend I was invisible for as long as he could get away with it? It seemed that he was. He was heading off to his car. I blocked his path.

"Tony, we need to sit down and plan a strategy."

"Not tonight. I'm booked."

"Tomorrow, then."

"There's no rush."

"There's every rush. What are you talking about? We're three days away from a strike here."

"Which means I have a lot to do."

"Tony, perhaps you aren't aware that I bill at seventy dollars an hour now. Is it worth it to keep me twiddling my thumbs?"

"Have it your way. Tomorrow at Yancy's diner. Breakfast. It's two blocks from the office. Is seven-thirty too early for you?"

He knew that I looked and felt awful in the morning. Fine. I'd take one of those valerian pills Louise had given me for traveling, and fall asleep by 10 P.M. I was going to be glowing and dewy as a new bride tomorrow morning, damn it.

"Terrific," I said, and turned my back on him before he could turn his on me. I could sense rather than see Hamner gloating somewhere in the background. Hamner was always caught between wanting to be like the straight-shooting cowboys in the organizing department—of whom Tony was a prime example—and wanting to see them fail. With me around for a scapegoat, I bet Hamner was already picturing himself as Tony's new buddy.

"Come on," said Kate. "You're hungry now, aren't you? Doug, is that a cigarette I see you with? Don't you have asthma?"

"It's not that bad," said Doug, but he dropped the cigarette hastily and stubbed it out with his shoe.

She turned back to me.

"Do you like Mexican?"

I didn't, but I was suddenly so hungry that it sounded mouthwatering.

Kate disposed of two enchiladas and half my chilis rellenos. She ate voraciously for such a slim person. We were in a Tex-Mex theme restaurant, which grew on me after we'd polished off our first bowl of tortilla chips and I'd had a margarita.

"Don't let Hamner get to you," Kate said. "Or Tony, either. Tony's actually a good guy, but I guess you know that."

"I've worked with him before."

"He told me. He told me you guys used to live together but broke up."

"It wasn't all my fault."

"Hey, it probably wasn't even half your fault. He's a stubborn one when he doesn't have it just his way."

"So how come he listens to you?"

"I don't know. Maybe I remind him of his mother."

"I don't think so." From his brief accounts of her, Tony's mother seemed to have been a soft, placid woman who had delighted in her three energetic sons but never had the knack of managing them. Tony was such a troublemaker in high school that he'd have been expelled long before graduation if he hadn't been on the football team. Of course, in his high school years his mother had been getting sicker and sicker with cancer, slowly dying in a family of men for whom John Wayne was the model of emotional communication. It was no wonder Tony had been trouble.

"So, Kate, how did you think he handled that reporter's last question?"

Kate scooped up some of my guacamole.

"I love this stuff. I know it's bad for me but I don't care. Tony did great, like I told him. It's easy for him to say all that stuff, of course. He isn't leaving any patients."

"But you are."

"I'm an oncology nurse."

"That's tough."

"My best friend's in there right now, in ICU. Pancreatic cancer. It's a bacterial infection she's in for this time. Chemo makes you vulnerable to those."

"I'm sorry. Really sorry. Will she get out soon?"

"Who knows. It's been one infection after another. Thank God, not pneumonia yet."

"Is the chemo working?"

"She hasn't been one of the success stories. You should see her, though. Eileen has more life in her sick than most people do when they're well. She does her needlework, which I have to tell you is incredibly ugly. She made this cap I wore tonight. She talks to a million people on the phone, she eats Tootsie Rolls by the bagful, she sits up and acts lively when her husband and her two boys come in every night. With me, though, I think she feels like she can let go a little."

I nodded. I wanted to say, "How long does she have?" but thought that would be a cruel question.

I said, "So her prognosis isn't the best, it sounds like."

"She has maybe six months, and she's only thirty-seven. And still she wants this strike. She's gotten pissed off on our behalf, can you imagine that? If I were as sick as Eileen, I'd be on a nice long cruise somewhere, to hell with everyone else."

I tried to think of what I'd do if I were terminally ill. The first thought that came to my mind was that finally I could eat whatever I wanted. The second thought was that my mother would make my last months of life feel like several years. Even if I were dying—perhaps especially if I were dying—my mother would not cease her attempts to hack my life into a shape that was pleasing to her eyes. She'd probably bundle me off to Lourdes or subject me to an experimental cure that involved a diet of Brazil nuts and sheep's urine, all the while talking me up to the doctors as her lovely single daughter.

"I can't imagine it, Kate. Your side of it. The stress. Worse than stress."

"Well. What can you do? Don't get the idea that Eileen's some plaster saint. When we were girls we fought all the time. Real fighting, scratching and punching. She gave me a black eye once, when we were ten."

She sighed.

"I wish to hell this was all over, or doesn't happen. The strike, that is. It would give Eileen a coronary if I crossed a picket line, and of course I'd never do that. But if we somehow reach a contract, then I could be in the hospital, I could make sure she's getting what she needs when she needs it."

I wondered what I'd do if Louise were in some hospital somewhere and I couldn't go see her.

"Let's change the subject," said Kate. "Will you feel strange, working with Tony?"

"We're both old pros."

"If you're both such old pros, then how come he was so self-conscious when he came to Clare and me and said, and I quote, that 'this old flame' of his was going to be coming in to work this campaign?"

"Sometimes he's straight out of Lawrence Welk, the expressions he uses. The expressions he used, that is. I don't know a lot about what he's like these days."

"I don't think guys like Tony change that much over the years. I don't mean that Tony's boring, I mean that he was well on the way to being who he was when you met him. My husband, Mike, and I, we got married so young that I felt as if he was turning into a different person right in front of my eyes at some points. Especially when he went through medical school. He's probably felt that about me, too."

"But here you are, still together."

"He makes me laugh. Consistently, which from what I can tell is pretty rare. The other stuff goes up and down, but that hasn't changed."

Kate slurped up the last of her watered-down sangria through her straw, and said, "How does anyone do it? What no one tells you when you're young is how virtually impossible it is for any two adults to live together without wanting to kill each other once in a while."

"You couldn't really call it living together with me and Tony. He wasn't home enough. Though I often wanted to kill him just the same."

"I bet. His job is his heart and soul, which is not healthy. Not healthy at all."

"He's a throwback to the old days when the union boys risked their lives to organize. Got shot by Pinkerton men and all that."

In the town where Tony grew up, the union meant the difference between making it into the middle class or staying poor. The union was what saved you from being fired a week before you qualified for a full pension, or from being tumbled into poverty by illness. Because the union took care of you, you could send your kids to college. You could get them out of a world where you punched the clock.

Kate said, "Not easy to live with, those true believers."

"No."

"Tony would be kind of hard to get over, I'd think."

"Yes."

I shook myself.

"But I had someone new. Well, I guess I still have him. If I want him. No one could say I'm pining away, since Tony."

"You're fine with all this? Being around him, working with him?"

"Hey, we're all hardwired to forget."

"If you say so."

But you can't forget someone who's going to be right in front of you fourteen hours a day, scowling and muttering and second-guessing you at every turn. I knew so much about Tony. I knew that he couldn't eat Italian without falling asleep right afterward, that two of his back molars were capped because the fillings had cracked, and that he spent the first half of the night on his right side and the second half on his left side. I knew that he'd never pay more than a dollar-fifty for a greeting card on principle, no matter how sentimental the occasion, and that there wasn't a movie in the world he'd wait in an hour-long line for.

Unlike the background material in Weingould's files, I couldn't see how any of this knowledge was going to do me any good in the coming weeks. I wished I had the sort of memory eraser that aliens use when they're returning abducted humans in science fiction films. But that's life, I guess. There's never an alien handy when you need one.

"Get some sleep," Kate said when we parted. "You look dead on your feet. I'm going to go home and say hello to my poor husband. He'll probably look at me and say, 'Your face is familiar. Where do I know you from?' My kids, on the other hand. This is soccer season. They barely notice I'm gone."

She took me back to the strike office parking lot, told me the fastest way to my bed-and-breakfast, and waited for me to drive off in my own car.

"Your lights aren't on," she yelled, before I even had the chance to find the right gadget on the unfamiliar dashboard of the rental car. "Your lights!"

It gave me the oddest sense of being watched over.

8

THE WHITE HART had started its life as a coaching inn during the Revolutionary War, but inside, the year was 1888 or so, the height of Victorian excess. Except for the plaster-and-beam ceilings, the entire place had been draped and ornamented within an inch of its life. The windows were invisible behind swags of brocade weighted with bobbled fringe. The plank floors were hidden by layer upon layer of faded rugs, and the couches well swathed in paisley throws. The walls were crowded with gilt-framed cardboard prints from the most sentimental of nineteenth-century British domestic artists. They depicted little girls in ringlets and pantaloons giving kittens a bath, or simpering lovers leaning against a churchyard wall, or mothers sewing tiny garments by lamplight.

My hostess, Mrs. Crawley, dressed with a blithe disregard for the fashion ideals shown in *Town & Country*. She wore a cheap silk blouse, obviously an inexpert Pucci knockoff. The blouse was anchored down with cascading gold chains, and her pearl button earrings were so large and sturdy they could have served on a winter coat. Her lipstick was fuschia, her eye shadow mauve, her rouge an unhealthy shade of lilac. The coal-black of her hair had obviously been dumped out of a bottle. I liked her on sight.

"Come up," she said. "You look beat."

Why was everyone saying this? How bad did I look?

My room resembled a New Orleans brothel midway through the Gay Nineties. It had a dressing table with a ruffled skirt and a three-way hinged mirror. The bed was huge and decadent, with curlicued brass knobs one imagined clinging to in order to achieve certain sexual positions. It was just my luck to be alone whenever I encountered beds like this. There was even a low armless sofa referred to as a fainting couch, shoved into a corner as if any three square feet empty of furniture created an unbearable horror of the void.

Mrs. Crawley handed me a key, informed me of her breakfast hours, and prepared to leave. Contentment stole over me as I put the inn key on my own ring.

"Your assistant called," Mrs. Crawley said. "She asked me to have you call her back at home."

The phone was a squat old black model with a rotary dial, concealed by the ruffled net skirts of a plastic shepherdess with the face of Ava Gardner and a broken crook barely holding a tiny gold note pencil.

"I tried you at the strike office," Wendy said, perky as ever at 10 P.M. "You weren't there, but I remembered where you were staying."

As Ron had arranged, Wendy was stepping in for me on the Christmas fund-raiser for Campsters U.S.A., and she was raring to go. Advocacy's main role on this one was to dogsbody for the fund-raiser committee chairwoman, Janet Stratton-Smith. Or Jantsy, as she liked to be called, for reasons I didn't understand. Did the prep school nickname bring back the happy days of her youth, or was it just that the Buffy-and-Muffy types looked and thus felt the same all their lives? The same pleated skirts and girlish-elderly hairdos and stingily applied makeup. Certainly Jantsy's style hadn't changed since she was fifteen. In fact, I think she still had a riding jacket from her teenage years that she wore sometimes, out of what passed for sentiment.

Jantsy had married at twenty to a corporate attorney who'd done very, very well for himself, thanks to her enthusiastic prodding. After raising three blond children, she'd cast about for something else to do. Blessed with the energy and political skills of Lyndon B. Johnson, she threw herself into charity work.

Jantsy's events were spectacularly well attended in a city where there is fierce competition for important guests, but she had an outrageously high standard of perfection. Her pet project was "A Campsters Christmas," a yearly gala to raise money so that city children who had never seen a cow could spend the summer in the Berkshires. She herself loved the great outdoors, which she knew in the form of golf courses, motorboats, and two weeks in Maine in August. I felt that the great outdoors was what my family had left the Old Country to escape, and found the Campsters event, and Jantsy, a worse trial with every holiday season that passed.

Wendy said, "I have a progress report for you." She thought this phrase sounded professional.

Wendy was horribly efficient, horribly cheerful, and horribly dedicated. Her office was filled with business-gal geegaws, from the bronze nameplate she'd had made for her door (Wendy Williams, Public Relations Coordinator) to her matching desk set and bulletin board. She even had a gold-rimmed porcelain tray for her business cards. Over her desk was a poster of the Alps at sunrise and the words, "You can reach great heights if you start at the bottom and work up."

Not only was her office more professional than mine, her clothes were too. I never wear suits, but Wendy had at least fifteen, obviously picked from the "Career Dressing" section of better department stores. Clearly this girl had been devouring *Working Woman* for hints when I was still discovering the joys of *Cosmopolitan* sex quizzes. Once I heard her talking about me on the phone to one of her friends. "Nicky doesn't even have a day planner," she was exclaiming sorrowfully. "Her address book is full of little slips of paper that are always falling out. I don't know how she manages."

The rest of us sometimes referred to Wendy as "P.R. Barbie," but Ron relied on her when I was gone. She was Advocacy, Inc.'s most tireless worker and its self-appointed morale officer. When we landed the Helpers in Homebuilding account, she baked cookies in the shape of little saws and hammers. On staff birthdays, she was always the one who ordered the cake and found the "From Us to You" birthday card. Every Holy Week she ran an office Easter egg hunt complete with clues on pastel index cards that read something like, "Your face will sure be wreathed in smiles / When you find jelly beans in a drawer full of files."

Everyone participated, of course. There was no harm in Wendy, no spite. She just didn't realize that for other humans, life was not the rah-rah, go-team affair it was for her. While Wendy waved her pom-pons, most of us couldn't figure out where the game was being played, let alone which side to root for.

"So how are the Campsters doing?" I asked.

"Jantsy's a little upset about the centerpieces. She thinks they aren't rustic enough."

Janet's idea was to do the whole ballroom in a homespun, country theme. She wanted the walls draped in spruce branches, which was no problem given the time of year. But she also specified huge bouquets of black-eyed Susans on each table, a feat no florist could perform in the middle of December.

"I told her twelve times, they won't be in season, Wendy. And black-eyed Susans are the Maryland state flower, so how would that relate to the Berkshires? We shouldn't be doing this shit anyway. We aren't party planners."

I could hear Wendy's little sniff on the other end of the phone. She felt cussing was even more unprofessional than not giving your full name and title when you answered your office line.

"Didn't she like the idea of big silver bowls filled with red apples? It's easy to do, and it works well with the spruce. Very Christmasy."

"Jantsy's afraid people will steal the bowls."

Janet had a point. Rich benefactors might be able to buy the earth, but they would still swipe the centerpieces if they could.

"Oh God," I said. "Remember last year when she decided on those awful—what were they?—tiger lilies the day before the event?"

"It was asters," said Wendy.

"Whatever. Can you talk to Davida at Parties Plus and see what else she can come up with?"

"Actually," said Wendy, "I had a suggestion. I thought we could set up a country scene on each table, with little toy cows and horses and trees, and mountains out of peat moss, and lakes made of blue and green cellophane."

"Like model railroad scenery except with wildlife? Hey, that's cute. That's really cute. Did she go for it?"

"I don't like to brag but she loved it. We're having lunch with Davida tomorrow."

"You're terrific. You saved the day," I said, trying to sound like the maternal, capable boss Wendy dreamed of.

"I just want to keep my end up while you're gone," said Wendy.

When she'd said a chipper good night I wondered why, when it took so little to keep Wendy happy, I was usually so surly with her. She got under my skin like chiggers, but that was no excuse for my frequent curtness. I resolved to do better, just as I frequently resolved to be more patient with my mother, more collegial with Ron, and more open-minded about Louise's latest trip into the realms of the weird on her continuing search for a religion half as crazy as the one she'd left behind.

Bent on putting my good intentions into practice, I phoned my cousin. She answered on the second ring, breathless.

"I just got in," she said. "Hub was in town, passing through on his way to Philadelphia."

Hub, the rich-boy would-be Arlo Guthrie. Louise's current lost cause. With all the men Louise met, you'd think she could find someone who wasn't a fanatic or a loony, but her tender blue eyes and tolerant sweetness drew the nut jobs like a magnet.

Hub's full name, as I've said, was Hubbard Everett Gruber III, but he revealed it only reluctantly. His grandfather was the Gruber in Gruber's Home Central, the big hardware chain, and Hub did not like it to be known.

"And how's Hub's band doing these days?"

"It's called Miss Molly's Stovepipe, as you very well know, Nicky."

I thought this was a superlatively silly name for a band. There was no Miss Molly and no stovepipe. Hub had been stoned when he thought up the name.

"He just finished a new song."

Hub wrote with a prolificness that was suspect in my eyes, but I think Louise imagined that his work was the result of long nights of torment, an outpouring of the soul.

"The title is 'Seeing Eye Dog.' It's about this guy who kicks seeing-eye dogs on the subway because he himself is in so much pain. Hub wrote it after his last girlfriend turned out to be cheating on him with his band manager for the past five years."

I sighed to myself. Couldn't Louise ever date anyone normal?

"How was it that Hub did not know this?"

"He was busy."

"It was five years, Louise."

"Hub is a trusting person. He thinks that if you put your faith in people, it nearly always pays off."

"There's a fine line between faith and stupidity, if you ask me. He didn't really go around hurting seeing-eye dogs, did he? Because I think you can be arrested for that."

"Of course not. It's a metaphor for how angry he was at his *own* blindness about Karen. He always says he didn't let go of the pain about her until the moment he looked up from the accident and saw me."

Louise never met any of her nonnormal men in a normal way. She'd first encountered Hub when he got into a car accident late one February night at the intersection near her apartment, which was the corner of Tenth and Pennsylvania. Louise had heard the crash and run out to be of what assistance she could. She fed Hub and the other driver sandwiches and coffee while they waited for the police to come.

"I still can't believe you did that, Louise," I said now. "Don't you know better than to flit out into the street at nearly midnight, in your neighborhood?"

"Nicky, I know my neighborhood. You think it's dangerous just because it's mostly black people, which is very narrow-minded of you."

"No, I think it's dangerous because it's mostly people with prison records. I don't care about the color of their skin, and neither should you. You should just stay inside and call 911. Remember when they raided that crack house two doors down from you and you stood on the sidewalk offering to feed the dealers' rottweilers for them until they made bail? I swear, Louise, please don't make me come down to the morgue and identify you."

My brother Joey referred to my cousin's living situation as "Louise's single-handed attempt to integrate Southeast." In her determination to rub shoulders with her fellow man, Louise had been mugged, burglarized, and had her butt grabbed by a fondle-and-run molester on a bicycle. My theory was that Louise had chosen her dicey neighborhood because it was as far from the rest of her family as she could get without decamping to the suburbs. And the rents were low, so that Louise could squirrel away her money in the event that someday the supply of lonely hearts gave out.

"Hub's band is playing D.C. and Baltimore all through Christmas and New Year's. Will you come hear them with me? We can go back-stage."

"If I'm home I'll come, sure."

"You have to come home. I want you to see him at his best, when he's performing."

It was hard to imagine that Hub could be any *worse* on stage than when he appeared before me in person trailing an aura of sweat, stale marijuana smoke, and sandalwood. He believed, Louise informed me, that deodorant caused cancer of the lymph nodes.

I plunged. I knew better, but I did it anyway.

"Louise, don't you think that any of this sudden intensity with Hub has even a little to do with Johnny?"

"Nicky, I wish you'd quit harping on that. No one could be happier for Johnny than I am. Let go of these girlish fantasies. We're all grown up now."

I tried to speak her language.

"Louise, don't you think maybe that the Universe wants you to save Johnny from spending his life with someone humorless and unloving?"

"You don't know that Betsey is those things."

"She doesn't laugh at his jokes. She'll make him live in some development in Gaithersburg."

"Many very nice people live in Gaithersburg."

"Many nice people live in Moscow, too, but that doesn't mean we want Johnny to be dragged there. I have a bad feeling about her, Louise. I just can't help thinking that all elementary school teachers have a little too much of the bully in them. I mean, one of these days she's going to tell Johnny he has to raise his hand before he goes to the bathroom."

Louise ignored me.

"How did you do, seeing Tony again?"

I had filled her in during a brief phone call while packing.

"Horribly. I don't want to talk about it. It'll just depress me. Tell me what you've been up to the last few days."

"Actually, I went with Betsey to see about the wedding flowers. Johnny's bugged me and bugged me to do something chummy with her, so finally I did that. It didn't go too well, to tell the truth."

Floral wrangles seemed to be the theme of my night. It transpired that Betsey was so enamored of natural simplicity that she intended to carry a bouquet of dried lavender and baby's breath in her tiny, doll-like hands. Apparently the fragility of dried lavender presented a real challenge, and the florist had doubted Betsey's chosen arrangement would make it through the ceremony intact. I could see her, shedding dead blossoms all the way down the aisle.

"She's such a pill, Louise. There's a reason why roses are the flower of choice. Is she cheap or something?"

"No, I think her parents are footing the bill and they're *quite* well off. She just has very specific tastes. It's her big day. I can't blame her."

Louise was being charitable. I knew her opinions on weddings: the gaudier the better. Louise's wedding, whenever it occurred, was sure to be as flaky as they came, populated by Quakers, Scientologists, palm readers, anti-vivisectionists, and tree spikers—guests from every cause or sect Louise had ever stepped foot in. But whatever her bridal excesses, you wouldn't catch her in a wilted linen dress like the one Betsey had chosen, or foisting carrot cake on her unsuspecting guests, as it appeared Betsey was planning to do.

"Betsey asked me if I thought Johnny would agree to get a professional manicure the day before the wedding. I told her I didn't think he'd be amenable to that idea."

Tactful Louise. I'd have laughed out loud. If you marry a mechanic, you'd sure better be okay with grimy fingernails. My father and brothers had always relied on an excellent snot-colored, oil-based concoction by the trade name of Glop, but no matter what you used, there'd be traces of engine oil and dirt that would never come out. It was ingrained in the skin.

"Louise, don't you see? It's happening already. Who does she think she's marrying here?"

"Nicky, in my work I've seen that it's not so uncommon for one partner to try to change the other partner at first. Many couples grow out of that."

"But we're not talking about her making an alteration in his table manners. We're talking about his work, his work that he loves. She's going to make him feel like a grease monkey."

"She must make him feel good about himself somehow, because he's marrying her."

"Her, not me" were the words she didn't say.

"Are you speaking to Johnny again? He told me you'd had a fight."

"It was nothing. I was a little emotional that night. Hormones."

"It's nowhere near your period."

"Work stress."

She said she was tired a moment later. After we'd hung up, I ran a bath in the clawfoot tub and lay there thinking about Louise and Johnny, and what could be done to engineer the happy ending they both so richly deserved.

Betsey was like the murder victims in my Agatha Christie novels. She was like selfish, spoiled Linnet Doyle in *Death on the Nile* or vain, cheating Arlena Marshall in *Evil Under the Sun*. Not as attractive or underhanded, of course—just, as they were, overpoweringly in the way. She had to be gotten rid of, but how? Louise was no match for her. Louise would keep kidding herself with men so odd and needy that their very oddness and neediness was a distraction from the fact that she didn't love them. All the while, Johnny was being frog-marched to the altar.

When I returned home for Thanksgiving, I vowed, something had to give. Don't interfere, Ma had said. But I wasn't so much interfering as inviting fate to use me as an instrument to set things right. Who could say that wasn't noble?

9

TONY ORDERED EGGS over easy, a disgusting dish I'd always hated watching him eat, the egg whites runny and almost translucent. I ordered blueberry pancakes with a side of bacon. Here we were, eating breakfast again together as we had so many times. Lovely.

Trying to appear not to be trying, I'd gone for a wholesome effect that morning—or as wholesome as I ever get. I wore a boat-necked sweater of dark gray fleece, and a pair of slim-cut charcoal-gray flannel trousers with a silk lining that felt like heaven against my legs. My only jewelry was a tiny dog tag on a pewter chain. Louise had given it to me. If you looked closely, you could see that the dog tag read, "goddess." Louise has a gift for giving presents that become talismans.

The morning light wasn't kind to Tony. Sitting across from him, I could see that the last five years, doing the work he did, had taken a toll. There were faint bags under his eyes that hadn't been there when I knew him, and lines around his mouth I didn't remember. He seemed not so much older as exhausted. Part of me was dismayed, but part of me was smug. I'd told him to slow down. Now look at him.

The morning light wasn't kind to this town, either. I had forgotten what it's like in places like this, where the ghosts of more prosperous decades seem to hang in the air around you. On my way to Yancy's, I'd driven past a hillside graveyard with an elaborate scrolled iron gate and hulking Victorian monuments. Winsack's rich had once counted on winding up here, side by side with people they wouldn't object to knowing in the afterlife. Now, except for one plain, modest marker on which someone had placed a vase of red plastic roses and an American flag, the weeds and keeled-over stones made it clear no one ever visited.

Down the street from Yancy's, rising four stories high (which was high for Winsack), was one of those old hotels for businessmen with the words "Prospect House: Clean Lodging, One Dollar a Night" still visible on the side of the building. The building was now a center for troubled youth. You could see that the five-and-ten, with its Egyptian-style Deco storefront, had once been a dazzling emporium, complete with a soda fountain sparkling with chrome. Now only the display of potted plants on the sidewalk revealed that the place was still in operation.

Aside from these shipwrecked remains, the business district consisted of small outfits whose dusty facades made you wonder how they kept going. For example, who patronized the "Topline Tuxedos" shop with its flyblown windows bearing the gold-stenciled motto "Serving Winsack Society Since 1963"? I felt, for a very short moment, sorry for Bennett Winslow with his elaborate black marble fountain in the hospital lobby. His dreams of grandeur were about fifty years too late for this town.

Yancy's was quiet at this hour on a Saturday. It was the kind of classic, uncompromising diner that all right-thinking people enjoy. Nothing had been jazzed up or spoiled. There was a luminous greasy film on the tabletop jukeboxes, and you could search the menu until your eyes ached and not find anything healthier than cling peaches in heavy syrup with a scoop of cottage cheese.

We sat in a big corner booth. At the counter was what looked like a delivery guy on a quick break, and a few booths down were two old ladies who were rather loudly planning a day of shopping at the new mall in Providence. No place in the world makes tougher old ladies than New England does, and these two were prime examples: flinty, soberly dressed, composed and unself-conscious as statues or thoroughbreds, speaking loudly not because they were ill-bred but because, it became clear, they were rather deaf.

"How's your bed-and-breakfast?" Tony asked with derision in his tone. Any lodging but a cheap motel made him feel inferior, reminding him that he came from a coal town where the only restaurants were a pizza parlor and the bowling alley snack bar.

"It's gorgeous," I said, although even this early in my stay I was get-

ting sick of the bright pink moire bedspread and the matching hang-
ings that were reflected, their color shrieking at my hair, in every one
of the five gilded mirrors in the room. The mattress was deep and soft,
though. I knew I looked fresh this morning, and better for our five
years' separation than Tony did. Take that! I thought, stabbing a stray
blueberry.

"I'll never understand why you'd stay at a place like that when you
could have something with all the modern conveniences."

"For the same reason you like those revolting eggs and I like a
breakfast that doesn't include the exciting possibility of salmonella
poisoning."

He mopped up a last streak of egg yolk and pushed his plate aside.

"Let's get down to specifics," he said.

"I'm not finished with my food yet."

He looked pointedly at his watch, then glared out the window
while I speared one small piece of pancake after another, chewing
with a ladylike delicacy entirely foreign to me.

Finally, I wiped my mouth daintily with a paper napkin and said,
"Okay, I'm ready. Where's Clare, by the way? I'm not kidding about
needing to speak to her today. The sooner the better."

"She was in negotiations all night. Still going on as of her last
phone call. You'll see her soon enough, either way. If talks break off
this time, we're going out as of midnight tonight."

"Why aren't you in negotiations?"

"No big reason," he said. "A squabble with someone on the other
side's team, that's all."

I'd have to ask Kate for details.

He took out a list written in pencil on brown mailing paper.
Wendy would have found Tony sadly unprofessional.

"Here's what we can get going with, for now," he said. "I marked
your part."

"I'm not doing any of Hamner's make-work, I can tell you right
now. I have other clients to juggle and I don't have time for his
shenanigans."

"You and Ron are that booked up?"

His tone implied that he was surprised that there were enough idiots, even in the idiot-crowded town of Washington, to keep Ron and me employed at our sketchy endeavors.

"This is a busy time of year."

He should have remembered that from our days together, though he'd never managed to be there in person to cheer me through the dreaded holiday season with its dozens of social galas on behalf of what Jantsy always called "those less fortunate." Tony had spent our first December together in Alaska, trying to organize employees of a large bookstore in Anchorage. Some big muckety-muck at the national union had thought bookstore chains might be an easy target. He'd been wrong, but at least Tony had been inside for that assignment, meeting people in coffee shops and hotel lounges. I would never forget the campaign to unionize South Dakota highway maintenance workers the following February. He'd almost lost a toe to frostbite, riding with the snowplow drivers.

I took up the brown paper list. A drop of egg yolk adorned it.

" 'Declare strike,'" I read aloud. "Okay, good start."

"Read silently," said Tony.

I read, " 'Assign picketing shifts. Meet with state senators. Meet with any possible U.S. senators and congressional rep., or staff. Strike newsletter daily, one page front and back. Pressure on hosp. board. Press outreach.'"

Next to "press outreach" he had put my name in parentheses. He had spelled it Nikki. He knew I hated that spelling.

" 'Radio PSA possible on questions patients should ask during any hospital stay? Flyers for picket line handout. Letter to editor, for Providence papers. Kennedy?' "

"Good idea, Tony. Patrick Kennedy is excellent on labor issues."

"Yeah, but actually I meant Ted. He helped settle that hospital strike in western Mass not too long ago, and the nurses won hands down. This isn't his turf, but you never know."

Tony's list continued: " 'Dirt on Jet-a-Nurse.'"

"What's Jet-a-Nurse?" I asked.

"Scab nurses," said Tony. "This company Jet-a-Nurse flies them in on really short notice from Nevada, pays them around sixteen hundred a week. The replacement nurses keep the hospital going, not at full census, of course, but enough for them to claim to the public that there's nothing to worry about—come on in for that thyroid operation or whatever."

"Are they good nurses?"

"Some. Some actually think they're rescuing patients by filling in. On the other hand, some of them just do it for the money and are really lousy. Jet-a-Nurse already has a couple of patient deaths on its hands from other strikes."

"We can make that record known. Where are we on testimonials from members and community leaders? Is there a Portuguese community here? Latinos? Any Asians? And we need a few mothers with babies or toddlers."

"Mary Grunewald has five kids under twelve," Tony said. "Husband's a landscaper, so they'll have it rough this time of year."

"She would be great. We'll take her picture with all the kids and run it on the front of an eight-by-eleven cardboard postcard with copy on back saying something like, 'Mary Grunewald listened to her conscience and went on strike. Now Mary's six kids—' "

"Five kids."

" 'Now her five kids may get nothing for Christmas.' We send it to key opinion makers, business leaders, legislators. No vitriol against the hospital. Just regular nurses and their children suffering on behalf of their ideals."

"This makes me want to retch, all this Clara Barton shit," said Tony.

"We don't have a choice, Tony. We have to take the high road."

"Blah, blah, blah," he said, and signaled for more coffee.

"How many of your people do you think will cross the line, Tony?"

"Not many at first. Eventually, maybe twenty percent. We already have a strike loan program in place. And we're putting together a list of area hospitals that want per diem nurses, for people who need to pick up work. The other problem will be guilt, of course."

"Yeah. I saw Louanne Reilly on the late news last night."

"Old Louanne really laid on the schmaltz," said Tony gloomily.

Louanne Reilly was the St. Francis director of nursing, who'd appeared on the Channel 8 news to say that any nurse "who chose to honor her professional commitments" would be more than welcome to remain at her post. She was gotten up as a Mrs. Santa Claus type, wearing a nubbly Kmart-ish sweater embroidered with daisies, and drugstore reading glasses on a chain. According to Kate, the woman owned Chanel shoes and Louis Vuitton luggage and did all her shopping at designer boutiques on Newbury Street in Boston.

The hospital was getting good advice from someone. Reilly's tone of sorrowful regret was the right note to hit.

"I'll keep the strike newsletter," Tony said. "Clare can record a new hotline update every day. You ghost a few op eds or letters to the editor from state senators and she'll get them in their hands for approval."

"I can do the newsletter, too, if a quick and dirty layout is okay," I said. "You're busy enough. And the testimonial flyers. We'll start simple, just one person, an older nurse, I think."

"Ruth Morgeski," said Tony. "She'll have them crying in the aisles. Two months ago her charge nurse interrupted her while she was assisting at last rites for a patient. She said Ruth was needed on the floor. Ruth is still fuming about it."

Tony talked to everybody. He remembered their units and their stories and their family situations, and what was more, he knew where everyone was in their commitment to the union. He knew who had the guts to wear a union button on his or her uniform, what unit was pissed off enough to sign a petition down to a woman (as ICU had been), which units had the worst charge nurses, and which had charge nurses who were sympathetic to our side.

Tony had no desire to be the guy who ran things from his desk at strike headquarters, waving to the troops from a distance. He would work round the clock on this strike, but he'd still be out there picketing with the rest some portion of every day. It was a job for two or three people and he wasn't twenty-five anymore, full of youth and the kind of full-throttle youthful energy you don't pay for later.

"Ruth wears a Miraculous Medal," said Tony. "Make sure it shows in her picture for the testimonial. We gotta play our end of the Catholic thing big time."

He was so involved in our propaganda planning that he seemed to have forgotten who I was: the woman who done him wrong. It was strange that when everything between us lay in ruins that were no longer even smoking, we still had this, the easy rhythm of our work together.

But then we had always had that. It was what we began with.

I met Tony in New York City. I'd been detailed to one of his campaigns by Swinton McClaine. Swinton was working at the time with a loose consortium of interests who wanted to prevent the expansion of a large, prestigious college—whose name I shouldn't mention—into six surrounding neighborhoods. This consortium, which consisted of businesses, brownstone owners, and community groups, was disturbed that the college was gobbling up real estate and failing to provide adequate security patrols. The college was polluting, too, and its students were loud and inconsiderate in Zabar's. It was getting out of paying city taxes. It was a bad neighbor.

Swinton was brought into the picture to assist these civic leaders in sticking it to this respected institution of higher learning any way they could. Our first opportunity lay in fanning the flames of a messy scandal-in-the-making: the way the college treated its clerical staff, whose contract was in the process of being renegotiated. These women were paid so little that many of them qualified for food stamps. They had bare-bones insurance coverage. They were cheated out of overtime by supervisors who instructed them to lie on their time sheets or find another job.

By the time I arrived on the scene that fall, negotiations had been stalled for weeks by a corporate type high up in the administration, a guy bent on chiseling the secretaries down to a 2 percent raise in order to demonstrate to his boss that he could play hardball. Some snotty Wharton Business School graduate.

It should have been a dream campaign for me. The administration fat cats on one side, women with children to feed on the other. A few Hollywood alumni already interested. A contact at *The Village Voice* who was fired up about the story. And, as frosting on the cake, support from the gay community, because the union's local president was a lesbian activist. I was assigned to help with leaflets, speeches, publicity gimmicks, and whatever else we could think of to make the college look like a worse employer than the California grape industry.

There was only one snag: I wasn't wanted. Tony Boltanski, the Toilers' national rep who was chief negotiator for this pink-collar unit, liked to play a lone hand.

"I really don't have much for you to do here" were his first words to me.

"I'll go shopping, then," I said.

"No offense, but I'm used to handling these situations by myself."

"I don't see a contract yet. Your boss said a writer would come in handy."

"You can stuff some envelopes," he said. "That's about it."

After that reception I didn't find him at all attractive. I generally preferred tall men—Tony topped me by only a few inches. I tended toward bookish types—Tony's idea of great literature was *The Science of Hitting* by Ted Williams. I favored dark men with dark eyes. Tony's light brown hair was coarse and curly and receded a little from his forehead, giving him what I felt was a completely undeserved look of intelligence.

I spent a week running the copying machine and drafting press releases that Tony vetoed. He eventually condescended to ask me to "glance at" a flyer he'd prepared, a flyer inviting students to a Rally for Fairness to Employees, to be staged at the university gates on the day a prominent human rights advocate was due as guest speaker in a lecture series entitled "Ethics in the Postmodern Age."

The union must be somewhat desperate, I concluded, or Tony and Sheila, the local president, wouldn't have taken the contract fight so public. Not that Tony had asked me to sit in on their meetings or begged me for ideas or anything like that.

The hall in which the lecture series would be held happened to be the site of one of the largest industrial accidents in the city's history. Presently the chemistry building, it had once been a trouser factory whose snow-laden roof had caved in one February night in 1916, killing forty-two seamstresses, some as young as fourteen years old.

Tony's rally flyer had a graphic photo of the Octagon Trouser Factory disaster and the headline, "Women suffered here then and they're suffering now. Don't let the bosses get away with it!"

"Can I make a few changes and get back to you?" I asked him.

Two hours later he was standing in front of my desk, glowering.

"What the hell did you do to this flyer?"

Using my handy computer layout program, I had changed the photo to one of Wilma Stevens, who worked in the library, handing a book to a student and smiling warmly. An inset displayed a chart comparing clerical salaries with the average cost of living in the outer boroughs. The headline now read, "The people who make this college run are only asking for a fair deal."

The copy ran: *We find that library book you're looking for . . . we make sure your financial aid comes through . . . we're there whenever you need us, in the cafeteria, the bookstore, and the health clinic. We're the clerical workers of _____ College, and we're hoping for your support.*

A caption under the salary chart added, *At _____ College, you can work full-time and still qualify for food stamps. That's just not right.*

"What is this bullshit?" Tony repeated, in case I didn't pick up on his opinion of my handiwork.

"Look, Tony, the kids who go to school here aren't going to remember the Octagon tragedy. If they come out for you on Tuesday, it's going to be for that nice lady at the dining hall salad bar, not to fight for the female underclass in the male patriarchal hegemony. Where do you think we're running this thing, Brown University?"

"This is the most namby-pamby piece of garbage I've ever seen," Tony said. "My committee's going to hate this."

"Sheila already showed it to them. They loved it. Because everyone loves Wilma, that's why."

I brought the flyer up on the screen and added a few words under Wilma's picture: *Wilma Stevens is sixty-two and has worked here for nearly forty years. But she's too poor to afford new dentures. Surely our college has too proud a tradition to treat its employees this way. Tell this administration, it's time for decency again!*

"Wilma doesn't wear dentures," Tony snarled.

I deleted "dentures" and typed in "eyeglasses." He stomped away.

"Let's print it in some really sweet color," I called after him. "How about pale pink?"

"This isn't getting printed," he snapped over his shoulder. "Decency, my ass."

I left the paste-up on his chair.

The next morning, stacked on the floor by my desk, were a thousand copies of my version of the flyer, printed by our members in the college print shop on pale blue paper and ready for distribution by our people in the mailroom. The pale blue was an even bigger concession from Tony than the copy itself, I knew. Pink would have been total surrender.

On the top copy in the stack Tony had scrawled, "We'll try it your way." I didn't know if it was a challenge or an apology. But we got five hundred students at that rally, and the visiting human rights activist asked some questions that were very, very embarrassing for the stuffed shirts who ran the place. He asked them again, a week later, in a letter to the *Times*.

After that, when Tony wasn't in bargaining sessions or meeting with the municipal unions to get their support, he spent every minute with me and Sheila, the local president, devising ways for us to up the ante on the administration. Sheila went home to her partner and her kids by 10 P.M., and Tony and I ate take-out Chinese and meatball subs in the office late in the evening, too tired to go out, too hungry to make it back to our separate hotels. Over sweet-and-sour pork one night, he gave me a brief history of himself. He was the oldest of three brothers. His father was a truck driver. His grandfathers were both mine workers; they both died of black lung before he was five. His mother died of a cancer he wouldn't name (ovarian cancer, I learned later) when he was twenty. His football career had been ended by a shattered kneecap at the state high school championship in his senior year. His heroes were John Lewis, Caesar Chavez, Franklin Delano Roosevelt, and Larry Bird.

He gave me a nickname: "kiddo." He talked me into going to a Rangers game one night on impulse, when we'd been up for forty-eight hours straight. He taught me how to eat hot chestnuts. And, three weeks later, when it became clear that the college was going to crack and I was ordered back to Washington, he took me out for lasagna at a little restaurant in the Village. We drank two bottles of red wine, and meandered the fifty-three blocks back to my hotel.

In the lobby he said, "I should walk you up to your room. This is a dangerous city." At the door of my room, he said, "I could check your room for you if you like, make sure no one's hiding under the bed." He was kissing me before we'd turned on the light. I wanted him so much I didn't even ask him if this was an end-of-campaign fling or the beginning of something.

"When you met me, did you ever think we'd wind up this way?" he asked me afterward.

"You were a pain in the neck at first, but I knew you'd think of something to do with me and my valuable skills."

All night long he thought of things, and I thought of some too. After the new contract was voted up by the unit with triumphant joy, I went home and Tony stuck around to wrap up loose ends. For a month I came up to see him in New York every weekend, and then he moved in with me, down in Washington. The plan was that he would fly off to his assignments during the week, and come home to me on weekends.

That first month in New York, how drunk we were, how crazy we were, with love. The only New York I know, the magic city, is the New York Tony showed me that September. When I go there now, I don't stay long and I don't walk around much, not for fear of being mugged but for fear of remembering.

My apartment, which is on the top floor of one of those shabby Beaux Arts buildings in Adams-Morgan, was more than big enough for his possessions and mine. In fact, for the first time the place was full enough that it didn't seem to echo. Living there with Tony was the version of grown-up life that children dream of. With Tony, I could eat with my fingers, or leave my smelly socks on the floor, or forget the coffee filter was in the pot until mold grew on it. With Tony, I could lunch on apple pie and take a three-hour bath at midnight if I liked. Slightly eccentric himself, he made me feel beloved, for the first time in my life, for my own eccentricities.

Tony had been away on a work assignment when I left him the

note saying it was over. I did the official dumping, but the truth is that Tony was really the one who left me.

When we first started living together, he was gone nearly every week but home on the weekends. Then he was away for two weeks at a stretch. Then he was always traveling, it seemed. At the end he was away even when he was standing in front of me, and I knew it was time to go. Tony had come home to a letter informing him that I'd gone to Louise's. Not even a long, tortured explanatory letter holding out hope of a reconciliation. Just a scribble on the back of the gas bill that read, basically, "I give up and I'm getting out."

I'd left because I couldn't think of anything else to do. Tony was slowly, surely being lost to me. What I hadn't understood in those heady weeks of the campaign was that his real life was lived on the road, in the high drama and moment-to-moment decisions of his job. I soon became a pleasant distraction he returned to for forty-eight hours every so often, or that's what I assumed I was to him, since he never indicated otherwise. When he missed my brother Joey's wedding at the last minute in favor of a rally for underpaid dockworkers in New Orleans, I cried for a week. He knew, he *should* have known, what it meant to me to go alone to that wedding.

"You have to learn to be flexible, Nicky," he'd said from a pay phone in Monroe, Louisiana. "You knew what my job was like when we got into this."

I think I began to give up hope at that moment. After all, if I'd wanted to live with someone who mocked my fondest desires and downplayed my disappointments, I could have moved back home with my mother.

The year after Tony and I split up, my father died of a heart attack. He was gone before I got to the hospital. My mother and brothers were there, but I'd been in some dull meeting and it took them a while to reach me. Before my father went, some corner of me believed that there was no such thing as a last chance, that nothing you really wanted was ever lost to you forever. After my dad died, I knew better.

*   *   *

I was closing my notebook with the list of tasks we'd agreed on when I saw Tony glance toward the door.

"There's one thing I forgot to tell you about," he said. "Our professor."

"What?"

"We just call her that because she gets a little hard to follow sometimes."

His voice sounded almost fond. Tony was not a nicknaming type.

"Weingould borrowed her from a friend of his at Hatcher and Draybeck, one of the big consulting firms in Boston. She's looking into Coventry's finances for us, digging up dirt with numbers to back it."

The woman approaching us looked nothing like any professor I'd met. She possessed a degree of exquisite grooming and quiet assurance that you don't see in people with harried schedules and stingy paychecks. She nudged Tony to make room on his side of the booth with a casualness that made me feel suddenly an outsider.

"Suzanne Perry," said Tony briefly. "Suzanne, this is Nicky Malone, who's here to help us with PR. She'll need a few facts from you, maybe in words of one syllable. They think in sound bites, these PR types."

I felt slapped. He'd sure been quick to put me in my place after our brief interlude of cooperation.

"Screw you, Tony," I said. "Try doing my job for a day."

"At least I'd have a chance to put my feet up."

"You were putting your feet up just a minute ago." It was true, his feet had been resting on my side of the booth, inches from my leg. Not that it meant anything.

Suzanne smiled calmly. She wasn't really pretty, but she was enormously attractive. Her eyes were hazel under heavy, sleepy eyelids, and though her nose was a little long it had an interesting tiny crookedness in the middle. She was slender, and wore small wire-rimmed spectacles which may have been an affectation, since she seemed to remove them at will during the ensuing conversation without the dazed expression of someone who actually relies on glasses to see.

She tucked a strand of hair behind one of her shell-like ears. Her gestures had a deliberate quality, so studied that they were almost stylized, as if she'd gotten Balanchine to choreograph motions for every-day social encounters. She slowly pulled the wrapper off a straw and twisted it into a ring shape, then discarded that ring and took another wrapper. Soon there were a pile of perfectly made rings next to her hand. I watched in fascination as she repeated the ritual over and over again.

Her heather-green wool sheath and polished black loafers were simple and excellently made, and I could tell that the store where she purchased them was one I wouldn't even feel well dressed enough to browse through. Her hair—a nothing-special medium brown—was cut in a long, sleek bob, the featured haircut of that fall, the haircut most women in Washington would be experimenting with several months from now. It was clever of her not to have gone blond, despite her fair complexion. This way, you noticed first those unusual hazel eyes, that clean jawline.

She was drinking out of Tony's coffee cup, then brushed her hand against his as she reached for a packet of artificial sugar. If she were a cat, I thought, she would now be pissing daintily on his side of the booth, marking her territory. I raised my eyebrows, deliberately, so briefly that only Tony saw.

"So how's it going so far?" I said, as Suzanne continued to say nothing. "What have you got for us?"

"There are areas I think bear investigation. For example, Coventry is moving money around in strange ways between the main corporation and its several subsidiaries. Thus far, I've found nothing illegal, but it's an unusually complicated setup, even for the corporate health care field. Their Medicare billings are also unusually high, but as you know, there's already a federal investigation under way there."

"The corporate finance stuff is interesting," said Tony. "But so far it only confirms that they can afford to have us camp out in front of the hospital all winter if they want."

"Monetarily. We'll turn up the heat in other ways."

I said to Suzanne, "Can you find me money that's being spent on inessentials? That silly waterfall in the lobby, for example, or executive salaries. Perks. Fancy cars, junkets to meetings abroad, extravagant entertaining allowances."

"They're paying the status quo for executives in this field. Six figures with generous, and I do mean generous, benefits is usual."

"The public won't like it even if it is the status quo. How far would one of those bigwig's salaries go toward medical equipment? A PET scan machine, for example."

"It's a simplistic argument," she said.

"I'm a simplistic sort of gal. As Tony just said."

"Let me root around a little, if that's what you want. It won't be hard. I'm based in Boston, though. So we'll have to do some of this by phone."

"Fine." By phone seemed a good way to deal with Suzanne, who might be less intimidating if I didn't have her right in front of me in all her tastefully packaged glory.

"But I manage to get up here pretty often," she added.

She was inspecting Tony's plate.

"Eggs again? I thought you were cutting down."

Tony did not meet my eyes. Well, what had I thought? That Tony was lying on his chaste motel bed every night mooning over my photograph?

Suzanne turned back to me.

"You know that Coventry is just one of several health care conglomerates that have emerged in the last decade, and by no means the worst. I can give you statistics on the increase in acquisitions of public hospitals by private companies in the past five years. Not to mention mergers, larger and larger health care networks, closings of community hospitals that serve the Medicaid and indigent populations. If Coventry is a villain, they've got a lot of company."

"We don't have to let them off the hook by talking about trends in the industry."

"There's something to be said for sounding factual and aware of the big picture."

"Most people don't give a damn about the big picture."

"I'll get the information, and you can do what you think best with it," said Suzanne, acting a little miffed, like a doctor advising a hefty patient to go on a diet with little hope that the patient will actually follow orders. Did she have to sound like such a snooty expert? I'm convinced that half the reason people get graduate degrees is to feel entitled to talk down to us plebes who don't specialize.

"There's something else that struck me as odd," said Suzanne, turning to Tony as if weary of my frivolity. "St. Francis is purchasing the bulk of its medical supplies from a small company called BioSupp, Inc. Does the name ring a bell?"

My mind flashed back to one of the folders Weingould had given me.

"They're a wholly owned subsidiary of Coventry," I said.

Suzanne nodded.

"And their prices are, I won't say suspiciously high compared to the rest of the market, but high enough that it caught my eye."

"So Coventry is siphoning money off St. Francis through the inflated prices the subsidiary is charging for medical supplies?"

"It's just possible. People will like that even less than high executive salaries. I have to do some checking, though. What do you think, Tony?"

"You're doing a great job, Suzanne, but I'm still hoping we won't have to use any of this. We can talk strategy more if it turns out we have to walk the line."

"Walk the line. Who are you, Johnny Cash?" I said.

I hated it when Tony acted like the Marlboro Man, all gruff and weathered without a three-syllable word in his head. He was *swaggering* in front of Suzanne.

"Suzanne graduated from Harvard Business School," Tony mentioned, as if she'd discovered radium. "We're lucky she's wasting her time on us."

Suzanne glanced down modestly into her coffee.

"Nicky went to Maryland," he added, as if admitting that I'd done time somewhere. As if his degree from Duquesne were suitable for framing. He'd barely squeaked through.

"Communications?" said Suzanne in the dismissive tone in which she'd have referred to a BA in Home Ec.

"Nope, studio art."

She gave me the first truly interested glance I'd had from her.

"Are you working now?" she said. "What's your medium?"

I didn't think she'd be impressed by the giant paper-doily dancing hearts I'd done for the St. Ignatius Valentine's Dance last year, though they had received a lot of critical praise from the attendees. They hung from the ceiling and were blown about by cleverly rigged standing fans so that they really seemed to be dancing. Ma had been delighted, but I didn't think Suzanne would get it.

"In school I did sculptural stuff mostly. I liked to play with forms built up mainly out of old mud flaps from sixteen-wheelers, especially ones with lewd images that I'd pick up off the side of the road, plus a variety of clays and resins. But I'm currently experimenting with rendering common household objects in a compound of plaster of Paris and shredded feminine napkins. A sort of Judy Chicago-meets-Dada thing."

She nodded thoughtfully.

"Just kidding," I said.

"Nicky. She likes to tease," Tony said to Suzanne.

"More coffee?" said the waitress.

As I held my mug up for a refill, the shopping-bound old ladies began bustling toward the door. One of them jostled the waitress's elbow, spilling coffee over my left hand and wrist.

When they offer you fresh coffee at Yancy's, they mean fresh. At first the burn felt like cold water, and a second later the pain was intense. In a moment, Tony was kneeling by my side of the booth, scooping ice out of my water glass and applying it ineffectively to my hand, from which it immediately slipped off. Suzanne, with a cooler head, was soaking napkins and trying to open a butter packet.

"Butter's not really good for burns," the waitress said.

"For God's sake," said Tony. "Get a bucket of ice."

"Do you need to put your head between your knees?" asked Suzanne.

Through a haze I could see the elderly ladies in the parking lot, placidly consulting a map. The waitress came back with an aluminum basin full of crushed ice, and Tony plunged my hand into it.

"I'm fine," I said to Tony. "Honest."

"Shut up and lean back," he said, using his hand as a lever to keep my elbow up and my hand and wrist in the ice bucket.

We sat there for a few minutes, Tony crouched by my side, Suzanne and the waitress discussing potential remedies. It was humiliating.

In the end, they smeared my left hand with some Pond's cold cream the waitress had in her purse, and wrapped it in an Ace bandage that had last been used for the busboy's sprained ankle.

"Ace bandages aren't for burns," I said, as Tony wrapped my hand up, pretty deftly and surprisingly gently.

"It'll keep this gluck on until you can ice it back at the inn."

"I'm not going back to the inn."

"You are so frigging stubborn."

"Let her decide," said Suzanne. "Can you drive yourself, Nicky?"

"She's a lousy driver when her hand *isn't* burned," said Tony.

"I'm not the one who made a U-turn in the middle of the Stockton Street Tunnel at rush hour," I said, remembering an exploit from one of Tony's past assignments out west. He'd sworn over the ticket, then put it in a drawer as if he expected it to disappear.

"Who had two accidents in the same parking lot in a year, Nicky? A parking lot!"

Suzanne was considering us with her head tilted to one side and her heavy eyelids especially sleepy. Her expression did not bode well for our working relationship.

"I'm perfectly fit to drive," I said. "Perfectly. And you don't have to keep holding my arm up, for God's sake, Tony."

He dropped my elbow with a thump.

"Excuse me for not wanting you to faint all over the booth."

"I fainted once, Tony. Once in the whole time you've known me, and that was after a flu shot."

He was being kind to me. Nothing is more galling, when you once had the power to move someone's heart to its depths, to endure disinterested kindness from him. His whole impervious attitude was an insult, a diminishing of what had been between us.

I was rooting for my keys when Suzanne's cell phone rang. It was the smallest cell phone I'd ever seen, looking more like a hip piece of jewelry on its leather cord than an actual communication device.

"He's right here," she said. "It's Kate. She said negotiations broke off twenty minutes ago."

Tony grabbed the phone. Suzanne looked from one of us to the other.

"So this means . . ." she said.

I could hear what Tony was saying now.

"It means Clare's made up her mind," I said. "As of midnight tonight, we're out on strike."

As we left Yancy's, I couldn't help but notice that while Suzanne was naturally slender with no hips to speak of, her butt was decidedly flat. Not attractive.

Tony had once told me I had "an award-winning ass."

I felt better.

· 10 ·

BACK AT THE OFFICE, there was the feeling of determined preparation that you see when people are boarding up in the path of a tor-
nado. Picketing shift schedules had been tacked on the wall, and Kate
was running off a phone tree list. Sky-blue-and-white buttons in the
colors of the local had appeared from somewhere. They read, "On
strike for safer patient care," and felt flimsy in my hand. Not bad for a
rush job, but if we lasted more than a week out there, maybe I could
talk Tony into something nicer.

Clare was still taking her coat off when we arrived. It was the same
sensible navy blue coat I'd seen her wearing in the video Weingould
had shown us, a workhorse of a coat that fell in one stiff sheet from
shoulder to midcalf.

"Good to see you," she said. "What happened to your hand?"

"Nothing serious. It's not my writing hand. And it looks worse
than it is."

I peeled off the disgustingly oily Ace bandage and tossed it in a
nearby wastebasket. Under it my wrist and palm showed pink but
unblistered.

"Margaret can help you type if you have any problem," said Clare.
"Is it possible to get a press release out in the next hour or two? I'm
already getting calls."

"It won't take me long at all, if you can go over the main points
with me."

"Doug thought that the three of us could sit down and outline a
few."

"With Tony?"

"Tony's rounding up his strike captains."

"Won't he want to be in on this meeting? It's pretty important, what message we lead with."

"Let's just see what we come up with first. Doug has a very good sense of what we're trying to do here."

I didn't like the looks of this, remembering what Kate had said about Doug using his blandishments on Clare.

What troubled me about Clare—what might make her vulnerable to Doug's machinations—was that from all accounts she had faced crises with such composure that the people around her probably forgot she needed shoring up occasionally. With his Iago-like sense of where people's weak points lay, Doug would be quick to spot Clare's need for understated flattery, eloquent silent sympathy, respectful appreciation.

Clare wore a thick smoke-blue cardigan and a straight, knee-length skirt with low heels. Her hair was clipped back from her face by a tortoiseshell barrette, her lipstick was minimal, and her only jewelry was a watch with a plain black band. She looked in every way to be the grown-up version of the kind of exemplary Catholic girl my mother had hoped I'd be. I could picture her face inside a veil and wimple with no problem. That was worrying. Inside every good Catholic girl who *remains* a good Catholic girl is a hopeful, obedient child working her damnedest for approval. Ideal prey for a plausible flatterer like Hamner.

Doug came sidling up. There was a trace of powdered sugar on his tie. He'd been at the doughnuts. Hamner's well-known greed for sweet things was one of the few likable qualities he possessed.

"Nicky thinks we might want to wait for Tony for this meeting, Doug."

"Oh, we can handle this, you and me," Doug said. "And Nicky, of course."

"Okay, then, we'll meet in my office," said Clare. "Ten minutes."

After she'd walked away, Hamner glared at me and said, "What is your problem, Nicky?"

"My problem is that you seem to be making an end run around Tony. Is that smart, Doug?"

"I know what I'm doing. I've worked a lot of organizing campaigns, in case you don't remember."

Yeah, who could forget that one last spring where he'd gotten those valet-parking attendants in Atlantic City a whopping ten-cent-an-hour raise. Phyllis, the receptionist at the Toilers, had kept me filled in on Doug in the two years since I'd had the nonpleasure of working with him. Phyllis resented Doug because, when he was in residence at the national office, he frequently ordered her to call him a taxi home in the evenings, even though there was a hotel with a taxi stand twenty feet from the entrance to the Toilers' building.

"Don't second-guess me in front of Clare," he said, breathing heavily. He was rifling through his pockets for something. He took out his asthma inhaler and put four pumps up each nostril.

"You're going to burn out your nasal cavity, Doug," I said.

"Your concern for my health is touching. Listen, you should be aware that I don't need to consult Tony every time I turn around. Obviously you don't know how things stand around here."

"Are you saying Tony's not in charge on this campaign? Because maybe I got something wrong. He didn't tell me anything about you replacing him on the big decisions."

He ground his little rodent molars.

"The Toilers are your client, if you recall, and I'm a national staff rep. Don't you think I'm entitled to a certain amount of respect?"

"Try it on some poor, scared twenty-two-year-old PR assistant, Doug. Not on me."

Clare's office had been a large broom closet when the local had leased the strike headquarters. A steel door in the far wall gave access to an area out back where the office garbage bins stood. Another local president might have grabbed the midsize room off the large central work area for her office, but Clare had given that room over to files, supplies, a coffee machine, and a capacious easy chair.

Her broom closet was barely big enough for her desk, some folding chairs, a small pine bookcase, and a very small sofa on which I was forced to sit uncomfortably close to Hamner during our meeting about the press release. He kept pinching his nostrils between his hands as if he'd just inhaled snuff—the effects of overusing that inhaler, I guessed—and clicking and unclicking his ballpoint pen. He directed most of his comments at Clare, occasionally asking me if I'd taken down some point of information, as if to convey that I was present at this meeting only by virtue of my shorthand skills.

"In the press release we should cite the recent Morehouse study on staffing ratios as a variable in cardiac outcomes," he began. "While the influence of staffing has to be teased out from the data, I think it makes our case well enough."

I said, "I think we should play to their common sense. We can provide the Morehouse data as backup. Maybe Doug could do a three-paragraph summary we could attach. But for our press contacts, we should simply give some dramatic examples about the reality in human terms of Coventry's move to fewer nurses and more patients. Does it mean that patients are ringing their call bells for half an hour? Does it mean a recovering stroke victim could fall in the shower in his hospital room and break a leg?"

"We don't call patients 'victims,'" Doug said prissily.

I decided to keep my eyes on the task at hand, tempting as it would be to snipe at him. Doug was such an easy target. He had so little self-awareness that he just stuck out all over with handles for mockery. I wasn't sure I liked the corner of myself that delighted in that fact.

"Tell me this, then. When there aren't enough nurses to care for patients, what happens here? For example, I would hate the idea of being in a hospital and not having someone there to help me to the bathroom and then soiling the bed and being found like that."

"That's disgusting," said Doug.

"I got that from the ICU petition, Doug. Right here at St. Francis."

Doug's pen clicks reached a cricketlike franticness.

"You'll have to meet Mae Carroll from the Gray Panthers," Clare said. "Mae's fielded a lot of complaints from her members in the past several months about what's going on at St. Francis, and she'll have some stories you can use. Plus, she'll gladly talk to the press, and so will her people."

"Mae is a little bit too outspoken, perhaps," said Doug. "She's not what people expect from a senior citizen."

"What exactly are people supposed to expect from a senior citizen?" said Clare mildly.

She seemed to find Doug amusing, as if his crotchets and pettiness were kind of cute. It's true that, for every nine women who find a man insufferable, there's a tenth to willingly indulge him. Thus it is that even the most unattractive men find mates without half trying. Not fair, really, when women too often prune and tweak at even our most minor faults in order to qualify for love and acceptance.

"Not a prison record, at any rate," said Doug.

I looked at Clare.

"Mae was arrested in draft protests during Vietnam, and then again in a sit-down demonstration over that toxic waste dump in Foster ten years ago," said Clare. "She was never convicted of anything, obviously. You're being silly, Doug."

"It would look bad if it came out," Doug added in a voice full of regret, as if Clare had been harboring a felon.

I wished I could deal with Clare without his poisonous presence. At random, I picked up a tiny cup that was sitting on her desk, clearly a favored ornament since it was in a grouping with the picture of Clare's border collies and a small figurine of Saint Anthony holding the Baby Jesus.

The cup was blue and white, light on my palm as a freshly baked meringue. The blue porcelain had a wavery, wet-inky look, and depicted two birds flying past a miniature gazebo. I turned it round gingerly, since it was clearly old. Yet it was without a chip, a small miracle of survival. There were several plates and cups of a similar blue and white china on the rickety shelf behind Clare.

"It's willow ware," said Clare. "I collect it. Not for value primarily. I have a lot of chipped and cracked stuff."

"My cousin Louise collects Depression glass. The cranberry color."

Doug cast an impatient glance at me. I handed the cup to Clare, who was now turning it in her hand.

"This one's Victorian. See the mark on the bottom? That tells us the manufacturer and country of origin. It was required on British exports after a certain date. I found this at a church bazaar for two dollars."

Her eyes went dreamy with a treasure hunter's remembered delight. I began to like her better. A minute went by. Doug went from clicking his pen to doing a complicated baton twirl with it in his right hand and pulling on his mustache with his left hand until I wanted to yank it right off his face. Clare put the cup down and said, "You want to try a draft on this press release, Nicky? I work better when I have something tangible to start with."

"Sure. And feel free to edit me. I'm used to it."

"We will," said Doug.

"I'm not worried," said Clare. "I know your work is good. Tony showed me some samples."

Tony still had samples of my old campaign lit? What a thing to keep. Of course, I still had a box of rock candy he'd once bought me on a trip through Paw Paw, West Virginia.

I left Doug in Clare's office, sketching out a diagram he had for the strike website. He envisioned a special section for reporters, listing research resources on health care policy issues. Most of them would ignore it completely, overworked as they were. They wanted easily digestible, verifiable facts, and we'd supply them, slanted our way.

It would keep Doug busy, though, and out of my hair. As I headed back to my shadowy, inconvenient corner, my left hand began to throb again, and my stomach to ache from the combination of tension and Yancy's pancakes. I was intercepted by a woman whose name I didn't yet know, but whose type was legion.

"I put a new stapler and pencil sharpener on your desk," she said. "I'm Margaret, by the way. I'm one of the stewards, and I'll be giving you a hand with logistics."

I have encountered many Margarets in my time. Every union, every church, every association, every Girl Scout troop, requires its Margaret. A Margaret was the glue of any collective endeavor. She would be the one who would still be full of practical solutions to knotty problems at the end of a four-hour committee meeting. She'd be the one who nagged people into volunteering for phone banks and who made sure the account books were in order. The one who kept the office in coffee and typewriter ribbons, and made sure the fire insurance was renewed. She was a scourge and a necessity.

Margaret provided me with the name of the nearest union printer, plus a file with the phone numbers of the local's executive board and strike captains so that I could bother them at any time, day or night. She had researched alternative hotels and their rates, in case I didn't find the White Hart to my satisfaction. She'd even typed out a selection of picket line chants for spontaneous use.

" 'Two, four, six, eight, patients before profit rates,' " I read.

"We want to make sure the chants stay appropriate," Margaret said. "Doug's been concerned about that."

Margaret's strawberry-blond hair, which could have been luxuriant and shiny, was cropped in a practical pixie cut. She was dressed for action in carpool-driving clothes: a cotton turtleneck with a pattern of tiny frogs, crew-necked navy blue sweater, jeans, and jogging shoes.

She said, "I think we should have a system for monitoring production. I can keep on top of the printer for you, and I've identified three of our members with vans who can help deliver finished jobs if the printer's lollygagging."

"I prefer to deal with the printer directly, but I *really* appreciate your having the foresight to think of that, Margaret. And those vans could sure come in handy."

For hauling the rest of us off to the loony bin after you've driven us all crazy, I thought to myself, but I infused warmth into my voice. I bet Margaret's parents had rarely praised her. She wouldn't be like this if they had.

A boy came up and tugged Margaret's elbow, none too gently.

"The Coke machine is broken," he said.

"This is Eric," said Margaret. "His mom, Mary Grunewald, is one of our members."

Mary was the one Tony had mentioned. A family of five and a landscaper husband. And Eric, if I remembered right, was the tyke who had inked the pornographic messages on my desk.

"It took seventy-five cents of mine," said the polite child, wiping his rabbitty nose on the cuff of a much-stained flannel shirt. You got used to members' kids being underfoot at union offices, but this was one of the most unappealing children I'd ever seen.

Margaret bustled off to attend to the errant Coke machine, a light of battle in her eye.

"You have Bozo hair," he said, turning his attention to me.

"Haven't you seen red hair before?"

"I like blond hair. I would do something about your hair if I were you."

"Mine's clean at least."

It's not that I forget children aren't grown-ups when I talk to them, it's that I forget *I'm* not a child still, being taunted by other children who are mean little beasts.

"You catch pneumonia if you wash your hair all the time," said the scruffy child.

If regular washing predisposed a person to lung problems, this kid was clearly in no danger of an early demise. Eric, whose age I guessed at ten or eleven, had in his brief life achieved a level of dirtiness and seediness beyond the wildest dreams of child anarchy.

His face was grayish with smudges that must date back a day or two. On his plaid flannel shirt I could discern egg yolk, crusty ketchup, chalk dust, and on the cuffs a slug trail of dried snot. He was skinny, with thin wrists poking out of his sleeves, though by the end of the day I had seen that he was forever eating or demanding to eat. His eyes were narrowed and watery, his nose dripped, and his mouth gaped open a little. Adenoids, maybe, or perhaps he assumed that vacant expression just to annoy adults.

"Shouldn't you be in school?" I said.

"I got suspended."

"Who'd have thought it."

"Eric," said Kate, who had spotted our little tête-á-tête with that sixth sense of hers, which seemed to operate even when she appeared to be absorbed in one of her many tasks, "I thought I told you to clean up that mess you made in the storage room. What did you spill in there, a milk shake?"

"I was rearranging things better."

"Arrange it back."

"I have a plan. It's a good plan."

"You heard me. Now."

He disappeared, but I had a grim suspicion that we'd be seeing a lot of him.

"What a devil," I said to Kate. "I'm getting my tubes tied."

"I think he actually liked you," said Kate. "Normally he torments newcomers unmercifully. We had a nurse in here the other day who's only been on the job six months and is just getting involved. She was helping Margaret make name tags for a meeting, and she asked Eric to take his outdoor hat, which is an incredibly filthy Bruins cap, off the table so she could spread out. He said, 'That hat was the last thing my father gave me before he died,' and burst into tears. Well, Gina reproached herself for a week. She lost *sleep* over it. Then she accidentally saw him with his dad in the grocery store and asked me if that poor little boy had a stepfather now."

I wended my way back to my chair, feeling, between Doug, Margaret, and Eric, that it had been an obstacle course.

"These came for you," said Tony, dropping two faxes on my desk.

"Thank you for doing first aid back at the diner," I said. "Especially the ice bucket."

"Forget it," he said curtly. "By the way, I'd appreciate it if you didn't tie up the fax machine too much."

"Hey, if you don't want me on the phone all the time, you'll have to put up with the occasional business fax."

"Yeah, *business*," Tony said.

"I don't know what you're talking about, but while I'm thinking of it I should tell you that Doug and Clare and I met about a press release for tonight. They said you were tied up."

"Good of you to look out for me," he said sarcastically, and walked off. I saw him approach Hamner and say a few short words, then go into Clare's office and shut the door. Hamner turned around slowly and stared at me, an ill-wishing stare.

The first of my two faxes was a missive from my mother, received at 9 A.M. that morning. It had been sent by the Advocacy, Inc. office manager, Myrlene. My mother must have dictated it to her over the phone. The nerve of the woman! I'd told Myrlene not to give way to her on such requests, but Ma had coopted our secretary long ago, using a mother's love as her lever, and now could rely on Myrlene as an efficient guilt conductor.

In a moment I saw what had put Tony in such a foul mood with me. The fax read:

Dear Nicky,

I hope your strike is going well. I will pray that you and the nurses come out the winners.

As you will be alone in your hotel room at night with nothing to do, just wanted to remind you that we need to come up with something for Betsey's shower invitations by the end of the week. I know you will think of a pretty and appropriate design.

Jeremy happened to stop by the other day. He isn't looking well. He must have lost ten pounds at least since you left him. Of course he asked after you, and was a little upset that you were up there working with that Tony. I told him he had nothing to worry about on that score, and that, thankfully, you had finished with Tony years ago, and wanted absolutely nothing more to do with him and had been very displeased at getting this assignment.

He asked for your number up there and I gave it to him. I didn't think that would do any harm. He seems serious this time, so the least you could do is speak with him.

Just wanted to let you know I had seen him. You can overnight the shower design to me. I am home most mornings.

Affectionately,
Mother

I gnashed my teeth over this epistle, which Tony must have read. It's impossible to resist reading something once you've seen your name mentioned in it. I'd have done the same thing in his place.

My mother had never liked Tony, though Louise had been won over immediately. Tony was too blunt for Ma's comfort, and unlike her own sons, he was not charmed by her or cowed by her. From him, she could never expect the courtly deference that she felt was a mother-in-law's due. And she suspected him (quite mistakenly) of being a member of the Communist party—an impression he may have deliberately given just to make trouble.

Jeremy, on the other hand, played up to my mother from the

beginning. He'd paid her muted, thoughtful compliments on her cooking and her home. He'd notice the care with which she arranged a bunch of tulips on the hallway table, or how the new yellow-and-white-striped curtains in the kitchen "brought light into the room." To give him credit, he was quite sincere in these observations, and he could get away with them because the sensitivities my mother would find suspect in an American male—an eye for interior design, or a talent for choosing a pricey necktie—were just part of his classy Englishness.

What my mother liked most about him was that he was a professional. Not just any old businessman, either, but a *professor*. In my mother's imagination, Jeremy had entrée to a world where people discussed Jane Austen over Madeira, surrounded by eighteenth-century portraits, hunting dogs, and family silver.

She determinedly ignored the uncomfortable facts: that Jeremy was the son of a Methodist schoolteacher and a train conductor, that he'd been raised in proverbially sooty Newcastle, and that he had taken both his degrees not at Oxford or Cambridge, but the University of West Anglia, one of the undistinguished government-funded universities that flourished in the years after World War II. All my mother saw was that he was ravishingly well-spoken, handsome in a style guaranteed to be distinguished in later years, interestingly melancholy, and, above all, respectful and appreciative.

I could have told her that Jeremy had been making good use of this caricature of an impoverished English peer since he first cleared customs at Kennedy Airport, but I didn't want to burst her bubble. A real estate mogul who longed to drape me in ermine could not have been more welcome in my mother's home than Jeremy was.

"What did he do?" my mother had said when I came over to announce I'd shown him the door. Her first action had been to make a pot of tea and put out some of her rock-hard shortbread. My mother is indeed a terrible cook. *Her* mother could make a veal scallopini that melted in your mouth and a tiramisu in which the rum and chocolate positively crooned to each other, but Ma specialized in overdone roasts, underdone chicken, watery stews, and singed, saggy cakes from mixes.

"He screwed around on me," I'd said, not giving the details because she'd have had the whole story from Louise already.

"A lot of men run around a little."

"Thanks for your sympathy."

"All I'm saying is that there's a difference between a man who slips up once and a man who makes a habit of it. Men are more physical than we are."

"Ma, this wasn't the same as getting plastered at some convention and winding up in bed with someone else. That I would understand, wouldn't even want to know about. It was five months of creative, repeated lying."

"Are you going to dump a successful, considerate, educated man like Jeremy in the trash can because of one mistake? A mistake he's very, very sorry for?"

"That's easy for you to say. You had Dad. He never even looked at another woman."

"He knew that if he ever messed around on me, he'd have to face your grandmother," said Ma placidly. Such a threat would keep any man in line. No afternoon of illicit passion could be worth risking the wrath of an infuriated Neapolitan matriarch with a meat cleaver in one hand and a rosary in the other.

"Give it time," Ma said. "You'll get over it."

"I don't think I *can* get over this. I can't trust him. Where am I then?"

"Trust is overrated," said my mother. "All this talk these days about honesty in relationships. Honesty this, communication that. It's nothing but trouble."

"You know, Ma, I don't want to be the heavy. I don't want to be some prison warden, or some wronged wife all noble and forgiving, like Norma Shearer in *The Women.*"

"She gets him back in the end, doesn't she? You know, there are plenty of other women out there for Jeremy if you close the door in his face. With those looks, he won't be left alone long."

The clear implication being that I, less endowed with attractions, could look forward to a winter of chicken pot pies for one.

*   *   *

Tony had his back to me. He was on the phone, pacing the length of the cord, the way he always did. He turned and met my eye, and turned again, deliberately away from me. How was I going to work with him when he couldn't even stand to look at me? Thanks for the fax, Ma, I thought. You're always looking out for your darling daughter, your only daughter, the apple of your eye.

The second fax was from Ron. It was in memo form and was titled "Preliminary Thoughts on Detroit Breast Campaign."

A few months before, Ron and I had landed an account with the Coalition for Women's Health, a group that focused on breast cancer prevention and treatment. CWH was launching a pilot program in Detroit in which a doctor-staffed van would provide free mammograms at community centers in the city's poorest neighborhoods. The coalition had called us in to assist them with strategies to get the word out about the "mammo-van" and to encourage women to use the free service.

Ron had faxed me his idea for a bus stop ad. According to the memo, it would feature a stylized breast with a red-and-black bull's eye painted on it, and the tag line, "Breast cancer will hit one in eight women in their lifetimes. Catch this deadly disease before it targets you."

I couldn't leave him alone for a second. How was it that sometimes he could be so brilliant, and other times so obtuse, so offtrack? He would never think of advertising a prostate cancer prevention campaign with posters of a giant limp penis and the headline "It could happen to you. See a doctor or kiss Mr. Willy good-bye."

Tony reappeared.

"I'll need that press release draft by one," he said. He grabbed a legal pad from a shelf over my head and stalked off to the food counter, where he stood jotting notes to himself and eating black olives. He'd gotten as far away from me as he could get without leaving the building.

· 11 ·

THE PRESS RELEASE was easy to whip out. The issues were clear, and the two sides so far apart that even a six o'clock news anchor could lay out their differences in a few sentences. In the last hours of bargaining, the hospital had refused to budge an inch on the deal breakers: safer staffing, no forced overtime, proper training of all nursing personnel before they were floated to other departments, and a 2 percent raise. Not outrageous demands, but the hospital continued to react to them as if the nurses had asked to turn the morgue into their own private underground squash court.

As I wrote, I could feel my blood stirring. I liked clients who were up against real stinkers. I liked the almost-hopeless cases, the stubborn fighters who wouldn't recognize a useless frill even if they could afford one. In my work life there were too many clients like Jantsy and her summer camp, or the outraged homeowners of Mallard Gardens. Too many clients whose causes seemed feeble and inconsequential, whose connection to those causes seemed a matter of leisure and choice.

For all Jantsy's noble hype, I doubted that being granted the privilege of stepping in cow manure on some brisk August morning in Vermont could possibly make a difference in the life of a child who had never had any other privileges at all. I doubted that if Mallard Pond became landfill, our fragile ecosystem or the glorious history of the War of Northern Aggression would truly be the poorer for it. But it made some sort of small, undeniable, concrete difference, what happened on this strike. And so it was beginning to make a difference to me that I was here for it, awful as it was to see Tony, awful as it would be to tolerate Doug and Suzanne and Eric.

So much of my life was spent in conference rooms and restaurants, at purposeless meetings and diplomatic parlays and staged nonevents. To get up in the morning, you had to feel that along with the 90 percent of your life that was long-windedness and strategy and boredom and formula—the 90 percent of your life that was making a living— that there was a 10 percent that was something else. Something that made you feel you had, from time to time, been one of those who fought on the side of the angels.

That had been one of the qualities that had attracted me to Tony. He understood the kick I got from the desperate cases, because he was the same sort of sucker for the underdog that I was, and spent a much larger portion of his life at it. No wonder he looked tired.

Still, I couldn't think of any job that would suit him better. Union organizers were a funny breed. Tony lived from election to election, contract fight to contract fight. Weingould had offered him a management job at the national office, six times over. But Tony had often confided to me his fear that once he was trapped behind a desk, he'd be dead of cancer or a heart attack in five years. He'd seen it happen to enough friends of his, guys who left the road to take it easy at long last, and then found too late that the road was what had kept them going. These days, when Tony got together with his organizer buddies, it was usually at a funeral.

Hamner strolled up to my desk with his own four-page version of my press release in his hand and a placid smile. He'd make me acknowledge that I worked for him yet, that smile implied.

"It needed major changes but you had the seed there," he said.

"I guess you'd better talk to Clare, then."

I handed him the copy Kate had just brought over, with "Perfect! Set to go," across the top in Clare's copperplate handwriting.

"As you can see, all she altered were a few commas here and there. And Tony signed off too."

Tony had tossed the draft at me and said, "Fine. Get it out of here."

"We can revisit the whole thing if you like, though," I said to Doug. "Let's get everyone together."

I beamed up at him, innocently helpful.

Doug folded up his stapled pages and put them in his vest pocket.

"Nope. No problem," he said. "If Clare is happy, I can be happy. And I found a great group here. If I don't have to fix this now, I'll have time to give them a call."

He ambled away, seeming suspiciously untroubled by losing this round. For a moment I was puzzled about what he meant by "group." Doug was not the personality type that shared its questions and failings in therapy. Then I remembered how he'd spent his spare time on that project in Oklahoma. He contra danced. Contra dancing, it seemed, was something like square dancing, only, as Doug had informed me once, when I'd confused the two, much more complicated. The figures of the dance were called out as in square dancing, but they were infinitely more intricate, according to Doug. There seemed to be a certain snobbism, in contra dance circles, about how well one could follow the figures and how many one knew.

Doug, of course, knew them all, and deeply resented the times when he was paired, or accidentally paired himself, with a partner not his equal in skill. This was puzzling, because, early in our acquaintance when we didn't hate each other yet, Doug had freely confided to me that he had taken up this hobby to meet women. I didn't see how he'd make any big conquests with this approach. Critiquing her dancing is not the best way to a woman's heart. Back in those early days in Oklahoma—ignoring the considerable demands of his work—Doug would often sally out to contra dances of an evening, only to tell me the next day that the women were not up to his standards in their dancing abilities, that he had spotted such-and-such a one but then been disappointed by her clumsiness on the floor.

After one of these post-contra reports, I had said to him, "Doug, does it matter so much how she dances if she's nice? If you think she's cute?"

He had given me a despairing look that implied he couldn't possibly explain to an ignorant novice.

"No, honestly, Doug. Is dancing all that important in the grand scheme of life? Unless you're a Shaker?"

"I happen to enjoy it. You don't know how annoying it is to be paired with an awkward partner who has no business trying figures at that level."

"Maybe she's hoping you'll teach her. Maybe she's hoping to meet some nice guy."

"If she wants to learn she can take a class. That's what I did."

Such attitudes did much to explain why Doug was still single eight years after his divorce. I doubted if even Louise's unblocking-your-path-to-love course would have worked with Doug. His main pleasure in the ostensible search for the woman of his dreams seemed to be the enjoyment of turning down hypothetical candidates for the job.

Doug's unruffled good mood seemed sinister to me. After all, the man had a direct line to Jerry Goreman, who'd love to see us all fall on our faces. I resolved not to escalate hostilities if I could help it. Despite my childish wish to aggravate Doug, I didn't want to cause trouble for Weingould or Tony or Clare. I'd try to be nicer. I'd pretend that Hamner was a mosquito who'd landed on my arm to be flicked away, a cockroach running along a kitchen baseboard that I could zap with one blast of bug spray. I had bigger problems than Hamner, whose revenges were always petty and whose nastiness was limited by his lack of imagination. Maybe he wouldn't bother us much. Maybe he'd be off dancing.

All day long the nurses came through the strike office, making picket signs, stuffing envelopes for a mailing to other St. Francis employees asking for their support, pooling information about regional hospitals with temporary shifts available. All day long I could hear people murmuring in groups of two or three, saying, "Something could come through before midnight," and "Clare might still pull this off." I heard a few asking Kate about her friend Eileen, the one she'd told me about at dinner the night before. Apparently Eileen was scheduled for a full-body CAT scan that day. Kate never flagged in the many tasks she'd set herself, but her narrow little face was tight with worry.

I'd been curious as to why Tony did not sit in on the very last bargaining session, until Kate informed me that there were still some hard feelings from the previous session, in which Tony had publicly referred to Louanne Reilly, the director of nursing, as being "dumb as dirt," a comment unfortunately picked up by the *Providence Journal*.

"If Tony could just remember to shut up once in a while," said Kate. "Not that it really made any difference. Management doesn't have any personal animus against us. We're in the way of their business plan, that's all. In fact, you should see Winslow flirt with Clare."

"With Clare?"

"Oh, yeah. He's the kind of guy who yearns after calm, motherly women. Of course, his wife is one of those blond, liposuctioned types without enough body fat to survive two days on a desert island."

"How's your friend Eileen?"

"I went over and told her we were about to go out. She said to win one for the Gipper. That's the kind of sense of humor she has."

"And the CAT scan?"

"They didn't tell her why, specifically. But you know they don't do those to see if you swallowed a safety pin when you were a baby."

"Maybe the strike won't last too long, Kate."

"Keep dreaming. If I were you, I'd get someone back home to ship you another box of winter clothes."

We got terrific coverage that night. All the network affiliates included us in their top story lineup, and Rhode Island Public Television convened a discussion panel about the St. Francis strike within the larger context of national health care reform on their 10 P.M. show, "Questions in Public Policy."

We arranged for three prominent doctors on the hospital staff, including their most renowned cardiac specialists, to release a statement saying they sympathized with the nurses' concerns. A female state senator who had once been a nurse was featured on the late news denouncing mandatory overtime for nurses as "a return to the fourteen-hour factory day"—a reference that resonated here in the mill towns of the Blackstone River Valley. Mae Caroll of the Gray Panthers gave a wonderful interview in which she actually uttered the words, "Shame on them! Shame!" The reporter lauded her as "a veteran crusader for social justice." So much for Doug's predictions that Mae would be seen as an aged hoodlum.

One station narrated the day's events over background footage of Clare at the opening of a nursing home two years earlier, holding the hand of a trembling Parkinson's patient in a wheelchair. After this came a nicely contrasting shot of Winslow leaving the hospital that evening, getting into his Cadillac accompanied by his attorneys, both of whom were plump, very well dressed, and sneering. It's funny how on television shows, lawyers are always attractive. In real life, the odds are more like one in fifteen. Washington is full of lawyers and yet it is definitely not a town of beautiful men.

The positive press buoyed all of us, but for the most part, we were just geographically lucky. Had we been pitching this strike to the media in Jackson, Mississippi, or Houston, Texas, we'd have gotten nowhere. Here in Winsack, supporting labor was like being Catholic. People didn't necessarily believe in the cause with the fervor they once did, but it was still what they came from, the venerable if frequently disregarded faith in which they'd been raised.

The next morning's *Winsack Eagle-Gazette* made no pretense at neutrality. Their lead editorial was titled "Why we're rooting for our nurses." I was dismayed, though, to see a full-page ad taken out by the "Winsack Concerned Citizens for Quality Care." The ad showed a photo of a nurse, in a cap and uniform-dress of the kind nurses hadn't worn in years, bending tenderly over the bedside of a wizened old man in an oxygen mask. The headline beneath the picture asked, in seventy-two-point type, "Who will be there for him now?" It went on to bemoan the fact that the nurses of St. Francis, "misled by higher-ups at union headquarters," had deserted their patients to tell experienced hospital administrators how to do their jobs.

The Concerned Citizens were a front group for the hospital. It wasn't an uncommon trick in labor disputes for the employer to invent a phony community group to feature in ads and direct mail, but how many other people would know that? The ad played up the one point on which we were vulnerable, and we had yet to get more than a reserved mention on the Boston stations. Still, it was a decent beginning.

"Great job so far, Nicky," Ron said when he called me at 6 A.M. "Weingould's hearing about our initial coverage and he's very happy."

"I'm glad he's happy, Ron, but a little local hostility isn't going to faze Coventry. They want to make an example of our crowd for the other facilities in their chain."

"Always so doom and gloom."

"I'm being realistic."

"You haven't asked about the Campsters."

"Damn. How could I forget them? You know what deep meaning that assignment has for me."

"Well, you'll be glad to know that Wendy's really dazzling Janet. They're best girlfriends all of a sudden."

I was sure Wendy made that clear to Ron several times a day.

"Janet's even having Wendy dog-sit when she goes to Bermuda next month."

I didn't envy Wendy that. I had met Jantsy's three German shepherds—Conrad, Heinrich, and Wolly by name—one ill-fated day when Janet had me drop by her miniature English manor in Potomac with a program layout for a benefit concert for Appalachian folk musicians. I like dogs, but these were big enough to saddle and ride, with expressions so ill-tempered that you wondered if they'd been trained with kicks and blows to hate every representative of the human species. Jantsy did not seem particularly fond of her slobbering pets. Perhaps she kept them on the assumption that they'd protect her from thieves and rapists who might somehow make it out of the city on the bus, coming straight for her house from the T9 stop down the street in order to attack her in her cozy kitchen, which had the approximate square footage of a major pharmaceutical lab.

I didn't want to compete with Wendy for Ron's approval. I didn't respect Ron enough for his approval to be anything but a matter of moral concern should I win it. So I said airily, "Wendy never lets us down. Did you get my message about the mammogram ad concept?"

"Yes, and you're overreacting. People understand that advertising is exaggerated."

"Ron, have you seen any of those TV ads about male impotence? They're as soft and evasive as feminine hygiene commercials."

"Sometimes you have to shock people into listening to you."

"If you're talking about gun control or drunk driving. Not if you want them to do something that's already scary."

"If you don't scare them, they won't show up for the, er, physicals."

"Mammograms, Ron. You were at the focus group. When the facilitator listed possible reasons for not participating in the program, what was it that three-quarters of the women there said they agreed with?"

"I can't remember. You know how many focus groups I go to in a month?"

"It was 'fear of finding out I have cancer,' Ron. So why would you think the best approach is to slap that fear six feet high on the side of their local bus stop shelter?"

"The graphic was great. Really eye-catching, with the red and black."

"Use it for something else. You and I both know it was clip-art you had someone doctor up. And Helvetica Bold isn't a typeface, it's an anachronism. Why do you *always* ask for Helvetica Bold?"

"It's a nice clean typeface. I like it."

"Like it on some other campaign."

He gave an exaggerated sigh.

"Fine, Nicky. I guess I was phoning it in a little. We're up to our necks in work here."

"What's the deadline?"

"We have a little time to play with. They liked our initial proposal. Thanks for that, by the way."

By the way. I'd given up three weekends for that proposal, just because I thought the project had such merit.

"Let me come up with another concept."

"How are you going to do that, Nicky? You'll be lucky to get five hours' sleep a night as it is."

"I want to do this. And no offense, but I get this one better than you do, Ron. Who's the woman here? Who has to stand in the shower feeling herself up every four weeks?"

"Okay, okay," he said hurriedly. When push came to shove, I could always embarrass Ron into capitulating. He pretended to be such a smooth, sophisticated operator, but underneath he had the shrinking sensibilities of a Tennyson heroine.

I told Ron that the construction trades and the Teamsters had pledged their guys to turn out. The firefighters were all lined up—and the public likes firemen almost as much as they like nurses. Tony had mentioned, in a brief moment of cordiality to me, that most of the lab techs, secretaries, and accountants on the hospital staff would likely come picket with us on their lunch hours. They knew that if nurses were being targeted today, it would be their turn tomorrow.

"Couldn't be going better," said Ron.

"Don't get Weingould too excited yet. This is not going to be a walkover."

"Did I say I'd promise him an easy victory? He knows what we're up against. But any good news will calm him down."

I could picture Weingould pacing his office, barking incoherent questions to Ron and wiping his forehead. He had reason to sweat. If this strike failed, Jerry Goreman would be the first to point out that St. Francis was the sort of expensive disaster that the union could expect if it persisted in the risky venture of hospital organizing. And with Hamner on site feeding Goreman all the dirty details, there was no chance that any mistakes on our end would be missed.

"The scab nurses are going to be arriving any second. Tell Wendy I'm going to need more background on Jet-a-Nurse. Anything and everything she can find. Tell her to try that strike in Seattle three years ago. There was something about a scab there giving a triple dose of morphine after an appendectomy."

"You've got it. By the way, how are you and Boltanski making out?"

"Only slightly better than expected."

"I heard Hamner is on the scene, too. Are you controlling yourself?"

"For now, but if he gives me any trouble, don't count on me not to rip him a new one."

"I wouldn't blame you, but try not to give him and Goreman any ammunition."

"They won't need me for that. Doug's probably on the phone right now, making St. Francis sound like potentially the biggest labor disaster since the Haymarket Massacre."

"You're a pro, Nicky. I know you can handle this."

Ron was happy with me. For now. Of course, if this strike didn't end in a blaze of glory, he'd blame me for everything in a mournful, I-expected-better-of-you voice.

· 12 ·

THE FIRST DAYS of a strike are always exhilarating. There are lots of people on the picket line chanting and shouting, and it seems the whole town has come out to support you. For the people on the ground, who've put in months of waiting, it's exciting to be taking action of any kind, at last.

I went down to picket every noontime, to do my bit and soak up motivation for what promised to be a long haul. The bright bobbing signs and camera lights gave the place a carnival atmosphere. There was a constant invigorating din of beeping cars past the hospital entrance, since a union member named Lester Sinclair had insisted on standing on the traffic island just opposite with a large fluorescent-green sign that read, "Honk LOUD if you support the striking nurses." The resulting cacophony was cheering, although Kate questioned the wisdom of letting Lester stand where he could startle drivers.

Lester's strike uniform was a brown corduroy coat, a hat of Russian fur that made it seem as if a chipmunk were nestled on his head, trousers in electric-blue polyester, and work boots that looked as close to hobnailed boots as any modern footwear I've ever seen. Someone—his mother?—had appliquéd "Proud to be union" in gold satin letters on the back of his jacket. He was a fearful sight.

That first week everyone came: the Gray Panthers, the St. Jude's choir, the firefighters and police unions, the faculty of Winsack Community College, and dozens of public school teachers, some of whom remembered the big teachers strike of 1978 when it was their jobs on the line and the nurses pitched in. Whole families came. While the sunny dry weather held, we had babies on every shift. Margaret decorated their strollers with huge helium balloons in blue and white.

A police cruiser and an officer or two were there every day, but they didn't interfere, even when a Mrs. Margot Lemura complained to the *Eagle-Gazette* that her elderly mother couldn't sleep in her hospital room because of the noise. A day later the *Gazette* discovered that her mother was in for a face-lift, which shut that story down fast. The cops stood by casually, leaning against the cruiser and telling jokes, warming their hands on the coffee we brought them and eating more than their share of muffins.

The other representative of the law was the hospital's daytime security guard, a big, jovial fellow named Bill Fitzgerald, who hung around on the periphery of the picket line with his guard dog, a husky named Punch. Punch's companion husky, Judy, sometimes appeared with him, but most days Punch was solo. Apparently Judy was a bit of a diva who left the grunt work to her long-suffering mate.

We all liked Bill, who was visibly sympathetic, and Punch was a big favorite too. He was lavished with our best scraps and amenable to petting. Only not in front of Mr. Winslow, Bill requested, since it might have perturbed Winslow to see Punch frisking around our team, trading his virtue for dog biscuits and tummy rubs. The only striker to whom Punch took an aversion was the demon-child Eric. Eric teased the dog endlessly, trying to "coochee-coo" Punch under the chin, attempting to make Punch beg for snacks or learn to play dead. By the third day the poor animal would turn skittish and growly at the very sight of Eric.

Winslow entered and exited the hospital through a side entrance, though sometimes he nodded at the picketers as if to say, "I'm pained that I cannot acknowledge you, but I remain the cordial, mannerly fellow you've all come to know." Other Coventry suits came and went, shadowy figures behind the tinted windows of airport limos. The replacement nurses arrived en masse the day after the strike was announced. With frightened faces, they scuttled out of vans and eventually reappeared in the windows of the hospital, peering out from behind the curtains of patients' rooms as if they expected rocks to be thrown at them.

Tony did stints on the picket line, too, but never when I was there. He'd review drafts of my flyers and strike newsletters and leave his changes in writing on my desk. Sometimes I'd see him joking with Suzanne, who seemed to me to be always underfoot. Didn't they need her at her big consulting firm in Boston? Every morning I had to steel myself to look unconcerned when I saw Suzanne consulting Tony about his daily whereabouts, barely pretending that she needed to know for reasons of business. Every afternoon she'd be perched on the edge of his desk for the duration of any short break he could spare, calmly appropriating his time, her low laugh sometimes audible through the din of the strike office.

It's not that I wanted Tony, I told myself. I just wanted to . . . even the score. When you meet an old lover, you should be on top of the world. At your goal weight, better dressed than in the days you were with him, more sure of your direction, and nourished by some hidden sustenance. Another man, perhaps, or great professional success, or the simple knowledge that you are lucky as hell to be quit of him.

Instead I was tired and overworked, limping with disillusionment over Jeremy's betrayal, living out of a suitcase. Suzanne was living out of a suitcase, too, of course, but it must have been a different sort of suitcase than mine. She remained beautifully groomed, with a varied wardrobe that it must have taken six bellboys to haul up to her hotel room.

If I'd been an objective observer, I'd have admitted that Suzanne and Tony made a good-looking pair. Suzanne stood about five foot five, and had those finely drawn features, that effortless slimness. She made Tony's stocky build and blunt nose and chin look rugged and muscular.

He'd never been so nicely set off when next to me. I was too tall to gaze up at him admiringly, as Suzanne did. And while I was no Brunhilde, I was definitely too sturdy to lay my hand on his arm very, very lightly when asking a question, as if it were a rose leaf that had just drifted there.

I'd have liked to tell Suzanne that Tony might seem like Secret Agent Man now, but she should see him when he had a cold. A sniveling baby, that's what he was, lying on the couch and sipping ginger ale through a curly glass child's straw. His wandering life might look glamorous and daredevil now, but wait until she had a family christening to attend and Tony was off in Gadsden, Alabama, busy searching through trash bins for the employee list of some chicken processing plant so that he and his crew could start approaching them on their off hours about joining the union.

One day Kate sent me to find the industrial-size staple remover, which Tony kept locked away because Eric had been caught with it too many times, inflicting damage on carpeting and furniture.

"I can't just go into his desk drawer," I said as Kate handed me the key.

"We have three thousand petitions here in these cartons, we need to get at them, and I'm not ruining Margaret's scissors to pry them open. She'd kill me."

When I opened the drawer where Tony hid the staple remover, a photo slipped from the space between the drawer and the desk frame and landed at my feet. It was a photo of Tony and Suzanne. Some kindly passerby had evidently snapped them arm in arm at a roadside produce stand, bushels of apples and corn at their feet. Suzanne was holding a makeshift bundle of wildflowers. They were laughing into the sun, which struck gold lights in Suzanne's hair. Suzanne was wearing trousers that resembled riding breeches (though I had never heard that she rode and doubted that she did), and a soft tweed jacket with a nipped-in waist. She had jazzed it up with a large silver horseshoe pin in the lapel, which on anyone else would have appeared hopelessly dowagerish, but on Suzanne looked whimsical.

Tony's coat I knew well, a dark green corduroy with patches at the elbows. I remembered walking in Rock Creek Park with him one chilly autumn day and his insisting on lending me this jacket because I had only a sweater. He'd said I'd looked better in that jacket than he ever did. He'd said I was beautiful.

I turned the photo over. On the back was a note in angular, precise handwriting: "Tony, a memento of our afternoon, not that I'll forget it."

I don't know how long I stood there, but Kate was at my elbow before I could cover for myself.

"What have you got?" she said. She read the inscription.

"Oh," she said.

"I wasn't spying. It fell out."

"I wouldn't care if you were. Are you okay?"

I grabbed the staple remover and slammed the drawer shut.

"It doesn't matter a bit to me who Tony's porking."

"Nicky."

"It doesn't."

"He's just passing time with her, Nicky. She would never fit into his life, and he would never fit into hers."

"Who *does* fit into his life? No one ever could, not the life he leads, so it might as well be Suzanne. I'm just temporarily bitter, I guess. It's not fair. It's not. Tony's romping around with Holly Golightly here draped all over his arm and I'm facing Christmas and New Year's Eve solo."

"Don't jump to conclusions about how well Tony's doing. I have more hope for you than I do for Tony, romance-wise," said Kate.

"What in the world would lead you to feel like that? Not the photo we just saw. Not my love life, God knows."

"I have more hope for you because you want the real thing. Lots of women would have taken this Jeremy of yours back by now. You're not satisfied with that, which means you'll find better than that."

"While Tony doesn't know his happiness is shallow and fleeting. Poor, poor Tony."

"Tony's gotten lazy. You just have to look at him to tell. He's not trying with Suzanne. He's *letting* her care about him. I'd guess that for the last few years, that's been his attitude toward women, and it's starting to show. Pretty soon it will be obvious to Suzanne, too."

"What will be obvious?"

"That Tony just takes whatever comes over his desk. So to speak. Now come pry open these boxes with me. It'll relieve your feelings."

Tony ignored me with chilling completeness, but thanks to the kinder, gentler approach Ron had asked me to adopt, Doug hounded my steps with lamebrained ideas: a sit-in at the state house that would stall government operations for days and land us on the evening news as heroes in the great New England civil disobedience tradition of Henry

Thoreau. A sing-along in front of the mayor's office, even though the mayor already supported us. A virus-laced e-mail chain letter that would flood Winslow's in-box and paralyze his hard drive.

I began to regret my efforts to be nice to Doug. He was learning the tin whistle and afflicted Kate and me with squealing rehearsals of "We Shall Overcome" and "Blowing in the Wind" for performance at some future strike rally. He had somewhere acquired a button-making machine and was convinced that we no longer needed to order buttons from our supplier, since it would take a mere two thousand man-hours to produce our own. He talked to reporters freely any time I was out of the office, improvising quotes that predicted, variously: an immediate end to the strike, a winter-long strike, or a strike stretching out past the millennium, depending on his mood that day.

To Hamner, I was a not-very-respected but convenient sounding board, a carping but graciously tolerated nag who preferred talking points to creative spontaneity. To Tony, I was simply a noise that would go away if he covered his ears and hummed. Tony made an art of avoiding me. When I crossed his line of vision, his eyes slid over me. When I drew near his desk to ask a question, he immediately picked up the phone. If I entered the break room for a cup of coffee, he left it as if summoned by telegram.

A week into the strike, I finally caught up with him as he was rushing out of the office, on his way to a meeting with one of the Department of Public Health officials who were setting up a monitoring office at the hospital. Tony was supposedly going to clue in the public health officer about the potential dangers to the remaining St. Francis patients from sloppy replacement nurses. We were getting this opportunity only because the guy was one of Clare's third cousins, and I wanted to make the most of it. But Tony wasn't really up to snuff on the subject. How could he be? He hadn't studied up on the material I'd given him, or even opened the folder full of damning research on Jet-a-Nurse that I'd left on his desk. I'd offered to prepare him a fact sheet, and he'd said, "I know what I'm doing, Nicky. Don't bug me."

Tony was in a foul mood that day. He'd been on his feet all morning, talking with his strike captains, revving them up, answering their questions, easing their anxiety as well as he could without being dishonest. At the end of the meeting, Hamner had insisted in trotting out a list of do's and don'ts for the picket line, including an objection to Lester's sign and attire. He remarked that Lester did not "reflect the dignity of this union." This comment was met with a hostile silence, and Tony had had to prolong the meeting another half hour to get his people back to the level of energy and optimism at which he needed to leave them.

"Nice work, Doug," he'd said after everyone had left.

"We have to be conscious of how we're coming off in the media," Hamner replied. "Those shots of that Lester guy in his deerstalker cap on the news last night were ridiculous."

"Guess what, Doug? Folks up here like that sort of thing. It's real. As opposed to you, in a suit, pulling out some Ross Perot flow chart."

The day before, Doug had taken an interview with the Channel 8 evening news against my specific instructions, and had waxed eloquent and incomprehensible on the economics of the U.S. health care system. I was out of the office making our case at an editorial board meeting in a neighboring town, or I would have tackled Hamner to the ground before letting him act as spokesman. Most unfortunate was the way that his mustache seemed to acquire a life of its own on camera, twitching out of sync with his words in a manner that recalled Japanese animation.

"There are people back at the national watching this strike," said Hamner. "We have a professional image to maintain."

"I guess we'd disagree about what's professional, Doug," said Tony. "Lester is out there every day when you're in here adding special scrolling banners to the website."

Hamner flushed purplish.

"Lester is ridiculous. He's an accident waiting to happen."

"At least he's walking the walk."

"I hope you realize that this isn't a lone hand you're playing, Tony. Or you either," he added angrily, as he saw me cracking up out of the corner of his eye.

"Come on, Doug," I said. "You sound like an outtake from *High Plains Drifter*. Lighten up. We're on the same side here."

"If we're on the same side, why are we stalled at local coverage? Why aren't you getting us national press?"

"We got the *Boston Globe*. We haven't been out long enough to rate national coverage. Give it some time."

"How much time? We should be thinking of something we can do to *make* the news. Where's our celebrity rally? We need an attention grabber."

"Charlton Heston said he'd clear his calendar if we were real nice. He might even lend us a few AK 47s for next time Winslow pokes his head out of the building."

"Be that way," said Doug, gathering his meeting notes together. Doug always spoke from notes at meetings, as if he were Henry Kissinger. "You, too, Boltanski. I'm only trying to keep you from making some big mistakes."

"Don't do me any favors," said Tony. Hamner flounced away. Few men can flounce, but Hamner did.

I'd had so many good intentions. In our most recent conversations, I'd asked Doug about the vacation cabin he was building in Tahoe, his views on reforming Social Security, and even his advice on whom to pick for our first testimonial. But it was no use trying to be nice to Doug. The second he felt threatened, he went for the jugular. He'd hit home, the little worm, with his comments about national press. I hadn't come through in a big way, not yet. But just yesterday I'd had a promise from one of the news-hour shows that they'd take a meeting with us if their schedule unjammed a little.

"A minute of your time, Tony," I said.

"Do you have to antagonize him, Nicky? I can fight my own battles."

"In case you haven't noticed, Hamner is on the phone to headquarters eight times a day complaining about how you're running this strike, and he's in that office with Clare the rest of the time telling her just how much he admires her, even if *you* don't always appreciate her leadership and vision. Or else he and Suzanne are baby-sitting each other, holed up at Yancy's, with Doug telling her how he rode the Freedom Bus back in 1964, even though he was only ten years old then."

"I know all that. Suzanne and Clare can see through him, I'm sure. And so can Weingould."

"But Goreman?"

"Let me worry about Goreman. And about Hamner. Don't declare World War III on the guy in public."

"Fine, as far as you're concerned, Tony. But don't think for a minute I'm going to let him take shots at *me*. How noble do you think I am?"

"Believe me, I don't think you're noble. Did you want something? Because I have this health department guy and then the firefighters, and I'm late already."

"I'll walk you out and tell you. By the way, if you're going to the firefighters, see if you can get five or six of them for a half-page *Gazette* ad I had in mind. I thought we'd get some of the teachers, some of the firefighters, some of the seniors, some of the moms, and do a big group photo with a head like 'We trust our nurses to tell us the truth about our community's care. Don't let them be silenced.' Can you float that idea and see if we can get some volunteers for the photo? See if you can include a few Irish-Italian hunks with blue eyes and black hair and broad shoulders. That sort of look."

"Fireman fantasies? I think you've been watching the late-night cable channel at your hotel a little too much."

"It's a bed-and-breakfast, as you know, and she doesn't have cable. Unlike some of us, I don't stay awake until three A.M. watching *USA Up All Night* on the off chance they'll flash some side boob."

"Was there something else?"

He was stuffing a fistful of papers into the weathered leather briefcase he'd picked up at the Goodwill when he first started as a union rep. Back then, he'd reassure his members by striding into grievance hearings and pulling "exhibit" after exhibit out of the bottomless case. Over the years, the briefcase had acquired tiny rips and frays at the seams, as if rats had been gnawing at it. The lock had broken long ago, and the leather handle hung by one hinge. But Tony still lugged it around.

"I have some new stuff for you on Jet-a-Nurse, Tony. You should use it at this meeting. A wrongful death suit in a strike in Pittsburgh, plus my assistant got a line on four doctors from two separate strikes who are willing to talk about how crummy the Jet-a-Nurse replacements were."

"Later, Nicky." He didn't even congratulate us on the doctor find, a miracle of determination on Wendy's part.

"Tony, at least show the public health guy this clip."

I waved the newspaper clipping in his face. It had a photo of an infant's scrunched-up face in grainy black-and-white. The headline read, "Striker replacement blamed in baby's death."

"See? A Jet-a-Nurse in a strike in Portland, Oregon, a few years back fails to properly monitor a newborn with breathing difficulties. She sends the concerned mother home with the infant, tells her that the child will 'perk up' after a week or so. The baby, who actually needs a complicated lung surgery, goes and dies two days later."

"Do you have to sound so gloating about it, Nicky?"

"Don't try that on me. Remember that grievance in Tennessee with the state employee who had the heart attack while his boss was yelling at him? You had the guy gasping and wheezing in front of the hearing officer until he got awarded double back pay on the spot."

"I have limits at least."

"Tony, just tell this person from the Department of Health what we found so far."

"Have you heard of libel, Nicky?"

"Have Weingould's lawyer check it out if you want to wait on the press end, but open your mouth in this meeting or I'm coming with you. You haven't even looked at the file. We've got plenty to support a public warning about Jet-a-Nurse."

I shoved the folder Wendy had overnighted me into his hand.

"You know, Tony, I've been asking you to review this information for three days now."

"Doug says it's too negative, and he may have a point."

"Oh, boy. You're taking Hamner's advice now?"

"Clare thinks it may be alarmist, too."

"What a surprise. I wonder where she imbibed that opinion."

"You were the one who kept talking about how we have to take the high road, Nicky."

"That doesn't mean we can't raise valid, substantiated concerns about the track records of the people taking care of our patients. Hamner has Clare so hypersensitive about a clean campaign that you have to wonder if he's trying to muzzle her."

"I wish I could muzzle someone," said Tony.

"This is good stuff, Tony, and you know it."

"If I agree to bring a few of these things up with the health department guy, will you leave me alone?"

"My pleasure. And bring that file back. It's my only copy."

"Yeah, yeah."

As he walked away, I saw that the backs of his lace-ups were scuffed thin, but the heels were in excellent condition. I remembered why. Instead of buying new shoes, he just had the heels replaced repeatedly. Tony had a good union pension and a fat savings account, but he was so scared that the Great Depression would return that he never opened his wallet for a luxury like proper footwear.

"You'll never make it through the winter in those shoes," I called after him.

He slammed the office door, the effect somewhat marred by the tinkling chimes Margaret had tied to it. I watched him climb into his rusty 1984 Oldsmobile Cutlass Supreme and take off, skidding a little on a patch of ice that had congealed in one of the ruts in the parking lot. Our relationship just kept getting better and better. At this rate, we'd be taking contracts out on *each other* long before these nurses ever won one.

"At least you're talking," Louise would have said.

· 13 ·

THE ODOR OF JEREMY'S lilies seemed to fill the whole office. They'd arrived on day six of the strike and now, by day ten, it seemed they'd never die off.

It was like Jeremy to have them delivered to the office, a show-offy thing to do when I was sure that my mother must have supplied him with the name of my inn. The flowers came tied with a fat white bow that looked strangely bridal. The card had only his name. Perhaps my mother had advised him to lighten up on the sentimental pleas.

"Those stink," Eric had commented, and an hour later he'd knocked the pot over "by accident on purpose," as we used to say when we were kids, only to have it rescued by Margaret. Tony said nothing aloud, though I'd heard him mumble something under his breath about the place smelling like a perfume factory. Tony was not the flower-giving type, though once he'd brought me home a sheaf of gladioli he'd lifted from a funeral parlor at the end of a wake.

I was grateful to Jeremy for making me look popular and admired, and for irritating Tony. But I did not call him. There was nothing new to say.

That second week of the strike was a low one for all of us. Cold and damp set in, a damp that struck to the bone. Two days of driving rain that turned picketing into a miserable chore. I began to see that Kate hadn't been joking when she suggested I stock more winter clothes. Washington's sunny Novembers and mild, fair winters with their sunny cold snaps bore no comparison to these penetrating fogs, these ungentle rains.

Kate was far too petite for any borrowed clothes of hers to fit me, but she came to the strike office on Sunday with a hefty cardboard box full of sweaters, tights, and leggings. The tights and leggings still had the tags on them.

"My sister Caroline is just your size, and she's surprise-pregnant with her third," Kate explained. "The sweaters are old ones but the rest of this stuff we just got at the outlets in September."

The sweaters were serious sweaters, in a different league than the thin cashmere cardigans and lamb's-wool vests that saw me through winters at home. There were two fisherman's-style pullovers, one cream colored and one slate-blue; a brown-and-cream Peruvian V-neck that shut the cold out as effectively as flannel underwear; and a luscious, coral-pink angora with tight sleeves that made me feel as if I were being hugged by a giant rabbit. Kate's donations layered over my own clothes kept me comfortable, despite the faulty heating of the strike office, which rattled through the office walls as if the whole building had a rumbling cough, yet generated a surprisingly paltry amount of warmth. The former-drugstore side of the office was especially cold, with its high ceilings and knocking, sputtering radiators.

On Monday, the hospital announced that, effective immediately, it was canceling health insurance coverage for every striking nurse. The Toilers' lawyer (I hoped for his sake that he was on a fat retainer) filed the appropriate court challenges, but the effect was chilling, as the hospital meant it to be. A nurse who had a young daughter with severe juvenile diabetes and one who had a husband dying of lung cancer crossed the line and went back in. Nobody blamed them.

The same morning, the *Newport Herald* ran an open letter from the archdiocesan bishop, calling for nurses "to promote harmony instead of strife, and remember that nursing is a profession of sacrifice by returning to their patients as swiftly as possible." Archbishop Kroehling, Clare explained to us, belonged to the same country club as Winslow, and was known for his often-voiced nostalgia for the dear dead days before Vatican II. But this same bishop had confirmed most of our members, and his rebuke was bound to sting.

Our only comfort was that the local parish priest, angered at

Kroehling's betrayal of his flock, stopped by to suggest that the Church of Sts. Jude and Rita host a Thanksgiving Mass and supper for the strikers and their families. Father Peter also offered to have St. Jude's "adopt" the St. Francis nurses as their Christmas effort.

"Our Lenten effort, too, if it comes to that," he said. "The bishop's seminary training must have left out Pope Leo's encyclical outlining the Church's unqualified support for workers' rights to organize. I'll have to send him a copy."

"The bishop won't exile you to Siberia?" Kate said.

"The old fossil can yammer on in the *Herald*, but he's not going to risk St. Jude's chunk of the annual funding appeal. Not on your life."

This cheered us all. Until the next morning, when Clare found taped to her front door a photo of herself on the picket line, cut from an article in the *Winsack Eagle-Gazette*. A thick black X was slashed with a marking pen over her face, along with a printed message, "Get back to work, bitch."

She showed it to Kate, Tony, Doug, and me in the privacy of her office.

"It's juvenile stuff," she said. "It could even be one of our own people. There are some in our own unit who definitely don't love me."

The hand that held the photo was shaking a little.

"No, this is the hospital's taking it to the next level," said Doug. "I expected this."

"Do you really think the hospital's behind it?" said Kate. "This doesn't seem like Winslow's style. He likes Clare."

"Hey, in one strike in California, management hired someone to toss the local president's bedroom, just to scare her," said Doug. "They broke the frames on her photos of her kids and threw her underwear all over the room."

"Those bastards," Tony said. "I'm spending the night tonight. Make up the couch for me."

"How is that going to look?" said Clare, ever the prude.

Margaret, who'd eased through the door as soon as she got a whiff of drama, suggested that Clare put up at a hotel for a while.

"That's even worse. As if I'm running away."

"Clare, nothing is worth your well-being," said Doug solicitously. He made a movement as if to put a protective arm around her shoulders, then seemed to think better of it.

"Don't you know that when you're being bothered like that you're supposed to report it to the police?" Margaret asked.

Margaret always followed procedure. She'd be a good person to have around during an air raid: calm and conscientious, with an iron nerve sustained by rules and regulations.

"If I show up at a police station with this scribble, I'm going to look absolutely neurotic," said Clare.

"Not with modern stalker laws," said Margaret.

"Clare is right," said Doug. "The police won't take this seriously. I'm going to keep an eye on you. We'll see if they try anything now."

The virility of this speech was marred by Doug's immediately choking on an overlarge bite of lemon Danish. Tony pounded him on the back, harder than strictly necessary.

"Mighty Mouse will save the day," I muttered to Kate.

"Clare can stay with Mike and me for a few days until we see what's what," said Kate firmly.

Doug seemed disappointed, but Clare did not, to my relief. Clare might have been vulnerable to the soothing blandishments about her leadership abilities that Doug constantly provided, but she clearly did not want to curl up on her sofa with him to sip sherry and watch Norma Rae on video.

Someone at the hospital must have put the lowlifes on a leash. After three days there was no more trouble, and Clare returned home. Tensions were running high, though. When word got out about what had happened, a few of our people took things into their own hands. Forty-eight hours after Clare found the threatening photo, every vehicle left in the hospital's executive parking lot after sundown had a tire flattened, including Winslow's Porsche.

Winslow remarked to a news crew in wounded outrage, "I don't even know our nurses anymore. They're acting like hooligans instead of healing professionals." Several of the nurses then showed up for picket duty in sweatshirts on which were painted the motto, "Proud to be hooligans."

"We need to set a more positive tone," Clare said in our morning meeting on Thursday. She was her calm self again. Once the first fear was past she had been eager to get back to her home and to her dogs. Clare might be a risk-taking politician, but she needed her lovingly arranged retreats to survive: her office with its willow ware and Saint Anthony statue, and the small Cape Cod with its fenced backyard and front garden.

Kate said, "Father Peter's going to hold a toy and clothing drive and start a Christmas fund for the strikers. Let's have him talk to the papers, give us a little cover."

"A bunch of church ladies isn't going to cow Coventry," said Doug, fingering his newly naked upper lip. He'd shaved his mustache the day after the infamous Channel 8 television interview, and when he wasn't talking he'd developed a nervous tic of drawing his index finger furtively across his upper lip.

"If the point is for us to shine through as the good guys, having a photo of Father Pete surrounded by donated stuffed animals and boxes of clothes is just the ticket," said Kate. "What's more, Christmas is only five weeks away. And the hospital's arranged a huge holiday bash for the scab nurses with prime rib and a raffle for a big-screen TV. We need to show our people the community is behind them. You know, " 'Local Church Rallies Around Valiant Strikers.' "

"This isn't *Boys Town*, you know. As much as we all like Father Pete, in real life Bing Crosby doesn't smile a twinkling smile and save the day. If something doesn't break by the end of December, we're going to have to rethink our options."

No one liked to consider this point. We knew, much as we hated to admit it, that Doug was right.

"So, have we got them on the ropes yet?" Ron asked at the beginning of week three, phoning from his chiropractor's office, where he faithfully shows up every Tuesday because he has a fixed belief that one of his legs is shorter than the other and needs to be stretched weekly.

"Not even close, Ron. We're still dancing around the ring."

We'd begun leaking the damning research on Jet-a-Nurse as each piece of data passed muster with the Toilers' paranoid lawyer. The hospital census went down as patients with elective surgeries postponed their procedures and patients with the option of choosing Providence hospitals went there.

"I heard Coventry might ask for a mediator," said Ron.

"That's just posturing. They're not ready to cave in yet. Nowhere near. Ask Tony if you don't believe me."

"No, no. I believe you." Ron didn't enjoy dealing with Tony directly. They spoke different masculine dialects. Tony's language was a gruff, cut-to-the-chase Morse code, and Ron's a needlessly embellished, confidence-man patter.

"Are you drowning back at the office, Ron? I know it's a crazy time of year, but I don't think I can work this one long distance. Much as I'd like to."

"I'm the person who sent you in there, I shouldn't complain."

"Think of your final bill to Weingould. That'll make you smile."

"Yeah. Hold on, this is the part that hurts."

I heard him moan as the chiropractor pulled on his hamstrings. For a second I wondered if that was what Ron sounded like in bed. It's funny how, even with men you despise, you sometimes think you'd like to give it one quick try. They say women are the monogamous sex, that we have fewer lustful thoughts than men do. Men must feel safer in this belief, which is why they cling to it.

"Fill me in now and then," said Ron. "I don't want to be blind-sided."

Ron frequently spoke as if his staff were engaged in an ongoing conspiracy to make him look foolish and ill-informed in front of clients. In reality, Ron's staff were always trying to get him to sit still for half a minute so as to keep him posted on late-breaking developments with their accounts. Memos didn't work; Ron refused to read them, a stance you had to admire.

I'd barely hung up with Ron when Margaret, who liked to man the switchboard, came over to announce, "Your cousin is on the phone."

She was wearing a clay brooch shaped like a pilgrim's hat. If there's one thing I hate, it's seasonal jewelry.

"Lou-lou, how are you-you?" I said, an old joke we'd found funny when we were ten.

"Wrong cousin."

"Johnny? What's up? Are you okay?"

"Of course I'm okay."

He rarely made phone calls from work. The place was far too loud and busy. In the background, one of the mechanics was testing an exhaust system. I could hear him revving the engine and the clearly audible roughness still left.

Johnny yelled, "Larry, make sure you tighten the joints on that intake pipe."

I said, "You guys used a replacement part, didn't you? He's never going to get it totally quiet now. I hope Larry told the customer. It'll save money but he won't get as quiet a ride."

"God, Nicky. Don't you think I know my business?"

"Most customers don't understand replacement parts. They worry they're getting shortchanged. You have to explain it to them up front, that's my feeling."

"I didn't call to hear your views on replacement parts."

"Why did you call?"

"To hear your lovely voice."

"Johnny. Spill."

"It's Louise. She's really hurt Betsey's feelings, and for no reason. I don't know what's going on with her these days."

"What did she do?" I hoped that Louise had thwarted Betsey in another tasteless wedding idea. I wouldn't put it past Betsey to try to incorporate her cat in the wedding party, perhaps as flower girl.

"She told Betsey she wouldn't be a bridesmaid, and she gave her no good excuse at all."

"A bridesmaid? Betsey already has all her bridesmaids, doesn't she?"

"One dropped out. She was waiting for her Foreign Service assignment, and she got it. So she'll be in New Delhi in June, and that's too far to fly back even if they'd let her."

"So Betsey thought of Louise, of all people? They aren't even close. They don't even go shopping together."

"She thought it would be nice to have someone from my family."

"And she didn't think of me?"

I made sniffly weeping sounds.

"She said that you once told her that you thought most weddings were hokey bourgeois displays and that you wanted to be married on Burnside Bridge at Antietam, at dawn, with only a battlefield guide or two as a witness. She said that you said the slaughter of the Civil War was a fitting metaphor for the future of most marriages."

"I was joking around. Although the Burnside Bridge is very erotic, Johnny. You should go there sometime with someone fun."

"Betsey said that you also said that you'd once deliberately exposed yourself to the Hong Kong flu to get out of a bridal shower."

"So I'm not on the short list?"

"Not even if she has to get Boy George to stand in, in full drag."

"Damn. And I was looking forward to wearing the dress."

Like most brides, Betsey did not want to be upstaged by her bridesmaids. Unfortunately, the linen potato sack that Betsey had chosen for the wedding dress left very few *less* appealing options for the bridesmaids' attire. Betsey had finally decided on a hideous button-down blouse and skirt combination, chosen ostensibly for its post-wedding usefulness. The fabric was a pale blue sailcloth, and the blouse had elbow-length sleeves and a wide pleated collar. You could upholster a sofa with all the excess material in the skirt. Not an outfit for Louise, whose pink-and-white complexion was washed out in anything but simple lines and subtle, warm colors.

"Betsey asked Louise very tactfully, she said, and Louise turned her down flat."

"Louise didn't even want to do a reading at the wedding, Johnny, remember? Why would she want to be a bridesmaid? Especially a substitute bridesmaid. Can't Betsey ask anyone else?"

"She decided that since her half of the wedding party is blond so far, she needs another blond."

"Well, how *could* Louise ever resist a compliment like that? What's gotten into the girl?"

"It's not that much trouble, Nicky. It's one day of her life."

"It *is* that much trouble, Johnny. That just shows how much you know. It's going to the damn shower, and buying the dress, and getting shoes dyed to match it, and getting measured for fittings once the dress comes in. And getting thingies to go in your hair."

"Thingies?"

"You know, silk rosebuds or a little tiara or whatever the bride inflicts on you. Betsey's so damn nature-loving she'll want them to stick hay in their hair, for all I know. Anyway, it's a pain in the ass of monumental proportions, being a bridesmaid."

"I think you're exaggerating."

"How many times have you been a bridesmaid? By the way, if she agrees to do this, who would you pair Louise up with?"

"Bob Sanders."

"Bob Sanders? Oh, yeah, she'll have a great time with him. His idea of conversation is reviewing the transmission problems of the 1972 S-Class Mercedes. Why not Dennis Flannery?"

"She's too short for him."

"Or he's too good-looking for her."

"Dennis goes through women like Kleenex, Nicky. I'm not putting Louise with him."

"Yeah, it would be awful if Louise got to spend your wedding with someone charming and self-assured and sexy. Could it be you're jealous?"

"I should have known better than to call you," Johnny said. I could hear Joey shouting for him in the background.

"Don't you dare get off the phone, Johnny. Now tell me, what do you want me to do?"

"Talk to Louise. Tell her to do this for me, as a favor."

"As a favor? Forget it. I'm not going to pressure Louise about this. Betsey can hire someone to be her bridesmaid if she's run out of Aryan-looking friends to color-coordinate into her wedding party."

"My own cousins aren't happy for me," said Johnny. "I don't expect you to ever give Betsey an even break, but Louise, I thought Louise would come through. It's lousy."

"Why do you keep trying to force Louise to clap her hands for you? I don't see you clapping your hands for her about Hub."

"Hub." He snorted ungracefully. "That little candy-ass."

"Oh, Johnny. You are so transparent, you know that?"

"Boy, you get an idea in your head and you don't want to let it go, do you? I'll just have to talk to your mother, then," said Johnny. "I didn't want to bring her into it. See you at Thanksgiving."

He rang off before I could say anything else. But despite its abrupt end, his call lifted my spirits. I felt that in some subterranean fashion, things were happening with Johnny and Louise. I was only sorry I couldn't think of a way to push them along.

The night before I left to go home for Thanksgiving, I was up until one o'clock folding gold paper napkins into the shape of turkeys, under Margaret's direction, for the St. Jude's "Strikers' Thanksgiving Mass and Gala Dinner." Eric was not part of these preparations, having been sentenced to a day of banishment by Kate, who'd caught him teasing the hospital security dog again.

"He came this close to being nipped," she said. "Bill turned his back for a second and Eric had his hand on Punch's collar, saying, 'I command you to heel, Punch.' He saw some show on public television on dog training. I hate to punish him, but the only thing that seems to cause him any pain is not being here."

"Punish him more, then."

"He's a good kid at heart, Nicky. I think he may be so smart that he's bored out of his mind at school, which is probably why he acts up. I'm going to talk to Mary about getting him tested for one of those gifted and talented programs."

"I'd like to get him tested, all right."

The day before the holiday I caught an evening flight home. I wanted to stay in Winsack for the dinner, which was going to be the parish's biggest blowout since its one-hundredth anniversary steamers-and-corn feast a few years earlier. I'd written flyers for the big event, gone with Father Peter to collect donations from area businesses, and helped decide the crucial issue of round vs. rectangular tables. I'd even done my time on the phones asking people to bring the dull but important supplies—paper cups for the kids, sugar for coffee, and foil wrap for the leftovers which Kate, with great tact, would make sure went to the families who were the most short of cash right now.

I was putting in a lot of nonbillable hours. Ron would have had an apoplexy if he had known just how many. Somehow I'd gone from being a PR flack with duties apart to being just another person Margaret bossed around in her party planning. It felt good that I did my own shift on the picket line and that Mrs. Crawley said every morning at breakfast, "Well, how are you nurses shaping up today? Any trouble expected out there?" although I'd explained to her again and again that I was not a nurse.

It felt especially good that Tony forgot the bad blood between us enough to ask me, almost kindly, when I'd be back.

"In three days," I said. "Try not to settle the strike until I get here."

I gave him a quick little grin to let him know it was not a criticism.

"I wouldn't dream of settling without you," he said, and in his voice I heard an echo of an echo of the old teasing affection.

"Well, you know where to reach me if anything comes up."

"I might call you just to run a few ideas past you," he said. For the first time since I'd come to Winsack, he wasn't staring over my head or frowning down at his feet. His eyes were weary but they were looking right into mine for the first time in five years.

"Tony, if you need me here, I can stay. My mother's turkey is nothing to fly home for."

"I remember her date-prune stuffing," Tony said.

"See? No great loss."

"You go. It might be the only break you get before Christmas. You've earned it."

He smiled at me. I could smell his aftershave, which is a brand that comes from the drugstore in a box with a cowboy on it. Once or twice, after we'd broken up, I'd actually opened a box of this cologne and sniffed it, homesick for him. But in the box the stuff had far too sweet an odor, whereas on Tony it acquired, somehow, a scent of cedar and wood smoke.

"Nicky," he said, "I know I've been—"

A hand fell lightly on his shoulder. It was Suzanne, wafting up the way she always did.

"You're still here," she said to me. "I wanted to talk to you about the hospital suppliers' issue, but I know you have to make your plane."

"I have twenty minutes."

"It's not important. Just another area of wasteful spending that belies their argument that there's no money for that two percent raise or for more staffing. Their purchasing process is positively byzantine. I don't think there's been any competitive bidding around here for years."

"Can we accuse them of some kind of sweetheart arrangement with the supplier, with the extra profits coming back to Coventry?"

"Maybe. But I don't want to be too hasty."

She spoke as placidly as if we had years ahead of us for a leisurely explanation of the iniquities of Coventry's sharp business practices. It was the fourth time she'd hinted about having discovered mud I could actually sling at Coventry, then prevaricated. I cast an impatient glance at Tony, but he was staring down at his hands, twiddling a pipe cleaner from a stack Margaret had left on the counter.

"Are you saying you have something we can use soon? I could whisper in the ears of a few reporters if so."

"Not yet. We shouldn't rush to judgment."

"It seems to me that if there was ever a time to rush to judgment, it's now."

I'd had it up to here with her. Here she was with Tony, a light work schedule that seemed to consist of riffling through the pages of audits and calling her cronies to gossip, and a wardrobe that I was ten pounds too heavy to look good in, even if I could have afforded it. Enough was enough.

"Suzanne, you've been here, what, a month? Please, for the love of heaven, give me something that's not embargoed. Give me this, or give me some other damning statistic or unorthodox pattern. Anything. If the feds are investigating these guys, they've got to be screwing up somehow. In that whole pile of papers and annual reports and computer printouts you've amassed, there must be something you can hand me."

She just smiled, and moved an inch closer to Tony, the inch that spelled the difference between business-collegial and intimate. That smile of Suzanne's. I'd disliked it from the beginning. That perfectly confident, slow, sweetly unkind smile.

"You're in such a hurry all the time, Nicky. Tony did warn me that you're sometimes too quick to make up your mind. He said it's your only fault. That you made a decision and that was it."

Now Tony looked up, finally. His eyes were guilty, and I saw that he had told Suzanne the tale of our romance and spared me not at all in the telling.

Well, I hadn't survived four years at St. Madeleine Sophie's to be cowed by a glammed-up bluestocking like Suzanne. I set down my suitcase and reached for a pen.

"I think I'd better take a later plane and go over the details of these purchasing irregularities with you, Suzanne, so that you'll feel comfortable with whatever we do with this. In fact, if I have to miss everything out of Logan tonight my family will understand. They're troopers. Besides, Father Pete said he wished I could be here for the dinner, anyway."

At the thought of forgoing the promised holiday from my presence, Suzanne grew arch for the first time in my acquaintance with her. Her moment of malice was over, having served its purpose.

"No, no. I'm sure we can put something together once you're back. You go home now to whoever that wonderful person is who sent you those lilies."

She gazed at me with that air of patient waiting that always made me wonder what the hell she was waiting for. It was that atmosphere about her of prolonged, entitled expectancy that made people want to rush in and fetch her whatever it was she wanted. I had seen it work on everyone here—except, perhaps, Kate.

I shrugged on the shearling jacket that no longer fit Kate's sister Caroline, feeling like a polar bear next to Suzanne in her size-two knit skirt and twinset.

Tony followed me to the door.

"Nicky," he said. "I was drunk one night and did some talking. I didn't know she'd throw it in your face."

"Then I guess you don't know much. She's obviously been waiting for the chance."

"She's jealous. It's been hard for her."

"Tell you what, Tony, you scamper on back and reassure her. Tell her you'd never carry a torch for someone as *pigheaded* and *judgmental* as I am."

"Nicky, I'm sorry."

"You have nothing to be sorry for. I'm a vicious bitch who threw you out on your ear without a word of explanation, right? I deserve everything I get."

Some part of me knew that I was being carried away by my own dramatics, but it was impossible to stop. Since I'd come here he'd insulted me and overworked me and, worst of all, ignored me whenever he could. In front of them all. In front of Suzanne. I was hurting him back at last—I could see how his whole face became set and shut, as if I'd aimed a blow at him—and it felt wonderful. It felt heavenly.

"If you would think for a minute, Nicky. When I . . . let my mouth run loose with Suzanne, I had no idea I would ever see you again. I had no idea she would ever meet you."

"I don't *have* to think for a minute, Tony. I *pride* myself in never thinking. You know how I am. Impetuous. It's part of my charm."

"Oh, Christ," he said. "Don't go home this way. Let me . . . let me drive you to the airport. You can leave the rental car here for two days. I'll keep an eye on it."

"No, thank you. I wouldn't dream of taking you away from your *work.*"

It wasn't a brilliant exit line, but it was enough to walk out on. In the parking lot I started to cry, but then I realized that if I began I would never stop. To be discovered by anyone—by Tony or Suzanne or Doug—sitting there weeping, wiping my snotty nose with the back of my glove and trying to rub mascara off my swollen face, would be simply too much humiliation for one day.

My last sight of them all through the strike office window, as I sat there snorting back sobs and defrosting the rear window, was of Margaret with an enormous box full of silver napkin rings, passing out polishing cloths. She handed one to Suzanne, who regarded it with puzzlement and walked away.

*　　*　　*

Logan was crowded with people who, like me, appeared as if they didn't especially want to go where they were going and wished the whole ordeal were over. Of course, I hadn't particularly wanted to stay in the place I'd just left, had I?

I bought an overpriced travel magazine at the newsstand and read it on the plane, sullenly drinking Bloody Marys and weighing the attractions of alligator watching in the Everglades versus an excursion to Macedonia for a firsthand experience of an archaeological dig.

In the taxi home from National Airport, the driver told me how he missed his family back in Ethiopa. I wondered why people who actually wanted to see their families were so often separated from them by chance or necessity, while those whose families exasperated and oppressed them were doomed to celebrate holiday after holiday in domestic discomfort.

My heart grew even heavier as I thought of all I was arriving without. I had no shower invitation design in hand for Betsey. I had no wherewithal to bake the two apple pies my mother had requested I bring the next day, so I'd have to run to the grocery, which would be no more pleasant than the airport was, on the night before Thanksgiving. I didn't even have a clean pair of tights in which to honor our Puritan forefathers.

Well, I could promise Ma a few sketches for the invitations by the end of the week. I could wash my tights in the sink and hang them over the radiator. And everyone, including my mother, would just have to settle for store-bought pies. They'd taste better than anything that ever came out of my oven, that was certain.

· 14 ·

MY MOTHER DID not see my point about the store-bought pies.

"You *bought* the dessert, Nicky?"

No hello, no "How is that exhausting assignment of yours going?" No motherly hug (she was never big on those).

"Ma, I was lucky I made it to the store last night to get these."

"These" were two very expensive apple pies and a cheesecake whose price amounted to highway robbery. Driven by an uneasy conscience, I'd skipped the local grocery and headed for one of those condescending gourmet shops that specialize in creating home-baked cooking for overworked professionals who are too pretentious or plagued by guilt to go to the bakery section of the supermarket. The gold cord with which this store's boxes were tied and the pale pink waxed paper that protected their delicacies from a cruel world should have told my mother that I'd made an extra effort—if not with my mixing bowls, at least with my wallet.

"We've never had store-bought desserts on a holiday."

"Ma, I did not have the energy. These will taste just as good. Better."

"They won't taste homemade."

Joey grabbed the boxes from me and stuck his nose inside.

"You're right, Ma, they won't taste homemade. Nothing Nicky cooked ever smelled this good."

But my mother wasn't to be cajoled by Joey, who can usually laugh her out of any wrongheaded notion or uncompromising mood.

"You can warm the pies up," I told her. "They'll taste fine warmed up. Perfectly fine."

She turned on her heel and walked into the kitchen, where

Johnny was leaning back on a chair drinking beer from the bottle and watching the football game on the tiny eight-inch black-and-white my mother kept in the kitchen so that should catch her soap opera even if cooking or cleaning.

"Stop tilting back, you'll get a skull fracture," my mother snapped, and then put a coaster under his beer bottle, all without missing a beat in the stage business that was intended to convey her deep displeasure with me: slamming cabinet doors as she pulled out dishes, rattling the silverware around in the drawers, and glancing disdainfully at my outfit for the day, a cream satin blouse with a notched collar tucked into my favorite pair of pants, boot-cut trousers in a very expensive, supple brown suede given to me years ago by a client in the apparel industry. I knew I looked good in those pants. Market research had shown me that. And I knew they were classy, since my former client had never given a tasteless gift in her life.

"You couldn't put on a dress for once, for the holiday?"

"You're not wearing a dress, Ma. And you look great."

I wasn't just buttering her up. A transformation had taken place. Always before for special occasions, she'd dressed in blouses a size too large in patterns too big for her small features, A-line skirts cut unflatteringly just below the knee, and the sort of "comfort" pumps that you knew would have a trademark name like "Flexi-Shoes," indicating that no woman had ever been propositioned while wearing them.

But today Ma had come into her own. She was wearing a sage-green crinkled organza tunic top over tapered, narrow pants in the same material. The shade brought out the green of my mother's eyes, the clarity of her white skin. She looked confident, elegant. She looked . . . my God, my mother looked sexy. I hadn't seen her this way since the parties she used to go to with my dad back in Boston when I was three or four, wearing a black net cocktail dress that she still kept in a clothes bag in the back of her closet.

My mother had gone to the lengths of putting on earrings and a bracelet made of scrolly silver wire, and flat ballet slippers in a silvery velveteen. Someone—I was beginning to guess who—had helped her with her makeup. She'd brushed on one of those new face powders that gleam a little, which softened and brightened her face. Louise—

I was sure now it had been Louise—had also found a very sheer shell-pink blush for my mother's cheeks, collarbone, and temples. Louise had always had a nice hand with cosmetics. The question was, why had my cousin suddenly pushed the issue? God knew my mother had never listened to any hints on updating her style before.

"You look beautiful," I said.

"Can't a woman get a new outfit once in a while without her whole family acting shocked?" said my mother.

"Not when she looks as great as you do," said Johnny. My mother gave him a melting smile, then turned to me and unfurled more grievances from the mental list she carries with her titled "Ways in which my only daughter disappoints me."

"Nicky, I asked you for one thing. One thing. To whip up a few apple pies."

"Ma, stop harping. I can't work ninety hours a week and be Julia Child in my spare time. These are good, good pies. These are expensive pies."

"You think money makes up for effort?"

"Money *is* effort, Ma. It's my effort at my job, transformed into apple pie. Transubstantiated, if you like to think of it that way."

"Don't be profane," said my mother in a cool, offended voice.

"Fine, Miss Lavinia Ann," I said.

We'd once had a tabby cat named Lavinia Ann (my mother's idea of a classy name, taken from a book). She was a cat of great age and dignity who, if petted too clumsily or startled from sleep, would turn her head away and lift her nose in the air just as my mother was doing right now.

I couldn't see why Ma was so upset. I'd never been the culinary star of family gatherings. In fact, two winters ago when I attempted ginger cookies for Thanksgiving, my brothers and Johnny had used them as pucks for an impromptu game of hockey on the frozen creek in the woods behind my parents' house.

"How much did you pay for these?" said my mother.

"I'm not telling you," I said.

"You'd better not. I think the price would make me sick. Who shops in these gourmet stores? Who pays that kind of money?"

At this point the kitchen door opened and Michael came in. He was wearing a deep blue fisherman's sweater and brown tweed trousers with loafers and argyle socks. He looked handsome and windblown. He was carrying two large apple pies with the juice bubbling out over the crust.

"I thought you might need extra desserts so I baked these this morning while the parade was on," he said, giving my mother a kiss and lifting me in the air in an exuberant hug.

"Look, Ma, your problem's solved," said Joey. "Nicky has no domestic skills, but Michael more than makes up for her."

He seized the pies from Michael and ripped off an edge of the crust to stuff in his mouth.

"Don't be a pig, Joe," said Michael. "You're such a godawful pig, you know that?" Michael made pig noises, grunting and oinking, and Johnny threw a roll at Joey, who continued to pretend to dig at the pie with his fingers.

"Joseph," said my mother, and Joey subsided.

"Your mom's just nervous because she has a new boyfriend, Nicky," said Johnny.

"A boyfriend!"

"Louise calls him her 'beau,'" said Michael.

"You don't have to sound so surprised," said Ma. "Louise knew a gentleman in her salsa class who has free evenings since he lost his wife, and she thought we might want to meet. So we had dinner at O'Donnells, and it was a very pleasant evening."

"And you're seeing him again?" The last time I'd mentioned the possibility of dating to her, she'd implied I was spitting on my father's grave.

"Yes, I am. He was polite and attentive and a wonderful storyteller, and I haven't enjoyed myself so much in a long time."

"Why shouldn't Ma get a little action?" said Joey, who'd balanced himself on my mother's cooking stool and was fishing sausage out of the huge pot of sauce she had simmering. Joey broke all the rules of my mother's house with impunity.

"Have some respect for your sainted mother," said Michael in a phony brogue, and grabbed the fork out of Joey's hands. They began singing a song Ma hated, "Mother McCree." Ma always winced at the line about Mother McCree's brow being "all wrinkled and weathered with care." Her own brow was smooth and unclouded, as befitted a woman who made her children's lives a misery with her nagging and thus slept every night with a sound and untroubled conscience.

"Louise has Aunt Maureen in her sights," said Johnny. "Louise won't be happy until she marries off the entire Western world. Except for herself. She's too busy hanging around with rock singers."

There was an unaccustomed sour note in his voice.

"Hub's not a rock singer, he's a poet of the people," said Joey. "That's what Louise says. I asked her if they *elected* him poet, or what, and she got pissed at me."

Joey and Louise disagreed on everything, but I think Louise actually found Joey soothing to be around. He saw through what he referred to as Louise's "Glinda the Good Witch routine."

"Leave Louise alone," said Michael. "She's not hurting anyone."

"She's hurting herself," said Johnny.

"I appreciate your concern," said Louise, coming in unexpectedly from the hallway, as if we were all in a play and she'd been scripted to enter at a dramatically awkward moment.

Louise, like my mother, looked different from when I'd last seen her over lunch. Usually for these occasions she showed up disheveled and late, with flour in her hair. Today she had piled her hair on her head with a few curls drifting around her face and neck, and she wore a deep plum, Empire-waisted dress of thin wool with a low scoop neck, extremely becoming in its simplicity and rich color. Where was my hippie cousin with her gypsy garb and her tinker's jewelry? Where were Ma's sleeveless polyester mock turtlenecks printed with daisies? I left town for three weeks and look what happened.

"What's your boyfriend's name?" I asked Ma.

"It's Ira," said Louise, as my mother didn't answer.

"Ira? That's not a—"

"Ira is Jewish," said my mother, as if she were admitting that he was married or worked for the CIA.

"And there's nothing wrong with that," said Louise firmly, ignoring the fact that for twenty years my mother had referred to Louise's parents as "a mixed marriage" because Aunt Pamela had converted from Methodism.

"You're surprised," said my mother defensively.

Shocked was more like it—not that Ira was Jewish, but at the suddenness with which my mother was breaking her own rules. This was the woman who'd once told Jeremy he'd have to convert if he wanted to marry me.

"I had a few older Irish Catholics on file," said Louise, "but none of them seemed just right for your mom. Ira isn't settling into his sixties, he's busting out of them."

"I guess you'd know about busting out," said Johnny. "Some dress. You've got a date later?"

I was speechlessly impressed that my mother hadn't taken a pass on the Ira opportunity in order to be set up with a dour Irish widower with sixteen grandchildren and a crumbling family cottage in County Meath that he visited every other year just to prove that six decades in America hadn't caused him to get above himself.

"Ira finds the difference in traditions intriguing," said Louise, pretending Johnny wasn't present. "It's such a myth that couples have to have everything in common."

"I bet that's not what he finds intriguing," said Joey. "It's Ma in her slinky new clothes."

"Enough," said my mother. "All of you, get out of the kitchen." She placed Michael's pies tenderly on the sideboard, shoving mine on top of the icebox and stuffing the cheesecake into the freezer, where it would be ruined.

To my mother, homemade pies were tribute, and I'd refused to pay it. That was the whole problem with us: I wanted her to like me for qualities she had never admired in women, and she wanted me to pay homage, the way the rest of my family did, to her never-unfeminine spunk, her efficiency, her immaculate housekeeping, her pep. I thought Ma could do with a lot less pep, and as a child had envied friends with dreamy, distant mothers who took tranquilizers or painted watercolors.

We dispersed—Michael and Joey to go outside to hold their weekly argument about whether or not the pine tree in front of my mother's dining room window should be cut down because it blocked the light, Louise and Johnny and I into the living room to eat black olives and hot peppers from the partitioned appetizer tray my mother put out every holiday. From upstairs we could hear Joey's wife, Maggie, babbling loving baby-nonsense as she put the little one down for his nap. In the kitchen my mother switched on the easy listening station she liked to cook to. Strains of "The Days of Wine and Roses" floated through to us, though not loudly enough to cover the uncomfortable silence between Louise and Johnny.

"So where's Betsey?" I said.

"Betsey is with her family in Stamford."

"Why aren't *you* there?" said Louise, in a cold tone I'd never heard from her before, at least not aimed at Johnny.

"I have six jobs waiting for me at the shop," said Johnny. "Not all of us can just leave what we're doing to go hang around backstage at the Swamp Hole."

The Swamp Hole was a local club where the floor was sticky with beer and you didn't want to use the ladies' room. Acts on the verge of making it played there. Sometimes groups that had hit it big came back out of sentiment. I hadn't been to the Swamp Hole since I was twenty-one.

"Hub's band played at the Swamp Hole?" I said. "Wow."

"Not yet. He's booked there for the Friday before New Year's," said Louise.

"Yeah," said Johnny, throwing an olive up in the air and catching it in his mouth. "He wrote a special song for it. It's all about how he didn't like the Mercedes his mommy and daddy bought him last Christmas."

"It's about the loneliness of a consumer society," said Louise. "It's called 'Christ Child in Suburbia.' I played it for you. Just because Hub's family has money doesn't mean he can't have a keen sense of social justice."

"It must be a nice life, writing about poor people and clipping stock coupons," said Johnny.

"You know, I've been nothing but supportive of your relationship with Betsey and all the ones before her. You could do the same for me for a change."

"I don't call it very supportive when you won't even be a bridesmaid," said Johnny. "She'll have to ask her cousin now."

"What a tragedy," said Louise. "Why can't you understand that I don't want to take on anything more right now? I'm really busy. I'm even thinking of hiring an assistant."

"An assistant? Where is an assistant going to turn around in all that clutter? You don't need an assistant, you need to get rid of some of that mess," said Johnny. "How hard can it be to set people up on blind dates that you suddenly need an assistant? It's not rocket science."

"What is your problem, Johnny?" I said. "Louise works as hard at her job as you do at yours. She puts a lot of flair and insight and imagination into it."

"I can see she has imagination," said Johnny. "She's got Aunt Maureen all tarted up until I don't even recognize her. We'll be lucky if one of those earrings Louise bought her doesn't fall into the spaghetti sauce."

Louise flushed, the deep angry flush we had learned to dread as children, the sign of one of her very rare tempers.

"If it does," she said, "I hope you choke on it." And she left the room.

I sat at the other end from Johnny on my mother's long sectional couch, a couch that would have been comfortable if it hadn't been covered in a rust-brown "French country" fabric whose strawlike fibers dug through to your skin. My mother refused to replace this upholstery hair shirt with chintz or linen "because it was still perfectly good." I put Johnny's feet up on my lap.

"What in the world is going on with you guys?"

"I don't know. Louise is angry because I won't come see her skanky boyfriend play on his little guitar in a few weeks. Like that's how I want to spend New Year's Eve."

He was picking twiggy bits off the couch cushions, not looking at me.

"Well, Louise goes places for you. She went with you to pay all those D.C. parking tickets a few months ago. That took all day, as I recall."

"She wouldn't go with me when I got measured for my tux. All of a sudden, she doesn't have ten minutes for me."

"Johnny, did you think about what we talked about on the way to the train station?"

"I figured you had PMS or something, talking crazy like that."

"In the first place, I hate it when men act as if PMS is some sort of excuse to avoid electing a woman president or taking female opinions seriously. A few slightly off days once a month is nothing, I repeat, *nothing*, to the eighty million testosterone surges you men have addling your brains every single hour. In the second place, it wasn't crazy of me to tell you that you don't have to marry Betsey."

"Of course I don't *have* to marry her. It's not like she's pregnant or anything."

No, when Betsey got pregnant it would be because Betsey planned to get pregnant, at just the right moment to take a pause in her career and devote herself to hunting up organic baby food and non-gender-determinant baby clothes.

"Betsey's good for me," said Johnny defensively.

"She's like a giant bowl of Brussels sprouts, huh?"

"No, she's a woman who has a little vision about where she wants her life to go. Unlike your idiot cousin."

"Louise has a vision. It just doesn't drive her like an engine."

"Nothing drives her. She just goes along, la-la, la-la, la."

"Since when has that bothered you?"

"Since all of a sudden this guy Hub comes and takes over her life. Just like David Dent."

Louise had wasted her senior year of college on David, who attended law school at Georgetown and spent twice as much energy making Law Review as he did on Louise. David wore his fair hair slicked back from his forehead, tortoiseshell glasses, and starched, expensive oxfords that always looked fresh from the dry cleaner's. His quaint formality, which the rest of us found unbearably mannered, charmed Louise. His Presbyterian forbears must have bequeathed him an unalterable sense of Calvinist responsibility, because I never saw him sway from his path of complete devotion to worldly success.

All of David's social activities were aimed at advancing his prospects. He engulfed Louise in tennis (at which she was clumsy), sailing (which made her seasick), and cocktail parties at pretentious little rooftop bars that David's well-connected, sheltered friends thought were edgy and daring. During the David era, Louise confined her lovely hair in unbecoming headbands and bought a number of unflattering outfits in the category that used to be called "sportswear."

When David tired completely of being youthful, at the age of twenty-three, he dumped Louise. She was left with a closet full of clothes that looked horrible on her and shelves of books she would never read again, books with titles such as *The Origins of Property Theory in British Common Law*.

"David was a pill, Johnny, but by now it should be no big surprise to you that, left on her own, Louise has bad taste in men."

"Her taste seems to be getting worse, which I didn't think was possible."

I pressed my palms against Johnny's toes. He pushed his feet against them, trying to force my arms to buckle, an old habit of ours from the days when he was a weedy fourteen-year-old and I was a fifteen-year-old girl as strong as he was.

"Are you maybe jealous of Hub, Johnny?"

"Jealous? Are you kidding?"

He sat up and glared at me.

"Jealous of that little poser? Why would I be jealous?"

"Geez, I guess because he has such a big amplifier."

"If Louise went for me at all she wouldn't be running around after this singer, talking about him as if he were the best thing since Neil Young."

"Louise isn't very good at admitting to unhappiness. I doubt Hub is making her happy. How could he? I've never even seen him smile. The man is melancholy personified."

"Louise has always treated me like a brother."

"Did you ever give her any other cues?"

"It's the girl who gives cues," said Johnny.

"What are we, still in high school?"

"Just forget it, Nicky. I'm not exotic enough for Louise. I shave every day, and I have a regular job."

"Louise has never judged your job. Your card is right on her desk, next to that massage therapist's she refers clients to."

"It's no problem for Hub to be exotic. He doesn't have to earn a living. None of the guys Louise hooks up with ever seem to have to earn a living. But some of us have to work for our money. We can't all have rich daddies."

Or even daddies at all, I thought to myself, remembering that Johnny's father had contacted him exactly twice since divorcing Johnny's mother when Johnny was eight. No wonder it galled Johnny when Louise mentioned that Hub's doting parents had built a tiny recording studio onto their house when Hub was still in high school, in order to nurture their son's fledgling talent.

I changed my tack.

"When you described Betsey just now, you sounded like a personal ad. You don't love someone because of a list of qualities."

"Can you leave me alone, Nicky? I know ten guys who'd give their teeth for Betsey."

"Let them marry her, then."

I doubted that there were ten guys who yearned after Betsey, but I did not doubt that Betsey would not have to search long for a man who wanted to be mothered, managed, and prodded into everything from regular physicals to retirement planning. There are many such men out there, which is one of the things that sometimes makes the life of a single woman so depressing.

"The thing is, Johnny, is it really fair to Betsey to marry her if she doesn't make your head spin? If you marry someone, you should feel that you'd rather, oh, I don't know, go pay parking tickets with her than go to a five-star restaurant with anyone else. Do you really find Betsey interesting, Johnny? Is she fun?"

I thought I'd gone too far, but it is one of Johnny's sweetest traits that, much as he might argue with those he loves, he rarely becomes truly angry with them. As Doug's disposition defaulted to nastiness and pettiness, Johnny's defaulted to a lighthearted flexibility that forgave me more, perhaps, than should have been forgiven me.

He got off the couch in a swift spring and kissed the top of my head.

"You try, Nicky. I know you try."

In a minute I saw him outside, tossing a football with my brothers. In playing Cupid, I had failed on every count. It seemed that Louise's talent for matchmaking did not come from the paternal side of her family.

My mother stuck her head in.

"Nicky, I need you to fill the ice bucket. And what did you say to upset Louise like that?"

Right about now, I thought, Father Peter would be carving the first turkey. Margaret would be lifting trays of rolls from the yawning industrial ovens in the church hall's kitchen and arranging them in attractive piles on the platters she'd brought from home. Clare would be walking from group to group like a conscientious bride. Tony would be cracking up the old ladies with his imitation of Bennett Winslow doing the lambada. Eric would have spilled something, broken something, accidentally sat on something, or all three. Perhaps he'd have dumped grape juice on one of Suzanne's designer dresses, and I'd missed it. I could have been there, part of all of it, lost in a group that didn't care that I couldn't cook or that I wore pants to family occasions. Instead I was filling the ice bucket for my mother.

Well, maybe that was the point of holidays with our families, to remind us that the rest of our lives wasn't so bad. I smashed the ice cubes into dainty fragments, the way my mother prefers. Surely there was another Nicky Malone somewhere, living out the adulthood I'd been supposed to have, getting ready for this blessed season in the leisurely way in which people who have their lives under control get ready for the holidays.

I could see this alter ego pulling the hand-painted family ornaments out of tissue paper, piping icing onto the gingerbread mansion she was donating to the school auction, hugging her husband for shoveling the driveway of their restored Victorian in Glen Echo, on a bluff overlooking the river. Somewhere there had to be some doppelgänger

Nicky Malone whose mother approved of her, whose ex-boyfriends sent fond Christmas cards instead of snarling at her over her desk, whose closest female cousin went to Sunday Mass instead of winter solstice celebrations held at dawn in vacant lots. When I caught up with that other Nicky, that impostor, I was going to slap her silly for grabbing the life I was supposed to have and putting me through all this.

· 15 ·

DINNER WAS A strained affair. Johnny and Louise weren't speaking to each other. Joey and Maggie were openly curious about their quarrel. Michael sat calmly, removed to whatever distant corner of his mind he takes refuge in when the rest of us fight. My mother said a prim grace and then got up twenty times to check the progress of the apple pies warming in the oven and the coffee perking in her elderly, plug-in electric pot that would someday ignite and catch the whole house on fire.

I babbled on about the strike in order to make conversation. Maggie chimed in with reports on the baby's progress and the optometrist's shop of which she's one-third owner, contributing anecdotes about the eyeglass frames she had to talk people out of. The turkey was praised repeatedly.

We have our salad after dinner, in the Italian manner. As we were finishing, the doorbell rang. My mother raced out from the kitchen, patting herself down. That should have told me, that nervous, girlish tic. A minute later she led Jeremy into the room.

"Houston, we have a problem," said Joey.

"Look who dropped by," said my mother in a false, hostessy voice.

I had been picturing him, in my bitter thoughts, as being commanding and Byronic and sexy as ever. Jeremy had the kind of looks that always made you think of him as standing at a cliff's edge, gazing toward the horizon while wind ruffled his heavy curls off his noble brow. It would have been too easy if he'd shrunk to the proper proportions, if he'd dwindled and gone seedy. He hadn't. In my current discouraged and melancholy state, Jeremy looked damn good.

"Hello, Jeremy," I said, standing up. Now I perceived why Ma had

184 ~ CHRISTINA BARTOLOMEO

wanted me to show up with proof of my housewifely prowess in the form of pastry. She knew Jeremy was coming by for dessert. It was a marvel that my mother could think for one moment that Jeremy could be fooled, at this stage of the game, by any show of domestic talent on my part.

He hovered uncertainly in the doorway of the dining room, being stared at by Johnny, Louise, Maggie, and Joey. Only Michael seemed unflustered.

"Sit down, sit down," my mother said. "We were just having dessert."

Everyone bustled around, with far more fuss and business than the production of dessert plates and forks warranted. Jeremy and I sat side by side, as if we were at the children's table.

He said to me under his breath, "This wasn't my idea but I couldn't think of another way to see you."

"So you enlisted my mother? Great move."

"It was an act of desperation."

He shifted in his seat. My mother's dining room chairs are a heavy pseudo-Spanish oak style with black leather seats from which you can hear guest's thighs unpeeling as they rise from a meal during the summer months. My mother had thought they were the last word in elegance when she and my dad purchased them in 1975, and she still thought so.

The murky light from the wrought-iron chandelier (bought to complete the Moorish-Spanish motif begun in the chairs) shone down on Jeremy's heartbreaking cheekbones, his deep green eyes, his lovely wide mouth. I felt a stirring of desire, but it must not have shown in my expression. I knew that because, as my family hunted up the good silver teaspoons at Ma's direction, and trotted out milk and sugar in my mother's wedding pitcher and sugar bowl that hadn't been used for years, Jeremy continued, too softly for anyone to overhear, "Haven't I told you I was sorry? Haven't I shown you I'm sorry? Didn't you get my lilies?"

"I don't need another apology, Jeremy."

"What do you need, then?"

"How should I know? I've been working fourteen hours a day for the past four weeks. You're lucky I remember your name, the state of exhaustion I'm in."

I could hear my brothers and cousins and sister-in-law conferring in low tones in the kitchen. Should they leave us alone or would that be too unnatural-looking? Drama queens, all of them.

"We're waiting for pie out here," I called.

"You're hurt now," said Jeremy, with a little of his old assumption that he was entitled to an easy pardon. "But you'll feel differently in another month."

"Don't hold your breath."

"This is about that man Tony, isn't it? The one you lived with. The one you're working with up there."

"I bet that's comforting for you, to assume it's about Tony. And not, say, your humping Virginia on that vinyl sofa in your office. Whatever happened to her, anyway? Why aren't you spending Thanksgiving down South, huh?"

My mother chose this moment to place the pies on the table with a flourish, accompanied by a dish of freshly whipped cream.

"You do like apple pie," she said to Jeremy, who agreed to a huge serving with a look of sickly resignation. I tackled mine with gusto. I'm like my mother in that during times of stress, we find sugar far more soothing than liquor.

My mother was tucking into her own portion. For such a tiny woman she could put away a lot of pie. Louise picked at hers, glancing sometimes at Jeremy with a look of pity, sometimes at Johnny with a look of resentment. Perhaps Jeremy could take one of Louise's cards on his way out the door. Perhaps Louise could find him a woman who combined my feistiness and backbone with Virginia's pedigree and cup size.

Maggie kept her eyes on her plate. She still felt somewhat like an outsider, thanks to my mother's frequent reminders that her daughter-in-law was an interloper who had carried away her darling baby boy. Joey once told me that before he and Maggie left their wedding reception for the honeymoon trip, Ma had remarked in Maggie's hearing, "I'm so happy for you, Joey honey. But remember, if anything ever goes wrong, you'll always have a welcome waiting for you back home."

Ma's attitude to Maggie made me grateful that she only had *one* daughter-in-law to insult and patronize. Michael's boyfriends—the few we met—she treated differently, rather like college chums who'd arrived for a brief visit between semesters. She liked to believe that all gay men were just really good pals, that the most they ever did together was hug.

Joey said into the silence, "We haven't seen you for a while around here, Jem old boy. What have you been up to?"

"This and that," said Jeremy. He stirred his coffee and examined his shirt cuffs.

"Watched any soccer lately?" asked Joey.

"Not every Englishman watches soccer," said Jeremy.

"You call it something else, don't you?" said Joey. "Football? Is that what you call it?"

"Yes," said Jeremy shortly.

"You like football?" said Joey. "Those Brazilians sure took you guys to school the other day."

"I don't follow it," said Jeremy. "Sorry."

"Don't mention it," said Joey in the faintest of fruity English accents. He seemed to take a fiendish joy in heckling Jeremy. He had once said that Jeremy made him feel as if all his grammar was wrong.

"I don't think soccer is a subject for the dinner table," said my mother. "All that violence. Why don't you and Jeremy go for a walk, Nicky?"

"Yeah, kids," said Joey. "You go off and have a good time." My mother glared at him. In ten minutes, when Joey was playing "Sonny Boy" on my mother's out-of-tune piano, my mother would be wiping her eyes and beaming.

The drizzle covered Jeremy's black hair with tiny raindrops and turned his eyes an even more serious green. He looked . . . oh, he looked so good, and I'd been so low, so tired of the face I saw in the mirror that seemed to me to have no freshness, no bright expectation.

The forsythia and lilac bushes were bare and dripping, and no one was out, not even walking a dog. I noticed through an uncurtained picture window that Mrs. McBride's married daughter had come to see her and had gained a lot of weight. I saw that the Luccianos had replaced their third Cadillac with an Audi, a sad move from buy-American patriotism to German. It appeared that Mrs. Hanlon and her daughter with cerebral palsy were off on their annual Thanksgiving trip to visit relatives in Naples, Florida. I was glad of that, for my mother would have forced me to stop in.

Eyeing the Hanlons' bright green front door, I remembered with a sudden, vivid rush of dread the scores of times during my childhood when Ma would drag me along on uncomfortable visits to Mrs. Hanlon and Marcie, who was my age. Ma would invent reasons to help Mrs. Hanlon in the kitchen, leaving me alone with Marcie in the living room. I would sit on the edge of the sofa stammering out nonsensical chat into the silence, hoping desperately that the grown-ups would come back soon.

If I had brought up this memory with my mother and asked her why she had forced these frightening times with Marcie on an impressionable child, my mother would have been truly perplexed. Shouldn't children be taught charity, compassion, generosity? Surely such things were a matter of overcoming a ridiculous and unkind squeamishness, a squeamishness Ma (a strong-stomached Christian) didn't feel and couldn't imagine. Ma would hold Marcie Hanlon's hand and watch figure skating while Marcie drooled and her head lolled sideways, all the while eating Mrs. Hanlon's horrible raisin cookies and drinking her watery coffee with her other hand. I admired my mother's practical goodness, but did she have to expect that everyone else be good in exactly the same way she was?

The leaves were matted and slick under our feet. Once Jeremy slipped and I grabbed his elbow to keep him from falling. He frowned and pulled away.

"Can we talk?" he said.

"I need to sit down if we're going to talk. I ate too much pie."

We took a path through the neighborhood park, which the citizens' association had wrested from the grounds of a huge department store. Hard won, the small enclosure was lovingly tended. There were swings, and an abbreviated jogging path that curved in on itself, and a ten-plot community garden pegged out with sticks and string.

It was funny how you could tell the personality of the gardener from each plot. One was measured out neatly in red brick, with an orderly stack of clay pots and a watering can hanging ready for spring. Another was sheeted over in dark green plastic, with four bright pink wind whirligigs staked at the corners to keep the plastic down. My favorite was the small square at the exact center of the garden, still glowing with the embers of the last chrysanthemums and marigolds. There were no flowers in Winsack this late in the season, and I hadn't realized how much I'd missed seeing the last of them here.

The picnic benches were warped and puddled, and speckled with bird droppings, so I wiped off a swing with a corner of my jacket and sat down. Jeremy stood above me, leaning on one of the iron poles of the swing set.

"You have ten minutes," I said.

"Virginia is over, Nicky."

"She is, is she? Funny, I know when she's over, but I had no idea when she began. And why is she over?"

"We had nothing in common, really. She's not, actually, a very deep thinker. She doesn't have your wit, your perception."

"So you want to get back together with me because, compared to fluffball Virginia, I'm Dorothy Parker? That's really flattering."

"How long are you going to keep punishing me, Nicky?"

"Oh, Jeremy, I'm not punishing you. I mean, I *was* punishing you but not anymore. Now I just want my mother to stop nagging me about you."

"That's all I am to you, one more thing your mother nags you about?"

"Of course not. You had really lousy luck, in a way. If I hadn't found out about your fling with Virginia, we might still be together."

"I think we would have been. I really do, Nicky. I know that this fellow, this trades unions organizer, has you a bit thrown off balance right now. Your mother told me."

"How would she know? There's nothing going on between Tony and me. And we don't say 'trades unions' over here."

He ignored this childish dig.

"I think that when you consider it rationally, you'll realize that we should have another chance."

"Jeremy, we had great moments, especially in bed, and I learned a lot from you about the Spanish Civil War and the economics of the fifteenth-century silk trade. Can't we leave it at that?"

"I still want you," he said, and took my hand. "I still think we have a lot to offer each other."

"I don't want half a loaf," I said. "I want . . . abundance. We don't have that. We'll never have that. It's not your fault. We're just mismatched."

"Mismatched? Can you really say we're mismatched?"

He leaned down and kissed me, holding my head gently between his hands and tilting my chin up. My mouth opened under his. He kissed me with passion and infinite patience, ravishingly perfect kisses. I struggled to my feet but once I was standing up, I didn't pull away. He had never conveyed such yearning, not even in our first months together, and it was sweet and warming. He held me tightly, reaching under my jacket to slide his hands up my back. It was intoxicating, kissing him. It always had been. I forgot, for those minutes, that you can't live on champagne.

"You see how we are together," he whispered in my ear. "You can't give this up."

Maybe it was the tinge of self-assurance in his voice. Maybe it was the thought of my mother back at home, smug and pleased to have engineered this little reunion. Or maybe it was just that mere desire and loneliness no longer seemed a good enough reason to put up with certain things. By which I meant this sense that Jeremy's love for me was the result of my passing a series of tests. If I were a little bit less intelligent, say by five IQ points, would I have failed to meet Jeremy's standards? If I were several shades less pretty than Virginia, instead of just a few, would he be kissing her in the rain right now, instead of me?

A qualm smote me. Maybe I just wanted to believe the worst of Jeremy because he'd hurt me. Maybe my ego was so bruised I couldn't be trusted to make a decision. Yes, Jeremy had cheated on me, but didn't every dog get one bite? My quickness to judge had lost me Tony.

He'd been in the wrong, and so had Jeremy, but if I left every time a man was wrong I might be single until the end of my days. I pictured myself at seventy, alone in a rent-controlled apartment, eating saltines for dinner and saving my money for scratch tickets and Aqua Net, knowing that some other woman was getting the fun of septuagenarian sex with Jeremy and enjoying his nice academic pension. What a fool I'd feel like then. On the other hand, I could easily picture Jeremy at seventy-two, making some feeble excuse about running down to the store for milk of magnesia when he was really sneaking off for a quick snuggle with some rich widow he'd met online.

"Jeremy," I said, "I'm not ready to go back with you. I don't know if I ever will be."

He started kissing me again, but I pulled away.

"This just distracts me," I said.

"I want to distract you."

"I wouldn't mind being distracted if I didn't pay for it later. Let me think about all this, Jeremy. I don't know if I'm being spiteful and vindictive toward you or if it's just that anything my mother wants is automatically suspect. Or if we've just gone too far to come back to each other."

"I haven't gone anywhere. You have. You've gone back five years, and you're letting Tony take you over again."

"No one's taken me over. What am I, Belgium?"

"I only know that you're different since you've gone up there and seen him again."

"I'm different since I discovered that you'd been playing me for a fool. And seeing Tony has had no effect on me at all, except to irritate me."

As I said this, I knew I was lying. Even if Jeremy and I had been selecting our silver pattern at Macy's, seeing Tony would have knocked me for a loop. But did Jeremy deserve to know that? I thought not.

"I'm not going to give up so easily," he said. "No matter what temporary dream you may have fallen into upon seeing this man again."

"I would call the past few weeks more of a nightmare. I do have a job, you know, and I'm working round the clock."

"Think of me a little, at least," he said. "Let me cross your mind once in a while. That's not too much to ask, is it? And then, when this strike is over, we can talk."

"Maybe. That's the best I can do. And it's a weak 'maybe.' "

"I'll settle for that," he said.

He kissed me again before he drove off in his blue Miata, a flimsy little toy car he loved with a solicitude surpassing any he'd shown me in our time together. I let him kiss me, and even told him he could call. Maybe we had a chance. Then again, maybe my weakening toward him was just one of the pernicious effects of the holiday season, a season which makes us think any love is preferable to family love. Family love takes all our energy from autumn to Christmastime, and throws us into the new year drained, dispirited, and unconfident. Romantic love at least puts a glow in our cheeks and a spring in our step from time to glorious time, and when we fail at it, the results don't hang around forever, reproaching us and sighing. Sometimes I felt that, at my final hour, when I stood before Saint Peter and the gates of heaven began to creak open upon Paradise, the echo of Ma's disappointed sigh would waft even to the apostle's ears and cause my name to be blotted from the heavenly roster.

"You didn't ask him in?" said my mother.

The house was quiet. I could hear the game playing behind the closed door of the den. Once in a while Joey or Johnny gave a half-strangled shout at a touchdown. My mother barely used the den since my dad's death. It had been his room, the only room in the house besides the garage where he could do just as he liked. I think one of the reasons my dad loved my mother was that deep down, my mother knew she was a bit much and that any man would have needed to get away from her once in a while to save his sanity. She never barged in on him in the den, and she never interrupted him when he had his head poked inside a car. In some ways, my mother was an extremely wise woman.

In some ways.

"Here it is, a holiday, and he's far from his family, and you don't invite him in for coffee and a little more pie?"

"Ma, he's English. They don't even have Thanksgiving, remember?"

"He didn't look good, Nicky. Is he eating? He didn't eat much."

"How's he supposed to eat when all of you are watching him like he's a zoo panda in heat?"

"I think you're being a little hard-hearted. The man is clearly distraught."

It was no use fighting. Instead, I put my arm around her and walked her down the hallway to the kitchen. I said, "Ma, let's talk about you for a change. Tell me about your date, about this wonderful Ira."

In the kitchen we found Louise drying the good wine goblets with a felt cloth. We made a big pot of tea and my mother and Louise discussed the virtues of Ira Stern, a former estate planner who now only took on a few favored clients, but who was very witty on the intricacies of the tax code and the inheritance penalty. According to my mother, he danced beautifully but not too showily, he played rummy but not canasta, and he'd voted a straight Democratic ticket since Truman beat Dewey. According to Louise, he'd been a good family man, was a loving grandfather of three, and couldn't wait, he'd said to Louise during her post-date check-in call, to see my mother again.

"I think he's under an illusion about me. I think Louise made me sound too good to be true," said my mother, who'd never been given a compliment without wanting to disown it.

"I'm a very honest person," said Louise, "so I told him you were wonderful."

They smiled at each other. I was glad my mother had Louise. Sometimes, affection between aunt and niece is easier than affection between mother and daughter. If it made me a little jealous, a little regretful, it also relieved me of the burden of being the sole repository of my mother's feminine hopes. If it seemed my marriage prospects were so dim that I'd need to use a walker by the time I made it down the aisle, my mother could always dream of Louise being married sometime soon in a hokey tiara veil and an eight-foot train.

I'd seen the magazines on my mother's night table, testaments to a faltering hope: *Today's Bride*, *Washington Bride*, and, lately, *Older Bride*. I could picture her leafing through the glossy pages with her drugstore reading glasses on, wondering if she'd ever get to wear a tasteful georgette mother-of-the-bride dress, or weigh in with her opinion on pale pink orchids versus tiger lilies, salmon versus chicken, a limo versus my uncle Bill's Lincoln Town Car, and a thousand other mouthwatering details.

As I watched Ma debating outfits with Louise for her date tomorrow night, putting away more than her body weight in semi-frozen cheesecake, I was filled with fondness. I was lucky to have such a mother, even when she made me want to shriek with irritation. How many people in the world had someone who cared about them enough to feed them, bully them, and deceive them for their own good?

The doorbell rang. Thinking that it might be Jeremy returning, I ran to answer it, beating my mother by a nose. I didn't want her to get to him first this time. I wouldn't put it past her to offer him my old room.

But it wasn't Jeremy. Instead, standing a diffident three feet back from the door as if fearful of his welcome, was a slight man of sixty-odd, with wildly curly gray-and-silver hair and an air of being not quite sure whose house he'd planned to visit.

"Ira!" said my mother, pushing past me. She'd forgotten what she'd used to teach me, which was that you always kept a man waiting a few minutes in the living room before you made your entrance.

Somehow I'd imagined someone genial and self-assured. Someone . . . bigger. My dad had been six foot two. In his high school pictures he'd looked gangly, and he'd always stooped a little as if in memory of the days when his height was new to him. My dad had large hands with long fingers, and big feet; he took a twelve in shoes. In the brief space of time that I'd been aware of his existence, I'd been picturing Ira as being like my father in physical type, but he couldn't have topped my five-seven by much. He was slim but not insubstantial-looking, as so many of Louise's male clients were. The hand that shook mine had a good firm grip. He wore very hip steel-rimmed spectacles and carried a huge box of chocolates.

"You shouldn't have," said my mother, clutching the candy to her chest. My father was not one to bring presents home. They didn't have much money for most of their marriage, and my mother was not a good receiver even on the biggest occasions. You could always tell when a gift disappointed her, and most gifts did, as her tastes were picky and exact. She would utter a die-away "Oooohhhhh," the essence of lukewarmness, and set aside the box in which the ill-chosen item was wrapped with a palpaple air of marking it down for a "return to store" errand.

Ira's chocolates, though, were a big hit, and so, clearly, was Ira himself. She whisked him into the living room, plied him with coffee and brandy, and offered him the first chocolate out of the box before selecting one herself with the deliberation of a five-year-old girl.

"You made it home," said Ira, smiling at me. I felt hulking sitting on the couch next to my mother and him, like a big Raggedy Ann doll on a shelf with a china shepherd and shepherdess. I'd never noticed before just how much my mother had to crook her neck to talk to my dad, to dance with him. Next to Ira, she finally seemed to be in the proper scale. This made me uncomfortable somehow.

"I made it home, but I'm going back tomorrow." My mother hadn't known about my imminent redeparture, but she barely blinked.

"Well, you're fighting the good fight up there, I hear," he said, with the mildness of someone who didn't need to tout his political opinions. A rarity in this town.

"So you still believe in the good old cause of labor?" I said. "A lot of people get in my face when they hear I work for unions."

"Oh, please," he said. "My mother almost named me Eugene, after Eugene Debs. My sister is Emma, after Emma Goldman."

"My second-grade diorama depicted the martyrdom of Sacco and Vanzetti," I said proudly. "Right down to the little electric chairs."

"She was awfully morbid as a child," my mother said, giving me a look that I didn't at first recognize. And then I realized that it was the same look I used to give her when she'd hang around the living room making polite chat when I had a date. I retreated to the kitchen, a little dazed.

Louise was in there nursing her tea and listening to a tape of Hub's last concert.

"His music never ceases to amaze me," she said. "It's so fresh, so completely original."

That it *was* music, I had to take on faith. I am not a big admirer of the school of vocal artists that includes Neil Young and Bob Dylan, but I will admit that at its best, it signifies something, even if I don't understand precisely what. Hub's stuff was a feeble imitation of those guys, his vocals reedy and thin, almost lost in the feeble, folksy guitar chords. No matter how nasty the words of Hub's songs were, his voice just ambled plaintively on, like a cat mewling persistently outside a bedroom window at three in the morning.

> The storm blows on
> And I'm out your door
> Leaving you there
> Like a cast-off whore
> Like a broken doll
> In a sewer drain
> Like a squirrel crushed on asphalt
> In the rain.

The squirrel song was followed by one called "Nuclear Winter," a departure from Hub's usual style, which consisted solely of his instrument making an effect like a tortured sitar.

"He has a real talent," I said to Louise. I did not say what I felt the real talent was for, so I wasn't lying.

"He'll never sell out, either. They wanted one of his early songs for a commercial for children's vitamins, but he wouldn't do it."

I reflected silently that it is easy not to sell out when you know where your next forty years of meals are coming from.

"You think he's a spoiled rich kid," said Louise. "I know Johnny does too."

"Rich doesn't mean spoiled," I said. "Not always."

But the truth was, I much preferred someone who'd had to scheme and compromise to make it, like Ron, to a stickler like Hub, who had pristine artistic values paid for with someone else's money. I knew that Ron was a fast-talking sleazeball who would be distracted by a waterfront real estate opportunity on his way to save a drowning man. It didn't matter. Whatever marginal virtue Ron possessed, he'd earned every scrap of it.

"And you and Tony?" said Louise, as the last song on Hub's tape skidded to a close. "How's that going?"

"Me and Tony, nothing." I told her about Suzanne.

"She sounds kind of coy and disingenuous. Tony was never coy. He may be too chicken to bring up the past with you, but he's not coy."

"The past is the past. He's moved on to a more sophisticated type."

"Well, that *really* doesn't sound like Tony. I've seen the man eat barbecue, and Roger Moore he's not."

"Hey, I'm happy for him. I'm glad he's found someone who'll think it's sexy and appealing when he rushes off in the middle of her birthday dinner to take a phone call from a disgruntled street cleaner in Toilers Local 102073."

"This Suzanne sounds so scripted. So phony."

"Tony doesn't think so. You know how flattering it can be when someone who's not your type suddenly goes after you."

"Not that you're jealous," said Louise.

"Tony could make mad passionate love to her on the conference table for all I care. He could ravish her on my desk. I would just pull my blotter out from under them so they wouldn't mess it up."

"Sure," said Louise. "I believe you. But just in case, be a little nicer to him and see what happens."

Ira stayed an hour, and when he left my mother stood on the porch waving him off. She'd never waved me off that way. Usually she'd shut the front door before my car pulled out of the driveway.

"He's nice," I said, and she shrugged.

"We'll see. It's early days."

Early days for what? I wanted to ask, but it seemed callous and cruel to spoil the fragility of new love with intrusive questions. If it *was* new love. If it was anything but two widowed people getting together for companionship. Who was I kidding? My mother was glowing. She'd never glowed for my dad like that.

She looked so elated that I didn't even get irritated at her when she said, "Were you pleasant to Jeremy at least, even if you didn't have the common courtesy to bring him in from the rain?"

I gave her a hug and said, "Ma, thanks for interfering."

"So it did go well?"

"Not really," I said. "But thanks for interfering anyway, Ma."

She squinted at me, thinking that I was being sarcastic. Then she grinned, the wicked grin so like Joey's but so rare in her that I forgot that's where Joey gets it, and said, "Any time, my Dominica. Any time."

16

Ron had said, untypically, he didn't need to see me before I went back to Winsack. Suspecting I didn't know what, I came by the office before catching an afternoon flight to Providence. I knew he'd be there. No one at Advocacy, Inc. took the day after Thanksgiving off. The weeks before Christmas were too crowded and hectic.

He'd instructed our secretary, Myrlene, to tell me he was too swamped to "take a meeting" with me, so I simply strolled in and sat on his desk, planting my butt on the stack of client proposals and contracts he was going through.

"Did Weingould approve the PR budget for St. Francis for December, Ron?"

"He's still dickering over it."

"He's had that budget on his desk for over a week."

Ron said, "We heard this morning that the hospital has Finchley and Crouse on board."

Bad news. Finchley and Crouse was the granddaddy of the union-busting law firms. They could shut down an organizing drive or scuttle a strike faster than you could say "unfair labor practice." Finchley and Crouse specialized in nastiness.

Who could forget the union organizing drive a few years ago at Humstock Canning, where F & C had come in quite late in the day? The union's vote was assessed at 80 percent of the unit, and the guys from Finchley had taken the whole thing apart by starting a rumor that if the union won, Humstock was going to close its operation in Wisconsin and set up shop in Mexico. They also started a rumor that the local union president was sleeping with his wife's sister *and* his seventeen-year-old baby-sitter. They bugged the employee break room. They even circulated a phony copy of the cannery's supposed agreement with the Mexican concern. A load of malarkey, but these were people who'd staked their lives on working for this company until the day they retired, and once Finchley started in to scare them, the fear spread like brushfire.

The union lost by only fifty votes, a real heartbreaker. They could have challenged the election results, but a runoff would only have given Finchley and Crouse time to get even more creative, so the organizers folded their tents and planned to return another day. Five years later, the patriarch of the Humstock family died of a heart attack while in bed with the Humstock mailboy. In the chaos of transition, and with a much more liberal son of the family in charge, the union tried again and won.

Humstock was a rare happy ending for a case in which F & C had figured. To stand a chance, we'd have to come back at these guys with all the firepower we had.

"Ron, we've got to get Weingould to approve that budget and maintain the overall level of funding. We have to turn up the heat. Those nurses can't stay out forever."

"The hospital said it might be willing to call in a federal mediator."

"You know as well as I do that that's a classic Finchley tactic. They'll tell management to go into mediation and offer something completely unacceptable, and then, when our side turns it down, the hospital will announce that the nurses aren't open to reaching an agreement. Why is Weingould sitting on this money?"

"Weingould's got a case of cold feet. He had a bad November. Now he's nitpicking everything I show him. He nixed the billboard, by the way."

"But he loved the billboard."

It had been Kate's idea: a large billboard she'd noticed a quarter mile from the hospital was currently blank. She'd hunted around and found out we could get it cheap. It would feature only a black-and-white photo of a young nurse cradling a newborn with absorbed protectiveness and the slogan: "For our patients. For our community. For our future. St. Francis nurses." No number to call, no mention of the strike. Just a reminder of who our nurses were and why they were out there.

"Weingould's getting pressure from Goreman to scale back finan-cial support," Ron said. "Goreman's getting some sort of inside infor-mation on the strike, from that waste of space Hamner, I'm sure, and Goreman's not pleased with our progress. And then there was the recent unpleasantness."

"What unpleasantness?"

"I thought you'd have heard through Boltanski."

"We're not exactly close, Ron."

"Well, last week, Goreman's executive assistant, you know, that little prick who wears the different suspenders every day, caught some of Weingould's staff in the lunchroom with that cardboard life-size fig-ure of Goreman."

"The one people had their pictures taken with at the Honolulu convention for a dollar, to benefit the political action fund."

It had been Ron's idea, an unexpected success.

"What happened was, Weingould's guys had this figure propped up in a corner of the lunchroom and were throwing food at it for fun, and one of them came up with this song, to the tune of the *Hawaii Five-O* theme."

"Sing it for me. I could use a laugh."

Ron cleared his throat and sang in the agreeable bass that had won him the role of Judd in *Oklahoma!* the spring of his senior year of high school:

> *His name is Jerry Goreman*
> *He's a union man*
> *Fighting for the memmmmm-bers*
> *He does the best he can*
> *THROWS crumbs to the oppressed and poor*
> *FROM his penthouse on the ninth floor*
> *That's Grief Goreman*
> *That's our union man.*

I snickered. Goreman was nicknamed "Grief" because of his habit of showing up to speak at members' funerals and then forgetting the name of the deceased.

"So," said Ron, "after Goreman heard the story from his little stool pigeon, he hightailed it down to Weingould's office and they had a big blowout, yelling and doors slamming and everything. And now Goreman is trying to make Weingould's life as miserable as possible."

"They've had dust-ups before, right? They always go back to their armed truce."

"Eventually. But in the meantime, Weingould doesn't want to go out on a limb for anybody."

"Are you saying that the national is no longer willing to give this strike its full backing?"

"Let's just say they're taking a wait-and-see approach."

"Are you going to push for us, Ron?"

"It's not my role to tell the client what to do," said Ron sanctimoniously.

"You tell clients what to do all the time. If anyone can stiffen Weingould's resolve, it's you, Ron. He actually listens to you."

"Nicky, I've pointed out before, you tend to get too emotionally involved in these campaigns."

"Listen. This Christmas season, while you're attending Kennedy Center benefits, I'm going to be up there in Depressionville, Rhode Island, freezing my tail off for what happens, incidentally, to be a very good cause. You owe me. You owe me big."

"What can I do, Nicky? It's out of my hands."

"Point out to Weingould that every union in the country that organizes nurses, every health care conglomerate, every hospital CEO, is watching this strike. We made the front page of the *Boston Globe* yesterday, remember?"

"Holidays are always slow news days."

"Ron, if Weingould cuts us off now, every hospital the Toilers go after in the future will be able to shut down the organizing drive with one flyer about how we hung the St. Francis nurses out to dry."

I could hear the soft "tucka-tucka" noise Ron's tongue makes on his teeth when he's mulling over a decision. I wanted to slap him.

"Ron! If this thing fizzles, you know who Weingould's going to blame, no matter what he's done or not done himself."

He leaned back in the two-thousand-dollar executive swivel chair

Dana had gotten him for his last birthday, his eyes closed, doing his usual reptilian weighing of his own self-interest. You couldn't even call it a thought process.

"I'll see what I can do," said Ron. "You have to remember, Weingould is in a very delicate position right now. If he pushes Goreman too far, there'll be a pitched political battle and Weingould could wind up losing. Not just this issue. Losing his job. His job is everything to him. Where's he going to go at his age?"

"I sympathize, Ron, believe me. But there are two hundred people in Winsack with a lot fewer options than Weingould has, counting on their union to stand in back of them."

I gazed at him soulfully, trying to convey that only his big, strong shoulders stood between the Mexican army and the women and children in the Alamo.

"I'll think about it," said Ron. "And now leave me alone. I have two proposals to write. Someone has to make us money while you're off being noble. I barely have time for lunch anymore."

He didn't look like he was starving to me. Ron always put on eight pounds over the holidays, then had them bullied off by Dana and a trainer in January.

"Aren't you going to fill me in on what you and Wendy have been up to with my other accounts?"

"Another time," he said, shuffling through his papers.

Was it possible his conscience was troubling him, that I'd roused it to a flicker of life? Yeah, right. That'd be the day. And my mother was at home right now feeling guilty about all the times she'd been too hard on me.

On my way out, I looked for Wendy. Her office was empty, though I saw she had acquired a new desk. A desk that was larger than mine, actually. A desk made of polished blond wood. My desk was constructed of low-grade, office-furniture steel with shallow, barely useful drawers. Wendy had also lugged in a tiny potted Christmas tree and hung it with white fairy lights and blown-glass globes. I thought of the two brownish sticks that passed for plant life in my office, and wondered why I could never achieve the sort of work environment I'd seen other women put together, those homey, welcoming sanctuaries with family photos, framed art, and wall calendars from museum shops.

I finally spotted my assistant rushing down the hallway, leafing through her executive-style folder as she walked, like some television-character rendition of a high-powered businesswoman. As befit the season, she had switched her panty hose from a summer sheer beige to a winter taupe. The taupe looked mauve and middle-aged. No woman has legs that color, so why wear it?

She seemed reluctant to stop.

"Wendy, you haven't seen my face in three weeks. Come talk to me for a second."

"I'd love to, Nicky, but I'm lunching with Janet."

Lunching? She sounded like a bridge-playing matron.

"Speaking of which, how's the Campsters thing going? Ron says you're getting along like wildfire with Janet."

She grew more forthcoming.

"We just thought of one more thing for the entertainment. We thought we'd have a table of potential campers, like we do every year, and before the speeches they could get up and sing a few songs. Something sort of woodsy and patriotic, like 'This Land Is Your Land.'"

"Is every table sold?"

"And then some. We're going to crowd the banquet room at the Shoreham, but I think the whole effect will be so festive no one will mind the squeeze."

She rushed off, leaving me with a twinge of foreboding as I tried to imagine how the little campers, some of them already accomplished junior thugs, would react to Wendy, in her Ann Taylor shifts and Pappagallo flats, leading them through "Don't Fence Me In." But Janet was happy with Wendy, that was the main thing. Face it, Janet was happier with Wendy than she'd ever been with me, and vice versa.

Wendy's efficiency inspired me to sketch out an idea for Betsey's shower invitations during the short flight to Providence. For the front of the invitation, I'd use a ragged-edged square of hot press watercolor paper glued onto heavy card stock, with a wash of pale green water-color across it, and, in the center, a heart shape made of tiny, glued-on seashells. We could purchase envelopes with a gold foil lining to match, and a tissue insert to protect the shells and prevent them from falling off and rattling around like lentils. Inside, we could keep it sim-ple, something like "Join us as we gather together to wish Betsey a joy-ous life of love and laughter." Something goopy. I knew a stationery store in Winsack that would carry the envelopes and card stock.

Only in the car did I stop to reflect on what a hack I'd become. Here I was, thinking about pleasing the "client" with a shower invita-tion design for a wedding that was going to blast the hopes of Louise, my cousin and best friend. How far would I go? Would I someday find myself getting all excited about an idea for rifle-shaped gift totes for some state NRA convention?

"I'm so glad you've gotten in" were Kate's words as I reached the strike office at 9 P.M. They did not suggest happy welcome so much as des-peration.

"What's up? How did the gala go?"

"Oh, that was fine. Wonderful. But now Tony's thrown out his knee. He's flat on his back at his motel."

"That's all we need right now. How did he do it?"

"Changing a flat tire on Suzanne's car."

"How manly of him."

"You know the woman, Nicky. She doesn't weigh enough to change the lug nut on a tricycle, let alone jack up a Volvo in the mid-dle of a rainstorm off I-95."

"She has Triple A membership and a cell phone, right? I've told him and told him to see a doctor about that knee. Now look."

"Okay, wifey," said Kate.

"Just tell me the rest."

"The hospital issued a letter begging striking nurses to return now to the patients who so desperately need us, as they put it, and promis-ing no repercussions on their mothers' graves. Then Winslow went on the six o'clock news tonight and said that the hospital would, and I quote, 'hold out a day longer than forever' rather than agree to the union's demands."

It was Finchley and Crouse, all right. They specialized in this one-two punch, this Victorian father act: first tender reproach, then stern warnings.

"It's just trash talk, Kate. Standard operating procedure."

"Maybe, but Tony thinks we need to get a press release out about how saddened we are to see this attitude on the hospital's part, since it doesn't show a spirit of good-faith bargaining and a commitment to patients' welfare. You'll have to write it now and run it by his motel. He wants it out first thing tomorrow morning."

"Fine."

Suzanne was probably there with him, putting cool washcloths on his forehead.

"There's more," said Kate. "Last night, someone smashed three of the back windows of the office."

"That could have been anyone. That could have been kids."

"Yeah, I know. And speaking of kids, Eric broke the copier taking pictures of his butt and now we're taking all our copying to that place down the street until ours is fixed. The repair guy's coming in tomorrow."

Perhaps Winslow was paying Eric as a double agent.

"Kate, can't we tell his mom not to bring him anymore?"

"Do *you* want to tell Mary that? She looks as if she's barely hanging on. She parks him here when she's working per diem at Mercy, over in Shelby Falls."

"Maybe we could just tie him up and leave him in the janitor's closet."

"You love the little darling, Nicky. Admit it."

"How do you cope with him, Kate? How do you do it?"

"I just say over and over to myself, he's only a child, he's only a child."

The Narragansett was a little better than the usual dumps Tony stayed in, but not much. It didn't actually smell of mold, as some of his digs had, and his room wasn't next to the ice machine or the coin laundry, and the stairs up to the second level were carpeted instead of cement, but that was about it, as far as any extra touches went.

I'd tried to talk Kate into dropping off the press release, but she'd firmly refused.

"Mike made dinner an hour ago, and his food isn't so terrific even when it's piping hot," she said. "And besides, I think the sight of you will perk Tony up. One way or another."

The desk clerk at the Narragansett was loathe to answer the bell that said, "Ring for immediate service." It was only on my third vigorous attempt that he emerged from a back room in a cloud of frying onions. He disclosed Tony's room number with a readiness that made me feel a little uneasy. I didn't like the idea that just anybody—say, operatives from Finchley and Crouch bent on giving him a black eye—could have this information for the asking.

Although anyone who wanted to locate Tony could have trailed him from the strains of Glen Campbell floating down the corridor. Tony liked true country music, not what he called "this new Hollywood-style stuff." During my time with him I'd memorized the words to "Galveston," "Kentucky Rain," and, my personal favorite, that George Strait classic "Amarillo by Morning." Tony also liked to sing along to Johnny Rivers's greatest hits, and would belt out "Mountain of Love" and "Secret Agent Man" in the shower.

"Door's open," he yelled at my knock.

"Are you crazy, leaving that door unlocked, Tony? Are you waiting for the hospital to send you a dozen roses?"

"I've had twenty people in and out today. I can't get up every time."

"Was one of those people a doctor?"

He was lying on the bed, eight or nine flat, lumpy motel pillows heaped around him, propping his back and leg up.

"This is just the same old thing, Nicky. I don't need a doctor."

"As I recall, your doctor told you that you should take it easy on that knee and that if it went out on you again, you were supposed to get yourself to an orthopedist."

"I don't know any orthopedists up here."

"You work with a hundred nurses, Tony. I think there's a shot that one of them knows an orthopedist."

He grunted to indicate he didn't want to talk about it anymore. Men are like that. A man won't call a doctor unless he is firmly convinced that his life or his potency is endangered. Perhaps men believe that the very act of picking up a phone to request a medical appointment is somehow registered in the collective unconscious of males all over the planet, who then send killer waves of derision and ridicule back upon the unfortunate coward who can't grit his teeth through a bursting appendix or migrating kidney stone. It's the same way about parking. A woman parking on a crowded city street will be satisfied if her vehicle winds up a foot or less from the curb. Men are engaged in some invisible, continuous contest in which nothing less than the Platonic ideal of parking is acceptable. I can't count how many times, when I was seeing Tony, I sat shivering in his underheated Cutlass while he inched back and forth, refining an already dazzling parking job.

"I don't have time for medical appointments, Nicky. And I didn't ask you here to be some kind of angel of mercy. I just want to see the press release and then you can go."

"I'll give it to you when I'm good and ready. I'm sure you'll love it. Now you answer a few questions. Has Kate looked at your knee? Has anyone looked at your knee?"

"Kate took a look at it."

"And what did she say?"

"None of your business."

He lunged for the press release but I held it away from him without effort. It was great to have him at my mercy. I was healthy, vigorous, and strong, and he was a wreck of a man dependent on my talents. It made me feel like Jane Eyre at the end of the book, when Rochester has lost his sight and she finally gets an equal relationship with him. On the other hand, a part of me hated to see him in pain. During my first winter with Tony he had bronchitis once, and I stayed up night after night into the small hours, unable to sleep because his breathing was so labored that I was afraid he'd stop breathing altogether. The shush of a vaporizer and the smell of Vicks ointment still reminded me vividly of him.

"Kate said to see a doctor, you fool. And what were you doing, changing a flat tire? Is there anything more guaranteed to throw your knee out?

"I'd promised to take Suzanne to Les Chauffroix that night and she was late getting back from an interview in Boston. She called to tell me what held her up, and of course I offered to come get her."

Les Chauffroix was the best French restaurant in Providence. When we'd been together, we'd eaten in places where you did better not to examine the silverware too closely.

"Why didn't she handle the flat and then call you? She had to know you'd rush out, like the fool you are."

"Maybe because she likes having a man around who will do things for her. Unlike some women, who know all about cars because they were born with a monkey wrench in their hands."

"Not that again. Get over it."

When we'd first moved in together, Tony had been dismayed at the extent of my competence in areas he'd clearly thought were going to be his bailiwick. I could snake a drain while he was still footling around with opening the cap to the Liquid Plumbr. I knew how to rig the coin laundry in our building to take Canadian quarters. When my mother's gutters needed cleaning, I didn't wait for Tony to come home for the weekend or my brothers to get a free hour or two; I could climb a ladder as well as the next guy, while Tony had a terrible head for heights.

His masculine pride had been especially humiliated when, on our way back from a weekend in Ocean City, we'd had car trouble and stopped at a mechanic's off Route 50. The mechanic said, "What seems to be the problem?" Tony had thought it was the radiator, but I'd been convinced it was the fuel injection line, and had said so. And had been right. Tony sulked all the way from Annapolis to Connecticut Ave.

He pulled himself up on the pile of pillows in an attempt to speak from a more dignified position, but because they were made of cheap, flattened foam rubber, he only succeeded in sliding down a few more inches.

"It's nice to be appreciated, Nicky. It's nice to have a woman say you're her hero instead of saying, 'Did you know your spark plugs are shot?' "

"What did you think, Tony? My father, my brother, and my cousin. All mechanics. Did you think I didn't know my way around a car engine?"

"Would it have hurt you, once in your life, to sit back and let someone else take the lead?"

"I'm letting you do that on this strike. And boy, you've got 'em on the ropes, don't you?"

This was a low blow. But I was furious that Tony would put his knee at risk just to prevent Suzanne from getting a snag in her twenty-dollar stockings.

"Just give me the damn press release."

I handed it to him, and roamed around the room while he read it, slashing away with a pen his brother had given him six years earlier, the clear plastic one filled with Austin's Amber Ale.

"Have you eaten yet, Tony?"

"I'll put something in the microwave."

"No, you won't. You can barely make it to the bathroom. I'm ordering you a pizza and waiting here until it comes."

"Don't trouble yourself," said Tony.

Tony traveled with his microwave, circa 1984. When he got an assignment, he loaded it in the trunk of his car and plugged it in wherever he landed, heating beef stew from a container late at night, irradiating frozen macaroni and cheese for breakfast. All food cooked in this contraption tasted sour and denatured, but Tony was so damn cheap that he wouldn't order room service. Or even stay in a place that offered room service.

I looked up Cangellosi's Pepperoni Palace in the Winsack Yellow Pages and ordered his favorite: black olives, green olives, and sausage.

"Here. I made my changes. You can go now."

"I believe I said I was staying until your food arrived. By the way, I'm not changing the press release, Tony. It's perfect."

"We sound too holier-than-thou."

"We sound like good, suffering Catholic women. If anyone can get that tone right, I can."

"Yeah, you can phone your mother for inspiration."

But he didn't argue, which meant he must truly be in pain.

I had to feel sorry for him, laid up in these dismal settings. There was nothing nautical or lightheartedly beachy about the Narragansett. The machine-quilted bedspread was a sour burnt orange with loose threads sticking up all over it. The bathroom counter was some sort of sawdust composite with fake wood-grained contact paper smacked on top. There was a chandelier of sorts, a plastic eight-armed contraption painted to resemble pewter, with "candlestick" lightbulb holders.

I sat down beside him.

"This quote from Clare is poetry, Tony. I almost cried writing it. Don't make me change it."

"Do you ever listen to me anyway?"

"Sometimes."

I leaned over so that my hair brushed his cheek for an instant.

"Your hair is in my face."

"It's nice, isn't it. You always liked red hair, you told me that once."

He sighed, and tucked a strand back into my hair clasp.

"Nicky, you rushed off before I could talk to you the other night."

"You seemed to be otherwise occupied. Suzanne must be a full-time job on her own without your having to try to be nice to me. Should I say, a tad nicer."

"You don't seem angry now."

"I'm trying to soften you up so that I can talk you into printing more bumper stickers."

"How was home? Are you going to give your Limey another chance?"

He said this lightly.

"Why should you care, Tony?"

"I care because you never gave *me* a second chance."

"*You* never asked for another chance."

"You made it very damn clear you'd never give me one."

"You know, Tony, I've been beating up on myself for years that I did that to you. That I walked out on you. But I'm getting sick of being the only villain in this story."

"*You* left, dammit. I didn't."

"Not physically. But you never gave me one signal that you'd be willing to change a single detail of your life for me."

"I moved in with you."

"What an honor. You moved in, and my place just became the new place that you left on Monday mornings."

"You don't remember any good times we had that year and a half? You don't remember that night we walked two miles to the cathedral and sat in the garden there?"

I did remember. It was August and the Bishop's Garden was cool and shadowy and scented with lavender. The Sunday churchgoers were long gone and the walled garden was deserted. We strolled among the roses, then Tony lay on the stone bench and put his head on my lap and sang "Jerusalem" for me in the twilight. He'd said he'd started to dread leaving me on Monday mornings. Of course, the next morning at six he left again like he always did, took the early flight though I begged him to lie in bed with me another hour. So much for Romeo and Juliet.

"I remember a lot, Tony. But why the hell didn't you fight me? Why didn't you show up at Louise's door after you got my note and tell me we'd find a way to work it out? If it's my fault I lost heart, it's your fault that you did nothing to make me *take* heart again."

"I know when a woman's through with me."

"I wasn't through with you. I was exhausted, that was all."

He said, "If I'd come back to you a month later, wanting to work things out, would you have even let me in the door?"

"I don't know. How can I know now?"

"You can know," he said.

"Then, yes," I said. "I was a mess. I'd have taken you back like a shot."

I kissed him, holding my weight away from him so that he wouldn't be jostled. He tried to put his arm around me, but his knee slipped off the pillow and he groaned. It wasn't a groan of passion.

"Damn knee," he said.

"I owe that knee. Would you have said what you just said if you weren't trapped here with me?"

"Give me some credit."

"Okay," I said, and then I kissed him again, on the forehead, on his pugnacious chin, on his stubborn mouth that I had longed to kiss since I walked in the door of the strike office and he shook hands with me with such heartbreaking coolness. We had kissed so long that my elbow was beginning to ache with the effort of not jarring against his poor, banged-up knee, when a muffled adolescent voice came through the door.

"Izza," it called. The *p* was inaudible.

I opened the door to an adenoidal young man who appeared supremely bored, and fumbled in my purse for cash.

"I don't have change for a twenty," he said.

"You don't have change for a twenty?"

"It's been a busy night. I can go down to the front desk and get change if you want. No one's there now, though."

"I love the security in this dump," I muttered to Tony.

"I could go to the Chinese place down the block," said the helpful youth.

I shoved the twenty into his hand.

"Never mind. Keep the change."

He departed into the night, and if the large tip gave him any delight, it did not show in his face.

I turned back to face Tony, who was sitting up alertly now and looking at me with a look I knew well. I dropped the pizza on the table and smiled at him.

"What are we doing here, Tony?"

"Let's do it some more and see."

I hadn't reached the bed when the knocking started again. Thinking it was the pizza boy returning with napkins or plastic forks or perhaps a thank-you for the eight-dollar gratuity, I flung open the door.

There was a lesson here for me about flinging open doors based on hasty assumptions, for standing there, not at all disconcerted, was Suzanne. She was carrying a bottle of red wine that, judging from its label, probably cost more than a night's stay in this lousy motel.

"Nicky," she said, and brushed past me.

She wore a pale blue cashmere coat, soft and spotless. In her other hand was a dark red leather makeup case with brass clasps, the kind

women used to carry on trains in the twenties. Behind her in the hallway was a suitcase on wheels. The suitcase was about the size of a
toaster. I assumed that the rest of her luggage was in the trunk of her
car and that she'd hauled these two pieces up the concrete stairs
because they contained jewelry or expensive electronic equipment.

"Are you going somewhere?" I said.

"Yes, I'm afraid so." She put the wine on the table next to the pizza.
"Why are you here?"

I pointed silently to the press release, crumpled under Tony's left
buttock.

"I see you've fed him," she said, as if Tony were her dog whom I'd
been looking after while she was on vacation. "Thank you, Nicky. I'm
in such a rush."

"Want some pizza?" said Tony feebly. He smoothed his hair down
and rubbed a palm against his mouth in one incriminating gesture.
The man was trusted to negotiate high-dollar contracts and he
couldn't bluff for beans.

"I have to leave for Boston, actually," said Suzanne. "They need
me back at the office."

Funny. They hadn't shown any signs of needing her for weeks now.
I wondered if she had read one of those 1950s-style books on man
catching and was at the section entitled "Maintain the mystery: when
your guy thinks he has you where he wants you, leave town."

She turned to me.

"I just wanted to review a few points with Tony before I go," she
said. "Have you finished with him?"

Tony said nothing.

"For right now," I said. "Someone will check on you tomorrow,
Tony, and bring you breakfast. Now eat that pizza."

"I'll make sure he does," said Suzanne, who apparently hadn't even
noticed my dishevelment or the room's general air of interrupted passion. Perhaps she considered Tony and me such slobs that our tousled
and rumpled appearance didn't seem out of the ordinary to her, to be
explained in me by recent travel and in Tony by his laid-up state.

A woman of more spirit might have made a stand for her man,
then and there. Certainly a woman of spirit would not have left the

room with a breezy wave of the hand, gently closing the door behind her. Then again, a man of spirit wouldn't have let me leave like that. I didn't pause to reflect that Tony wasn't in the best shape for leaping up and rushing down the stairs to clasp me in his arms.

The desk clerk was at his post, leaning back in his swivel chair and watching a special about botched police chases. He did not glance at me as I left. I could have been an ax murderer fleeing the scene covered in arterial blood for all he cared. The announcer of the cop chase show observed, "Whoa! Have you ever seen a minivan spin like that? Bad move, dude." The clerk chuckled unlovably.

In my car I pounded the steering wheel with my fists. Damn the man. After all these years. He must think that he had only to crook a finger in my direction—and why refuse a free roll in the hay with an old flame? If he thought I was a fool for him, he wasn't far wrong. Tony hadn't bathed for two days, and there he was in that seedy motel, ensconced in the arms of a scheming vamp, like Mike Hammer or something. And I still wished we hadn't been interrupted.

Maybe I was just suffering that strange malaise that affects people who have seen a love end badly. It was powerful and enchanting, this wish to rewrite history, this wish to make it all come out the way you thought it would when you first found him, when you were all in all to each other.

Maybe I'd been seeking to rescue the past in those kisses. But it didn't feel like that. Tony, in his threadbare sweatpants and his three-day stubble, his voice, his hair, his scent, his arms—he wasn't the kind of man who fades politely into sepia tones. The thought of him made me smile, and it wasn't a reminiscent smile, or a rueful smile, or a resigned smile. What I'd felt back there had been suspiciously like delight, and I hadn't felt it to this degree since I wrote that note to him and packed my bags five years ago. How smart of me to realize this, at a moment when it couldn't do either of us any good.

Any couple with a past like ours could come together in nostalgic affection. Any couple could lapse into a wistful passion for ten minutes.

But Tony and I were not just any couple, and it hadn't been just any kiss, said the side of me that does all my wishful thinking.

You're reckless and foolish and completely banal, said the guardian angel of common sense. So I drove the car back to the White Hart. I unpacked my bags and said hello to Mrs. Crawley, and brushed my teeth and flossed. I got into bed and finished the first chapter of *Death in the Air*, the next Christie on my rereading list. In *Death in the Air* a wealthy, ruthless woman is killed with a poisoned thorn dart in full view of rows of her fellow passengers on the noon flight from Paris to London. I entertained a fantasy of ordering a blowpipe and similarly dispatching Suzanne, with a spare dart left over for Doug if he didn't watch his step. I could probably blame the whole thing on Eric. Poisoned blowpipes would be just his style.

Then, because I had a long day ahead of me tomorrow, I put out the light. I was too old to be bamboozled by a kiss, said the sensible angel. A kiss changed nothing. A kiss was a bonbon, a daisy petal, a bunch of cheap ribbons from a country fair. So the sensible angel contended.

She must have retired for the night soon after I closed my eyes, for she made no appearance in my dreams.

17

"Betsey loved your invitation idea," said my mother on the phone, in the surprised tone that shows I've actually pleased her.

"Fine. I'll get going on the rest."

"I know you're busy," said my mother, with an unusual deference to my work schedule that was explained by her next words.

"Have you heard from Jeremy?"

"We've spoken a few times, Ma."

Jeremy's ardent phone calls were sops to my ego, for Tony had made no move toward me in the days after that night in the motel. He'd simply delivered a blunt announcement to all of us that Suzanne had been called away on business and did not know when she'd be returning. And everyone in the office assumed that Tony would be the first to know when she got the green light to come back.

Perhaps he'd been doped up on painkillers that night, or weak with hunger. Perhaps I'd been mistaken, and I was the one who'd done all the kissing. I hid my wounded pride and treated Tony with impersonal friendliness.

I couldn't summarize any of this for my mother, so I said, "Jeremy's trying."

"But you're not."

"Give me a clue as to how I could try, Ma. I'm sure you can think of ways for me to make up to Jeremy for having cheated on me."

"Sulking. You never grew out of it," said my mother unfairly. "That time Louise was a flower girl in your cousin Mona's wedding and you weren't, you fussed for days."

"I was five years old, Ma. And, if you recall, Louise threw up ten minutes before the ceremony and I had to go on in her place. With the dress all pinned together in the back."

"Well, don't dig your heels too far in about Jeremy. Resentment is a lonely road."

"You sound like a fortune cookie."

"Ira and I were talking the other day about how, as you get older, your grudges and old spites seem to matter less."

She'd reached the stage where she had to mention his name all the time.

"Is Ira treating you all right? Should I ask him what his intentions are?"

"I have to go," said my mother. "I promised Betsey I'd look at some Butterick patterns with her. She needs resort wear for the honeymoon."

I could picture my mother and Betsey at the sewing shop, poring over the unwieldy pattern books in search of the right flower-splashed trousseau items. Johnny had booked tickets to Antigua and reserved a "honeymoon cottage" in a complex of such cottages. How unromantic—newlywed copulation in a hutch, with a bunch of other horny-rabbit-filled hutches all around you.

Probably this was a choice made with Betsey's preferences in mind. Left on his own, the Johnny we knew would never drink mai tais on a white sand beach. He'd said a few months ago, in a conversation with Louise and me, that his idea of a perfect honeymoon was a trip by motorcycle up the West Coast from northern California to Seattle. I remembered the way Louise turned her head to hide her hurt expression. Louise would have loved a free-form, unstructured honeymoon like that. She'd have loved any honeymoon that included Johnny. Men are such stupid, cruel idiots sometimes.

"Don't get Betsey sewing up a storm, Ma. Who knows what could happen."

"I'm starting to take a liking to Betsey. At least she expresses an interest in sewing."

"You mean, an interest in getting married."

"You can't deny the fact that you were raised a certain way, Nicky. You can't escape your upbringing. You need a man who wants to marry you. You need some security."

"No, Ma. *You* need a man who wants to marry me. If Jeremy's so wonderful, marry him yourself. Better yet, maybe you can talk him into switching teams and foist him off on Michael. Think how pretty the children would be."

"I give up," said my mother. "I give up. But I only want you to have the things you should have."

"Then we're in complete agreement."

"When can you ship those invitations?" said Ma.

I would never learn. Conversations with my mother were like those basketball hoops at amusement parks and carnivals. "Sink a bucket, win a prize, three tries for a dollar," the sign would say. It was only when you walked around the side of the hoop that you saw it was a flattened circle that rendered it almost impossible to score a basket. The game was rigged with Ma, the hoop eternally flattened. Still, I'd keep forking over my dollar bills for one more try.

The St. Francis strike was now in the second week of December, and flagging. It wasn't that we'd lost support from any quarter. We had our rally, and it gave us the expected bump in the press. We had the mayor, plus two state senators, a retired folksinger, and a celebrity nun who was active in animal rights causes. Even a minor movie actor stopped by on his way to Bangor, Maine, to film a comedy about ice hockey.

The town did not forget us at this festive time of year, either. Sts. Jude and Rita had already set up a Santa's workshop in the basement of the rectory, where strikers' kids could buy donated toys for a dime each. Tokens of encouragement kept pouring in: a Christmas tree from Clare's uncle who had a tree farm in Vermont, a basket of gourmet coffees that the office coffeemaker transformed into the usual rusty water, a carton of paper clips and binders in Christmas green and red from a sympathetic office supply store down the street. The defunct doughnut counter in the strike office was still laden with baked hams and layer cakes. Outwardly, we were fighting the good fight.

But our people were starting to get weary. The picket lines thinned a little. We were trudging along out there, and the cold was a horrible reminder of what the hospital said in their letters: Come back in, where it's warm. Come back in, where people need you. All is forgiven. Six nurses crossed the line in the first week of December. Tony reminded us that we hadn't yet lost even the 20 percent we had predicted would cross, but it was depressing all the same.

There were a few diehards. Lester still stood out on the traffic island every morning, and the cars that passed him still honked and waved thumbs-up. Margaret still snapped endless photos on every conceivable occasion, so that none of us would forget these times of our life. We even managed to ignore the unsettling incidents that kept occurring.

One morning we arrived to a horrible odor and found that a hunk of Gorgonzola had been taken out of a gift basket of cheeses and salamis that had been sent from the IBEW a few days before. It had been left in bits and pieces in various hidden places around the office. Another night, Margaret left three rolls of film on her desk to remind herself to take them for developing, and in the morning they'd been pulled open and the spoiled contents looped festively over the men's room stall doors.

Seeing Bennett Winslow humming and hawing in the news like an actor who's muffing his lines, I found it hard to believe that he was authorizing such petty persecutions. Puny gestures like these weren't Finchley and Crouse's style, either. By all accounts, if they intended to scare you, they made sure they really scared you.

The mysterious occurrences seemed to wear away at our last reserves of energy and optimism. Clare was taciturn with weariness, saving all her energy for bucking up the picket line and meeting with politicos and the press. Tony's knee healed, but it still pained him; you could see it when he stood up suddenly or insisted on carrying a box or moving a piece of furniture. I had a cold that seemed to be in the running for immortality. And Kate was low, though keeping up a good front.

"How's your friend Eileen?" I asked her as we came in from our picketing shift and huddled over coffee on a particularly bleak afternoon in early December. We were soaked and shivering from a driving cold rain that turned to ice at intervals. For the past hour, it had been blown straight into our faces by a fierce northeast wind. A nor'easter, they called such storms up here.

It had been too many days since I'd thought to ask Kate about her friend. She never mentioned Eileen.

"Not so good," said Kate. "She went home for a week, but now she's coughing and rasping and they put her back in the hospital, in case of pneumonia. The pain meds make her pretty woozy. Sometimes I'm not sure she knows who I am when I call."

"God, Kate."

"Those nurses up there. I don't know how they can even call themselves nurses. Barry, her husband, tells me that he'll go there after he gives the kids dinner and ask her when a nurse was last in and she'll say, two hours ago. You and I know how low that damn census is now. They have the time to check on her. ICU is a ghost town compared to what it was. And Eileen's no introvert. She doesn't want to lie in that hospital bed reviewing her life. She needs human contact."

"Do her other friends visit?"

"Oh, sure. But everyone has lives. Children to pick up from school, and work deadlines, and family holidays. If I could be there, it would make a difference. I'm sorry to complain, Nicky. I get down about it all."

"Kate, go see her. Everyone on this side would understand."

"Even if they did, the hospital would probably kick me out in ten minutes."

"Is your face that well known?"

"Not by most of the managers, but my own charge nurse knows me, of course, and Winslow, and Louanne Reilly, the director of nursing."

"You have to chance it."

"And risk a scene with my being escorted out of Eileen's room by security guards? She's been through enough."

"You're the last one I thought would patronize her just because she's sick. She sounds like she'd get a kick out of it. And they can't arrest you. Even if they did, Clare would understand. We'd hold a candlelight vigil outside your cell window. Talk about great press."

I squeezed her forearm tentatively, uneasy with the gesture since she never invited reassurance or sympathy. Kate looked out the window. We could hear the icy rain hissing and spattering, and a rumble of winter thunder.

"We could go in the middle of evening visiting hours," she said. "Less conspicuous."

"We?"

"Come with me, Nicky. Please. I can't ask Mike. He'd do it, but he's a doctor and this is a small town. I don't want any grudges held against him when this is over."

"Kate, Winslow's met me in person. And Reilly's seen me outside, talking to the press, several times now."

"Winslow's never around that late. He goes home for cocktails at six P.M. sharp. It's legendary. And Reilly's hardly ever on the floor. She prefers paperwork and management meetings."

"Kate . . . I have no credentials in this situation. She's not my friend. If I'm caught with you, it will look weird."

"We can sneak in through the staff entrance, the one at the side, not the one Winslow uses."

In the end, I said I'd do it. I had never crossed a picket line in my life. It was worse, in my family's book, than eating meat on a Friday during Lent or leaving your chewing gum in your mouth when you went up to take Communion. But this was an undercover mission, not a white-flag-waving surrender. We'd be going in behind enemy lines, for the best of reasons.

It is almost impossible to refuse a request, wrung from awful circumstances, of someone who rarely asks for help. If Kate was asking me—our flippant, self-reliant Kate—it was because she had no other choice.

"And Nicky," she said, "can you do it at a moment's notice?"

"Sure."

"Because it might have to be soon."

The same day, Margaret announced her latest plan to raise our spirits.

"We're going to do Secret Santas," she said, appearing before me with an ancient fedora in which scraps of folded typing paper were jumbled. "We regulars."

"Margaret, do they say Secret Santa anymore?"

"Oh, I'm publicly calling it Holiday Elves."

"I really don't have time for this, no offense. Give me a pass, could you?"

Margaret shook the hat.

"Everyone else is participating," she said. "You know how it works, right? Pick a name, then for the next two weeks before Christmas you do little nice things for that person. It really lifts morale. We're putting on a thirty-dollar limit. Me, you, Clare, Tony, Lester, Kate, Doug, Mary Grunewald, and Marjorie."

"Who's Marjorie?"

"The UPS gal. She's here every day, I can't believe you don't know her name. Most of us are friendly with her so we thought we'd include her."

I had seen Marjorie, and fervently prayed I didn't draw her name. She was a solid, beefy marine reserve captain with a tattoo on her left bicep that read, "Death before dishonor." She had no line of chaffing camaraderie, as the overnight mail people usually did, and no matter how lovely or exciting the seasonal gifts she'd begun to bring, she was unflappable and silent. I was, frankly, afraid of her.

"Come on," said Margaret. "And don't try to see the names, Nicky." She shuffled the hat again.

"Close your eyes and pick," she commanded.

The scrap read "Doug," in Margaret's schoolgirl handwriting.

"Doug! Let me pick again, Margaret. You know we can't stand each other. Let me have Marjorie."

"If you can't stand each other, this will break the ice."

"I don't want the ice broken."

"Sorry, no do-overs," said Margaret.

It was not motivating, being Doug's Holiday Elf. Over the next week, I showered all varieties of small gifts and good deeds on him, gritting my teeth. I sneaked out and cleaned his car after a light snow, and he complained to Margaret the next morning that his Elf had maimed one of his windshield wipers. I left a milk chocolate Saint Nick on his desk and he ate the head and picked out the sugar eyes and belt buckle, leaving the headless corpse lying there for days until Eric consumed it. The travel mini-shaving kit I bought him from the local drugstore was dismissed under his breath as "cheesy," though I'd intended it as a delicate compliment on his new clean-shaven look. Other tokens met with similar disdain. Doug had clearly had great hopes of his Holiday Elf. Ridiculously, I began to dread his childlike disappointment in my offerings.

I had no idea what I'd buy him for the big finale.

"Your problem is that you're not having enough fun with it," said Margaret.

"Fun is the last thing I want to have with Doug, Margaret. He's hardly been gracious. I heard him tell Kate that he wished he had *her* Elf."

Margaret beamed. We all knew she was Kate's Elf, actually. The homemade orange-and-clove pomanders had tipped us off, along with the découpaged pencil holder.

"I can't help it if I don't have a flair for this sort of thing," I whined.

"Here, take a half hour tonight and go shopping with me. I'll show you."

Margaret dragged me to Beach's Emporium, a novelty-and-sundry store out on the old two-lane business route that held every wish of the human imagination. It had an aisle of ribbons, thread, and skeins of yarn, another of plastic tablecloths and machine-crocheted place mats, and still another of children's toys and coloring books, some of which appeared to have been gathering dust since the previous generation stopped believing in Santa Claus. Margaret led me down a short flight of stairs into a stifling back room marked "Gifts."

"How much money do you have left in your Elf budget?" she inquired.

"Twenty dollars or so."

"You're lying."

"Okay, about fifteen dollars."

"You can absolutely go to town in this place for fifteen dollars."

Ten minutes later she had filled my basket with the following surprises for the unsuspecting Doug:

A hundred-page crossword puzzle book. ("I've seen him do them, Nicky. Crossword addicts are always running out.") A pair of Groucho glasses and mustache. ("He has a playful side, Nicky. . . . No, everyone does.") A paddle with a rubber ball attached to it with an elastic string. A game that consisted of a pocket-size frame in which square plastic numbers had to be moved around until they were put in their proper sequence. A bag of Tootsie Pops. ("He's quitting smoking, Nicky, he'll love them.") A snow globe depicting a miniature castle surrounded by a blue enamel moat. Red wool socks with individual toe holes. And, to top it all off, a pair of singing lobsters mounted on a fake sand dune (the sand was depicted by glued-on sawdust). The lobsters wore name tags that read "Clawrence" and "Shelley." The Shelley lobster wore two pink bows on her feelers.

"Clawrence and Shelley, get it?" said Margaret. The Shelley lobster was the girl, she explained, in case I didn't catch the significance of the bows.

Clawrence sang "By the Beautiful Sea," and Shelley sang "Under the Boardwalk," in tinny, Martian voices. They set me back three dollars. In total, my purchases came to nine dollars, and the owner threw in a bunch of plastic mistletoe for free.

"You still have about six left over for your final present," said Margaret. "I'll put my thinking cap on."

"Thank you, Margaret. Will he like these? He's kind of picky."

"Anyone would like these," said Margaret confidently.

Humiliatingly, Margaret was right. Doug had turned up his nose at my tin of Almond Rocha, but he was soon never seen without a Tootsie Pop hanging out the side of his mouth.

"This is more like it," he exclaimed when he opened the Groucho glasses. He even wore them to a staff meeting. He became expert at the paddleball game, annoying all of us with the thuck-thuck-thuck sound of the ball against the wood. And he took to Clawrence and Shelley from the moment he saw them, setting them in the place of honor at the front of his desk and pulling their singing strings every ten minutes.

"You see?" said Margaret. "He just wanted to be a kid again. Pretty cute."

I was taken aback by Doug's childish delight in his presents. When I thought about it, I realized that all he'd wanted was to be treated as one of the gang, a likable guy whom coworkers referred to with the words "good old" in front of his name. Margaret had seen this, but I had not. Margaret, whom I liked to make fun of because she was so mercilessly bustling and practical, had turned out to be a better student of human nature than I was. More than any other event of the strike, this shook my faith in myself. Doug's glee was a constant reproach. I began to pray, after the fiftieth rendition of "Under the Boardwalk," that a sad accident would befall Clawrence and Shelley.

Our days dragged on, full of chores and events but empty of real progress toward ending the strike. Eileen took a brief turn for the better. Over the phone, she told Kate she'd be home in the next day or two. Twelve hours later, she was too ill to take telephone calls and the doctors were shaking their heads. They weren't even promising that Eileen would make it much past New Year's.

"We're going in," said Kate, attempting to joke.

That evening at dinnertime, with Kate holding a large, shielding poinsettia and I engulfed in a bouquet of helium balloons printed with smiling teddy bears, we walked nonchalantly through the staff entrance like lost and unobservant visitors. We both wore mufflers well up to our chins, and Kate had covered my hair with one of the knobbly knitted caps Eileen had produced back in the old days.

I said to Kate under my breath, "If anyone asks, we're on the way to maternity. That's why I ordered the balloons with these ugly teddy bears instead of something tasteful."

The hospital corridors seemed the length of football fields. As we passed the statue of the Blessed Mother guarding the chapel door, I thought I saw a mild rebuke in her downward-looking gaze. We turned two corners, then a third. It swallowed us up, this place that was a world unto itself.

I don't like hospitals. I don't like their smell of laundry and urine and sad waiting. I don't like how the floors never look truly mopped and the walls look pallid and sweating, like the walls of underground caves. I don't like the food or the coffee in hospital cafeterias, with their smeary silverware and entrées left over from the night shift.

Please don't let me die in a hospital, I prayed, although I knew from one of the many studies Weingould had dumped on me that most Americans *do* die in hospitals. A car accident or plane crash came way up on my list. Something quick. Johnny once told me and Louise, in a sleepy, tipsy late-night conversation, that his ideal death would be standing in the old Boston Garden as the Celtics won the championship, with the rafters shaking and the floor pounding beneath him because the crowd would be stomping so hard. As the buzzer went, he'd sink to the floor from a stroke or heart attack, and that would be it.

Louise had nothing to contribute to this discussion, as she rarely worried about death. "I figure I'll go on, in some capacity," she said.

"Well, doesn't it matter to you in which capacity?" I said. "Do you care if you're formless ether? Or what if you're reincarnated in some terrible place like Calcutta or Boise, Idaho?"

"I'm not picky about the details. I'll think I'll still be myself in some sense."

If you asked me, Louise's happy-go-lucky faith that she'd arrive, identity intact, in the world to come was akin to trusting an airline to get your luggage to the right place on a trip with two short connections. Her belief in the afterlife was based on various fuzzy psychic experiences of her own, and the assurances of wacko chums who were allegedly in constant touch with the departed. An AT&T operator would have better success connecting with the dead than Louise's importunate friends, who were bound to offend the spirits since they certainly got on the nerves of those still among the living.

Yet Louise's *own* contacts with the beyond did offer strange comfort. A few months after my father's passing, she related to me that she'd had a dream the night after his death in which he was standing in her living room trying to remember the third verse of "Kubla Khan."

Louise was convinced that the dream was a message from my father on his way to the next astral plane. All well and good, but what in this world or the next was my father trying to convey? In life, the only poetry he'd known by heart was "The Highwayman" and "Casey at the Bat."

Kate nudged me in the ribs. There, tapping down the hall toward us, was Louanne Reilly, the director of nursing. She was dressed like a bank director, of course. The nubbly sweater and grandmotherly pearl brooch of her television interviews were nowhere in evidence. Louanne was sporting what was either an Armani suit or an expensive knockoff, and a pair of killer Ferragamos. Sadly, she had actually looked more attractive in her grandma clothes; the sharp, perfect lines of her severely tailored jacket only emphasized the grooves worn by stress and ill-temper around her mouth. She'd have done better "with a little softness around her face," my mother would have said.

Kate buried her nose in the poinsettias as if enjoying their nonexistent scent and I allowed the balloons to rise up around me a few inches. Reilly strode past us without a blink. In the elevator, we stood shoulder to shoulder, giggling. I felt daring and triumphant, like a member of the French Resistance.

On Level Three, two floors from our destination, the ponderous doors opened and Bennett Winslow stepped in. Kate stiffened next to me and moved back. The elevator was long and cavernous, as hospital elevators are, and the acoustics were such that we could hear Winslow humming "Begin the Beguine" under his breath. He unearthed a tin of hoarhound cough drops from his pocket and unwrapped one. A fusty, molasses smell filled the elevator. Winslow seemed to take in our presence only as fellow passengers. I blessed the convention that one never makes direct eye contact in an elevator.

It seemed we should have shot up twenty floors in the time it took to reach the ICU. When we arrived, finally, Winslow stepped aside and put out a hand to ensure the door stayed open, with the rather florid chivalry that seemed to be second nature to him. We were still behind him, steeling ourselves to walk past, when he said quietly, "I hope your friend feels better, Kate. If anyone gives you any trouble, have them call me."

Kate stopped dead in her tracks.

"Come on," I said, pushing her forward. As the doors shut, I turned around and raised my hand discreetly to Winslow in acknowledgment. He raised his own hand in return.

I stayed in the room just long enough to see Eileen's face when she perceived Kate, the delight that shone through the immense exhaustion.

"Katie," she said, and held out her hands.

To Kate, who remembered the lovely, rambunctious woman Eileen had been before her illness, the change in her friend after an absence of weeks must have been a shock. If Kate had had any slight hopes of an improvement before, Eileen's colorless face against the gray hospital pillows, the thinness of her shoulders visible through the chenille robe she was wearing, the translucence of her skin, all gave Kate an answer. Only her friend's eyes, huge brown eyes full of humor, resembled the face in the photos Kate had shown me.

I left them alone together and retreated to the floor lobby, where I leafed through old *Time* magazines and tried not to think about the germs lurking on the sticky Naugahyde sofa. Kate's visit would last forty-five minutes; we'd planned for her to leave with the general exodus at the end of visiting hours. Waiting for her, I hid behind my magazine and watched a few of the patients walking their families and friends to the floor lobby. One or two trundled their IVs behind them. Everyone was so cheerful. You'd have thought that they were all saying good night after a dinner party. For the first time, I thought that my father at least hadn't had to face the ravages of sickness or old age. He'd had what I'd said I would choose, that speedy exit.

When Kate came out at last, I could see she hadn't been crying. I should have known she wouldn't be crying.

"How'd it go?" I asked in the elevator, since that is what you ask in these situations.

"It went very well."

"Nice of Winslow, huh?"

"He has his moments."

"We can visit again. As often as you want to."

"That might not be too many more times," said Kate.

"She might surprise us."

"And she might not."

I wanted to go home and take a shower. I wanted to forget the sight of Eileen Grogan, so obviously once a vivacious, pretty woman, now lovely only to those who loved her.

Kate said, "I know you hated doing this, Nicky."

"Who said I hated doing this?"

"I can tell you hate hospitals."

"I love hospitals. They're fascinating. They really bustle, you know? When I get home I'm going to volunteer as a candy striper."

"I don't think that's a good idea. But this meant a lot to me. In case you couldn't tell."

I put my arm around her.

"You don't have to do that," she said. I kept my arm around her anyway.

"Don't let me cry in this elevator and have mascara all over my face."

"I'll do my Jimmy Durante impression."

"You're a very kind person, Nicky."

"Yeah. Just look at how I'm making every day Christmas Day for Doug."

She laughed a little then.

"You've outdone yourself for Doug."

"Who told you it was me?"

"No one had to. Only someone who *really* didn't like him would have bought him that corny shaving kit."

That night, when Louise called to say that she had agreed to be a bridesmaid after all, I was very kind once again. I did not say, "What in the world are you thinking?" I did not tell her how hideous the bridesmaid's dress would be. I only said, "Louise, are you sure you know what you're doing?"

"No," said Louise. "But I couldn't hold out against the nagging anymore."

"Just tell Betsey to go to hell."

"Not Betsey. Your mother."

"I'm sorry I haven't been there to back you up, honey."

"It doesn't matter," said Louise. "The dress is kind of expensive, though."

"They should pay *you* to wear it."

"Like Johnny said, it's one day out of my life."

"This is your busiest time, and here you are trying to find a place that sells dyeable satin pumps for next summer."

"In a six wide, which isn't easy."

As the year drew to a close, loneliness and family taunts pricked people harder than usual, causing them to show up at Louise's door with last-minute hopes that Louise did her best to fulfill. She even held two mixers, one for Christmas/Chanukah, another the night before New Year's Eve. (After one disastrous experiment, she had concluded that a party on New Year's Eve itself rendered the stakes too high.)

"You can still back out," I said.

"It's Johnny's wedding. I can't let him down."

"No matter how wrong it is? I defy you to say you like Betsey, Louise. That you even *like* her, let alone want to see Johnny stuck with her for life."

"Even if it's a disaster in the end, I still have to be there."

"The way you always are for him. You know, Louise, if you'd been on the *Titanic*, you'd have been the page turner for the band. I can picture you refusing a place in the lifeboats and humming along as they made their way through 'Abide with Me.' "

"It was 'Nearer My God to Thee,' " said Louise. "And you're wrong, Nicky. Don't sell me short."

"You're selling yourself short without any help from me."

"This is not my doing," said Louise. "It's Johnny's."

"It's Betsey's doing. You two are just going along for the ride."

"Some things aren't meant to be, Nicky."

"And some things are, if people will just help them happen."

"You believe that, and I don't. It's the difference between us," said Louise.

"We're not so different," I said. "You believe it, too, only not for yourself. Believe it for yourself, Louise. We're not very different at all."

· 18 ·

IT SNOWED FOUR inches the night before the federal mediator arrived for the charade that Coventry and the boys at Finchley and Crouse had planned for us. Mediation would be purely formal, a chance for the hospital to take potshots at us in the press, a chance for them to send the message that this fiasco would last longer than the siege of Leningrad if we were waiting for them to surrender an inch.

The evening news ran a clip of Clare marching in the picket line with a scarf tied over her head and snowflakes in her hair, a nice Mary-on-the-way-to-Bethlehem touch. Luckily the news crew hadn't panned back enough to show our paltry numbers. The next day there were fewer nurses on the line than on any day of the strike so far, only ten or eleven. It wasn't our members' fault. A lot of them were picking up per diem work at regional hospitals to make ends meet. Those who *could* afford to go without day work were picketing in longer shifts so that we were covered around the clock.

We conferred quickly before Tony and Clare went into mediation. After that, they'd be as unreachable as a sequestered jury—if things went well. If they didn't, we'd know within hours.

Tony was businesslike with all of us. I could see him drawing in his forces, preparing for battle at the bargaining table.

"Nicky, I think we need to issue a statement from Clare that nurses remain hopeful that the hospital will realize the seriousness of the patient care issues involved. You know the sort of thing."

"Is that the right note to sound?" said Doug. "We may need to leave ourselves some wiggle room here."

Tony ignored him. Tony had been ignoring Doug a lot lately. He could have been simply tired of Doug skulking around like a one-man

Greek chorus, predicting a terrible end to the strike. Our resident Cassandra, Kate called him. But I thought the new rift between him and Tony was more than a natural annoyance with a grumbly and defeatist coworker on Tony's part. The usual coolness between them had deteriorated to open hostility.

"I've been talking to the head of the HMO that the Winsack teachers are signed up with, HealthStar New England. The teachers have offered to pressure HealthStar to make a public statement calling on Covenant's CEO to step in to end the strike."

"A good percentage of St. Francis patients come to them through HealthStar," said Kate.

"It's nice of the teachers," said Tony. "Very nice. Although we still don't have whatever killer move we'd need to get Coventry to take us seriously. They're not gonna buckle under in Rhode Island when we can be made an example of for every other facility in their chain."

"We'll see what they counteroffer in talks," said Clare. "We'd agree to a mandatory overtime clause of no more than four hours."

"They'll never go for four hours," said Tony.

"We have to offer something," said Clare.

"I know, but they'll never go for it. They're just wearing us down."

"What else have we got?" said Kate.

"Precious little," said Doug. Kate, Tony, and I glared at him, but Clare sat with her head bowed, turning a plain silver bracelet round and round her wrist.

"We had a few other things we haven't tried yet," said Tony, pretending to glance down a list he knew by heart. "There's a rumor that the Rhode Island secretary of state is going to call for an investigation by the inspector general into the way state licensing officials hurried their review of the licenses of the scab nurses. We have Mae Carroll and the seniors to thank for that."

"The IG and the old folks brigade. Great backup," said Doug.

"If you have any other ideas, Doug, feel free to share them with the group."

"How about facing the facts?" said Doug.

"What facts?" Tony, when angry, speaks very quietly. Those who are wise don't press him at such times. Doug wasn't wise.

"We all know that Weingould and the rest of them at headquarters want us to wrap things up. I've been honest with Clare already; we've had a good run and now it's time we started talking about ways and means for winding down."

"Clare's decided to see what mediation brings," said Tony. I was sitting next to him, and saw his hand ball up on his thigh under the table.

"You know it'll bring zero, Boltanski. Zero. We need to get realistic. We owe these people that much."

"Speaking for my people, we appreciate your concern," said Kate. "But don't do us any favors."

"How many paychecks can you easily miss, Kate?" said Doug. "Your husband's a doctor, right? You're not clipping coupons yet, I bet."

Tony put up his hand and said, "I wouldn't continue with this, Doug. I mean it."

"Or what? You're going to tell Alan Weingould on me?"

"This meeting is over," said Clare, and stood up and left without a glance at Doug.

Doug's plump cheeks went heart-attack red. I'd noticed that he surreptitiously unbuttoned the top button on his trousers before he sat down for the meeting.

"Have you had your blood pressure tested lately, Doug?" said Kate sweetly. "We run a free program down at the Shop and Buy."

"Laugh. Go ahead," said Doug. "But don't come crying to me, any of you, when this thing blows up in your face."

What had happened to the Doug who was so sweetened and calmed by his Holiday Elf gifts? Even for Doug this behavior was extra antagonistic. He must have been rejected by a lady dancer at one of his contra nights, or been told by Goreman that he wasn't delivering the goods in his fifth-column activities. But surely even Goreman had to be pleased by how few strings were left in our bow. There was no need to harry and depress us any further.

"I can't imagine *anyone* coming crying to you, Doug," said Kate. "Not in a million years."

*   *   *

Clare and Tony went into mediation at four P.M. At nine I was still at the office, more for the comfort of Kate's company than because I had any remaining St. Francis work to do.

"Five hours," said Kate. "Is that good?"

"Don't get your hopes up. I have a feeling we'll see them back here only too soon."

"Without a tentative agreement?"

"Without anything. Through no fault of their own."

While she ran off the next day's picketing flyers on the copying machine, I played around with photos and copy for the Detroit bus stop ads that Ron had bungled so badly, the ones that were going to get women to drop what they were doing and make a mammogram appointment.

Wendy had e-mailed me some stock-service photos she'd scanned, shots portraying African-American mothers and daughters together. One photo in particular caught my eye. It depicted a mother in a business suit and a daughter in modern-dancer clothes walking down the steps of the daughter's high school. The model playing the mother looked proud, fond, glad to enjoy this marvelous child's company. My mother had never looked at me like that. In most photos of us from my childhood onward, she was clearly examining me for flaws, her lips pursed and her nose wrinkled with worry.

I dropped the scanned photo into a layout template and wrote a main head, "Show her that smart women take care of themselves." The copy underneath could run: "You've taught her so much. About working for the future. About hairstyles and high heels. Now set a good example for the rest of her life. Get a yearly mammogram after forty."

But the picture and head together gave the impression that the mother was about to hand the daughter birth control pills or a mutual fund prospectus. I flipped through the other choices. They were too affluent, too posed and cheery. Most mothers and daughters in inner-city Detroit did not shop together at pricey designer boutiques wearing affectionate smiles and matching linen separates. Nor did they hang around their patios on Sunday mornings lingering over cups of coffee, with gardening implements at their feet and spaniels cavorting on the lawn. Wendy had obviously chosen photos that appealed to *her* ideal of the mother-daughter bond. In the demographic we were targeting, it made more sense to don a bulletproof vest to go outside and pass up the spaniels in favor of a pit bull.

"I'm going," said Kate. "And you are too."

"I've got hours left in me."

"You're high on cold pills."

"I'm high on life and on this strike, Kate. It's the party of the century."

"Tony said we weren't supposed to stay in the office alone," Kate said.

"Tony is not the boss of me. I have pepper spray and a telephone and we can double-lock the doors when you leave, okay? Tony will never know."

"I don't like it," said Kate.

"I have to get this mammogram thing right before Ron comes up with another screwball idea. A wet T-shirt contest or something."

"If you're not gone by midnight I'm telling on you, Cinderella. And I will call and check. And I *will* know if you're just not answering the phone, so don't think you can get away with that."

"Okay, okay."

For the next few hours I lost myself in playing with typefaces and logging on to photo-library sites. I found an oldies station broadcasting out of Providence on Tony's vintage portable radio, and cranked it up, wearing the headphones so as not to disturb the sleeping residents of the apartment building next door. It was cathartic to warble along to "Back Field in Motion," "Arizona," and "Five O'Clock World" without worrying if anyone thought I was off-key. Before I knew it, it was almost eleven o'clock. I'd mapped out a few more concepts for the client, any of which would be an improvement on Ron's, but nothing that gave me that zingy, bells-ringing feeling you have when you know you've got it right. I'd let it all percolate in my sleep. Sometimes that did the trick.

I was zipping up my computer bag when I heard a noise in Clare's office. Kate and I had checked it earlier, but the office was way in the back of the building and had that separate steel-doored entrance onto the back alley, an entrance that could have been tampered with without my hearing, given my stupidity in putting on the headphones. I grabbed my pepper spray and was dialing 911 when the noise repeated. It was a cough, a prolonged, throat-clearing cough, and I knew whose cough it was. Doug's cough. I put down the phone in a rush of relief, mingled with fury at him for frightening me this way.

I didn't particularly want to talk to Doug after this afternoon's events, and he would want to spout off a few more of his dark prognostications. He was a regular Tokyo Rose, the way he seized any opportunity to try to convince us that this whole foolhardy enterprise was all washed up. I cracked open Clare's office door and called softly, "Don't want to startle you, Doug, but I'm heading out."

He had his back turned to me and didn't hear. I pushed the door wider, and that's when I saw that there were papers all over the floor. Files had been pulled out of Clare's drawers and tossed on the shabby old carpet. Her three African violets had been upended, and clumps of potting soil were strewn from corner to corner of the room.

"Doug?" I said. "What are you doing?"

He turned around. His face went slack.

"What are you doing?" I said again.

"It's none of your business what I'm doing," Doug said in a soprano squeak.

"Look at this place. Oh, my God."

"Keep your voice down. Someone might come in."

In a better-scripted life, I'd have pointed a finger at him and said, "I see it all now! It was you! *You're* the prankster!" For of course it had been Doug behind all the dirty tricks. He knew our habits and hours and had a key to the office.

These thoughts didn't come to me with any coherence at the time. There was only the certainty that Doug was doing something repulsive even for him. There had always been a reposeful quietness about Clare's office, the sense of a peaceful, orderly soul at work. Doug had stepped into that quietness and laid waste to it. Clare's photos of her border collies had been swept to the floor. Doug had rubbed potting soil into the finish of her oak desk chair and upended the small bookshelf where Clare kept her textbooks from nursing school.

The willow ware was still intact. I like to think Doug wouldn't have broken the willow ware.

Tonight he must have parked out of sight and come in the back way. He'd have seen that the parking lot was empty; he wouldn't have spotted my car because the lot had been full that morning and I'd parked around the corner. He'd have waited for Kate to leave before beginning his mischief, probably stayed slouched down in his car for a good while after she left, to make sure the coast was clear. Bad luck for Doug. His good luck had been that I'd been playing the radio so loudly and wearing headphones. Thus I hadn't heard him tearing Clare's room apart, and might have left none the wiser if not for that very recognizable cough.

Doug put his hand on my shoulder and said, "We can talk about this in the morning, Nicky. I think we'd both better get out of here now." He spoke as if we were jointly guilty of the mess around us.

I did not like the feel of Doug's hand, its hot weight through my thin sweater. I could smell onions on his breath, and the sickly odor of the nicotine-supplement gum he chewed.

"I don't think so," I said. "I think you'd better explain."

"This is all okayed. I'm authorized," he said. "By . . . by people who know what they're doing."

"To wreck Clare's office? Her cherished possessions?"

"I'm doing her a favor. I'm just hurrying up the inevitable for the sake of everyone concerned. This is sanctioned by the very top. The very top."

I removed his hand from my shoulder.

"I suppose you mean Grief Goreman. Weingould would never allow this."

His eyes flickered, and I knew I was right.

"You people can't wait, huh, Doug? Does Goreman hate Weingould that much? But you guys are a little early, aren't you? We're not waving the white flag yet. It must drive your boss crazy, the way we're hanging on. Lord, I can't believe you did this. No, forget it, of course I can believe you did this. I just can't believe none of us cottoned on to you earlier."

"God, you are so self-righteous. Underneath that liberated exterior, you're just a prude, you know that? You can't just look the other way, oh no. You'll have to go running to Tony. Tattling. One more thing you can do to try and get him back."

My cheeks burned. Doug's breath and the musty smell of his sweat overwhelmed me. I backed up a little.

"Making eyes at him at meetings. Ratting on me."

"I'm not the rat, Doug."

"Tony's just laughing at you, Nicky. He and Suzanne. Suzanne especially. She just finds you pathetic, you know that? She told me so."

I felt as if my legs were filled with lead ball bearings being slowly deposited in my ankles and feet, weighting me to that spot as Doug's mouth continued to move and move and move. I didn't want to breathe so close to him, to inhale his smell.

He was wheedling now.

"Nicky, don't drag Tony into this just to get a pat on the nose from him. It's not in his best interest, really it's not. If he keeps his head low he can come out of this no worse off than when he came in."

I backed up farther and took a deep gulp of air. For a moment I believed him, believed him completely. I *was* pathetic. The truth had been brought home to me, by Doug of all people.

But none of it mattered, suddenly. It didn't matter that I'd kissed Tony in his hotel room without any sequel, that I'd sneaked around the hospital with Kate, that I'd tried and failed to fix my cousins' lives. I was an idiot, and a laughingstock. What the hell. If you loved anyone at all, if you went out into the world with any hope, you were going to be a fool now and then. It wasn't fatal; it was just the opposite. I laughed out loud, in great relief.

"What are you laughing at?" Doug yelled. "*What* are you laughing at?"

"Nothing," I said.

"You're laughing at me," he shouted. "You're laughing at me!"

This was how he must have looked as a small boy, plump and despised, railing at some playground bully to stop tormenting him. There was a quality of despair to those shouts. What was Doug, after all, but a still-despised and frustrated kid, an errand boy for the despicable Goreman? We were the only two people awake on this whole deserted, run-down street, and Doug was shouting at me in this empty office that was really a broom closet, his little hamster hands waving in the air, his face gone babyish in its sorrow and frustration. Suddenly I had had enough of making fun of him, of making him the enemy.

"Doug," I said. "Doug, relax. I'm not going to tell anyone."

"Sure, you're not going to tell anyone. You can't *wait* to tell everyone. To tell Tony, especially."

"Why don't you get out of here? I'll keep my mouth shut. Go back to Washington and feed Goreman whatever explanation you want to. Tell him we're on our last legs. Tell him whatever he wants to hear."

He was gasping. I began to be afraid he was having a heart attack.

"Doug, are you okay?"

He sat down in Clare's rickety swivel chair and put his head between his knees.

"I'm fine" came his voice from under the desk.

"Doug, are you having pain in your arm? Does your chest feel heavy?"

I should have taken that CPR course.

He raised his head and pulled out his inhaler.

"Shut up. I get a little dizzy when I get upset, that's all. Asthma, nothing else."

I picked up his wrist to take his pulse, though I wasn't sure how. He flung my hand away.

"For heaven's sake, leave me alone. You terrible woman."

"But I gave you those lobsters," I said stupidly.

"That was you? I thought it was Margaret. There was no one else who would have . . ."

He rolled the chair away from me, backing it up until it hit the wall.

"No, me. Margaret helped, though."

Doug slumped there with his head in his hands, breathing loudly and slowly, for minutes and minutes. If an outsider had walked in it would have seemed that we were parting lovers, Doug's pose was so classically heartbroken.

Clare's carriage clock struck the quarter hour from under the desk. He raised himself heavily to his feet. His hair was damp with sweat.

"I've never liked you," he said. "You can keep the fucking lobsters."

He walked out the back door of Clare's office without another word. I heard his car start and roar away.

I hadn't finished cleaning up when I heard the characteristic shudder of Tony's engine and the cling-cling of the main office doors. I poked my head out, and Tony came in and surveyed the carnage.

"I saw the lights on," he said. "What's up?"

"An accident."

"What sort of accident?"

"I don't know."

"There's a poltergeist phenomenon in this office no one bothered to tell me about?"

He looked at me. I looked blandly back at him.

"That little shit," said Tony, with no inflection. "I bet you felt sorry for him."

I said, "How's mediation?"

"Trying again tomorrow. What were you doing here in the first place?" Tony said.

"Working. On the Detroit project."

"Damnit, Nicky."

"I had my pepper spray."

"Which you haven't tried out since 1992, when you bought it secondhand from that woman at your office."

"I could have taken him in a fight, Tony. I mean, if anyone had been here."

"You are the stupidest woman I ever met."

"I've always regarded *you* highly, too."

"Well, as long as I'm here, let me get a broom. Don't step in that glass."

We had to guess about where Clare's files belonged. She had her own idiosyncratic filing system. With Tony's help, only twenty minutes passed before the office was back in a state of reasonable order.

"I think that's it," I said.

"Give me the trash can. I'll empty it out in the big bin so no one will notice."

When he came back from the alley I was sitting on Clare's smallish sofa, which was so small it was almost a love seat. The encounter and the cleaning-up had worn me out.

Tony parked himself beside me. I did not scoot over. Let him scoot if he wanted to.

He said diffidently, "Suzanne called. She's not going to be in Winsack for a while."

"Oh, yeah?"

"They're transferring her to New York. It's a promotion, really."

"How nice for her."

"She wants me to come visit when all this is over with."

"Well, you've always liked New York."

"I used to like it," he said.

If he was trying to explain that he was all tied up with Suzanne and therefore could not follow up on our kiss, the message was coming through loud and clear. If he was trying to say anything else, the message wasn't coming through clearly enough. He could have been saying, "Our brief time in New York together was magical, but we both know, adults that we are, that it could never be repeated. Therefore, I am moving on with my life." Or, he could have been asking me if I missed him and yearned for him and wanted nothing more than to roll time back to those wonderful autumn evenings when we rambled through the streets of Manhattan without even seeing the garbage on the sidewalks.

Then he said, "Suzanne's very excited about this new position," and I decided that I had had enough of men for one night.

"I'm going home and catching some sleep," I told him.

"I thought we could get some pie at Yancy's."

Lovely. Yancy's for pie. He'd taken Suzanne to Les Chauffroix, and I got pie at Yancy's.

"I don't think I should eat pie late at night with someone else's boyfriend. Just save your appetite for New York, okay?"

He began to pace around the room, pushing at his forehead with the heel of his hand, a gesture left over from when he'd had more hair there. "Cut me a break, Nicky. What was I supposed to do, keep myself pure on the off chance you'd drop into my life again, like Mary Poppins floating down on an umbrella?"

"Of course not. You don't owe me anything. You didn't even have to feel obliged to send me a sympathy note when my dad died."

He blinked, and stopped pacing.

"I didn't know your dad had died until a month after it happened, and I went back and forth for another month wondering if you'd want to hear from me."

"They had no phone service where you were assigned at the time?"

"I thought about you a lot, Nicky."

"Much good that did me."

In an issue of *National Geographic*, I'd once seen a picture of snow-fields stretching on and on. Was it in Siberia? Nepal? That's how I felt in the months after my father's death, as if I were trudging across vast, snow-stilled wastelands. That's how part of me still felt, when I missed my father. And seeing Tony standing there at a loss for words, I knew that I had held against him every single mile of the distance I'd traveled without him.

"You could have reached me," I said. "You could have sent some message, somehow."

"I was afraid I'd call and you'd hang up. Or worse, be all cold and polite."

"Well, there you have it. Lock up after me, will you?"

"Nicky . . ."

"I need some sleep."

But I wasn't destined to sleep for a while yet. When I got home, Mrs. Crawley said, "You have a visitor." For a minute I thought it might be Doug, come to extract further promises of secrecy from me. Then Mrs. Crawley said, "I put her stuff in the little room off yours. We can add twenty dollars a night to the bill and call it even."

I followed her into the parlor, and there was Louise.

She was wearing a favorite coat, a creamy-beige wraparound tie-sash coat with a fur collar she'd gotten at the Next to New shop in

Bethesda. Vintage fur didn't trouble Louise's conscience since the minks had been dead a long time. Her golden hair was splayed out over the collar, and she'd even remembered to bring a hat, a camel-colored cashmere beret I'd given her last Christmas. She didn't look well, though. Louise's cloudless blue eyes were circled in shadows, and she'd lost at least ten pounds. She had a large box of cinnamon buns tied with string in her right hand, and her rubber inflatable travel pillow in the other.

When we got to my room I said, "You look like you're running away from home."

"I had some news I thought I should tell you in person. It's about your mother."

"Ma? It's Ma? Oh, my God."

"No, no, it's not bad news."

She took off her coat and looked around her, taking in my Edwardian boudoir in all its glory.

"Great room," she said.

"Jesus, Louise!"

"Your mom and Ira got married," said Louise in a tone of tremulous pride.

"They got married?"

"Yesterday morning. By a judge in Upper Marlborough. They're going to have a Mass, with a visiting rabbi, too. Sometime later."

"My mother got married to someone I've only met once?"

"They did it on the spur of the moment. Um, Nicky, could I have a glass of water? The plane air is so dry."

"In a second. This was his idea?"

"It was his idea to get married. It was your mother's idea to do it on the spur of the moment. I brought you cinnamon buns from the airport stand. I know you like them."

"My *mother's* idea? Wait a second. My *mother's* idea?"

"She's crazy about him, Nicky. You saw at Thanksgiving. She didn't want a big fuss. It was just her and him and me and Johnny. As witnesses."

"You and Johnny? You and Johnny but not me? The blood tests and license must have taken a few days. Why didn't someone tell me?"

"She made me swear to keep quiet. Even Michael and Joey didn't know. I think she was nervous. About how all of her kids would react. Maybe you especially. You were always your dad's favorite."

"Well, I sure wasn't *her* favorite, was I? Why didn't she tell me beforehand? Or call me afterward?"

"She said the eloping was because, for once in her life, she wanted to do something free-spirited. The truth is, I think she was anxious. She loves him so much that I don't think she wanted to wait for any arrangements at all, for fear he might be snatched away from her like your dad was. I'm sorry this was sprung on you this way. She was going to tell you tomorrow. They spent last night at an inn in Annapolis. A mini-honeymoon."

"Let me get you that water. You look like hell. When was your last good night's sleep?"

"I've been busy. You know how the holidays are."

"Have you eaten lately, Louise?"

"They gave us something on the plane."

"Peanuts. What about real food? Did you eat dinner?"

"We have these cinnamon buns."

I took her for a late dinner at Yancy's, but she hardly touched it. Overwrought from my tempestuous day, I demolished a chicken pot pie and most of Louise's Yankee pot roast. I had never seen her so dejected, so listless. Our Louise, who always had a Plan B for life, and never acted as if Plan B were a jot less wonderful than Plan A.

"Louise. Did you come all this way to break the happy news to me or was there some other reason?"

"What other reason? I figured I owed it to you to tell you in person. Aunt Maureen doesn't know I'm here, by the way."

"Does Johnny?"

"Since when do I report to Johnny?"

"Since always. Since he's driven you to the airport ever since you took your first airplane trip by yourself."

That had been for an exchange program in France that Aunt Pam had insisted Louise try when Louise was a miserable eighteen-year-old recovering from her first serious boyfriend. Louise hated flying, to the point that she'd been known to leave the plane ten seconds before the doors closed. For that trip she'd been doctored up on pain medication left over from the removal of her wisdom teeth, regaining full consciousness only on the Paris-bound shuttle from De Gaulle. We'd frog-marched her on board, and Johnny had insisted on staying at the gate until we saw the flight take off.

"Johnny isn't my keeper."

She was making a small construction with her french fries, as if she were laying sticks for a fire.

"God almighty, Louise. Talk to me. I'm your only close girl cousin."

"You shouldn't have to listen to my problems when you've just gotten this news about your mother."

"My mother can wait. Besides, she's just gotten married, not buried. Aren't you, of all people, supposed to be gamboling around with joy when a matrimony takes place?"

"I'm not in much of a gamboling mood these days."

"I can see that. You look like grim death. And stop fiddling with those french fries. Give them to me. I'm hungry even if you're not."

She switched plates with me and began making tiny Celtic-looking circles and crosses with her fork in the remains of my mashed potatoes.

"Nicky, do you think that there's just one person for everyone? That you get one chance and that's it?"

Now she had to ask me this burning question, at one in the morning after a day straight out of Dante. I wanted to reel off some confident answer, some snappy dialogue from the penultimate scene in one of those movies where the heroine realizes that the guy of her dreams is about to get away and races to catch him at the airport. But more and more these days, I didn't know what I thought about anything. In the space of the past six months it seemed that I'd unlearned every certainty I'd won since adulthood. Maybe that was what happened. More and more idols crumbled until whatever mattered was left standing in the debris.

But my cousin shouldn't be treated to this jaded view. She was a pilgrim, a seeker with a mind so open almost anyone could walk in if the timing was right, and she was hoping to hear some wisdom that would restore her faith in love. I was lucky she hadn't asked some Hare Krishna at the airport. I came up with the best answer I could.

"Louise, you know my opinion about you and Johnny. But if for some reason it doesn't work out with him, then, no, I don't think your whole life will be ruined. You know how to love, so if it isn't Johnny, it'll be someone else. Eventually."

She sat back, relieved or disappointed, I couldn't tell which. Perhaps I should qualify my soupy reassurance.

"But if you were at your business, Louise, and someone like you and someone like Johnny walked in, wouldn't you leap up and say, 'Eureka! Look at these two. They'll be so good for each other'? That's what you'd say, wouldn't you? As a professional."

"Maybe I'm not the person Johnny thinks would be good for him."

"Men don't have the foggiest idea of what's good for them. He loves you, but he's a chicken. Everything matters too much with you, whereas Betsey will let him keep himself at a remove. Where his mother always was. That's where he's comfortable."

"Maybe that's the only kind of love he'll ever be able to tolerate, long-term. Who are we to judge what people do in the pursuit of a love they can live with? You have to have love that lasts, love that's for everyday use."

"That sounds really nice, Louise, and if you ever decide to take up greeting card poetry, I will remember it for your future use. In the meantime, this is your life we're talking about. Are you going to wait to bring this matter up with Johnny until you're sixty and Johnny's been through two divorces?"

"You're exaggerating, Nicky."

"You know I'm not. Either she'll dump him or he'll get more and more daredevil, because he's the kind of person who's just going to tear around trying to outrun how bad he feels. He doesn't know any other way. If you won't approach him for your own sake, how about for his?"

"I did approach him," said Louise, shutting me up but good.

"You did?"

"I more than approached him. I slept with him."

"Boy. Oh, boy, oh, boy."

"After your mom's wedding I drove him home, because he'd had a lot of champagne. He was drunk and I seduced him. On purpose."

"Oh, my God."

"That's what I said, when I woke up yesterday and there he was. And then the phone rang, and it was Betsey, and as soon as he heard her voice he gave me this look of . . . I can't describe it, Nicky. It was a look of horror. A look that said, what have I *done*? So I grabbed my coat and ran out while he was still on the phone and headed for the airport."

"Are you sure it was a look of horror? Maybe he was just startled."

"It was horror, all right. It was like that scene in *The Godfather* when the guy wakes up with the horse in his bed."

"I think it's just the horse's head. And I can't believe Johnny would feel that way about waking up with you. Maybe he just needed to throw up from all the champagne."

"Maybe. But he didn't stop me from leaving."

We sat over the cold dregs of our coffee for ten more minutes. I was stumped. Had Johnny been that drunk? Had he been even as drunk as Louise thought he was? My cousin Johnny could hold his liquor better than any man I'd ever known. It would take more champagne than he could drink in an afternoon to sucker him into sleeping with Louise if he didn't want to.

"And what about Hub, how's that been shaping up?" I finally remembered to ask.

"I broke up with him two weeks ago. I tried to call you a few times, but this intimidating woman told me you were on the phone with reporters and she couldn't disturb you. She got really annoyed when I wouldn't leave my name."

That must have been Margaret. She thought every caller was a secret spy or a condo time-share salesman.

"I broke up with him the day I went to get fitted for my bridesmaid's dress. I was standing there, on the little stool you stand on so they can do the hem, and all around me were these wedding dresses on hangers, dresses the shop was working on. And I thought, I can picture myself in a wedding dress. I can picture the veil I'd want, and how I'd do my hair. But try as hard as I could, I couldn't picture Hub standing there at the altar, with his hair slicked back, waiting for me."

I couldn't picture it either, mainly because it was hard to believe that even for his own wedding Hub would consent to take a bath.

"He might clean up very nicely, Louise," I said tentatively.

"No, what I meant was that as hard as I tried, I couldn't picture driving away with him. I couldn't picture buying a coffeepot with him, or going on vacation with him sitting next to me on the plane and patting my hand during the turbulence. I couldn't picture any of it. So that night I called him and I said, 'Hub, when you think of us five years from now, what do you think of?' and he said, 'I never think five years ahead about anything.' And I thought, this is just not enough energy to carry us along."

"How'd he take it?"

"Not well."

"He'll get over it. He's probably already writing a song about it."

"Probably." Louise sighed. "That's the last time in my life that anyone will ever write a song about me, I bet."

"Hey, all those sonnets and serenading are overrated, if you ask me. Look at Helen of Troy. What good did it do her? And don't quote me Yeats about Maude Gonne, Louise. I might just throw up."

"Is my mother going off on a real honeymoon?" I asked Louise before we went to sleep. I was sleeping on the fainting couch, my cousin on my bed under six blankets with a hot water bottle (Louise doesn't adjust well to cold). She'd been too lonely to sleep in the adjoining room.

"She's leaving tomorrow afternoon. The Greek islands."

"I'll call her tomorrow morning and congratulate her."

Congratulate her, my ass. Not invited to my own mother's wedding. Left to handle the Louise-and-Johnny mess alone. Suddenly she was the wayward one, and I was the heavy. And I didn't like it. I didn't like it one bit.

I tried not to think about Tony's face when I'd left tonight, or about him and Suzanne roaming New York together, holding hands and window-shopping and taking a buggy ride in Central Park. Not that Tony would do any of those things publicly. At least, he'd never have done them with me.

Perhaps I should invite Jeremy to visit. Tony probably thought Jeremy was one of those whey-faced Englishmen who have bad teeth, probably pictured Jeremy as a pasty, stoop-shouldered consolation prize. I'd show him.

· 19 ·

THE NEXT MORNING, I left Louise in an exhausted sleep. When I got to the office, Margaret, Lester, and a couple of unhappy-looking conscriptees were practicing a few ditties to perk up the troops on the picket line, from a mimeographed booklet Margaret had dug up entitled "Sing Along With Labor."

"Just like a tree that's planted by the water," caroled Margaret a half step out of pitch, "we shall not be moved."

"I never got that," I said to Kate, lowering my voice so as not to hurt Margaret's feelings. "Why wouldn't you be able to move a tree that's planted by the water? The roots would be all muddy. I'd think that would be the easiest kind of tree to move."

"It keeps her happy," Kate said. "And I had to find some way to get Lester inside before he succumbed to frostbite."

"Is Clare still in mediation?"

"I hope so. She's not here, anyway."

"I need to borrow her office to call my mother."

Clare's office looked almost as if it hadn't been tampered with. I wondered what Tony would tell Clare about Doug's absence. Knowing Clare, she would put two and two together. Perhaps she already had. It would account for her sudden coldness to Doug at yesterday's meeting.

Doug's Elf gifts were still lying on his desk. Perhaps I should buy a singing lobster for my mother as a wedding present. Maybe the store stocked some for every occasion. I might even be able to find a lobster couple in a tux and bridal veil that sang a duet of "We've Only Just Begun" and "Oh Promise Me."

*   *   *

"We didn't elope," said my mother. "We merely decided to handle it the simplest way possible. At my age, I'm not waiting to see what David's Bridal has in stock in my size. We wanted to get on with things."

For the first time in my life, I couldn't imagine what my mother was looking like on the other end of the phone. I could hear how she *sounded* . . . carefree and happy. I just couldn't picture her *looking* like that.

"Who are you," I said, "and what have you done with my mother?"

"Is that any way to talk to me the day after my wedding?"

"You couldn't have let me know?"

"I told you, it was a sudden decision. Spur of the moment."

"You are not a spur of the moment person."

I could hear, very faintly, the crackle of tissue—my mother always packs her suitcases with layers and layers of tissue between her clothes, a special thin, rustling-sounding tissue. I don't know where she buys it.

"Ma, this is so unlike you. You didn't even get married in the Church."

"I'm sure God will understand."

"You didn't say that when Michael's friends had that Mass-and-barbecue to celebrate their lifelong commitment. You said, and I quote, 'I don't know what the Church is coming to. These liberal priests. No standards anymore.'"

"That was a long time ago."

"That was three *months* ago. You didn't even know Ira three months ago."

"You're going to like him even more when you get to know him," she said firmly. "We're going to go to the Greek isles for a week or so. Can you believe that? I bought a two-piece and it's the middle of December. I paid sixty dollars."

My mother was married. That was amazing enough. She'd married a Jewish man—my mother, the most insular Catholic since Torquemada—and what was more, she'd gotten married in a civil ceremony, without blessing of clergy of any sort. It almost defied belief. But even more startling than all these revelations put together, my mother had purchased a two-piece. My mother, who still owned a bathing suit with a little skirt on it.

"Anyway, honey," said this person, "we'll be back in two weeks unless we decide to stay and do the Holy Land. You wouldn't believe the packing a trip like this requires."

No, I wouldn't. My mother and father had never traveled farther than Cape May, New Jersey, on a vacation.

I said, "Ma, you take care of yourself over there. Wear a lot of sunscreen."

"I packed it already."

"And don't forget nights could be chilly."

"Ira got me a pashmina. Betsey said that you shouldn't buy one of those, that they hurt the mountain goats, but Ira said he got a cruelty-free one, and it's lovely."

Ira, Ira, Ira. She was really in love.

"Do you have your passport up to date?"

"Ira has a friend at the State Department. I don't like how my picture turned out, though. They wouldn't even wait for me to put on lipstick."

"Ma. This was so quick."

There was a pause.

"You know, sweetie," said my mother, who never in my memory had called me that, "the past few years, my life just hasn't been very interesting. Since I gave up the shop, I started to feel like a cliché, like one of those widows over at St. Ignatius that you see sitting in the back row every morning at Mass, the ones who are there because they have nothing better to do with themselves."

I couldn't think of anything to say. She hadn't known what to do with herself partly because I spent so little time in her company. Maybe that was her fault, but maybe my skin could have been thicker. To me, Ma's judging remarks had been like arrows in the flesh. But to my mother, criticism was just a medium through which she conveyed information, anxiety, possibly even affection.

She was saying, "For the first time in my life I wasn't worried about money and could sit back, but what was I going to do, learn to play canasta? Then Louise came up with this idea, and I thought, well, why not? Just for a social companion. And see what happened."

"I guess it's true, that you always find love when you're not looking for it."

"No, that's not true, not for someone your age. You should be out there. Ira knows any number of men who'd love to take you out. Gentlemen, just like him. But younger, of course. Older than you but still young. Young enough."

Great, I thought. With Ma locating dates for me from among Ira's geriatric set, I'd find myself settled down with a nice peppy sixty-two-year-old before the year was out. Ten years from now I'd be trimming his toenails and driving him to his monthly urologist appointment. Whoever said that bit about how it was better to be an old man's darling than a young man's slave had obviously never considered the varying expectations of the two roles.

"Ma," I said. "Don't you worry about me. You whoop it up out there in the Greek islands and you go on to see the Holy Land. How often do you get that chance? It's a once-in-a-lifetime kind of thing."

"That's what I thought," said my mother. "I thought we could take in the Wailing Wall and the ruins at Petra and maybe even hop over to Egypt."

"Ma, congratulations. I mean it."

"You're not angry? I didn't do this to hurt you, Nicky. I had the big wedding when I was young, and it was perfect. With Ira, it didn't matter how. And Johnny and Louise were so handy."

"Travel safely, Ma. Enjoy yourself and take a lot of pictures for me."

"When I see you at Christmas I'll have a suntan."

I didn't remind her that her pale Irish skin burned even in May. Ira would bring sunscreen and buy her wide-brimmed straw hats.

If my mother was happy, really happy, she wasn't as likely to mind what I did with my life. Okay, that was a pipe dream, but maybe she'd mind less, distracted by Ira. This concept was a little scary—as if I'd suddenly been informed that God actually *wouldn't* be too bothered if I robbed a bank or cheated on my taxes—but on the whole a great relief.

I tried to picture my mother camel-riding in the Valley of Kings, or fox-trotting with Ira as the ship's jazz combo played "Walking My Baby Back Home." I tried to imagine it, but I couldn't. Some things, as my mother had always told me, we have to take on faith.

When I emerged from Clare's office, Louise had arrived. She was applying felt lettering with a glue gun to a banner that a contingent of our nurses would carry tomorrow, when Clare or her designee went to the state house to testify before a subcommittee on a new needle-stick safety law. The law would require Rhode Island hospitals to switch to retractable needles within the next three years, and Clare had played a large role in drafting the legislation.

The banner read, "Safe Needles Save Nurses' Lives." Louise was jazzing the lettering up with some "alarm lines" around the edges of the words when I came up behind her.

"I see they put you to work."

"I asked for something to do. I want to hang around for a few days, if you don't mind."

"Mind? It'll be great."

She began to draw an exaggeratedly pointed needle next to the banner slogan, and made it drip with tiny scraps of red-felt blood. On the scene for an hour and she was already a natural.

I returned to my desk to discover that Eric had ornamented my keyboard with a large *E*, executed in painterly fashion with white correcting fluid. I spied the tail of his shirt disappearing into the men's room, and went right after him.

"You can't come in here," he said. He was wearing the same shirt he'd worn the day before, a brown and black stripe that had probably been bought at the Salvation Army. His skinny wrists stuck out of it. Suddenly, I wanted to take him to a department store and buy him a warm pullover, to scrub his little face and show him how to brush his hair. Someday, when he put a little weight on him, he'd be a handsome kid. Now he was a scrawny brat with exhausted but loving parents who couldn't keep pace with him. Why did people have so many children if they weren't up to it?

By a social worker's standards you could not make a case that he was neglected, but Eric was not thriving. Someone should say something before it was too late.

I sighed. I had been born with an urge to interfere even stronger than my mother's, it seemed.

"You can't come in here," Eric repeated. "Didn't you see the sign? Men's room. No girls allowed."

"I'm here, aren't I? What did you do to my screen?"

"I was just expressing myself."

I pulled two dollars out of my pocket.

"You express yourself by going down to the pharmacy right now and buying me a nail file."

"I don't know what a nail file looks like, Torchhead," he said.

"Ask the lady at the counter. Then you're going to sit with me while we scrape that off."

"I have homework."

"I'll help you with your homework afterward. Is it English? If it's math, Kate can help you. If it's English, we can ace it, me and you. Bring it on."

"You can't tell me what to do. Only Tony and my mother can tell me what to do."

"You want me to call Tony?"

"Give me another two dollars for Pop Rocks," he said. Pop Rocks were a rather frightening candy that sizzled and popped on the tongue. Eric liked to open his mouth while consuming them, to display the never-failing wonders of this process.

I pulled out a five. Some days you have to know when you're beaten.

"There's plenty. Now go," I said.

"I have to piss."

"You piss when you get back."

He departed with a smirk of satisfaction on his face that robbed me of all triumph.

Talks were broken off that afternoon, less than three hours after the local and the hospital went into mediation.

"It was a joke," said Tony. "We offered two hours of mandatory overtime, then four. They stuck to eight hours of overtime, on demand, per shift. That means sixteen-hour shifts for nurses at management's request. And they wouldn't discuss staffing at all."

An impasse was declared. On the evening news, every local channel showed Bennett Winslow standing in front of the hospital, saying, with the kind of shameless bravado that was a Finchley and Crouse signature, "Why did nurses return to the bargaining table if they weren't willing to negotiate? Why did they waste our time?"

Winslow was beginning to perk up as he sensed the nearness of victory. Assurance was returning to his mellifluous voice, and he no longer visibly cringed at the tough questions.

"I'm bringing them back in," said Clare. We sat around the conference table, not looking at each other.

"Another three days," said Tony. "That's all I'm asking. If we go back in then, it'll still be before the holidays."

"Won't that be a jolly, forgiving season inside the hospital," said Kate. "I'm sure a lovely Christmas spirit will prevail."

"At least we'll manage to get them a paycheck in time to buy presents for their kids," said Tony morosely. "Or pay the heating bill."

We all sat there silently and pulled apart an enormous braided rye that the Ironworkers had sent over.

Another loss for Tony, I thought, not sure I could bear seeing that.

Late in the afternoon, Eric returned with the nail file, three packages of disgusting beef jerky, and a bag of Pixie Sticks, a powdered candy in a paper straw that I remembered from my youth. The drugstore was out of the exploding confection he'd have preferred. He proceeded to spill sticky orange granules all over my keyboard, causing my fingers to smell like baby aspirin all day.

It took me half an hour to painstakingly, delicately scrape his decoration from the screen, where it left a visible shadow. After six minutes of "helping" me, he hightailed it off to the office supply store with Margaret. The only thing that cheered me up was that Margaret later reported that Eric had embarrassed her by asking loudly in the check-out line, "Margaret, do you pronounce it *clitoris*, or *clitoris*?" Margaret was so mortified that she forgot paper clips and masking tape and had to make a second trip just when she was going to sit down with me about her idea for a Christmas recipe corner in the strike newsletter.

Perhaps there was some good in the kid after all.

20

"THEY LIKED YOUR idea on the mammogram stuff," said Ron. "They think they can work with it, anyway. And Wendy had an inspiration that we'd give every woman who participates in the mammo-van program a free coffee mug with a slogan on it."

"What sort of slogan?"

"I think she wanted something like 'I Got an A+ in Breast Responsibility.' I couldn't tell if the client went for it or not."

"I hope to God the client didn't go for it. Would you want a mug that said, 'Kiss me, I passed my prostate exam'?"

"I'm too young to worry about my prostate," said Ron defensively.

"What was Wendy doing sitting in on that meeting anyway? It's not her account."

"She has everything but the last details wrapped up for the Campsters banquet and she was bored. Besides, I need to have staff beside me in these meetings. We don't want them to think we're some rinky-dink mom-and-pop operation."

"No, we wouldn't want them to think that."

"I hear you have your little cousin helping you out up there," said Ron.

Louise had picked up the phone the night before when Wendy made one of her bedtime calls.

"Louise is pitching in, Ron. For free. Is there a problem?"

"No," said Ron. "I think it's cute. I just want to warn you that I have no idea how much longer you're going to be able to stay up there. Goreman thinks you're an unnecessary expense."

"Those designer suits he wears are an unnecessary expense, with that pudgy figure of his. I don't get paid enough to be an unnecessary expense."

"You don't know how bad it's gotten over there. Goreman and Weingould aren't even speaking. Goreman is having his secretary communicate with Weingould on everything."

Even I had to feel sorry for the beleaguered Weingould. Goreman's secretary, Beatrice, was fiercely loyal, even though it had been years since she and Goreman used to sneak off for expense-account nookie trips. Beatrice had gone to one of those old-fashioned secretarial schools where they teach you a freezing, formal business etiquette that daunts the unwelcome caller and deflates the out of favor. She still called Weingould "Mr. Weingould" after a decade, claiming that it was a mark of respect.

"Ron, I don't like that mammogram pitch," I said. "It's not my best work. It's weak and mediocre."

"The client's happy, Nicky. I'm happy. Wendy is happy. Everyone is happy. By the way, I'm thinking of promoting her."

So low was I that this news didn't even depress me further, though it should have. Wendy at every key account meeting, making suggestions for upping the perkiness quotient of Alzheimer's bike-a-thons and abortion rights rallies. Wendy in the big office right next to mine, installing tailored peach window shades for that warm but energy-efficient look. Wendy pushing for a staff retreat in some cabin complex outside Lynchburg so that we could review our personal and career goals with the help of a corporate facilitator. It was almost too much to bear, but at that moment, I didn't take it in. There would be time later for cursing and throwing things.

"Do whatever you want about Wendy," I said to Ron, since he would anyway. "But keep me up here if you can."

"There's such a thing as cutting your losses, Nicky. We knew what the odds were on this one."

Louise had stayed with me three days now, taking care of her clients in a long-distance, listless way that would probably drive scores of them into cloistered orders. This was horribly unlike Louise, a veritable Sugar Plum Fairy who normally loved fussing happily over her holiday client roster and sending recycled-paper Christmas cards to every one of the couples who, through her good agency, had tied the knot in the past year.

Every day she spent a few hours at the strike office, typing mailing labels for Margaret or playing game after game of checkers with Eric, who always won because Louise was constitutionally unable to plot more than two moves ahead. Then she'd disappear, wandering over to the public library or taking my car to the huge Providence mall. Strange behavior.

None of my galvanizing comments seemed to rally her at all. Louise huddles into herself in moments of despair, and all you can do is stand by.

Without her permission, I had phoned Johnny at home, at an hour when I knew he'd be at the shop, and left a message that Louise was vacationing on her own, but had asked me to let him know she was safe. She wasn't ready to talk with him, I said, and had given me no number where she could be reached, but she'd sworn she was fine and in good health and desired only a space for solitude at present.

I thought this sounded like something Louise would say. There was no sense in Johnny being driven crazy with worry while Louise decided what to do. If Louise ever decided what to do. If she stayed here much longer she could apply for her own library card.

I'd have worried that Michael or Joey would grow concerned about her whereabouts, but for the fact that they'd assume Johnny was keeping tabs on her. Sometimes men's inability to convey crucial information to each other comes in handy.

Clare's deadline went by, day after day, hour after hour. Tony began by arguing with her every twenty minutes, then he gave up and sat at his desk, shooting rubber bands, one after another, in a grim, unbreachable silence.

I'd drafted a press release with a stalwart quote from Clare about how every one of the St. Francis nurses was going to continue to try to provide the best care possible to their patients, and how the union would persist toward the goal of a safe and well-staffed hospital. "We are giving up the battle on the picket line, but we are not giving up the fight," I had her say, cornily.

By two o'clock on the last day, I'd done what little I could to get us press-ready for settlement. For caving in. I knew that Clare was doing the responsible thing, but I wished she'd be less mature and composed about it. I never saw her lose her temper, slam a door, throw a paperweight. It was admirable. It was unnatural.

She'd taken even Doug's sudden departure with equanimity, not even blinking at Tony's explanation about Doug's being needed at the national to chair a committee on OSHA violations in the deep-south states. Clare had probably been on to Doug's tricks before any of us. Right now, Doug's defection was the least of her worries.

I never spared a regret for our two comrades in the trenches. Without Suzanne and Doug, the office felt less crowded to me, less wearing. My cold cleared up. Tony—well, he didn't look like he was pining away to me. Perhaps, away from Suzanne's intoxicating presence, he was giving some belated thought to what life with her might be like in the long-term, a life filled with staged play readings, underattended gallery openings, and summer visits to writers' colonies where he'd be reduced to taking the bird-watching course for spouses. Odds were, though, that he was concentrating his entire being on averting the defeat that lay before all of us.

"Come on," I said to Kate when the press release had been typed and vetted and lay folded like a Dear John letter on Tony's desk. Clare had already put in a call to Winslow asking for a meeting. "Let's go over to the hospital and walk the picket line one last time."

"God, Nicky, you talk like we're already beaten."

"I'm a pessimist by nature. It keeps me on an even keel."

"You're full of baloney," she said. "The woman who still thinks this might be the year for the Red Sox. Okay, I'm coming. At least when this is over I won't have to go sneaking around the back elevators any longer."

"You were starting to get a kick out of it."

Louise was already over there. She'd been taking it upon herself to bring coffee out to our picketers once every shift, good coffee that she picked up at the local Starbucks, not the slop we produced in the office. Eric was there, too, seeking new frontiers in which to misbehave. Worst of all, Bennett Winslow was expected any moment for one of his "curbside chats."

Winslow had begun this practice a week before. He'd descend from his office periodically and attempt to make conversation for a few minutes with the picketing nurses, asking them how they and their families were doing, giving news bulletins about doings inside the hospital. The nurses met his overtures with stony silence. He'd give it the old college try, and retreat upstairs again.

I pitied Winslow. He had never wanted to draw lines in the sand or be portrayed on the evening news as the man who was snatching the Christmas toys out of the hands of Winsack's tots. He'd much rather be the guy who made the toast when the ribbon was cut on a new hospital wing, the guy who led the fund drive for the children's burn unit, the guy who had the considerate thought of taking all of his secretaries to the best restaurant in Providence on Secretaries Day. Given his true druthers, he'd probably have preferred that the strike end in victory for the nurses, so that more people would smile at him when he walked down the halls.

It was a cold day, so cold that despite my heavy cabled turtleneck, my thickest corduroys, two pairs of tights, and fleece-lined snow boots, I was beginning to be chilled, a deep chill that would still be lingering after hours inside. Soon I'd begin to shake all over with the cold, like a dog that's just been in the water. To think I'd ever complained about winters back in D.C.

"I can't believe this is our last time," I said to Kate, as we approached the line.

"Will you and Tony stay in touch?"

"God knows."

"You should."

"You seem to forget he's Suzanne's property. They're very well suited. I'll watch their future progress with interest."

Kate peered out at me from the enormous puffy hood of her down coat.

"Pride goeth before a fall."

"Are you suggesting that I should be a credulous fool twice for that man?"

"Do you have anything better to do?"

I pushed her shoulder lightly, and she pushed mine. We were giddy with despair. Up on the line, anticipating Winslow's entrance on the scene, Lester had begun to sing the old Woody Guthrie tune "Union Maid," and Kate joined in, in her croaky alto.

I loved "Union Maid." I loved how the union maid in the song "never was afraid" of company bullies, how she'd give the men around her an example of courage, how she even stood up to the National Guard. No one messed with the Union Maid.

"You can't scare me, I'm sticking to the union," Kate sang, and then Margaret chimed in, and then a few of the others, including Louise who had been taught the song at my mother's knee. I was laughing, and jumping up and down a little to keep warm. None of us was paying much attention to anything but this few blessed seconds of clowning around.

What happened next appears in my memory as a frozen tableau, everyone moving with jerky precision, like those mechanized Christmas displays in department store windows depicting elves on the assembly line. It wasn't like that, of course. It was just a series of accidents.

The mill tower clock chimed three. Louise was handing out her last few cups of coffee. Bill, the hospital security guard, had arrived, accompanied by the guard dog Punch. It amused all of us that Winslow always demanded the presence of Bill and Punch when making his visits, as if he feared these mild-mannered nurses would rise up in a body and attack him. The dog Judy, as usual, was getting her toenails polished or something. She had the day off, at any rate.

Eric had been staying away from Punch, this extraordinary obedience the result of the one-day exile imposed by Kate and some solemn threats from Bill.

But today Bill, who had a soft spot for Louise, had half turned to take a cup of coffee from her hand. His moment of distraction was long enough for Eric to seize his chance. He approached Punch with one of the sticks of beef jerky he'd gotten at the drugstore. I saw him poke the meat toward the dog, in a fruitless attempt to get Punch to jump for it. I saw Louise, a foot away with the tray of coffee, looking suddenly alarmed, and Bill catching her expression and glancing back.

Then I saw Winslow emerging from the lobby doors, stepping toward the circle of picketers on the icy sidewalk. I saw the beef jerky jab Punch in the eye as Eric's foot slipped a few inches on that sidewalk, saw the dog's growl and instant snap at Eric's jacket. Bill ran forward, but Louise beat him to it, dropping her tray and grabbing Punch's collar. She dragged the dog away from Eric, and then Bill took over, reassuring Punch with soft words and brisk pats. Punch, thank God, was unhurt. And I saw, as one of our nurses examined the cursed child, that the nip hadn't broken Eric's skin.

What I didn't see was the stringer from the *Providence Journal*, catching the whole thing on camera.

21

OUR FAVORITE HEADLINE by unanimous vote, and the one that Winslow threatened to sue over, was, "Hospital sets canine on striker's child."

It was a slow news week. The picture made the front page, *over* the fold, of the *Eagle-Gazette*. It made the front page, *under* the fold, of the *Providence Journal*. It made the national sections of three of the major East Coast papers. The *Globe* used it to spearhead a series about the modern hospital in a new era of public scrutiny.

"This photo couldn't have been better if we'd staged it," said Tony.

In the picture, you couldn't see that Eric had been teasing the dog; the beef jerky wasn't visible at all. All you could see was the dog lunging at the boy, the child's terrified face, the security guard immobile, and golden-haired Louise throwing herself between husky and child. And, best of all, in the background, Bennett Winslow smiling smugly. Winslow was smiling smugly only because that was his normal expression in preparing for public appearances. But, through the camera's magic, it looked as if Winslow were smiling in approval as a small child was attacked by one of the hospital's guard dogs.

Where we'd sat in gloomy conference the morning before Eric's bite, we sat two days afterward, gloating over the press cuttings we'd been able to get our hands on so far.

"It's Bill I feel sorry for," said Margaret, ever-thoughtful.

"Don't worry about him," said Kate. "Mike and I are going to find him something, maybe with one of the vets around here. We owe it to him."

Bill had been amazingly discreet when asked by reporters if Winslow's story of Eric "provoking" the dog was true. He'd said that the incident was "regrettable," implying that the hospital was guilty as sin of, at the very least, reckless endangerment. Clare, to her credit and our annoyance, tried to give the press the plain facts about Punch's lapse into ferocity, but the photo was so damning that her explanation had little weight. Especially since even the true version indicated that Eric, angel that he was, was trying to share his beef jerky, the precious snack of a hungry little striker boy, with the dog.

"What are the odds they're going to try to ride this out, though?" I said. "It's a minor scandal. It'll be forgotten next week."

"It might be enough," said Tony.

"We'll wait and see, anyway," said Clare, who looked as if she'd gotten her first good night's sleep in three months.

The media fuss over the biting of Eric might have proved to be a flash in the pan. It might not have affected the final outcome of the strike if it hadn't happened that four days after the incident, the feds announced that they were launching a major investigation into alleged Medicare fraud at three of Coventry's largest facilities, including its flagship hospital in Orlando, Florida. Shocking stories surfaced. High-level Coventry players were implicated. The *Wall Street Journal* ran a sinister pen-and-ink sketch of the Coventry CEO. Suddenly, the guys in suits were too busy trying to avoid prison terms to care much about a dragging labor dispute at one of smaller hospitals in the Coventry chain.

The company had billed what appeared, from preliminary reports, to be hundreds of thousands of dollars in services to Medicare recipients, services that had not actually been provided. As unkindly as the federal government views that sort of thing, the public views it with even less tolerance. The outcry over Coventry's defrauding of the elderly was intense, sustained, and promised to go on as long as the investigation and ensuing trials (or, more likely, plea bargains) lasted. Most of the news stories on the fraud investigation also referred to the Punch incident, with the implication that Coventry engaged in a wholesale and coordinated effort to harm the widow and the orphan, so to speak. Less than a week after Eric's historic moment in the spotlight, we knew and they knew that it was over.

"Back to the bargaining table," said Tony. "And this time they're going to deal."

They didn't merely deal. They rolled over. Winslow tried to put a good face on it, telling the papers that he was pleased that nurses had "finally been willing to come to a rational agreement with the hospital," but every story that covered the strike settlement noted that the agreement reached was nearly identical to the proposal Clare had brought to the bargaining table more than a year ago. Under the new contract, St. Francis nurses could each be required to work up to three hours of overtime three times a quarter, but no nurse could be required to work more than forty hours of overtime per year. The contract further stipulated that *any* nurse could refuse an overtime request, at her own discretion, if she felt that fatigue or illness would prevent her from providing adequate care.

The hospital, eating large helpings of crow, also agreed to staffing minimums that were especially specific in regard to the intensive and constant care units. A committee with an equal membership of nurses and management—an unheard-of concession—was established to come up with staffing guidelines within three months. Thereafter, staffing violations would be enforceable under the contract, with a very small amount of wriggle room for the hospital in emergency situations such as snowstorms.

The nurses also won a 3 percent raise, an increase in their dental and family coverage, and the usual "no retaliation" clause that would guarantee that the hospital would attempt no reprisals against any striking nurse.

We weren't worried about Winslow holding a grudge or permitting recriminations against our nurses by other managers. He seemed only too happy to be back in his role of genial patriarch. At the contract signing, he told Clare that she looked more lovely than ever, despite the strain of the past weeks. And Eileen informed Kate that Winslow had been stopping by the ICU every day or so, making what Eileen called "remorse visits." When she was well enough, Eileen made a habit of beating him at gin rummy.

Eric was made much of by everyone at strike headquarters. We knew what we owed him. If we'd walked back in on the day Clare had earmarked for her deadline, chances are we'd have had a tentative agreement all mapped out, with a hundred concessions, before everything came out about the Medicare fraud. Eric bought us crucial time.

"He'll be *doing* time one of these days, if he keeps up the way he is," said Louise. Even for her, Eric was a bit much to take, though she was glad she'd saved him from being chomped by Punch.

I knew it was time to call Jeremy. In the back of my mind, I'd been keeping him in reserve, but now this tactic seemed selfish and stingy. I couldn't recall my old, effort-ridden love for Jeremy. It's tempting fate to try to hedge your bets; as some Chinese philosopher Louise liked to quote at me said, "Leap, and the net shall appear."

But when I heard Jeremy's voice, his low, lovely, caressing voice with its beautiful diction, its knee-weakening, murmured *a*'s, I almost lost my resolve. His voice brought back unwelcome memories of desire, of that dark and riveting place we went to when his skin touched mine.

"I thought you might call," Jeremy said. "I read about the strike's ending. Well done."

He had never praised my work when we'd been together. The thread of hope in his voice made me feel like a cruel tease.

"It's no use, Jeremy," I said without preamble. "We can't fix it. My heart's not in it."

There was a long pause. I could hear him breathing, could picture him leaning against the sill of his dining room window, one leg up on a chair. I could picture his green eyes clouding gray as they did when he grew sad or angry. I would miss those changeable eyes.

"I can't believe that," he said. "You're too tired to think clearly."

"It's not a matter of thinking. Please, Jeremy. No more."

His morose acceptance seeped like steam out of the receiver. I waited through the silence, feeling squirmy with guilt.

"I certainly have no one to blame but myself."

"Jeremy, it's not that. Really, it isn't. Forgive me for putting it this way, but I'm not maternal enough for you. What you need is some woman with backbone who will push you around and support your career untiringly. And I don't have that kind of drive. I'm not saying I was thrilled about it, but maybe Virginia happened because deep at heart, you needed someone entirely different from me."

He said some line in French about the heart having reasons of its own, but since it always annoys me to hear English people speaking French with their blatant, the-sun-never-sets-on-the-British-Empire disregard for rules of French pronunciation, I didn't pay any attention.

"There's no question," I said, though I didn't believe it, "that we were both at fault."

"If you insist on being generous. Still, I don't come off as a very admirable figure in all this."

Seeing him at a distance, I knew I was right about the kind of woman who would make him happy. Jeremy, like many beautiful and weak-willed men, didn't need a lover enthralled with his beauty and entranced with his melancholy. He needed a woman who'd take charge. A bossy, vital, confident woman who'd brook no nonsense, who'd protect him from his own vacillations, and steer him to the safety and security in which his easily jarred scholarly genius could shine.

"Jeremy, if I came back today, in a week I'd be getting on your nerves again."

He didn't argue with this, which was a little insulting.

"I'll miss you, you know," he said.

When he'd hung up I sat for a moment drawing cubes and spheres on my blotting pad. No, I could not fix it with Jeremy, not in this life, not as we two were and were likely to be. We each ought to get ten or twelve lives simultaneously, and in each life have the chance to live out fully every love that crosses our path. Every love.

That's easy to dream of, you see, when the one person for whom you'd gladly sacrifice other visions of happiness is not yours to make that sacrifice for. I had never stopped loving Tony, though I tried to ignore it for a while. Only with him, of all the men I'd known, did I feel that ease, that lack of constraint. If Tony and I were to part and meet again ten years from now, we would resume our conversation as if we'd spoken only the day before. If we were disguised in other faces, other bodies, in the wrinkles of old age or the damages of illness, we would still recognize each other. Always, always. In any life to come or in any future world, if such worlds and lives existed, Tony and I would find ourselves, eventually, right where we were in this one, in the middle of our endless and endlessly fascinating conversation.

You see couples like this. You see them at a coffee shop or walking slowly along a paved path at the river's edge, or helping each other up the steps of a medical office building, talking and talking. I wanted to be half of one of those couples, and I wanted to be that with Tony. I wanted code words again and secret language, midnight fights and long car rides filled with mishaps. I wanted that joyous ease.

It was December 20. Two nights before, the nurses of Toilers Local 302 had voted on a new contract, and there had been only a few dissenters, snide, discontented critics who'd always had it in for Clare. If she'd kept them on the line until the Utopian deal they demanded was achieved, they'd have said she hung them out to dry. That was all right—the moaners and complainers, like the poor, would always be with us.

I still liked Clare, and respected her, though I was less in awe of her than I'd been when the strike started. She'd turned out to be, as many politicians are, a little hard to get to know, a little lacking in humor. I wondered how that single-minded seriousness would affect her happiness down the years. My guess was that the right kind of man for Clare wouldn't be bothered by it. He would find her very inability to see a certain kind of joke endearing. Women dream of finding a kindred soul in a man, but men, I believe, are often looking for something else. A contrast, a balance, someone to hold them to one specific place on the earth lest they wander off too far. Clare could do that for someone. She would, I thought, end up with the kind of marriage people refer to as "solid." And it would make her happy.

That night, in the parish hall at Sts. Jude and Rita, a Christmas party was being thrown. It would be part belated holiday spirit finally bursting loose, part farewell for some of us, and part sheer triumph. A victory celebration complete with champagne, dancing, and mistletoe. The mistletoe was Louise's idea. Even in the depths of her own depression, she feebly reached out to matchmake. Oh, Louise. Our true believer.

"Dress up," the party announcement had said baldly, so Louise and I went to the mall, wandering its endless sterile halls and finally finding outfits in the Juniors section at Filene's. If you stay away from the teen-slut styles, Juniors can be very rewarding, and much cheaper than the women's section for nearly identical merchandise. Louise got a rosy pink taffeta with a low scoop neck and a flirty tea-length skirt overlaid with pale pink chiffon. It had a little rose velveteen stole thrown in. Thirty bucks on sale. I found a long, sinuous shrug of a dress in corded black lace over beige silk, with tight elbow-length sleeves. I even sprang, full-price, for a pair of strappy black sandals.

"We're crazy," said Louise, as we rifled through jeweled hair clips at one of those discount accessory stores where you never see anyone over twenty-one. "I buy the perfect dance dress when there's no one I especially want to dance with, and you get dolled up like Mata Hari when Tony probably prefers you in one of his old flannel shirts."

"This is not for Tony."

"Then maybe you'd better erase the words 'Eat your heart out, chump' from your forehead."

"May I remind you, Louise, that I'm going home in a few days. Tony will forget me faster than he can get his next assignment. He's forgotten me already."

"We'll go home together," said Louise. "Don't think I'm leaving before you do."

I found comfort in the thought of Louise and me on the train, reading *Harper's Bazaar* and *World of Interiors* and eating a big box of Russell Stovers. She likes the nuts and caramels, I like the soft centers, and we both leave the peanut butter crunch alone.

For days Tony had been busy, on the phone, or closeted with Clare working out details of the tentative agreement. That week, a gushing feature about him appeared in *Today's Hospital Nurse*, usually a very conservative publication, with a sexy black-and-white photo of Tony in action at our rally.

Though not as gushing as the *Nurse* article, Weingould had additional words of praise for Tony when he telephoned to express his congratulations.

"Plenty of people told me I should have gone with a bigger firm, but I told them I'd gone with the best," Weingould said in a forty-second phone call, the longest discussion he'd ever had with me. "And plenty of people told me I should take Boltanski out of there, too, but I wasn't listening to them. I have faith in that guy. I have faith in you both."

(When I reached home a few days later, I found a holiday card from him in my mailbox, one of those printed business holiday cards, to which he had added, in a sprawling script, "All good wishes to you, Micky, and Happy New Year." I helped save his butt for him against his own best efforts, and he called me Micky. Well, Ron would have said, that's what they paid us for.)

The strike victory had been a huge shot in the arm for Weingould and the union's diehards. The Toilers were now going ahead with previously stalled nurse-organizing campaigns in six states, and Goreman was putting a good face on it by attempting to claim that his leadership had supported and inspired the St. Francis local to endure until this milestone contract could be won. But those in the know were aware of who deserved the credit. Tony was golden, no doubt about it. There were even rumors that he'd be tapped to head a pending, all-out campaign to organize the strawberry workers in Sampsonville, California.

To Tony, this kind of assignment was better than a vacation. It would be dangerous, difficult, and prolonged. He would be off to new adventures, headed to California without a word to me about what had happened between us on this strike. Well, what *had* happened between us? A stray kiss? A few heated words? Just remnants, in his eyes. As for me, I would take up my life again on my own. I wasn't as scared as I'd been five years earlier, when we first separated. I knew now, as I hadn't fully appreciated then, that I wouldn't really be alone.

I had Louise, I had my brothers. I had Johnny, if he ever spoke to me again after the way I was hiding Louise. I had friends. I felt that my life was a caravan in which I traveled with these people so dear to me. Sometimes it was a pretty shabby, raggedy caravan and sometimes, rare times, it was splendid and triumphant. In my twenties, the end of a romance could plunge me into despair. Now, having survived unhappily concluded love more than once, I knew that it wasn't in any man's power to leave me completely bereft. Still, my heart, my chicken heart, was dreading the departure just the same.

It felt good to be getting ready for a party with Louise. All our lives we'd been preparing for festivities together. We'd made our first Communions at the same time, at the same parish, Louise in a simple batiste dress embroidered with white daisies, me in my mother's idea of a junior wedding gown, complete with a scratchy crinoline and a tucked elasticized bodice that left marks on my skinny chest.

Neither of us had gone to St. Madeleine Sophie's prom, but during my senior year of high school, when I'd gotten a little prettier and Louise had gotten cleavage, we were sometimes invited to formals at the boys' school down the road. Often our dates would be boys who were friends with each other, and so Louise and I would get dressed at my Aunt Pamela's house and be picked up there. I never thought at the time of how this must have hurt my mother, never wondered if she'd been disappointed that I didn't dress at home so she could see me teeter off on my high heels.

Louise and I had chosen together our first little black cocktail dresses, back when we went to the loud dull parties and unamusing receptions we thought were required of us in our twenties. It had been Louise who got me ready for my father's funeral, who'd run out and purchased for me a simple navy shift that would suit my mother's ideas of propriety, who made sure I had a coordinating shade of hose and matching shoes.

Tonight she looked about sixteen in her pink party dress, standing in front of the mirror trying different ways of draping the velveteen stole. I'd bought her a present, a fresh, sweet-smelling Crabtree &

Evelyn cologne called Savannah Gardens, so light that she could spray it on in abundance. Louise likes lots of perfume.

As I was buckling my sandals, struggling with a strap, Louise said, "I think I might take a trip."

"A trip? Where?"

"Anywhere. Maybe Central America. They say that Costa Rica is lovely."

"Who says that Costa Rica is lovely?"

"Well, I'm sure it is."

"I'm sure it's filled with mosquitoes and bad drinking water. Catching malaria is no way to forget Johnny."

"I need an adventure, Nicky. Something so difficult that it'll take my mind off things."

"How about learning Russian, or Chinese?" I regretted this idea as soon as it was out of my mouth. Leave it to Louise to meet some louche, insinuating type the moment she stepped foot in class, some Eastern European lothario who took languages in order to pick up credulous American girls. Washington seemed full of such types right now.

Before Louise could reply, Mrs. Crawley stuck her head in and announced, "Louise, you've got company. And this young man does not look happy."

Mrs. Crawley had been touchingly pleased with our contract victory. She seemed to attribute it to the nourishing breakfasts she'd been feeding me all along, and had been regarding me with a proprietary, pleased air, as if I were a niece who'd done something clever. Now, though, she looked apprehensive and dubious. I was afraid this mysterious visitor was some Coventry flunky bent on intimidating Louise about casting blame on the hospital in press interviews. One had tried already.

I followed her down to the parlor. There, among the bric-a-brac and ottomans, looking crowded, miserable, and blazingly annoyed, stood Johnny.

Louise didn't say anything. The woman who'd had such presence of mind when flinging herself between a frightened child and an angry attack dog was reduced to immobility by the appearance of a man she'd known her whole life.

"What are you doing here, Johnny?" I finally said. "And how did you know where Louise was?"

"How do you think I knew? I saw her picture in the *Montgomery County Record*."

The *Record*, a venerable Maryland weekly, included small features on county natives who'd made good.

I turned to Louise.

"When did you talk to them? I didn't know about this."

"It was a five-minute interview. I forgot to tell you. They didn't ask me much."

Johnny took a clipping, much tattered, from his pocket. The article was in error about Louise's age, the college she'd graduated from, and her present occupation, noting that she ran a catering firm. But there was Louise in the famous picture, quite identifiable, with an account of what Kate was now calling the Unfortunate Incident.

"That stringer must be making a pretty penny on this photo. It's all over the place," I said. Johnny glared at me.

"So this is where you were," he said to Louise. "I might have known. At least Nicky had the consideration to call me even if she did lie. I was out of my mind for twenty-four hours. You didn't answer your machine, you didn't answer your intercom at the apartment, you didn't answer your e-mail."

"Why should you care where I was?" said Louise, darting a glance of reproach in my direction for my betrayal of her whereabouts. "Did you think I'd rat you out to Betsey?"

"To hell with Betsey," said Johnny. "You go off, don't leave word with anyone. You disappear, which is something I've never done to you. Then I find you up here, getting into God knows how much trouble."

"In the first place, Johnny, I am not a child. I don't 'get into trouble.' "

"As you can see from the photo, she knows how to handle herself in an emergency," I observed.

"And in the second place, you had no right to know where I was. You have no rights in my life at all. Not after the way you treated me."

"The way I treated you? You didn't give me a chance to treat you any way at all. You were out of there like a bat out of hell."

"Because I saw how you looked at me."

"I think it's reasonable for a guy to look startled when he's in bed with one woman and the woman he thought he was going to marry calls on the phone."

"You didn't look startled. You looked like you wanted to scream with horror."

"Not over you. Over the situation. There you were, right next to me, and somehow here I was committed to marry another woman. It was like that nightmare Nicky used to have all the time, the one where Aunt Maureen forced her into a wedding with some faceless stranger. It was my not being free. I never wanted it to happen for us that way, don't you get it?"

"So you wanted it to happen?" I inquired.

"Shut *up*, Nicky. I don't know why you're wearing that outfit, but clearly you have someplace to go, so why don't you go there?"

"We both have someplace to go," I said, taking Louise's arm. "Unless you think Louise lounges around here in formal wear every night. Come on, Louise."

Johnny looked alarmed and desperate.

"Louise," he said entreatingly. His expression would have melted me, but Louise was made of sterner stuff.

"No," she said. "I don't think I can listen to you right now. You act as if I'm an idiot. You condescend."

"I left Betsey," said Johnny.

"I don't see what that has to do with me," said Louise, and walked out.

I had to pity my cousin Johnny as we left him in that parlor. He had a lot of explaining to do, and Louise would probably make him crawl. Then again, if a man takes a woman for granted for years and years and the only price he pays is a little minor groveling, he's getting off lightly.

· 22 ·

The auditorium of Sts. Jude and Rita parochial school was glowing with Japanese lanterns, dozens of them strung along the walls and bobbing up high in the rafters. The lanterns were coral and pale yellow, with delicate flower patterns. They cast a soft glow on the shabby hall with its liver-colored linoleum and cinderblock walls. The auditorium doubled as a lunchroom during the week, but Margaret had somehow purged the odor of stale milk and pink crystal disinfectant that hung over every school cafeteria I'd ever visited.

"I decided not to go with a Christmas theme," she said as she greeted me at the door and handed me a carnation dyed in local's signature sky blue. She waited while I pinned it to my bodice. Its size and awkward droop made me look like someone's grandmother at a high school graduation.

"I thought these colors would be springlike and hopeful," Margaret elaborated.

"It's lovely. The whole place is lovely," I said, and meant it.

The ugly square folding tables on which the kids ate lunch were transformed with pale green tissue tablecloths and simple, elegant centerpieces consisting of varying sizes of white and pink candles set on mirrors, so that the light reflected gently up into guests' faces. In the side room where the volunteer mothers usually served pizza or hot dogs once a week, Margaret had arranged long trestles of food and drink, including two giant turkeys sent all the way from Jennings, Mississippi, by the poultry workers union Tony had helped organize down there ten years earlier.

Some of the parish teenagers were circulating with hors d'oeuvres. I grabbed a chicken dumpling and a crab-stuffed mushroom. Food on moving trays always makes me feel greedy and frantic. I'm ashamed to say that I gobbled down a spare rib, a miniature quiche, and a mozzarella stick before I looked around for Tony.

"I should have known you'd be scarfing down the appetizers," he said when he found me.

He was wearing the navy blazer he'd bought for his brother's wedding six years earlier, and his one pair of dress pants, a fine dark-gray wool purchased for his first interview with the Toilers.

Tonight his dress shirt was so bright a white that I concluded it had been purchased for the occasion, and his dark red tie was nearly impeccable, except for a tiny unraveling thread hanging down to his waist.

"What took you so long?" he said. "You look like something in that dress, by the way."

I blinked. What was this all about? The man hadn't given me a compliment since I'd walked in the door seven weeks earlier.

"You, too. I never thought I'd see that blazer off the hanger again."

"Hey, be nice to me. I've been asking where you were for twenty minutes."

"Johnny showed up. Louise's picture turned up in the *Montgomery County Record*."

"Swift of him. It didn't occur to him before that she might be up here with you?"

"I might have misled him about that."

"And now they kissed and made up?"

"Nope. She's over there."

Louise was dancing with Bill, the security guard, looking up at him with a limpid, admiring gaze, one of the most useful tricks in her impressive repertoire.

"I promised Lester I'd drag you out on the floor," said Tony. "He's afraid no one will dance."

"Where is Lester, by the way?"

"Up there."

And amazingly, it *was* Lester, right in front of us on the auditorium stage, playing the saxophone accompanied by bass, piano, and percussion. A sign on the music stand read "Lester Sinclair and the Swingtime Boys."

"Lester plays?"

"Incredibly well," said Tony. "We were all surprised. Except Margaret. She met him in the music store once when her kid was buying a clarinet, and when she heard he was musical, as she put it, she went to one of his gigs."

"He plays for money?"

"He does a weekend thing with these guys, apparently. Small clubs, weddings, reunions. He brought a date tonight, too. Some woman he met on the strike. She used to see him every day on her way to work, when he was standing out on the traffic island. Lester said that a few weeks ago she started bringing homemade muffins for him out of solidarity, and they got to talking."

Close to the stage at one of the small, intimate tables Margaret had set in clusters around the dance floor sat a skinny, lank-haired young woman in draggled black chiffon, looking up at Lester with unmistakable adoration.

"Talk about meeting cute," I said.

Kate and her husband were sitting at the table with Lester's date. Kind Kate, who never overlooked the stranger in the group. Look how good she'd been to me. Her husband, whom I'd never seen before, was a large, hearty guy with a head of hair almost as red as mine, and a big mustache. He had his arm around her and she leaned back into it with the casual affection of a happily married woman.

There was such an air of earned, relieved joy in this dolled-up auditorium tonight that I felt my throat close up. Clare was there, being congratulated and hugged and actually looking as young as her age in a blue jersey skirt and top. Mae Carroll and her gang of octogenarian agitators were there, and our state senators and the mayor and the editors and reporters from the *Winsack Eagle-Gazette*, and Frankie and Paul, our landlord and printer, who might finally get paid now. Even Lester and his unsuspected talent made me feel sentimental. Shorn of his hunting cap and boots, and with a proper haircut, Lester didn't look half bad. He looked a little like Buddy Holly, in fact.

The band embarked on "They Can't Take That Away From Me," putting a little swing into it as their name promised. Tony dragged me to the edge of the floor, his preferred spot from of old. Three other couples were twirling smoothly in the center, showing off dancing class moves. Tony did what he always did, an imprecise two-step varied by unexpected attempts to spin me out and back again.

"Not bad, Malone," he said, as I corrected for his enthusiastic double twirl with a bit of neat footwork.

"You're awful friendly tonight."

"I'm a friendly kind of guy."

He spun me out again and pulled me up close to him, cradling my hand in his, holding it against his chest.

"Why the silence this last week, Tony?"

"I like to have things all sorted out in my head before I present them to you."

"Present them to me?"

"I have a clear, logical thought process. Unlike some people I could name."

"I guess we've forgotten who helped you through your taxes that August when it looked like you weren't going to make even the extension deadline because you'd lost the Schedule C and couldn't make sense of the mileage deduction."

"I'd have figured it out sometime that night."

"You'd have been chasing the mail truck down the street, just like you did every year before you met me."

"Then you'll be happy to know that after we broke up I finally went to one of those quickie places that whip them up for you for a hundred dollars. Now shut up and dance with me."

We made it through "In the Mood" and "I'll Be Seeing You," during which I looked around the room and got embarrassingly choked up, though I tried to hide it by pretending to sneeze.

"I hate the leaving part, too," said Tony.

"It gets to me. All the stories I won't know the endings to."

"I think Kate will keep you informed."

"If we can keep in touch."

"You have no trust in people."

"And I'm proved right a gratifying amount of the time."

"You talk such a good game, and you're such a marshmallow underneath."

I was about to hotly contradict this smug statement when he said, "I want to talk to you for real."

He led me out of the hall, out into a corridor with a steep stairway that led up to classrooms and the principal's office. Even here Margaret had been at work. The stairway was lit up and down with more coral and yellow lanterns. Crepe paper carnations were entwined in the stair railings.

"For all of us who didn't make it to our senior prom," said Tony.

"What are you talking about? You went to your senior prom with Mary Jo Selznak, and you got to third base with her by dawn."

"Do you have to have such a good memory?"

"It comes in handy."

"Sit down with me, Nicky."

I sat gingerly by his side. He had polished his shoes, I saw. The uppers still looked disgracefully worn, but he had polished them.

"I've been an idiot," he said.

"About what?"

"About pretty much everything."

"Go on," I said primly. I could see the candlelight flickering in his eyes, and was amazed that I'd ever thought Jeremy's eyes remarkable.

"If it hadn't been for Eric pulling my irons out of the fire, all these people would be cursing my name right now."

"They would never curse your name, Tony. And Eric gave you a hand, maybe, but you kept this thing together long enough for something to break, which was the real achievement."

"Would *you* curse my name?" said Tony.

I looked at his hands, his mouth, his hair, which was already rumpled, his irremediably scuffed but polished shoes.

"Not now," I said.

"Do you know that I love you?" he said. "I'm not sure I've made it clear."

"Not very clear, no."

"How do you feel about me?"

I put my hands on his shoulders. We regarded each other solemnly.

"Tony Boltanski," I said, "I love you, too. In spite of myself. Against my better judgment. With incredible stupidity and a complete lack of attention to what has happened between us in the past, I love you."

He kissed me. I had longed to truly kiss him for weeks, to kiss him without the hampering presence of motel pillows, bum knees, pizza delivery boys, and MBA girlfriends of ambiguous status. This night, this kiss—we'd earned it. It was more thrilling, more knee-weakening, more truly passionate, than our first one five years before in that New York hotel room. What was lost was not only found again, but it had transformed itself. Our first passion, back in New York, had been the passion of hopeful lovers, fairly young lovers who were confident that nothing within our own human control could part us. We were not as young now—though we were "still young"—and we were not as confident, and it made love doubly precious. Ours to have, ours to hold on to. Ours also to lose.

He pulled away from me for a moment.

"Had to make sure it was you," he said. "Finally. It's been such a long time."

We hadn't lifted a finger to help things along, God knew we fell far, far short of deserving this second chance, and yet here we were. Here we were again. It seemed to me that until that moment, I hadn't understood the meaning of the word "glory," because that was the only word that described this feeling. Glory, glory, and again glory.

"I could kick myself," said Tony. "I should have been braver five years ago."

"So should I. We've wasted time."

"Suzanne. That was nothing, Nicky."

"Weren't you pleased that she was so handy to make me jealous with?"

"If I was, she got her own back," said Tony. "You should have seen the letter she wrote me from New York."

"As long as I get my own back," I said.

His hand on my neck was cool and the callus on the right thumb that had always been there was still there. We kissed for a long time.

I thought I had missed him. What had I known? How had I breathed and eaten and slept, when I'd missed him so much?

Minutes later, I said reproachfully, "You've been pretty hard to read."

"The truth is, I knew I had feelings for you even before that night at the motel. Pretty strong feelings. I was a mess."

"You never let on."

"That night we kissed, I told Suzanne about it on the spot. I told her I couldn't shake you. You were like the flu or something."

"Thank you so much."

"Hey, you were getting deliveries every other day from that Jeremy, that joker. You never said a word about not planning to take him back."

We forgot about Suzanne and Jeremy for several minutes, until a stray noise from the dance floor caused us to pull apart.

"Tell me the rest," I said. "About what happened with Suzanne. I need to know."

"Don't you always?"

"Tell me."

"Suzanne was upset, but she asked me to think hard about it. She asked me to give us a little time, as she put it. She said she thought we had a good beginning to build on. She said maybe I was just carried away by memories. But even before she'd reached the airport, I knew she was wrong, and I called her on her cell phone."

"How'd she take it?"

"As she put it to me, she doesn't like not getting things she works for."

"Is she angry at me?"

"Let's put it this way. If Hatcher and Draybeck sends you a fruitcake at your office this Christmas, I'd have someone else take the first bite."

"I'll ship it to Hamner."

"So, Nicky."

"So, Tony."

"Do you have room in that apartment for me? Again?"

"I'll clear out a drawer."

"I swear I won't neglect you for my work. Most of the time. The great, great majority of the time."

"You'd better not. But if you do, I'll remind you and you can shape up."

"And, of course, you'll be there for some of it. We can talk about that later."

He started to kiss me again, but I pushed him gently away.

"Back up a second. I'll be there?"

"Ron didn't tell you? I heard it days ago. Weingould wants you for the strawberry pickers' campaign. There won't be much internal lit, but he thinks you'll have plenty of press work. He said he doesn't want to break up a good team."

"Out of the mouths of babes," I said. "Or rather, directors of organizing."

That was when Kate came to get us.

"They're looking for you two," she said. "They're breaking open the champagne."

"We'll come for the toasts but we're not staying long," said Tony.

"I can see that," she said. "I thought you guys would never figure it out."

"What are these, pine cones?" Tony said as we creaked our way up the stairs and he saw the silver bowl on the window seat.

"Yes, those are pine cones."

"Geez, will you look at that chandelier? What do you think that thing weighs?"

He had additional comments to make when we reached my room and he noticed the crystal jar of bath salts, the turned-down bed with its wealth of goose-down pillows, the candle lights in each window to celebrate the season, the thick lace-trimmed towels that made me feel like a princess each time I stepped out of the shower.

"Like any guy would dry himself off with these," Tony scoffed.

"She does have male guests, and I don't see any of them complaining. You should taste her breakfasts."

"What is this?" He'd picked up the ruffled chintz shower cap Mrs. Crawley provided, a fresh one every week.

"It's a shower cap. I don't use them, but it's a pretty touch."

"You and your touches. Gotten *awful* fancy since that Englishman. What is that in the corner?"

"It's called a fainting couch. It was to catch women when they swooned."

"Perfect for you. I thought you were going to keel right over when the waitress burned you with the coffee."

"Are you nervous, Tony? You're nervous, aren't you?"

"Of course I'm not nervous. We've done this before."

"I'm nervous. And we haven't done exactly this before."

The floor creaked as he walked over and took me in his arms, and the bedsprings creaked as we lay down together. For the first time in weeks I felt completely warm.

We were clumsy, we had forgotten each other, and almost fell off the bed twice, knocking elbows and tangling legs. We were hurrying, and imprecise, and when he came inside me, it wasn't lyrical passion, but I didn't care. Lyrical passion would arrive again in time. This was more, more than our early love, more than those few fraught nights of renewed desire that had given me hope in the last weeks we lived together. That first time, in the hotel room in New York, I had been still too full of the confidence of youth, that greedy, grabbing confidence that doesn't know that all love can end one way or another. And when I'd been on the verge of leaving him, I'd held him close to lift despair, held him for comfort but not for joy.

These moments were a passion I'd never thought to have with him, the passion of finding what was lost, and finding it not as a resumption of the past but as its own astonishment, its own delight. I recognized our gestures, and the murmured words were those we'd murmured in the past, but they were all turned golden and mysterious, like the Winsack church spires in the light of sunset. I wanted to shout with happiness, I wanted to cry with relief.

And when he said afterward, "You know what I feel like saying over and over again? 'Thank God.' Just 'Thank God.' That's romantic, huh? But I just want to say it over and over." Then I wanted to tell him all he was to me. I had the words at hand, they were coming to me in fleet eloquence, phrase upon phrase. I turned in his arms to look up at him, and he was already half asleep.

I switched off the bedside lamp and put a water glass where he could reach it when he woke up thirsty, as he always did. Then I pulled the covers over him, although I knew he would kick them off sometime in the night, and worn out with celebration, closed my eyes.

The Dresden china alarm clock, covered in rosebuds, showed 3 A.M. with its glowing gilt hands when a noise woke me up. Tony slept on. He had never been a light sleeper.

The sound woke me because it was familiar. A sound like an owl with whooping cough. It was familiar but out of context. Then I remembered back fifteen years, to when Johnny would stay out past his curfew and stand under my window and call this signal, which he flattered himself sounded like a night bird, to get me to let him in. My parents knew the whole time, of course. They were afraid to crack down on him lest that strain of wildness he got from his mother should take hold, and Johnny should break loose entirely. That never happened. They'd kept Johnny safe, my parents and Louise.

I ran to the window, like the Christmas poem says, and flung open the sash.

"Johnny?"

He was standing there in a dark blue raincoat. His hair was wild, and the belt of his raincoat was dragging in the mud left in Mrs. Crawley's backyard by the recent rains.

"Nicky, you have to get Louise for me."

"It's three in the morning."

"I know what time it is. Get Louise."

"She's asleep. She came in after me."

"Get her. I have to talk to her."

The cold air was like river water flowing around my neck and shoulders. I was about to run down the stairs and let him in when the window next door to mine slid open, and I saw Louise's head and shoulders parallel to my own.

"Johnny!"

"Louise, just listen to me."

"Go away. You woke me up."

"You can sleep again after you hear me out."

Louise was not a swoon-inducing sight in her nightdress, a purple and yellow tie-dyed burnoose. But Johnny didn't care. Not Johnny. It had taken him a long time, but he'd always dived in headfirst once he decided to take a plunge.

"I know I made a lot of mistakes, Louise. I know I've treated you offhandedly, that I've hurt your feelings."

"That you got engaged to someone else," Louise said slowly and distinctly. The air was so still I could hear every word clearly. It felt as if it was going to snow.

"I didn't mean to," said Johnny.

"I suppose it was just an accident."

"I wasn't thinking clearly. I didn't know what you were to me."

"You made me feel fat. For years."

"Never on purpose. You were more important than I knew back then. You're so important, Louise. You're everything."

"If I count for so much, why didn't you wake up smiling that morning after Aunt Maureen's wedding? Why didn't you?"

"I was afraid. I was . . . stunned."

Louise turned her head to look at me.

"Nicky, do you mind?"

I pulled my head in but kept the window open. Like my mother, I have excellent hearing.

Louise said, "You've always taken me for granted. You've always assumed I had nothing better to do than be at your beck and call."

"I'm not taking you for granted now," Johnny said.

I could hear other guests stirring below me, and a few windows going up. Tony slept on. Someone yelled, "Hey, Romeo!" at Johnny, but he paid no attention.

"You talk a good game," said Louise.

"I'll prove it to you," said Johnny. "I'll stand out here all night. I'll stand outside your window every night for the next three years, if that's what it takes."

There was no sound from Louise.

"I love you," said Johnny. "Did you hear me, Louise? I love you. I loved you when I was fourteen, when I was sixteen, when I was twenty-one. I loved you through all those silly girls in college, and it doesn't matter that I didn't know it, because it's true, and that's all. I was a fool, and a jerk, and a screw-up, but I love you, and deep down you know that, Louise. You *know* that."

I heard a snort from the other room, but I couldn't tell if Louise was crying or being derisive.

Johnny was expressing himself pretty loudly by now. Lights went on in a few neighboring houses.

"You love me too, Louise. You know you do. Aunt Maureen and Nicky both told me you did."

My mother had told him that? She hadn't mentioned it on the phone. My mother was a deep one. Tony turned over in bed, mumbled, and went back to sleep.

"Louise? Talk to me. Give me a chance, Louise. You have to. Louise, Louise, Louise, Louise."

He stumbled around the lawn, crooning her name.

I stuck my head out the window again. I could see her, her arms folded on the sill. She was so still that I could pick out the exact pattern of the tree branches on her pale face and arms.

"Louise!" I stage-whispered. My throat hurt from the effort not to scream at her. "Are you crazy? Get down there."

She disappeared. I waited for the sound of the window slamming shut on Johnny's pleas, but there was nothing. Then I heard the door of Louise's room close with its distinctive thud. There were footsteps on the stairs. The side screen door banged. I saw—the whole neighborhood saw—Louise run out to Johnny and put her arms around his neck. He staggered backward, than staggered forward. They looked drunk, reeling around together, but they were only drunk with love. And they had a better right to be drunk with it than most people. They'd waited much longer.

It wasn't until she took his hand and led him inside that I realized my fists had been pressed to my mouth to keep me from shouts of jubilation. I wanted to whoop and holler. What a near miss this one could have been. Somewhere in Greece my mother was probably smiling as she dreamed next to Ira.

I crawled back into bed and curled against Tony, nuzzling my face into his chest. When my cold feet touched his, he turned on his other side, but in his sleep he kept hold of my hand, so that my arm went around him and was tucked firmly under his. I pressed my face against his warm back, and fell asleep at last.

IT WAS SNOWING as I walked down Connecticut Avenue, a small-flaked persistent snow that was already sticking to the streets. I was going to the Advocacy, Inc. office. I'd promised Ron a briefing before I signed out for two weeks of vacation.

If the snow kept up, the federal government would close early and hundreds of men and women in thin business shoes would be standing by the curbs, hailing taxis with a desperation that the denizens of other cities save for blizzards. I liked this kind of weather, though. Tonight after the rush hour this soft, unexpected snowfall would reveal the secret, quiet Washington so rarely seen, as the auto-free silence of a hundred years before fell over the city.

I was glad to be home, though I missed them all. Kate and Margaret and Lester and even Eric. . . . Well, I would miss Eric when time in its kindness had dimmed his memory.

Kate had come to see Louise and me off on the train. Kate's friend Eileen had finally gone home from the hospital. She had gone home to die, I knew without Kate telling me.

Eric had wanted to come to the train station to say good-bye, but he was scheduled for yet another afternoon of evaluation by his school district. Clare had arranged it. She said Eric would surprise us all, and he did. The experts said he was testing off the charts in verbal, reading, and logic abilities and might qualify for an accelerated, high-prestige district program for a handpicked group of kids who were far too smart to be left in a regular classroom to suffer as other children did.

As a parting send-off on our last morning at the office, he'd attached a very realistic model of a hairy tarantula to the zipper of my suitcase, but Louise removed it before he could see me jump. This disappointment caused him to appear nearly as sad as everyone else looked as we made our farewell rounds at the office.

We'd left for Washington a day before Tony. He was flying in that night, if the snow didn't get too bad.

I was so unbearably glad Tony was going to be with me that I couldn't think about it directly. I thought about arrangements instead. Clean towels. Space in the medicine cabinet. Fresh sheets on the bed and lots of food in the icebox. Men consumed such large amounts of food. I wanted to do what would make him feel welcome, but not go so overboard he'd be self-conscious. The apartment was spotless, and all morning I'd wandered around it, hoping it would be a luckier place for us this time around.

I was saying good-bye, too, good-bye for now to my solitary self. Though I would be alone again, by choice and by default, in whatever years to come Tony and I might have, I would not know the solitude with him that I'd known in the time since we'd first parted. Half of me had treasured that solitude. It's not that hard for women to be alone, actually. We're better at it than men are. We form routines, cook for ourselves, and see friends, and travel. Men alone tend to mope, and grow depressed, and then marry unsuitable young women or get cancer. Men fare better when they have company in their lives. But women give up something real and precious when we decide to say to a man: Here, live with me. Sleep with me in a bed that will now be our bed. Eat your meals with me at a table that will be our table. It's a risky step, because there is so much in any man that's alien, so much to get used to, to keep getting used to, year by year.

I didn't pity my friends who were single women in their forties and fifties. Of all my friends, they seemed most content. It was my married friends who phoned me in tears, who exhausted themselves with the burdens of work and home, who wondered what the hell they were doing with their lives. I felt a rush of fear when I thought of myself as a woman paired. But the fear subsided when I considered that I'd lose much more in doing without Tony than I would in taking this chance with him. And I knew we hadn't seen all that was good between us, all that was possible. We'd barely scratched the surface.

*   *   *

Being in the office with Ron was a relief. In my business persona, I was far less vulnerable to nervousness and second-guessing.

"You people sure pulled that one out" was Ron's only comment on the strike, but I hadn't expected anything along the lines either of thoughtful regret at his lack of faith or delighted congratulations.

Ron appeared elegant and beautifully packaged as always. I sat down in one of his office chairs, an enormous squishy cube upholstered in a flat, fuzzy gray wool that felt as if it should have been carpeting material. Ron's desk was littered with holiday gifts from vendors and invitations in gold-foil-lined envelopes. On his windowsill was a large poinsettia like the one Kate had carried into the hospital that night, with a card attached that said, "Merry Christmas From Duke's Printing." Hovering over this greeting in upraised gold acrylic was what I assumed the owner thought of as a ducal crest.

Either Duke's was aware of Ron's Presbyterian roots, or unconcerned about offending its Jewish, Muslim, and atheist customers with a wholesale Christmas message and gift drop. It must be lonely to be an atheist during the holidays, I thought. Like being the only one at a wild party who didn't drink. I tried to imagine what kind of God Ron believed in. Was he an austere and critical parent like Ron's late father, keeping in touch only when it was necessary to register disapproval? Was he one of the boys, a Big Guy who'd go round a few holes and laugh at Ron's jokes when he'd had a couple of drinks back at the clubhouse? Did Ron pray? I couldn't imagine it.

"You want one of these raspberry caramels before Myrlene puts them out in the kitchen?" said Ron, holding out a silvery tin decorated with a Currier and Ives scene.

I grabbed a handful and stuffed them in my purse. You never know when you'll be stuck in traffic and want something to nibble. Ron didn't blink at my tackiness. That was one of the traits I liked most in him: deep down, he knew he wasn't any classier than me, that he was just some Midwestern guy who now owned a few nice suits.

It had been so many weeks since I thought of him without anger that I was startled. Sure, he hadn't come through for me on the strike, but he'd never billed himself as someone who could be counted on for that kind of support. He'd delivered, as usual, exactly what he'd promised. I relaxed into the depths of the chair, feeling I'd been gone for months and months.

"You're coming this Friday, aren't you?" said Ron.

Friday was our office Christmas party. Unlike other, more budget-minded bosses, Ron didn't believe in playing Chipmunk records and getting toasted on inferior punch in the comfort of our own premises. Instead, he invited each of us and a significant other to an overpriced steak house on Fifteenth Street, where you could get a prime rib for thirty bucks and be condescended to by waiters who didn't thaw for anyone lower than a cabinet member. No one enjoyed these gatherings except Ron, who drank too much and made sentimental toasts until Dana carted him home.

"I guess. Yeah, I'm coming. I'm bringing someone, too."

"I know who you're bringing."

"Stop smirking, then. How'd the Campsters event go?"

"Mixed results," said Ron, his face growing far sadder than it had appeared when he contemplated pulling the plug on the St. Francis strike. "There was a scuffle among the kids about who got to hold the American flag during the singing, and one of them got a black eye. And then the silent auction was a real bust."

"Why? Those usually go over."

"Wendy may have taken the woodsy theme a little too far. They were auctioning off stuff like a weekend in an unheated cabin in New Hampshire, and snowshoeing lessons in Labrador. Really rich people don't ante up to be as uncomfortable as that, at least not East Coast rich people. I think we should have gone for a little more conspicuous consumption, maybe left out some of that rustic shit."

Poor Wendy. I'd thought all along that this could only end in tears.

"How did Jantsy take it?"

"She's frozen Wendy out, basically. It won't last. No one else would put up with her the way Wendy does. But Wendy can't see that, and she's been moping around a little. She'd even made Jantsy a Christmas present, some sort of knitted throw rug."

"An afghan?"

"Yeah, that was it."

"I should have kept on top of that Campsters benefit, Ron, but I thought Jantsy was thrilled with Wendy, and neither of them wanted my interference."

"It's not your fault," said Ron in a burst of rare generosity. "No one can handle Janet Stratton-Pole-Up-Her-Snooty-Butt-Smith close up, let alone long-distance."

It wasn't like Ron to be understanding if blame was handy to throw around. Something was up. Here it came.

"Nicky, I have a proposition for you."

"Shoot."

"Weingould is very hepped up on you, as you know. He wants you on this strawberry fields campaign."

"Strawberry pickers. He sure does. He gave me a call a few days ago, even though he knows he's supposed to talk to you first. I think he may even come out there himself for a week or so."

"He's very excited. He didn't think the Toilers would have a chance to do this campaign. Goreman has been against it for years now."

We both knew why. Low-wage workers didn't amount to much in dues money, and thus their plight was uninteresting to Jerry Goreman, man of the people. Weingould's getting the green light on the Sampsonville campaign was a coup appropriate to this season of miracles.

"Well, as you know, Wendy has been wanting to get more experience in the field for some time now, and I think I can talk Weingould into taking her instead of you. I thought it would get her out of Jantsy's way for a while and cheer her up."

I couldn't believe my ears, a phrase you often hear but which I'd never fully known the meaning of until now.

"Cheer her up? You've got people risking their necks out there in California just to join the union, and you want Wendy assigned for therapeutic reasons? What's she going to do, make pretty name tags? This is serious stuff, Ron. She's not ready for it."

"Boltanski can bring her along. She learns fast. And I need you here. We might have a whole new sideline going with historic preservation groups after the Mallard Pond effort turned out so well. They're always trying to build shopping centers over battlefields out in northern Virginia. I can really see a market. I know you have something going with Boltanski, but I hope you'll agree that shouldn't affect our business strategy."

"Ron, I don't care if you're convinced I'm going to California so I can be Tony's on-site cupcake. As it happens, I would love to work with him on this one if we don't kill each other first. But that's beside the point. The point is, I can do this campaign and Wendy can't. She is not up to this one. Not in a million years."

His expression, bland and confident, didn't change.

"Wendy needs the experience, Nicky. She can't play social secretary forever."

Why did I think that he was quoting Wendy herself here?

"Fine. Then send her out there with me, and I'll make sure she gets her feet wet. Or wait for something less challenging than Sampsonville, and give her that."

"She wants this one," he said, almost as if he'd forgotten I was there. "This is the one she wants."

A nasty idea that had been knocking around in my unwilling subconscious suddenly, with huge reluctance, took form.

"You're sleeping with her."

He ruffled through the invitations on his desk. I saw one decorated with dancing penguins in tuxedos. Original.

"God, Ron. Wendy? It's bad enough that you're running around on Dana. Did it have to be Wendy?"

He swallowed, and for the first time in our acquaintance I noticed his Adam's apple.

"There's an attraction there, Nicky. It's like nothing I've ever felt before."

"It's called turning forty-five, Ron."

"Do you think that for one second you could talk to me like a human being?"

I stood up.

"You weren't straight with me, Ron. She's sitting in there with a fancier desk than I have and a nosy little finger in all my campaigns, and now we *both* know why. And it stinks. You're screwing over the two women who've been with you longest—your wife and me—all for some twenty-five-year-old nookie at lunchtime. You're such a little shit."

I was about to leave when he began to cry.

He didn't cry like a child, which would have been preferable. He cried silently, trying to stop the contortions of his face, putting his palms up to his eyes—the way men cry who never cry, which breaks your heart.

"Oh, for God's sake," I said, and pulled out a dozen tissues from the guest box on the coffee table. I shoved them into his hand but he ignored them. I went over and put my arm around his shoulder. It felt warm and damp, and less muscular than I'd thought it would be, and I had a chilling intimation of Ron's later years, as he lost his good looks and had to rely more and more on his facile charm.

"Okay," I said. "Don't worry. We'll figure something out. Okay."

"I am so fricking messed up, Nicky. I've wrecked my life. I've wrecked it. I'm in love with this girl, or obsessed with her or something. I can't stop it even for my business. Even for my wife. My wife who's been so good to me, do you think I don't know that?"

Maybe it was hard to have a spouse who was good to you. Who you'd come to rely on as stronger than you were. It must make you yearn to look wise and sophisticated to someone fresh and lovely who thought you had things to teach her.

Wendy would eat him alive. In that moment I felt very, very sorry for Ron. I even stroked his hair, a gesture I later squirmed to remember.

"It will work itself out," I said. "Everything does."

"You don't believe that."

"Maybe not, but in any case I'll be around. As long as—"

"As long as I don't let this thing with Wendy screw you up, too. I get that. I'm sorry. She pushed and pushed on this California assignment. She wants to play in the big leagues."

The big leagues. Definitely Wendy's words again. I wanted to ask Ron where she got these expressions, but it wouldn't be kind to him in his current distraught state.

"I'll tell you what, Ron. *Do* send her out there, but with me. She can't get into too much trouble while I'm keeping an eye on her, and it'll give you a break to sort out your . . . to sort things out."

He looked up, finally saw that he was holding tissues, and blew his nose.

"That would be one answer. You'd really be willing to do that? I know you two aren't the best of friends."

"But I'm *your* friend. It's too late now to change my mind about that. So pack her off to California with me, and take it from there. What the hell."

At one-thirty that afternoon, I left the Advocacy, Inc. office to meet Tony, who was coming into Dulles on a four o'clock plane. From K Street I caught the Washington Flyer, a big coach-bus that usually whisks you out there in forty minutes or so. But the snow that had seemed so beautifying and benign when I'd been striding down Connecticut had turned into a major storm. Flights from the north were reported by the airline as late, then canceled. No takeoff time was yet listed for Tony's at my last check before boarding the Flyer.

We sat on that bus for three hours, ten of us. There was a French-Canadian couple speaking a specific regional dialect with now and then a word I recognized, pronounced in a way I didn't expect. There were two American University students going home for Christmas, each weighted down with a duffel bag full of presents, talking about final exams and pre-Christmas breakups on their dorm hall. There was a guy in dreadlocks who was reading Kant, and there were two businessmen who tried to look blasé but kept checking their watches and calling their wives. Last to board was an old lady with teased white hair, carting a John Grisham thriller, a bucket of fried chicken, and a cat in a carrier. The cat yowled miserably and finally, looking around a little nervously, she took it out of the carrier and held it in her lap, feeding it bits of white meat. It was a Persian, with fur as white as its owner's hair, and it looked out indifferently at the white world we were traveling through and suffered itself to be petted.

Running from the office, I hadn't brought as much as a magazine, though I did have the raspberry caramels to chew on. I had never met Tony at the airport before. He'd never let me, years ago. He'd used to say that the time between airport and home was his decompression time. Now when I offered, he said, "That would be great. It's a drag to get off the plane with no one waiting for you."

Louise had offered to go with me, but she had enough to handle right now, making up for lost time both at her business and with Johnny. Louise and Johnny were dating. Actually dating. Louise felt they had to go back to the beginning and do it right, or, as she put it, "our relationship will have a psychic blight on it."

My mother, who had called from Jerusalem the night before "just to check in," had predicted that they'd be married by summer. She'd set all the wheels in motion, and now she was looking forward to bossing Louise into a June bridal.

"I'm betting on fall, so rearrange your thoughts about the location and color scheme," I said. "Never underestimate Louise and her stubbornness. And Ma, I should fill you in on something."

I told her about Tony. It didn't take much time, but it seemed as if I recited the story of Tony's and my happy reconciliation for hours, because my mother said nothing at all while I was talking. I tapped the receiver with my fingernail.

"Hello? A reaction would be good here."

"As long as he makes you happy," she remarked in pinched tones.

"How should I know if he'll make me happy, Ma? We just got back together. There's every chance that he'll make me *un*happy. Every once in a while. And very, very happy on occasion. We'll see how we do the rest of the time. He's a difficult guy, you know."

"You're not exactly easy yourself," she pointed out.

"Now you're siding with him?"

"I'll be back for New Year's Eve. We'll have a big party at the house."

"Could you try and like him, Ma? I'll try to like Ira."

"What do you mean? No one couldn't like Ira."

"You're right. Ira is a saint, a living, breathing saint. You be even more of a saint and give Tony a chance, or he and I will be celebrating the new year with one of those Holiday Inn champagne weekend packages. I hear they're pretty nice, and you don't have to drive on New Year's Eve."

"Don't get huffy with me. Louise says he's improved a lot, so we'll see. Since there's no talking you out of this." Of course she'd already hashed it over with Louise. Why had I wasted my breath giving her the news?

"If that's the best you can do, Ma . . ."

"Have I ever been rude to a guest in my house? I said bring him, and I meant it."

So, God help me, I had a place to go for New Year's Eve, and even a date.

I'd looked in on Wendy on my way out of the office. She was wrapping Christmas presents for all the secretaries. I hadn't even bought one for my own secretary yet. Her energy amazed me. She could wreck Ron's life and scheme her way to the top, and still find time to pick up tiny muslin sachets to tie into the ribbons of her gifts.

Career robot, I thought. But when I looked again, she seemed to be another person entirely. Just twenty-five, just young and making every mistake her character and situation could predictably work toward. If she stayed with Ron, she'd be taking on a man far more confused and weak-willed than she realized now. If she left him, the break would be ugly, painful, and public, since I would bet that every employee in the place knew what was going on, and had probably known sooner than I had.

At Wendy's age I had yet to meet Tony. Or Jeremy. My father was still alive. I thought I knew all there was to know about love and work and friendship, and I'd barely started on my way.

"I hear we're going to be traveling together," I said with false joviality.

She stared at me.

"California," I said. "I wasn't going to let Ron throw you to the lions out there. I'm coming, too."

There was disappointment in her smile. I wanted to throttle her. Then I saw a package on her desk, a package marked "For Nicky" in bubbly schoolgirl handwriting. Wendy had gotten me a present. The stupid kid. The poor, stupid kid. I'd have to buy some suitable basket of overpriced toiletries at the duty-free and wrap it tonight, though I had no wrapping materials at home except tinfoil and the Sunday comics. Also some duct tape and a leftover shirt box from Macy's. It would have to do.

"We'll have a good time in California," I said. "It'll be an adventure."

She nodded.

"Are you going home for Christmas?"

I hadn't asked her about her plans before this. Why hadn't I? Wasn't that just the normal kindness you'd show to anyone you worked with? For all I knew Wendy was an orphan, with nowhere to go for the holidays.

"I'm staying with my mother, in Aspen."

"Skiing?"

"I don't know how. My mom can't believe it. She's always bugging me to take lessons, because skiing's what she does all day and she doesn't like to leave me alone. My dad's in Vermont, and he said I could come up there, too, but he and his wife have a new baby, so I thought Aspen would be better all around."

"My mother just announced she's having a big New Year's bash, if you're back by then."

"Maybe," she said, and smiled at me, a quavery smile completely unlike the practiced teeth flashing that was her usual office smile.

"Great food," I said, reminding myself to make sure to force Ma into ordering party platters and sheet cake from the grocery store. "Dancing. Think about it."

Then I left before I could ruin even this feeble beginning. It was painful, somehow, to think of Wendy by herself in some condo in Aspen, thumbing through *Vogue* and pining after Ron, maybe calling one of her girlfriends, only to get the answering machine. I couldn't feel angry at her for this mess with Ron, when I'd made many an equally sorry romantic mistake in my time. Only luck and chance had thrown me back together with Tony. Otherwise, I might be just like Wendy, taking what I could get from a man who didn't have much to give.

Maybe Louise was right. Maybe it wasn't for us to judge what other people did in the pursuit of love.

In that underheated bus, staring into the snowstorm, my feet curled up under me, I was paralyzed to think that it wasn't a sunset Tony and I were walking off into, it was the mess of complications that any sea change brings. If I could have rung the bell for the bus to stop and dashed out onto the highway, I think I'd have thumbed a ride to Florida or some other silly warm place and not looked back. I was that frightened that we were asking for disaster. Disaster had been our modus operandi up to that point, you could say.

Louise had advised me almost two months earlier to make room for love in my life, and here I was, literally doing that. It might even work out. My brothers would welcome Tony instantly as one of them, as they had before. My mother would accept him when she got it through her head that he wasn't going away. I had a misty vision, suddenly, of us all pooling our money to buy a cottage somewhere on the Eastern Shore, for weekends and vacations and bird-watching, should any of us ever learn to identify a heron or an osprey. We'd get a pair of communal binoculars and fight over who got to use them, though only Michael would ever spot anything other than a possum. Ira's grandchildren could come down on summer vacations and teach Joey and Maggie's current and future babies—and Johnny and Louise's?—how to swim.

I had an imagination and it could take me that far, even if I didn't have the optimist's blissful certainty that everything would be fine. Louise will always be the one of us who peers ahead with trust and confidence. The gift of hope was not a gift that the godmothers laid in my cradle, but if I ever learn it, at some creaking and advanced old age, it will be because of my cousin. My cousin, my companion, my ally until the end. My undeserved blessing.

There was a foot of snow on the roof of the airport, big drifts of it that looked as if they'd bring down the whole tentlike structure. It seemed to take hours to crawl from the airport entrance road up to the Flyer drop-off spot. I was out of the bus while the others were still assembling their bags, stopping to tip the driver five dollars for getting us there alive.

Tony's flight was due in ten minutes, the arrivals board said. I felt that the whole airport should know this, that all the hurrying, clamoring, self-obsessed people should stop their noise. What did they know? Could anyone on any plane, traveling toward this place on a thousand converging flight paths, could any traveler be more important? I wanted to shove aside every baby carriage, every luggage trolley, every twittering tour group in my way. I stood on the people mover, cursing every passenger who darted in before the door could close and we could lumber to the correct terminal. Airports weren't fast places, I remember thinking. Not really. They just looked fast.

And then I was at the gate, in an anxious, pressing crowd. We waited a long time, people milling about, inaudible static on the PA system, clots of angry customers for the next flight out of that gate mobbing the gate agent. Then the airline rep announced that Tony's flight had touched down and was on its way to the gate, as if this flight were no more unusual than a pleasure trip on a sunny June day. The crowd pressed forward once again. The passengers came off the airplane, so many of them, all strolling from the plane as if they had infinite leisure, the lazy worthless bums. The selfish pigs. One after another they plodded up the carpet and were claimed and made much of. And still no Tony.

Then there he was, at the top of the gangway, lugging the largest duffel bag ever allowed in carry-on. It must have held every possession he owned. I don't know how he'd been able to lift it, with his bad knee. When he saw me, over the heads of the jostling, clumsy crowd, he dropped it there and came to me and held me tightly.

"I thought you'd never get here," I said.

"As if you'd be that lucky," he said, and kissed me over and over again.

No one noticed. He recovered the bag and we each took a handle, although Tony protested that he could carry it himself. We joined the crowd heading down the long corridors, so numerous and slow-moving it looked like a procession. A procession of the unwittingly fortunate, I knew in my rejoicing heart. Of travelers who—this time at least—had arrived in safety, and were heading home.

READING GROUP GUIDE

1. Why is Nicky drawn to Tony, who is very different from the quiet father whom she has recently lost? Is Tony a hero or a hack, or a little of both?

2. Nicky's mother is very intent on her finding a husband and "settling down." Is the mother-daughter relationship in the book accurate for today's mothers and daughters?

3. At the beginning of the novel, Nicky has left her lover Jeremy after a year because he cheated on her. Over the course of the novel, Jeremy repents and tries to show Nicky that he wants to start over. Should Nicky take him back? Or is she right to feel that one such lapse so early in a relationship is one too many?

4. Why does it take Nicky's cousin Johnny so long to recognize his attraction to Louise? In novels, movies, and television, the story of friends who slowly realize they are in love is a perennial favorite. Is this a true-to-life plot scenario, or are today's men and women more alert to romantic possibilities in their friendships?

5. What is the dividing line, in the book, between learning to forgive others and navigate in a morally cloudy world, and standing up for what's right? How does this theme relate to the book's title?

6. Tony is a "working-class stiff" and Jeremy is "sophisticated." How does the novel represent class and money issues in modern relationships? Discuss.

7. There are several secondary characters involved in the strike: Clare, the reserved union president; Kate, an activist nurse with a wry perspective on even the most serious issues; Doug, the on-site snoop for a conniving politician; and Margaret, the office Type A. What role do these secondary characters play?

8. The novel ends on a hopeful note, in the tradition of romantic comedies. But there is an awareness on Nicky's part that romantic happiness is hard to find and precarious. Looking ahead to the future, what joys and challenges do you anticipate for Nicky and Tony, and Johnny and Louise? What knowledge or new insights have these characters gained over the course of the novel that will improve their chances of lasting happiness?

For more reading group suggestions visit
www.stmartins.com

St. Martin's Griffin

Turn the page for an excerpt of
Christina Bartolomeo's next novel

Snowed In

Coming soon from St. Martin's Press

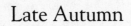

Late Autumn

One

Courage is not my leading virtue. I've always avoided change of any sort, operating on the principle of safety first. I married a "safe" man. I've made my living performing humdrum work, work that bored other people so much that they'd pay someone else to do it. All my life, I've watched those around me—my sister Delia, my friend Marta—dash forward to seize the day. I've admired them, cheered them on. But, if threatened by opportunity myself, I make sure to hide under the covers until the moment passes.

Evade life's twists and turns this assiduously and the Fates will get their revenge by quietly ambushing you. When the alarm clock squawked 7:30 on that sullen October morning, I had no clue that by nightfall I'd finally be ready for what Marta refers to ominously as "taking steps."

Marta takes steps when an express mail package fails to arrive on time, or her morning toast is served up a shade too brown at the coffee shop. She plunges into eloquent, daunting reproaches, she storms out of rooms—only to return an hour later, cheerful and unaware of any ill-feeling she might have left behind. My sister, Delia, is equally assertive but calmer. If her husband Tom casts an admiring glance at a passing woman, the stray look of a faithful husband noting the scenery, she merely says briskly, "Snap out of it," and carries on. She doesn't pout or bluster, but neither does she let things slip by until she slips right down under them, as I do.

But for me, all acts of bravery are overthought, and anger is a feared eventuality, a thundering waterfall away from which I'm always frantically paddling upstream. But that October day, in a city that was still strange to me—Portland, Maine—I began, in spite of myself, to inch toward something different. Well, not even "toward" anything. Just away from what I had. Coward that I am, I took the smallest of steps. Life being contrary, and life being kind, that's when things finally started to happen—small things, with large consequences.

The Monday morning when everything got to be too much, my still-new husband Paul and I woke up cold, as usual. Our radiators had mysteriously shut themselves off during the night. This had become a habit with them, and one of us was going to have to talk to the landlord about it. The one of us who was going to talk to the landlord wasn't going to be Paul.

"You handle him better," said Paul, who always shied from minor confrontations. He'd never challenge a waiter about a miscalculated bill, or ask a hotel for their best room rate, or require that his office manager commandeer him a desk chair that didn't collapse when he leaned forward. Paul had been trained early in the stiff upper lip. He could have led troops over the top as an officer in World War I, or survived a winter at Valley Forge without a fuss, but he got weak in the knees when required to act "pushy."

That was why, since our August arrival in Portland, I'd been steadily getting to know our landlord Donald, who was also the resident plumber, electrician, roofer, and tile layer.

Summer had departed with a suddenness that surprised us. Over the course of my first few attempts to get the heat fixed, I'd heard the history of Donald's early career, the sad tale of his first marriage, the vicissitudes of his twenty years of motorcycle ownership, and his difficulty in getting his dog to breed with his friend's dog. Paul hadn't had to listen to any of this. He was intimidated by Donald's surly, obtuse air and liked to disguise it by saying I had "a way" with him. No one had a way with Donald, unless it was his second wife, who was rarely seen but often referred to with fear and respect.

It wasn't Paul's fault, really. Paul was already burdened with fighting the tiny battles of someone else's life—his mother Patricia's.

When I first got married, my new mother-in-law made me uncomfortable, but I'd believed our relationship would improve with time. "My friends all call me Pepper, and you should, too," she'd said when we met. I'd thought then that we'd ultimately be friends. But

Pepper didn't want any more friends. She wanted a certain kind of daughter-in-law, and I wasn't it.

Pepper *was* peppery, in a perky, blond, tight-mouthed way. At fifty-eight, she was entirely competent to take care of herself and her catering company, Comfort Foods. Unfortunately for Paul and his brother James, Pepper was a woman who expected things of men, old-fashioned, manly things: handling income taxes, cleaning out the gutters, and dropping a lady off in front of the restaurant before going to look for a parking space.

In the five years since Paul's lawyer father had died quietly from a heart attack, Pepper had formed the habit of calling on her sons to look after her in any number of petty and large matters, as if she were a consumptive young widow at the turn of the century. Thus, any spare time Paul had for disputing electric bills and writing letters to county property tax assessors was already claimed. When it came to the sticky administrative details in our married life, I was usually tapped.

This was good practice for a person like me, whose main goal in adulthood has been avoiding raising her voice in any consumer situation.

"So you'll get on the phone to Donald, right?" Paul said.

He was standing in the bathroom, jerking his tie into place under a row of flickering fluorescent "vanity" lights Donald had installed in a strip above the sink. We both looked green under those lights, but Paul didn't mind that. For men, getting ready to go out seems to be a question of establishing order in their appearance: shaving, knotting the tie, zipping the pants, and tying the shoes. Battening down the hatches to face the day.

"Should I call from the office and remind you, Sophie?"

"No, I can remember that it's cold."

He sighed and brushed a bit of lint from his pants cuff with a re-proachful look in my direction. True, I hadn't dusted under the bed lately, but neither had he. Paul's quotient of these "why haven't you" looks had risen sharply since Natalie had been hired at his office, Natalie, the career gal who was also a domestic whiz, Natalie, the living embodiment of the idea that there's always one woman so perfect that she spoils it for the rest of us.

"I'm not trying to boss you, Sophie."

That had been my accusation to him in a recent fight.

"Yes, you are."

"It's just that I don't have time for this maintenance stuff."

"And I do?"

He paused, comb in midair. Even when fighting with him, I was sometimes struck by the handsomeness of my husband. It was a handsomeness that (under the theory that people wind up with their approximate physical counterparts) my own on-again, off-again attractiveness didn't merit. Paul had regular features, thick, light brown hair, and hazel eyes. His chin was nicely square, and his muscles were the well-defined muscles of someone who grew up playing tennis and swimming. His gaze met an onlooker's gaze head-on; even here, where we were so new, he was often stopped on the street for directions. He had a clean-cut, fearless, Protestant American face, a face that only generations of upper-middle-class sureness can create. When he smiled, you could see evidence of a saving sense of humor. He wasn't smiling now.

My own looks were unimpressive. Everything about me was almost-but-not-quite. Eyes: an unspectacular medium blue. Hair: darkened to ash from its childhood gold. Skin: pale and usually colorless. When all was right in my world, I was attractive in an offbeat, unphotogenic way. All had not seemed right with my world in a while. My face and hair seemed drab and dim—though it could just have been the lighting in that bathroom.

"You know what I mean," Paul said. "Your time is less . . . structured."

"I have a major layout to get out the door today."

"So how long does it take to call? You can work while he's here. You don't have to give him coffee and scones or whatever you do. He's the landlord, not your friend. Be firm."

He was pulling a V-necked sweater over his shirt and tie, his new office attire for Portland. Natalie had advised him on this. She was full of opinions on matters of style. I myself preferred him in the light gray and navy blue suits he'd worn in D.C. He'd seemed so lovable to me in those suits, like a boy dressed up for a cousin's wedding. I'd met him at a wedding, in fact; he'd been sitting, well behaved, in one of his very nice suits, his hair slicked back with water and his elbows off the table as he'd been taught. He'd looked very young. He would in some way always look young in that he frequently had the appearance of following rules he didn't truly understand, rules made by grown-ups whom he didn't think to question but didn't sympathize with either.

"Most people manage to handle a job and these other things that come up in life," his voice came at me through the sweater.

I said nothing. I knew whom he meant by "most people." However, I didn't think even Natalie—or any other superwoman of the new century—could hurry Donald up.

"You have to show him you mean business, Sophie. You have to show him who's in charge."

"I think Donald and I both know who's in charge."

"That's because you're too soft on him."

He was rifling through the black canvas bag that had replaced his calfskin briefcase, the one I'd gotten him for his thirty-fifth birthday. No one in Portland carried a briefcase, apparently.

He smelled nice, of witch hazel and the hard-milled soap Pepper sent him from Caswell Massey. I've always been partial to men whose own particular smell makes me want to bury my nose in their necks. My first love, Rory, had sometimes smoked a cigar, a youthful affectation that meant Rory's sweaters had often smelled faintly of the best Cubans. Even today, that smell floating outside a restaurant or from the jacket pockets of an elderly man strolling by could turn me weak at the knees.

Paul was outlining what I would say to Donald, the magic words that would turn Donald's current benign tolerance of me to awed obedience.

"You just put it to him simply. You say, 'Donald, this is far below the housing code standard and I want it fixed immediately.' Don't say, 'Oh Donald, it would be so nice if you could see your way to getting us a teensy bit more heat.'"

It wasn't fair. Paul knew I wasn't a take-charge type when he married me. Confronted with dilemmas that demand a confident tone and a commanding gaze, my voice squeaks and my eyes dart around furtively. In this state I can appear a little wanting—in fact, downright moronic. "Speak up!" the nuns at St. Catherine's would say. I knew even then, though, that speaking up got you in trouble far more often than *not* speaking up did.

I'd also learned young that stupidity was my best defense. My mother was a determined social activist and good-deed doer. Early on, I figured out that when Mom needed me to man a ring-toss booth at the muscular dystrophy carnival or fill in as a Roman guard in the church Passion play, she'd soon grow discouraged if I seemed slow and scattered, if it promised to be more trouble than it was worth to enlist my services.

My sister Delia, older by three years, was louder in her refusals. Her first word had been "no" and she'd been saying it to Mom ever since. Someone had to. My father found his wife hugely entertaining in all her altruistic endeavors, and I'd always been too awed by the sheer force of my mother's personality for anything but the most passive resistance.

When you've spent your childhood hiding under a rock, hoping to avoid being dragged along to benefit folk concerts and dawn tree plantings, it's hard to mature into an incisive, self-possessed woman who can stare down a Motor Vehicle Department functionary and say, "I've been standing here for three hours. I am *not* going back to Table A for that form." My friend Marta was capable of such feats, but then she worked on Capitol Hill and was used to kicking up a ladylike dust until she got what she wanted.

"Like I said, I'd do it but it's gonna be a hell of day," Paul finished, dragging his coat on. It was a navy pea coat with a red-plaid flannel lining, bought at a rugged outdoor store in Freeport. I remembered with a sigh his Washington coat, tweed with a silk lining.

"Try not to be timid with Donald," were his last words before he left. Then he kissed me, quite tenderly.

How, I wondered as I watched him drive away, could you kiss

someone like a lover while criticizing her like . . . like a husband. Criticism, I'd begun to conclude, was a side effect of marriage. Then again, I visibly bit my tongue a lot with him. Marriage meant biting your tongue.

Still, we hadn't grated on each other this way back home. They said the first year of marriage was the hardest, but this second year was more difficult by far. I'd liked our first year. I was thirty-three and I'd been, let's face it, so damn relieved to have someone. I'd positively rejoiced in our little domestic rituals. Grocery shopping together, painting the bathroom, buying mixing bowls. Other lovers had broken my heart and disappeared; Paul had stayed around to participate in the purchase of a hand-held vacuum cleaner.

Paul was charmed by my faults back then. He'd called me "charmingly soft-spoken," not "timid." But now, as we approached our second anniversary, his morning embraces were being steadily replaced by a list of important tasks I should consider completing before his arrival home. And "Did you have a productive day?" were his first words of greeting at night, accompanied by a tepid, G-rated hug.

This overseeing of my schedule was probably on the advice of Natalie, Paul's workmate. I brooded over Natalie as I made the first of many pots of coffee of my day. They said coffee gave you jitters, but it had little effect on me.

Natalie. I'd had a few years of practice hating Pepper, but in three short months, Natalie had almost caught up with my mother-in-law on my secret list of the top ten people I'd like to see shipped permanently to a research station on a polar ice cap.

Paul had taken to implying that, unlike me, Natalie managed her life. She was beginning to manage Paul, too, in all sorts of small, slightly sinister ways. In her high, clear, confident voice, Natalie had probably reminded Paul that depressed stay-at-home types need action to lift their moods. I should be prodded for my own good.

The trouble was, I didn't want to be prodded. None of this was really my fault. No natural laziness or gloom had brought me to this low point. I was stuck at home, working in solitude and chill, and I'd never intended that when we moved to Portland. I'd had plans, lots of them.

First off, I'd hoped to give up freelancing for a "real job." But we soon discovered that any position available in Portland's tight employment market wouldn't pay half of what I made on my own, at inflated Washington rates. So: no new job. This was daunting, but what the heck. I'd explore in my free hours, discover Maine, make the most of the short year we'd have here. Paul was going to leave me the car sometimes.

Then it turned out that a car was essential for Paul's work. He had meetings all over the region, last-minute demands, unpredictable hours. No roving up and down the lovely coast but only as far as my legs could take me.

That left joining things. Getting involved, which is hell itself for a shy person. So far, I'd attended one meeting of the local community group, West End Forward. The discussions there centered on homeowners' grievances: zoning regulations, property taxes, dogs messing on lawns. I nodded and smiled, but they could tell I was a fake.

A child would have led us to places where parents make friends with other parents, but we'd decided to put children off. Paul thought we should be married for at least three years before attempting parenthood. It was too bad that renting a child occasionally wasn't an option. People can place you if you're holding a kid by the hand: you're a neighbor, a community member, a good citizen who'd produced another miniature good-citizen-to-be.

These obstacles had temporarily deflated me and made Paul touchy. It was his fault for dragging us here, he said. No, no, I replied. We'd miscalculated a little, that was all. We'd thought Portland would be a smaller Boston, a bustling metropolis with lots of ways in for the just-arrived. We were wrong. Portland was a town, not a city, an old-fashioned town with an understandably reluctant attitude to newcomers, especially spoiled urban professionals who talked about Maine's stunning natural beauty, then left after their first winter. The handshakes at the community meeting were courteous but brief, the faces polite but wary. Standing there with a falsely vivacious smile, holding a West End Forward mug full of tepid coffee, I'd felt as if I were trying to infiltrate a secret society.

Yet, despite these discouragements, I wasn't depressed. I was a little stymied, a little homesick, but not the hopeless moper Natalie clearly pegged me as. My listlessness wasn't related to the move. I had other woes, and they came down to one un-ignorable fact: Paul had changed. Since we'd arrived in Maine, the easygoing, affectionate husband I'd known was disappearing fast. "My man," as Billie Holiday sings in that old standard, "was not the angel I once knew." He was different, and the difference boded ill for me. For us.